Joshua Appleby
and
The Ruby Dragon

www.kimlangley.com

Copyright © 2022 by Kim Langley

First published in Great Britain

an imprint of kimlangley.com

Kim Langley has asserted her right under copyright, Designs and Patents Act 1988 to be identified as the author of this work.

This book is a work of fiction and, except in the case in the of historical fact, any resemblance to actual persons, living or dead, is purely coincidental.

The moral right of the author has been asserted.

A CIP catalogue record for this book
is available from the British Library

Artwork Copyright © 2022 Kim Langley

Cover design by Claire Baker

Cover Copyright © 2022 Kim Langley

All rights reserved. No part of this publication may be reproduced, stored on a retrieval system, or transmitted, in any form or by any means, electronic, mechanical, photocopying, recording or otherwise, without prior permissions of the author Kim Langley

The book is sold subject to the condition that is shall not, by way of trade or otherwise. Be lent, re-sold, hired out or otherwise be circulated without the author's prior consent in any form of binding or cover other than that in that in which it is published and without a similar condition including this condition being imposed on the subsequent purchaser.

All rights reserved.

Hardback ISBN: 978-1-8383277-5-0

Paperback ISBN 978-1-8383277-4-3

E-book ISBN 978-1-8383277-6-7

Joshua Appleby
and
The Ruby Dragon

First Edition

BOOK TWO IN THE
JOSHUA APPLEBY SERIES

Kim Langley

BLUE HARE PUBLISHING
www.blueharepublishing.com

DEDICATION

To Raven, Saoirse & Lucia.

Keep dreaming of stars, the wonders of magic and follow the path which is true for you.

Roger Langley whose magical wisdom glitters our life together.

Acknowledgement

I would like to express my immense gratitude to my husband, Roger Langley, a dreamer who helped me along the way.

A profound thanks to Joanie Bassler, Mary Calderbank and Alison Atkins who patiently read this book and offered their advice.

Claire Baker using her artistic skills in designing the book cover.

And of course, my readers, in the hope you will enjoy the journey too.

CHAPTER 1
SOMETHING IN THE AIR
NOVEMBER 1963

Leaves rustled their winter song as they were tickled by the whispering wind. Alone in a small glade, stood a white wolf, enjoying the gentle breeze with closed eyes. Tendrils of white fur blew back against his face, his eyes flicked open, exposing intelligent amber eyes under white lids. He gracefully stretched out his lithe body, and yawned, large paws sank into the leaf strewn floor, his tail swished to and fro. He shook his heavy coat and padded around and examined undergrowth in the small clearing.

Come, come now, pull yourself together, there is no one here. This place is empty of Dark Magic. Sylvester Bluesky chided himself, he licked his coat irritated that he had spooked himself.

With a characteristic toss of his head, he lifted his nose a little higher and sniffed the crisp winter air. A heady sent of wild herbs and moss filled his nostrils, he found the sent pleasing. Fur blew against his whiskers and tickled them; he shook his head to push away the irritating strands.

There is no danger here. We will be safe practicing Earth Magic, he mused to himself.

Golden shards of light, shone through the gaps in the leaves, from the branches above. His eyes narrowed; a small growl escaped his throat. The sun was high in the sky, it was past noon. He hated waiting; he still struggled with the feeling of impatience.

Prudence, he grumbled to himself, *you are late, again!*

Just as the words left him, he heard a feint rustle of leaves from behind. He made a disapproving gesture with his head.

Sorry, Sylvester Bluesky. I was delayed. Her distinctive high-pitched voice, pushed gently against his mind. He felt the undercurrent of an apology, and breathless excitement. He whipped around and looked down at the slight figure of the blue hare.

Yes, you are late, it is very rude of you, Prudence. He sent his rebuke and watched her ears droop crestfallen.

Well, what are you so excited about? He couldn't be cross with her for long. She was not the most graceful of magical creatures, but she was faithful and honourable; to him and her human companion, Joshua Appleby.

I haven't got all day; he growled gruffly and watched her twitch from foot to foot.

She raised her face to his amber eyes, they stared down at her and crinkled at the sides.

You must come and see. Prudence stood a little taller on her hind legs. *I cannot explain it. So much colour!*

He looked away from the young hare, trying to hide a smile. He knew it frightened her a little when he bared his teeth in humour. It was difficult sometimes dealing with sensitive magical creatures. It was his burden; he was the elder of them all. They relied on his disposition, his wisdom, and his authority to explain Earth Magic law and give guidance. It was lonely, he was really meant to live as a pack, a large family. That had been taken away from him long ago when he was a mere cub. Now, he was the leader of a magical animal family. His thoughts turned to how magical animals and humans communicated with each other. *Telepathy,* the humans called it. He had never known another way. It was true he did not understand non magical creatures in the same way.

Come on, have a look, and tell me what it is! She became impatient, stamping her back foot in excitement.

What exactly have you seen that has made you so excited? He turned back to her.

That's just it, I am not sure what it is! They went past me on large lorries and houses on wheels.

Houses on wheels? he thought for a moment, a gleam of light cracked the mystery. *Oh, you mean caravans. Houses on wheels are called caravans.*

He watched Prudence struggle with the idea.

There was a big lorry with red and white colours. And bright lights on the front! She blurted; her foot gave a soft stamp, her ears pointed stiffly upwards.

I see. Sylvester Bluesky had an inkling of what Prudence had seen.

Well, don't you want to come and investigate? He could feel her impatience bubbling up.

I think we have more important things to do than follow some caravans.

The wolf watched the combination of expressions crossing her face and thought they were quite comical. He sighed; they did have other things to get on with.

Earth Magic.

Sylvester Bluesky wanted to make sure Prudence was ready for the battle ahead. The Appleby's needed their guidance, more now than ever, given the happenings over the last year.

If we have time, we will find the caravans later. Sylvester Bluesky offered.

No, you need to come with me now. There is something very strange about them. I could feel magic. Prudence waited for the news to drop.

Magic? His ears pricked up.

Yes, magic that was neither Earth Magic or Dark Magic. It felt very strange. She stuttered, one ear became lopsided, giving her a comical look.

I see. He said thoughtfully and sat down. *Where did you see them?*

On the road towards Tetbury. By the junction of the mighty oak tree. She gestured in the direction the caravans had taken.

He chewed over the news. Not Earth or Dark magic. Unknown magic? Magic from another time, place or even another realm? His mind raced as he chewed over ideas. Prudence impatient stamping cut the silence between them.

Well? Her nose twitched wildly.

This may be important.

He licked his paw and looked at her upturned face, her ears twitched. *We investigate together. You will always follow my instructions. And Prudence, if there is any talking to do, let me do it.* He looked around the glade and continued. *You have found yourself in all sorts of trouble by trying to do magical things your own way. We have rules on magic for a reason.* He finished with a growl. *I need a reply that you understand.*

Prudence flinched, the hair on her shoulders raised.

Yes, of course. She sounded a little offended and looked away, *Did I not come to you first?*

Sylvester Bluesky stood up and turned his head a little at the jibe. He chose to ignore it.

Let us go. Lead the way. He turned his nose in the direction they should go and watched Prudence saunter ahead of him.

Soon they arrived at the edge of the wood and walked along the road to the old oak tree. In the distance they could hear the beating of a drum.

This way. Sylvester Bluesky headed to a hedge and padded over to a small gap. His large body struggled to squeeze through the tight gap, the branches scratched his fur, he gave a final push and found himself in a newly ploughed field, the soil was dark and rich. Sylvester Bluesky placed a paw hesitantly onto the soil. He lifted his muddy paw and shook it; the soil was too wet to go straight across the field.

We go around the edge of the field. He looked down at Prudence and turned his head, motioning the direction with the tip of his nose.

Prudence bounced along, picking up speed with each leap. She skidded along and came to a wobbling stop.

Don't run Prudence, you will slip! he grumbled at her.

Well, we can't go any further anyway! Prudence sniffed haughtily pointing at a hedge blocking their path.

The air erupted with the beating of a drum. Prudence jumped startled and slipped. Sylvester Bluesky stopped her sliding into the slushy pool of mud at her side.

Thank you. Prudence looked up at him gratefully.

They stood in silence, listening.

A deep voice split the silence, 'Pu-l-l-l-l!'

The drumbeat kept it's beat. 'Pull!' came the voice again.

What do you think is happening? Prudence asked.

Sylvester Bluesky raised his nose and sniffed the air.

Wait here. The wolf gave Prudence a quelling look.

Fine. She replied huffily, her ears lowered down her shoulders and she looked away from him disappointed.

He gave her one more look before examining the hedge. He noticed a small gap a few feet away and gingerly crept towards it. His body taut, like an arrow he edged his way to the gap. Glancing back at Prudence, he gave her a 'stay put' look. She raised a paw at him edging him on. The hedge was too thick to see through, so he slowly pushed his nose to the edge of the gap. He made a few tentative sniffs. Nothing. No Smell at all. His head shot back, and he sat back on his haunches. There was always some sort of scent. Sometime strong, faint, or pungent. But no scent at all, not even the smell of old scents. Prudence had been right; this was very strange.

Well, I was right wasn't I, an excited whisper touched his mind.

He looked back at her, sighed at her impatience, and beckoned her with his head. He was glad she was light footed, only the blades of grass moved beneath her. Once again, he pushed his nose around the corner and plucked up the courage to look at what was happening. He gulped at the vision in front of him. A large pink-haired woman in flamboyant green harem trousers and a flowing pink jacket, her thick arms waved up and down as she beat a drum. A taller man stood to one side of the pink lady; he had the appearance of an eastern mystic. A long black braid of hair fell down his back, a thin handlebar moustache graced his upper lip and a pointed goatee beard on his chin. Dressed from top to toe in purple, in one hand he held a whip. He lifted his arms, like the conductor of an orchestra, and shouted at the top of his voice, 'PULL!', and crack his whip in the air.

'HEAVE!' came the reply of a unison of voices.

Twenty people stood around a red and white structure, each of them with a very thick rope in their hands. Sylvester Bluesky was mesmerized by the sight of the giant creation uncoiling like the eruption of a giant jelly fish, sliding taller and taller, at each pull.

Wow, I say! Prudence pushed her head between the hedge and his body. *What is it?*

I told you to stay there. He snapped.

Yes, but what is it? She ignored his stare.

The wolf took a moment to reply. It was the magnificent sight as the structured unfolded before them.

That Prudence is a Big-top. He smiled at her.

A big-top, why is it called a big-top? Prudence looked the ginormous structure up and down.

Sylvester Bluesky looked down at her, *A big-top is a gigantic canvas tent.*

What does it do? Came back her quizzical reply.

He took a moment before he replied. *It doesn't do anything, except for looking splendid. It's what goes on inside that is exciting.*

Ohh, can we go, and see? She whispered with excitement. *I want to see inside!*

No, Prudence, this is a place for humans, not us. Sylvester Bluesky looked down at her upturned face.

What I am more interested in is the magic you sensed. He looked back at the big-top.

It was a strange feeling, it's hard to describe. She babbled.

He wasn't listening to the young hare. He was thinking how silent it was.

'Good afternoon, nice to meet two magical creatures.' a rich deep voice interrupted.

Prudence shrieked and Sylvester Bluesky whipped around. The tall man from the big-top was standing with his hands on his hips, his whip wrapped around his shoulder. A grin touched his lips and his moustache quivered as if he was holding back a laugh.

'I am the ringmaster of the Forrest's Circus.' he bowed and waved his hand with a flourish. He raised his face to the stunned duo. 'You may call me Forrest. Whom am I addressing?' he inquired politely.

Forrest, what a strange name, Whispered Prudence. *He won't hear me, will he?*

The wolf shook his head disbelievingly. *Be sensible please.*

The wolf raised his head and looked Forrest in the eye. They were dark, almost black. He had never seen that colour in a human before.

My name is Sylvester Bluesky. This is Prudence, he waved at the hare.

They waited in awkward silence for Forrest to reply.

'Wonderful, wonderful!' Forrest clapped his hands and clicked his cuban heeled boots together, 'Splendid! Come and meet the others,' he waved his arms expansively towards the big-top.

You can hear me? Stammered Prudence, looking up at Forrest earnestly.

'Yes, I can hear you both.' he raised an eyebrow.

Sylvester Bluesky stepped closer and flinched. He recognized the magic exuding from Forrest. *I know what you are!* He whispered to Forrest so Prudence couldn't hear him.

I humbly ask you will not tell anyone. Forrest looked down with a dangerous glint in his eye.

They locked eyes, Sylvester Bluesky was falling into two deep pools of midnight blue, he felt the pull of Forrest's magic. Not Earth Magic and neither Dark Magic. Magic, he had not felt for centuries. Magic from another realm.

I agree to keep your secret. The wolf nodded.

Thank you. Forrest bowed his head slightly, never leaving Sylvester Bluesky's gaze.

'Now, come and meet the circus family!' he waved his arms affably towards the big-top, spun on his purple boots, and walked ahead leaving them staring after him.

Can we go? Prudence jumped up and down.

Sylvester Bluesky sniffed the air once more.

Forrest has given us an invitation to see the circus, I think it would be rude not to. He moved off in the direction Forrest had taken, looking back at the hare, he said cautiously, *Prudence, keep on your guard, something is not quite right here.*

Forrest stood outside the entrance to the big-top with a beaming smile.

'Come in, come in. There is one act practicing in the ring.' he waved them inside.

Prudence jumped back in surprise as a woman in a bright pink checkered dress came out of the big-top. Her frizzy green hair piled on top of her head, a white painted face, with huge orange lips and two red dots on her cheeks.

'Move out the way!' she shouted grumpily to Prudence.

Forrest raised an eyebrow at her. 'Now, now, Gladys. Don't be rude to our guests.' Forrest turned to Sylvester Bluesky and Prudence. 'I would like you to meet Gladys one of our clowns.'

Gladys stopped in her stride. Looked Prudence up and down. She gave a little bow. She opened her hand and a small daisy lay in the palm of her hand.

'For you.' Gladys handed the daisy to Prudence.

'Thank you,' Prudence uttered in awe.

Prudence put her nose to smell the Daisy, her nose twitched, it didn't smell familiar. *Poof!* The daisy exploded into small petals and floated down on the hare.

That was amazing! Prudence stamped her back leg excitedly.

Gladys's lips twitched. 'Enjoy your tour.' She cast an eye at Forrest, nodded and walked away.

'This way.' Forrest pushed open the red canvas material which acted as a door and went into the dimness of the big-top.

Sylvester Bluesky followed him in and adjusted his eyes to the dimness. Forrest sat in the front of a row of yellow painted benches. His large hands patted the seat beside him welcomingly.

When have you ever seen a wolf sit on a seat? The floor will do nicely thank you. Sylvester Bluesky beamed with good humour.

You are a very big example of your species, no offence. I think the floor would indeed be better. Forrest smiled at Sylvester Bluesky.

I will sit next to Forrest, much better view! Prudence rushed ahead and jumped up on the seat next to Forrest, missed her spot and crashed into him.

'No harm done.' Forrest held up a hand, 'I admire your energetic enthusiasm!' he laughed a deep hearty laugh.

In the circus ring were men dressed in blue silk costumes doing acrobats. A drum rolled sounded and the men climbed on top of each other and made a human pyramid. Symbols clashed and the man at the top of the pyramid held up his hand and a firework flashed above it.

Brilliant! Brilliant! Prudence shouted.

Sylvester Bluesky looked at Forrest and sighed. *She is still very young.*

'The circus makes everyone feel young. The magic, mystery and the impossible. It's all here for you to see.' Forrest cast his hand towards the ring. 'Come with me, I will introduce you to some more of our circus family.' Forrest got up and walked.

Sylvester Bluesky and Prudence found themselves in a small changing room. There were all sorts of costumes hung up neatly. Feather boas and glittered chiffon scarves littered the clothes racks. A small man, wearing a bright green suit came forward from behind one of the clothing racks.

'Hello, you're friends of Forrest are you. My name is Magnus Wintertree, I am the wardrobe master.' he gave a little bow, 'I look after all the costumes and make up.' He brushed down a dress which was hanging up.

Do you do the clowns make up; they look a little scary! Prudence asked.

Forrest conveyed her question to the wardrobe master.

'Oh no, never!' Magnus Wintertree threw up his hands in horror, 'Each clown has designed their own makeup for their face. No two clowns have the same face. Watch carefully when you meet them.'

'Thank you, Wintertree, we couldn't give such a good show without your dedication to the costumes!' Forrest patted him on the back, Magnus Wintertree beamed under Forrest's praise.

'Now to move on.' Forrest waved then on.

Sylvester Bluesky shook his head, *Sadly, we have no more time. We must go. This has been enjoyable.*

Prudence looked as if she was going to argue but the wolf gave her a stern look.

'Understandable, we are just setting up. Why don't you come on Saturday or Sunday and watch the show?' Forest said amiably.

Yes, we will be here! Prudence bounced up and down excitedly, she stopped under the quelling look of the wolf.

We would be honoured to accept your invitation. Thank you, we will see you on Sunday. Sylvester bowed to Forrest. *Come Prudence we must get on with your training.*

'By the way, you know we have met before. Some time ago, I would never forget a magical white wolf.' Forrest waved at them as they started to go.

Sylvester Bluesky looked at Forrest quizzically, a glimmer of a memory surfaced.

Yes, I remember, that was a very long time ago. You had a different name. The wolf looked at Forrest trying to remember his name.

'Indeed, I did.' Forrest went back inside the big-top.

CHAPTER 2

THE LURE OF DREAMS

Clarke Sharma slammed the door behind him, glad to be standing in the sanctuary of home. His eyes adjusted to the dim light of the pink wallpapered hall. Water dripped onto the floor from a black violin case he was carrying, he was careful it didn't touch the walls and mark them with muddy water. Wiping his mud caked wellington boots on the hairy doormat, he gave a wry smile, at the smears of mud coating the bristles.

'Better clear that up before Mum gets home, she won't be too pleased with that mess.' A picture of his mother's disapproving face shot into his thoughts.

A rivulet of water trickled down his cheek. He wiped his face roughly with the cuff of his coat, not that it helped much, it was saturated with rainwater. Heavy rain beat against the door behind him drummed its crazy beat, cracking the silence of the dim lit hall. Pulling at the wet toggles of his coat with numb fingers, they slipped off the fastenings smooth surface.

'Come on,' he willed the toggle to slip though the leather strap, 'I hate toggles!' He pulled at them angrily.

Finally, they were undone, he wiggled out of his coat, he eyed the row of dry coats hanging on their black metal pegs. He shrugged his shoulders, and let the sodden coat fall into a wet heap onto the floor. He shivered against the cold. His boots squeak on the floor sounded loud in his ears as he walked down the hall. A large wooden captain's chair stood in one corner, it was old and rickety. Grabbing the chair's arm, he sat down heavily; a sharp creak moaned under the burden of his weight. Setting the black case onto the floor beside him, he was glad not to have to carry it any further. He flexed his fingers to get some life back into them. Leaning back into the chair, he pushed his booted toe against the heel of his mud caked wellington boot. His face screwed up with the effort, the boot was firmly stuck on his foot. There was a whoosh of air and eventually his boot came off. Clarke did the same with his other foot, this time he used his socked foot to wedge against the boot. A sensation of cold and slimy mud seeped through his grey sock onto his skin, he shuddered. After a struggle, he was rewarded with the sound of a 'thud', as the boot hit the red tiled floor.

'Thought they would never come off.' He spoke to the empty hall, he blew out his cheeks, thankful he would not have to spend the rest of the day in wellington boots.

He stretched out his legs and wiggled his toes. A sharp stab in his calf, the muscle bunched up hard.

'Ahh,' his high-pitched scream filled the hall.

He bent over the edge of his chair and massaged the offending muscle.

'Why do I always get cramp when I take off these boots!' He eyed the dirty boots accusingly.

The cramp settled down and Clarke sat back enjoying the silence of the house. He let out a satisfying sigh. Clarke enjoyed the freedom of an empty house. Glancing at the tall grandfather clock, the black hands told the time. Twelve-thirty. His parents were not due back for several hours. They both worked at the local hospital. He glanced over to the spot by the door where they kept their leather medical bags. Clarke smiled as he remembered some of the tales his father told him about hospital life. His mother would chide him for not being professional.

'Doctors do not discuss their patients' she would rebuke him. Usually there would be a smile playing on her lips, and a dimple in her cheek taking some of the sting out of her rebuke. His smile turned to a frown; his thoughts turned to his mother. He worried his lower lip with his teeth. She had been angry with him this morning. Every Saturday he had a violin lesson, this morning he had forgotten. He was not too keen on the instrument, but he worked at playing it because he knew it made his parents happy. Anyway, he thought, lesson with Mrs Monte-Vela had been accomplished. An hour of her breathing over him and chastising him for not practicing more in her heavy Italian accent. The route back home via the ford had been tempting, he had stopped and watched the turbulent, muddy water rush by. The water had risen above the small bridge which straddled the ford. As he had walked across, he lost his footing, slipped and some of the water had gushed over his violin case. He had shaken off most of the water, but it didn't matter, the rain started to come down in thick sheets, blinding him as he walked home. Closing his eyes to rest a little. He clenched his fists, once more rest illuded him. Memories from last year pierced his mind, thick and dark it roamed, freely and unbidden, reminding him of the betrayal of his friends. Sucking in his cheeks he stood up from the oak chair. His stomach reminding him he hadn't eaten today as he had rushed out for his lesson. He went into the cramped kitchen, opened a cupboard, and inspected the contents. Reaching in he grabbed a fresh loaf of bread, out of the larder he balanced cheese and butter on the bread, slapped them down onto the kitchen counter, and proceeded to cut a thick slice of bread and broke off a chunk of cheese. He scoffed the food noisily, and watched the antics of a small brown bird, darting around the garden from the window. He looked around the kitchen, his lip curled, they had moved to this small cottage from the market town of Malmesbury.

'Because of what had happened.' Clarkes eyes narrowed; the memory tapped at his brain. He stopped eating and stared unseeing at the floor. The recollection of that fateful day crept back, scratching to be seen, memories he tried to forget, but never could. Smacking his tongue against the roof of his mouth, the food tasted dry, he was no longer hungry. Throwing the remnants of food back into cupboards, he slammed the pantry door with more force than he meant to, the door complained, it wobbled on its hinge, the crack of wood splintering sliced the silence of the kitchen. He poked his finger against the door, to makes sure he hadn't damaged it too badly. The door looked fragile on the hinge, he decided he would find a screwdriver later and fix it. Lines creased his forehead, and he wrinkled his nose, his mother would notice the disfigured hinge, but there was nothing he could do about it now. He gave the door one more prod, it didn't move under his fingers. Clarke grunted and made his way out the kitchen to the stairs. His fingers traced the smooth wood as he ran up them, grabbing the banister just before he reached the top, he vaulted over it, with a cat like precision and softly landed on the carpet. It was a great feeling to be in control. He marched down the small landing to his small bedroom, kicked back the door, crossed the room in a few steps, and threw himself onto his bed. The mattress was soft and gave way easily under the weight of his body. His eyelids felt heavy, he closed them. His mind wandered, a memory thrust images at him beneath his lids, he struggled to beat them away. The memory from that fatal day won, a terrible day, when his teacher Mooremarsh had killed the school caretaker, Ankleridge. That was the day he had discovered his best friend had Earth Magic. Clarke drew his hands into two fists at his side. Joshua Appleby, he scoffed at the thought of him. His best friend had Earth Magic and had never told him. He had found out one terrible cold snowy afternoon, in a damp barn, that his friends, Joshua and Milly Appleby had magic. Worst still, Delvera Mooremarsh, their teacher, it turned out, was a dangerous woman. She practiced Dark Magic. Clarke had found out that if you didn't have Earth Magic, Dark Magic was where you turned if you wanted to possess magic. A voice pushed behind his eye lids.

Do you want magic? The question slid easily.

'Yes, don't we all?' he called out into the silence.

An uneasy sleep crept upon him. The stillness in his head stretched out its hand what seemed like an eternity. He dreamed the same dream. He was lying in a hospital bed. His skull throbbed an aching beat against his skull. Feverishly turning in the hospital bed, he struggled under the covers. The presence of a woman drifted into view. She laid her cold hand on his brow and sang to him; the sound of her voice calmed his raging mind. His eyes half opened, through a fringe of his eyelashes, he found himself gazing up at a face he recognised. It was craggy and framed with frizzy white hair. A terrible face, fearsome, he knew he should have been afraid, but for some unfathomable reason, he wasn't. Clarke's hesitation melted away under her gaze, she was a vision of frailty framed with kindness. He didn't care about the contradiction of goodness or evil, he just wanted the song to go on.

'Your friends have lied and failed you, my child,' the voice purred at him through thin blue tinged lips.

'No, they wanted to help me,' Clarke had half-heartedly croaked back from his hospital bed. 'You were there, you saw how they tried to protect me.'

'They will not share their magic with you. They could have if they had wanted to. Instead, they let you come to harm,' The voice was smooth in the darkness. 'Not great friends I would say!'

The taste of bile in his mouth, bitterness, like thick black oil, coating, and staining, seeping its way up inside him. Had he been betrayed by his friends? Had Mathew known?

'Of course, Mathew knew. He never got hurt, did he?' The woman read his thoughts and fed putrid maggots to his fears.

She flinched in pain as she raised her hand and caressed his brow.

'Forget, forget,' she mumbled under her breath.

'I know you. I just can't seem to remember where from.' He had muffled under the stiffly starched bed sheet.

'I will teach you. Do not fear. I am here for you. You should not have been hurt. Sorry about that. My power will protect you.' The voice was edged with regret. It became fainter, he felt cold, bereft at the silence which followed her departure. He wanted the voice to be with him forever.

'Don't go.' He whispered into the dark silence.

He was terrified he would not hear it again. His body trembled violently.

'Are you sure you want me here?' Her voice broke the silence. 'After all the horror? You are very young.'

'I am thirteen and a half!'

He heard her laugh as he uttered 'and a half!'

'Yes, I want to hear your song.' He was glad to hear her laugh. 'What is your name.'

'Come, come now, don't you recognise me? I am Delvera Mooremarsh.'

Clarke felt a corner of his mind recoil and shrivel up. He knew the name should have stabbed cold fear into his heart, but it hadn't. He was too caught up in her magic to want to flee.

'I want you here.' He coughed into the silent ward.

A sickly-sweet smell engulfed him; it made him gag.

'I need to leave; I will teach you Dark Magic. Powerful magic. We will destroy the Appleby's together.'

'Yes, I would like that.' He had trembled at the thought of the power he would have if he had magic.

Fury swept through his bones as he lay in the hospital bed, the flames of hatred for his old friends licked his body, consuming every thought in his head.

Yes, I want to see the Appleby family destroyed.

'I will teach you magic when you dream. Till we meet next time. The way of Dark Magic is now yours. You must not share this with anyone. Do you understand.' She had whispered insidiously into his ear.

'Yes, I understand.' His brow had felt feverish again.

She had nodded and left him alone in his dreams, her song playing in his head.

A dark icy wall wrapped its way around him, drowning any happiness he felt, strangling any hope, leaving him cold, alone and bitter.

Clarke's eyes snapped open.

'I hate you all. You will all see. I will destroy your world.' His voice echoed around the room.

Sleep. Sleep and learn! He recognised the voice in his head.

Mooremarsh had kept her promise. She had returned in his dreams, to teach him Dark Magic.

Are you sure you want to learn the art of Dark Magic? Once you have the knowledge and used it, there is a costly price, but the rewards are unmeasurable.

'Yes, I want to learn.' He whispered back to her. 'I want to learn everything.'

There will be no going back. The law of Dark Magic, it is yours forever, you will lose some of yourself to it, but it will make you powerful.

Clarke felt heavy and his head rolled to one side. He stared unseeing at the wall.

'I want to learn.' He mumbled.

We will continue your lessons then, listen carefully to my words

CHAPTER 3
THOMAS HOBBES HIGH

Milly Appleby sat in her favourite corner of the playground; a book perched in her hand. A yellow title blazed across the front, Celtic Chieftains. She had a fascination with the 'old ways' as her mother put it, this attraction had started after the last winter break when she had discovered she possessed Earth Magic. Milly had devoured as many books on the subject as her mother would lend her.

'Read them slowly, savour the instruction within their pages.'

She wanted to read and learn as much Earth Magic as she could. It irritated her when her mother limited the range of books she could read. Her thumb nail scratched the page lightly, the wave of annoyance dampened, replaced with the memory of her battle with Mooremarsh, how her fury had driven her magic, and nearly cost her everything.

You know I am here. A warm whisper flitted in her thoughts.

She felt the presence of her 'fire bird' as she called her affectionately, though her name was Miskunn. The bird's golden feathers shone like fire, yellow eyes like two small topaz jewels, and a razor-sharp beak, Milly would never want her fingers near it. She smiled to herself and pretended not to notice her feathered friend.

Milly! Miskunn ruffled her feathers.

Milly looked over the top of her book and at the beautiful golden bird.

Miskunn, you should not be here. Milly pursed her lips at her beloved companion.

She cocked her head and examined the creature. Miskunn had been with her forever. Putting the book in her lap, she leaned back against the cold brick wall behind her.

Miskunn, why am I the only one who can see you? Milly asked.

A vivid memory stabbed at her, the day when she realised no one else could see Miskunn, the recollection still stung her. She had been three years old, picking mint leaves in the garden with her mother. Excitedly, she had pointed and called to Miskunn when her golden friend had circled above the trees in the garden.

'Look it's Miskunn, Mummy. She is my eagle. Isn't she beautiful!' Milly had clapped her hands as Miskunn had swooped down and perched beside her.

'Miskunn' she had called and pointed at her so her mother would notice her friend.

But her mother could not see Miskunn.

'Nice game Milly, come and see which herbs you can name.' Her mother pointed at mint leaves.

'No, here is Miskunn, she wants you to say hello.' Milly had giggled.

'Bring your imaginary friend with you, and after we have finished harvesting this mint, we will look at the different herbs.'

'Say hello to Miskunn, it's not polite to ignore her.' Milly had sobbed, not understanding why her mother could not see the bird.

She never mentioned Miskunn again.

Now she had Earth Magic, an ancient magic, she had sworn to keep secret from those who did not possess it. When she discovered her magic last year, she feared being even more different than others. Her awkwardness made her seem standoffish. It transpired that she was not the only family member to have Earth Magic. Her mother, Alana Appleby and twin brother Joshua had magic too. They had remained silent at the time of her magical emergence. She had thought she was losing her mind. It was Christmas eve when Sylvester Bluesky materialized in front of her, the shock had been too much. She had fainted! Milly brushed out her creased skirt with agitated hands. She had not gone through the night struggle. *Nox Certamen* they had called it. Terrible nightmares, everyone who had Earth Magic went through the *Night Struggle*.

During the dreaming, the choice between good and evil was made. She had never made the choice, she had never experienced *Nox Certamen*. How could she know which she would have chosen, Earth Magic over Dark Magic without the dreams? Seven Elders had been sent for to determine if her magic was pure or if it should they should bind her magic. Memories of her mother's worried faced floated under her closed lids. After a lengthy interview of her and her parents, the Elders had decided not to bind her magic. Milly knew she should have told them about Miskunn during the interview. She had been afraid that they would think the firebird was a dark omen. Sylvester Bluesky, her mother's animal guide was chosen to be Milly's magical guide, whilst they found an appropriate creature.

Miskunn, why did you not help me when I did battle with Mooremarsh? She shuddered at the memory of the battle of Earth Magic against Dark Magic. She had nearly lost herself to Dark Magic, Sophia and Sylvester Bluesky had talked her down. She could still feel the coldness of standing on that abyss as she faced Mooremarsh in battle. A choice between Earth Magic and Dark Magic. For a heart stopping moment, she nearly walked in the path of darkness. When she had needed Miskunn most, she had been absent.

You did not tell the Elders or your mother about me! The firebird stung her, sounding hurt. She flew around her in circles. *You must tell Sylvester Bluesky about me. He will be sorry, but he will understand.* She replied cryptically.

Milly shook her head sadly. *I think I have left it too long to tell the truth about you.*

Have courage and be strong. It will only get harder. Tell the truth, you are not a coward. Staying silent is as bad lying.

With that, Miskunn disappeared.

That's easy for you to say! She replied huffily.

Milly shrugged her shoulders and went back to her book. So absorbed in her novel with the image of mighty men and women that she did not notice anyone walking up to her.

'So, you have magic do you,' sneered a tall girl called Lavinia, her hands were placed on her hips.

Milly snapped her book shut and stood up from her comfortable place in the corner of the playground.

'I don't know what you are talking about!' Milly could feel her heart racing. How could they know?

'We were told this morning before school by a friend of yours that you have told him you have magic.' Lavinia turned and put her forefinger to her temple and rotated it to give the 'mad' sign at her friend and turned back, 'So, show us some magic. Or are you just telling people you have magic to get some friends other than your brother and Mathew Anderson.'

Both the girls started laughing.

Milly's eyes narrowed; anger flushed her cheeks. Who told them such a thing, told them her secret?

Calm Milly, remember anger is never used with Earth Magic. Sylvester Bluesky's voice coaxed her. *There is strength in eye contact, the weak cower from it.*

Milly stood a little taller and looked Lavinia in the eye. The eye of a bully. Like most bullies she would not like being stood up too.

'Once again, I am telling you someone is pulling your leg.' Milly felt she was telling the truth as she had Earth Magic, which was very different to the parlour tricks seen at parties. She stared deeper into Lavinia's eyes and watched her with satisfaction as she turned away from her.

'Well, that's not what Clarke says. He says you are creepy, that's why no one likes you,' Lavinia laughed, Milly noticed an air of doubt in the laugh.

'Come on Milly, you said that you had used magic to stop Miss Mooremarsh stealing the Flaming Sword and the Chalice.' Scoffing sounded behind Milly she turned to the voice she recognised so well.

'Clarke, I don't know what you are talking about!' Milly glared at him. 'Didn't your mother tell you to stay away from me? You really are a pathetic idiot.' Milly looked at the two girls standing beside him and continued scathingly, 'Guess it's the only way you can find friends,' she nodded at Lavinia and started laughing.

Milly looked at him steadily, raised a condescending eyebrow, threw a sarcastic glance at the girls, and walked away.

'Milly,' Joshua Appleby was marching towards her with Mathew in his wake. 'Thought we would find you here,'

She tucked her book a little tighter under her arm walking towards him.

'Clarke giving you trouble?' Mathew looked across the playground broodingly at the boy.

'Nothing I can't handle! Come on or we will be late for English,' she pulled his sleeve and they all walked in the direction to one of the small buildings.

The trio had started at Thomas Hobbes High a few months ago, and for Milly it had not been an easy transition. For the first time she shared the same class as her twin brother Joshua, and in many ways, it was nice, but she often felt she was in his shadow. Milly pushed away feelings of resentment. Her brother's easy nature and engaging manner meant he made friends quickly. She on the other hand found it hard to make friends.

'Watch out, Mrs Allcart is coming towards us,' Mathew looked at Milly and made a face. He found her mathematic lessons a nightmare.

Milly looked towards the waddling teacher bearing down on them across the playground. The heel of her black shoes clicking on the black tarmac floor, the sound echoed around the now empty playground. Following in her wake was a tall dark-haired girl.

'You three, stop.' Allcart's bored voice called to them.

Obediently, they stopped and waited. Milly hid a giggle at Mathews contorted face. The teacher was puffing slightly when she caught up with them.

'This young lady is in your class for the rest of the term. Her name is Eleanor Redfern.' Mrs Allcart said in a breathless voice. She pointed at the girl with her thumb. 'Take her with you.' She looked at each of them, 'Mathew Anderson, tuck your shirt in!'

Milly put her hand over her mouth to stop a giggle, Mathew had automatically put his hand on his shirt to tidy it up. The teacher walked away leaving the four children looking at each other.

'My name is Eleanor Redfern. They call me Nori.' Her accent was strange, her manner bold. Green eyes smiled at Milly.

'So where are you from?' Milly asked trying to be friendly. 'We live a couple of miles outside of Malmesbury, just past a village called Easton Grey.'

'My family travel a lot. Last year France, Spain, and Germany. This year Ireland, Wales, Scotland, just come from Edinburgh. We are in the west-country for a while.' She answered looking at them all. 'So, which way are we going?'

'This way,' Milly nodded in the direction, 'History next.' Milly was just about to walk away when she saw her brothers face. His cheeks had flushed crimson, he looked away when he saw Milly's questioning look.

'Come on Nori, you can sit next to me if you like.' Milly asked shyly.

'That sounds good. It's never nice starting a new school, and I have attended a few.' Nori replied affably.

Nori linked her arm through Milly's but let go quickly, like she had been scorched. The two girls stared at each other. Milly thought Nori was about to say something when the holler of teacher's voice spoilt the moment.

'Get to lessons!'

She felt a tug on her shoulder as Mathew pulled her towards the school entrance.

'Come on Nori, follow us!'

They reached their history lesson just as the teacher had opened the door to the classroom. Milly stood in front of Nori thinking about the energy she felt when she had put her arm through hers. It wasn't Earth Magic, but it was something else, magic she did not recognise.

'You don't want to sit with her!' Lavinia called out to Nori, 'come and sit here.' She pointed at a vacant seat next to her.

Nori ignored Lavinia and followed Milly to a table.

'I know you want to ask me.' Nori whispered to Milly.

Milly rested a gaze on her.

'Ask her what?' Mathew asked sitting the other side of Nori.

Nori gave Milly a conspiratorial grin.

Before Milly could reply, the history teacher tapped the board with a piece of chalk. The lesson had started. But Milly had been left with a bigger question. What type of Magic did Nori use?

CHAPTER 4
WHAT EVER HAPPENED TO DELVERA MOOREMARSH?

A tattered fragment of a newspaper quivered in the wrinkled hand of Delvera Mooremarsh. A black and white image of a man, with a large grin, leaped out from the page she was holding. The only thing that interested her was the small object that was neatly balanced in the palm of his hand. The title above the picture quoted:

Ruby Dragon is back at Overhill Hall and will be exhibited soon!

Mooremarsh gazed at the picture, her hand trembled uncontrollably. She recognized the statue.

'Idiots, its full title is The Ruby Dragon of Craig Isle.'

Mooremarsh angrily crushed the fragment and pushed it deep into her pocket. She picked up her self-fashioned walking staff off the park bench. It had been her home for the past week.

'Nobody takes notice of a down and out,' she snorted, 'in fact, they always look the other way.'

She shuffled out of the small park, wincing with pain each step she took.

'The library will have what I need to research where to find the Ruby Dragon.'

Excited she tried to pick up the pace, leaning heavily on her self-fashioned staff, ignoring the ripping pain in her legs, she marched as fast as she could towards the library. Soon she got to the bottom of Park Street, her breathing came in gurgling rasps. After some time, she stood before the gothic looking entrance of Bristol Central Library.

Mooremarsh stood for a moment to catch her breath, it had taken a lot of energy to make the short walk.

'I will have to be careful and conserve the little life force I have left,' she leaned heavily with sweaty hands on the thick staff. Glancing at the shriveled hand, her upper lip curled.

'You made a miscalculation dealing with the Appleby's' she murmured to herself, remembering the fight. A face hovered in her thoughts. 'Never thought the child would be so powerful, thought it would be the boy or even the mother,' Rubbing the frail hand with her slightly healthier one she thought about her appearance, she was disheveled, and her skin was sallow, wrinkled, and thin like parchment. Mooremarsh had been on the road for months, sleeping in doorways and vacant buildings to avoid the police.

Delvera Mooremarsh was a murderer... and practiced Dark Magic!

Her hand straightened out her dress as best she could, and she stumbled into the warmth of the library from the cold of the winter afternoon sun. Standing for a while, she let her eyes acclimatize to the darkness of the foyer, soon enough, everything was clear again. She looked around and found what she was looking for, a sign which pointed the way to the Reference Library.

'That's where newspapers would be kept.'

In the quiet of the library, the tap-tap of her staff, ruptured the silence. She let out a heavy sigh when she saw the flight of stairs. She clambered up each stair, breathing heavily as she went. Tightly clutching the smooth wooden rail to steady her on each tread, she growled at the effort it was taking her to reach the top of the stairs.

'Eventually!' she moaned when she had climbed the last stair.

She stood a while and caught her breath. Taking a deep breath, she shuffled her way through a large glass door and went from the gloominess of the hall into the bright reference library. The brightness from the large windows blinded her, for a moment she was disorientated, she covered her eyes. She could feel the heat of the sun through her lids, it made her nauseous. Her hand slipped away from her eyes, and she opened them.

A young Librarian sat on a high stool behind a desk stamping books. The librarian stopped for a moment and Mooremarsh felt her stare at her bedraggled state. Mooremarsh watched the librarian's eyebrows make a furrow in a smooth forehead, her disapproval oozed throughout the room. Glaring back at Mooremarsh, she heard her give a loud sigh, making it obvious, that she thought her quiet sanctity had been disturbed.

Mooremarsh stood taller, turned away from the librarian's waspish face and spied stacks of neatly laid out newspapers, upon a heavy oak table. Behind the table stood tall mahogany drawers, which held months of past newspapers. The smell of wood and paper filled her nostrils and lingered, reminding her of a time when she had been a teacher. Not any teacher, Joshua Appleby's teacher.

How could she not have detected their magic? Earth Magic smelt so sweet. She pushed the thought to one side and focused on the task at hand. Find all the information she could about Overhill Hall, so she could steal the Ruby Dragon of Craig Isle and use its power for herself.

Ignoring the unwelcome stare of the librarian she made her way to the table with the newspapers. She pulled out a chair, it made a teeth-jarring sound as it scraped along the wooden floor. Satisfied she had pulled away far enough, she sat down heavily with a thud and gave out a loud sigh.

'Tut, tut!' the librarian's lips puckered as she issued the rebuke.

Mooremarsh ignored her and smiled, she knew the librarian would be watching her irritated. It gave her some pleasure in her miserable state that she had annoyed her. Reaching out a wrinkled hand, she grabbed the first newspaper. Turning the pages, a noisy grunt issued from her lips when she had found the last page.

She threw the newspapers to one side and repeated the action with each one she read. She had rummaged through several issues before she found what she wanted.

'Yes!' Mooremarsh shouted hoarsely.

Her finger stabbed at a picture of a large ruby dragon.

'I thought it was you.' She sat back in the chair a long bony finger tapped her tooth.

'Another family heirloom!' her loud hiss caught the attention of the librarian.

Mooremarsh started to tear the page out of the newspaper, an irritated voice spoke over her shoulder.

'What are you doing, newspapers belong to the library!' came the reproachful voice of the librarian.

Mooremarsh turned and looked directly at her. Behind her stood a young woman, her lips were pursed, her eyes accusingly glinted back at her.

'Yes, and now it belongs to me,' her slow quiet menacing reply should have warned the librarian of the oncoming danger.

Mooremarsh's eyes flickered in the sunlight like a reptile.

'You are oblivious to your situation,' Mooremarsh's tongue darted out and licked her dry lips.

'You need to go and leave the newspapers on the table.' The librarian's foot tapped impatiently.

Mooremarsh sat still, her eyes darted around the room. They were the only two in the room. A thin smile stretched across cracked lips. She pushed against the table with fragile hands and stood up and faced her accuser.

'Come on hurry up,' the clipped voice caught in her throat as she looked at the old lady. She knew something was wrong, cold fear seeped down her neck.

Danger!

'It is unfortunate you have approached me and have been quite rude if I don't mind saying so,' Mooremarsh looked at her name badge which was clipped onto her shirt and read it out to the vastness of the Reference Library, 'Miss Moss,' her voice clipped sarcastically.

It is forbidden. A voice tapped at Mooremarsh's mind.

I don't care, I want it. Mooremarsh screamed back into the darkness recess of her mind.

You won't like the consequences.

When have I ever cared about consequences? Leave me alone. Mooremarsh screamed in her head.

She looked at the young woman, her freshness, her youth. She could smell her light perfume.

Stop me if you think it's wrong!

Mooremarsh feigned fainting and fell forward and collapsed onto the librarian.

'Come on, I will help you out of the library -' the librarians voice caught in her throat.

She felt Mooremarsh's fingers painfully digging into her arm, she was mumbling something under her breath. The librarian could not make out the words, but she felt weak, the room was getting darker. As quickly as the nauseating pain began it was over.

Miss Moss, the librarian, was dead.

A crack split the air. Mooremarsh turned her head in its direction. A red haze in the corner of the room shone in the shape of a door. It opened a crack and she thought she saw a shape slither through it. As quickly as the door appeared it disappeared. She swallowed hard and looked around the library. The warnings tickled the back of her mind.

You won't like the consequences. You are mine now!

The sensation of being struck with a hot ball of fire covered her body, she could feel the presence of someone else in the room, but she could not see them. There was only silence.

'Well, that was an interesting aftereffect!'

Delvera Mooremarsh stood up and stretched out a cat like stretch. She looked at her fingers and wriggled them. There was no pain, and they had the appearance of youth. Stretching her arms upwards and she gave a low evil laugh. She felt the energy of youth careering thought her body, the energy she had stolen from Miss Moss. Mooremarsh looked down at the now still body by her feet. The body was shriveled and yellow, a puddle of ash surrounding it.

'Miss Moss, I do believe you look like an Egyptian Mummy!' she put her finger to her lips and made a noise. '*Shhhh*'.

A loud crackle of laughter exploded from her now smooth lips; she pushed the body with the toe of her foot and noticed for the first time the tidy, clean clothes Miss Moss was wearing.

'Well, Miss Moss, it looks like you are to provide me with a wardrobe of clothes as well today!' looking at the still form, her callous laughter filled the room.

'I suppose it would be rude of me not to thank you for your youthful life force, even though it will only feed me for a while.'

Mooremarsh changed into Miss Moss's clothes and left her dirty ones in a heap on the floor. She looked up at the clock, the minute hand cut the silence. She had spent too much time in one place. Quickly gathering up the pages of newspaper she had torn she stuffed them into the pocket of her newly acquired jacket. Nimbly tip toeing to Miss Moss's desk, she snatched up a bright orange handbag, sitting forlornly on the floor beside the desks foot.

'Your too bright for these surrounds,' she stroked the soft leather, 'Time to go!'

She felt energy flowing through her veins, as she walked out of the room, 'Haven't felt like this for a long time!' she cackled, 'Why didn't I take a life force sooner?'

A small shard of uncertainty dented her newfound confidence. What would be the price for using such powerful Dark Magic?

She had become a *life-force vampire*.

Mooremarsh thought hard. Had she ever come across any writings in her books about them. They had rarely been discussed by her family. Even when they had, it had been in hushed tones, whispers frightened of being overheard, the subject was taboo, she had questions, but had never asked.

Her feet ached in the new shoes, she tried to wriggle her toes, but the shoes were too tight.

'I need two things,' she murmured looking down at her feet.

'New shoes, I won't be able to walk far in these! Most importantly, find out who has my books!' She slapped the handbag against her side.

'I will need them in the weeks ahead. All my recipes for my spells,' she pushed her foot out in front of her, examining the ill-fitting shoe.

'And my heritage, the notes in the books scribbled by generations of my family.' She gave a final look at the shoes and made her way out of the door.

Mooremarsh came face to face with a gold framed mirror at the top of the stairs. She paused in front of it. Her hair was a rich dark brown, it was untidy about her face. Her hands darted up and tied the dark locks into a lose bun at the nape of her neck.

She opened the bag and rummaged through its contents. She found what she was looking for. A handkerchief. Looking around to make sure she was still alone, she carried on. Spitting on the handkerchief she used it to clean the grime off her face.

'Presentable,' She sniffed the air, 'but my dear, you do need a bath,' she grinned at her reflection, and skipped down the stair and made her way out of the library. It was when she had got out of the library she realized. She had forgot to look for a map of Overhill Hall.

'Too late now. I don't want to be around if they find the delightful Miss Moss!' She decided the risk was too great to go back.

Mooremarsh made her way back down the street, taking occasional glance at herself in shop windows. Reaching the park, the iron gate was shut. Her long fingers grasped the rusty gate and shoved it from its latch. The gate gave out a loud high-pitched squeak as it gave under her hand. The flutter of pigeon surprised her; she raised her hands to protect her face. The birds had been alarmed by the sound and flew out of nearby bushes. Their wings flapped and beat hard against the air, warning off the predator who had surprised them.

'Disgusting creatures.' She spat at them, her feet treading lightly on along the path.

Her fingertips caressed the leaves as she walked past the bushes, they felt rough as they curled and were dying in the winter sun. Soon she spied the familiar bench she had sat on for many days.

'I may be cold, hungry and tired. But my revenge keeps me burning.' She drawled as she sat down.

Drawing out the crumpled fragment of newspaper, she read the article again. The image of the Ruby Dragon at Overhill Hall hypnotized her.

Only she knew its power and how to *use it*.

Her grandfather had shown her its magical properties. Unfortunately, her grandmother had sold it before he could harness its power when he most needed it.

The statue had the power to give the owner *Eternal life*.

It would have kept him alive and combated the ravishes of using black magic. He had died young, just as her father had.

'Not me, I will live forever.' A cackle escaped her lips.

Mooremarsh pulled the orange bag she had stolen from Miss Moss closer to her and began to rummage through its contents. Finally, she found what she was looking for, a purse. She unclipped the clasp and emptied the money into her lap.

'Good, enough money for a ticket to Malmesbury, and a much-needed pair of shoes. My house should be safe to enter now that I look so young,' she rubbed her hands together gleefully, 'this is going to be fun.' She put the notes and change back into the purse, clipped it shut and threw it back into the bag.

'Even better still, that stupid boy, Clarke Sharma, thinks I will teach him Dark Magic,' her voice raised, 'does he really think I would pass onto him a lifetime of learning. Never, but the lie will keep him under my control. You always need a useful ally and spy. This has turned out to be a delicious day!' clapping her hands.

Her head turned quickly to the sound of the gate screeching open. Her heart skipped a beat. A man in a blue uniform and black helmet walked into the little park. His pace was even, and the shingle crunched beneath his feet. Mooremarsh turned away and covered her worried expression by busying herself with the contents of the handbag. Her eyes caught sight of two large, booted feet which stopped in front of her.

'Afternoon, miss.' A deep cheery voice greeted her.

She raised her face and put her hand above her eyes to shade them from the low sun.

'Afternoon, officer.'

The police officer looked at her. 'Nice day to sit in the park.'

'Yes, it is.' She replied bored, she wanted him to go so she could get on with her journey.

'Lovely spot to feed the birds.' He said conversationally.

'I do not like birds,' she replied waspishly.

Something caught his attention, he looked away from Mooremarsh, and in the direction of a shrill sound coming from the direction of the library.

Someone has found the body! Mooremarsh smiled to herself.

'Sorry, miss, I have to go. Duty calls.' He raised his hand to his helmet and ran away towards the sound of the whistle.

She stood up watching the policeman running away.

'And I, dear sir, have a bus to catch.'

CHAPTER 5
NORI REVEALS A MYSTERY

Joshua stuffed dried peppermint leaves into a brown paper bag. The sweet smell mingled with the aroma of herbs his mother was packing into a bag opposite him. She carefully wrote out instructions on two labels and licked the backs and stuck them firmly on the bag.

'I hate the taste of glue.' She smacked her tongue against the roof of her mouth.

'Deliver these to Mrs Keats,' she raised an eyebrow at Joshua's impatient stare, 'after that you can go to Saturday morning cinema.' His mother laughed at him.

Milly burst into the room and grabbed an apple from the bowl.

'Starving! Are we ready yet? Don't want to miss the first film.' She looked at the table, littered with herbs.

'Yes, let's go.' Joshua pulled on his coat and grabbed the two packets of herbs.

'Remind Mrs Keats that its one teaspoon of peppermint leaves to each cup of hot water, if she wants to add honey, only add a little.'

'OK Mum. See you at lunchtime.' Joshua waved at her.

'Be back by twelve-thirty, we have to get to Grandad Rose this afternoon.'

Milly nodded, grabbed Joshua's elbow, and pushed her brother in the direction of the door. Joshua tumbled out of the front door, looked up at the sky, it was a winter blue with a lemon sun. He pulled his scarf over his mouth, the morning air was crisp, and pinched at his nostrils.

'Hurry, we don't want to be late.' His sister marched on ahead, her arms swinging as she walked.

Soon they arrived at the corner of the lane which led to the Anderson Farm. Mathew sat on a concrete milk stand, beside four milk churns. He jumped down when he saw them.

'Cutting it a bit fine!' he moaned tapping his watch.

'We have to deliver this first.' Joshua saw the mutinous look in Mathew's eye. 'You and Milly get in the line; I will deliver this. If I don't get there on time, go in but save me a seat.'

'No, it's ok, we will all stick together.' Mathew raised his eyebrows.

'Come on run, that way we will pick up some time!' Milly started to run ahead.

'Will give it a try, I didn't sleep very well last night.' Mathew shrugged his shoulders.

'Still having nightmares?' Joshua turned away guilty, wanting to tell his friend the meaning of them but knowing he couldn't. He heard Mathew shuffling, he looked back at his friend.

'Yes, they are horrible, I wake up in a real sweat!' Mathew looked at his feet not wanting to relive the terrors of the dream.

'We need to catch up Milly,' Joshua changed the subject, 'she will never let me live it down if she gets to the cinema first!' Joshua held the bags a little tighter and jogged in pursuit of Milly.

Soon they were turning into a small street lined with stone cottages.

'The label says Mrs Keats, Number 19.' Joshua said examining the brown package.

'Over there, the one with the white door.' Milly pointed.

Joshua crossed the street and knocked on the door. It seemed to take ages before the door opened a crack.

'Yes,' wheezed a woman's voice.

'Hello, Mrs Keats?' Joshua asked.

'Yes,' replied the wheeze.

'I am Alana Appleby's son, Joshua. She has given me some preparations to deliver to you.' He held out the two brown bags.

'Oh, Alana, lovely woman. Wait I will just get the money.' The door shut; he could hear her scuffing down the hall.

He looked across the street at Mathew who was pointing at his watch. He heard the woman returning, the door was opened enough to pass the bags through.

'Mum said not to add too much honey.'

'Thank you, I have put an extra three pence for you lad.'

'Thank you!' Joshua waved as the door was shutting.

'Come on, we will just make it if we run!' Mathew started running in the direction of the Cinema.

There was still a queue of children when they arrived at Athelstan Cinema.

'Great,' Joshua punched his fist up in the air.

As they took up their place at the back of the line, a voice called out to them.

'Milly!'

'Hi Nori,' Milly stepped forward and put her arm through hers. 'Are you coming to the pictures?' Milly asked.

'Yes, thought I would go, haven't been to Saturday morning pictures for ages!'

'I got a tip, so thought I could buy us some treats.' He looked sideways at Nori, 'Is there anything you would like?'

'Liquorice.' Nori rested her eyes on Joshua, 'Please'

Joshua felt a strange sensation in his stomach, it always happened when he was near Nori.

'Could you get me some dairy buttermints if they have them.' Asked Milly.

'Chocolate nut bar for me if you are buying' Mathew put his thumb up at Joshua.

Joshua thrust out his hand to Milly, 'You get the tickets for us, I will go and get the sweets.' He went to walk away, instead he turned to Nori, 'Do you want to help me?'

Mathew sniggered. Joshua threw him a dangerous look.

'Yes, if you need help, I will come,' She handed Milly her money for her admission fee.

Milly watched them walk away and raised an eyebrow at Mathew.

Inside the cinema, Joshua waited in line at the confectionary counter. He tried to think of things to talk about with Nori, but nothing came to mind. The silence seemed to stretch on forever.

'I understand your dad owns a garage?' Her silvery voice floated to him above the din of all the excited children.

'Yes, he is a mechanic, pretty brilliant one at that.' Joshua racked his brains for a topic to talk about. He felt a bit of a fool just standing there. The silence was unbearable.

'And your mum, she a healer?'

'She is an herbalist. She treats illness with plants.' Joshua racked his brain, but his tongue was stubbornly still, words caught in his throat.

He looked at Nori, her eyes held a question, her lips were beautiful.

'Well?' A voice broke his thoughts, 'I haven't got all day. You can gawk at each other when you are inside.' A tall thin woman, her mouth moved quickly as she chewed gum, her hands held the counter.

Joshua felt awkward and rattled off the list of sweets. Nori took each bag as it was handed over.

'Got the tickets, we better get inside I can hear the advert starting.' Milly took a bag of sweets from Nori and headed towards the entrance.

Inside it was gloomy. Milly found two seats and sat in one, Mathew sat down next to her. She twisted her head around to see Joshua and Nori sitting two rows back.

'Do you want to sit next to Joshua?' She asked Mathew.

'I don't think he would be happy with that,' he laughed.

An usher shone a torch at him. 'If you can't keep quiet you will have to leave!'

Mathew settled back in his seat. The picture on the screen changed, the words to a song and loud music started. The whole cinema erupted with children singing the Minors Cinema Song. Everyone clapped at the end and the film started.

Joshua didn't watch much; he was aware of Nori sitting next to him.

'I hope they do a film about the collie dog. I love those films.' She whispered to him.

He merely nodded in reply.

The last cartoon flicked across the screen, bright lights flooded the theatre, a mechanical clunking sound whirled, the heavy red velvet curtains slid across a rail and covered the blank screen. Joshua caught a movement out the corner of his eye, Milly waving furiously to them. Nori waved back. She turned to him and took his hand. Joshua jolted as if an electric pulse shot up his arm and throat.

'Sorry Joshua, it won't do, it just won't do.' Nori smiled sadly at him.

Milly came to their row and Nori made her way towards her.

'I need to get back now.' Nori said never taking her eye off Joshua.

'Why don't you walk with us? We are going home now.' Milly grabbed her arm and pulled her up the aisle.

Outside, the light stung Joshua's eyes. The change from darkness to brilliant light made him a little queasy. He heard Milly laughing and followed the sound of her voice. They were soon away from the crowds of children and heading along the hedged land out of town. Joshua listened to the others talking excitedly about all the films and cartoons they had just seen.

'This is me. See you this afternoon.' Mathew crossed the lane and went up another.

They walked on for a while. Milly and Nori chatting as they went. Joshua saw Chestnut Cottage in the distance.

'I have something to show you both.' Nori stopped and looked around. 'I can show you as you have magic.'

Joshua heard Milly gasp.

'It's not what you think. I need to show you.' Nori stepped to one side. 'This is who I am.'

Nori wiggled her shoulders and stood a little taller.

Joshua and Milly gasped in unison.

Wings as tall as Nori flashed out of her back. Fine, threads of gold and blue weaved throughout her wings. An incandescent glow radiated about her.

Milly stepped back; her jaw slacked and her mouth opened wide.

'Wow!' she trembled at the shock of seeing a fairy standing before her.

Nori's wings rustled behind her. Milly walked closer to the delicate wings.

'Can I touch them,' Milly whispered excitedly, her eyes met Nori's hopefully.

Nori tilted her head to one side.

'Yes but be gentle. There is nothing more awful when someone tugs at my wings,' Nori shuddered dramatically, then laughed a tinkering laugh.

'Can you fly with them; they look so delicate?' Milly asked in excited tones, her quivering hand stroked the gossamer wing. She was in awe of the fairy standing in front of her.

Nori's eyebrows arched, she swung back her head laughing.

'No point in having wings if I can't fly!' she raised her eyes mockingly.

'A fairy as a friend, bet not many people can say that!' Milly let go of the wing and feasted her eyes on Nori's exquisite form.

Milly shook with excitement. A fairy, standing in front of her!

'Are there many others?' Milly looked about her.

Nori gazed at Milly, the smile fell from her face, she sighed.

'Yes, we normally live in a big family group. It's only my parents and I now,' she put a hand and silenced Milly.

'What do you call a group of fairies then?' Milly changed the subject.

Nori giggled, glad of a change of topic.

'Our family travel around so much I suppose you could call us a troupe of F*airies*.'

Nori smiled mischievously at Milly, 'however, I have heard us called a frollick of fairies though.'

Nori's lips twitched and she burst out laughing. Her wings shook and a light refracted and sparked around her. She caught her breath and stood a little taller looking at them both solemnly.

'So, we will keep each other's secrets about the magic world.' Nori held out her hands.

Milly immediately took Nori's hands in hers.

'You shouldn't have to ask it. Of course, we won't tell anyone,' Milly looked over at her brother, 'that is except our parents and the Elders.'

'Well, that seems fine then.' Nori let go of Milly's hands and fluttered her wings.

Joshua stood transfixed by her beauty. His heartbeat rapidly, he was surprised she couldn't hear it. He felt breathless and lightheaded at the sight of her great beauty.

'Well, now you both know that I am a fairy.' Nori held her hands up matter-of-factly, she turned to Joshua, 'and you now know why you are attracted to me. Humans usually are. Easy to charm a human you know,' she winked at him.

Joshua looked away feeling confused. Nori shrugged her shoulders nonchalantly and folded her wings back. She looked at Joshua waiting for him to say something. He stood tongue tied, wanting to say something, but the words would not flow. He felt his face flush and he bit his lower lip willing for something intelligent to spring to mind. Nothing came to him, he stood in silence, his hands dangled at his sides. A slow smile spread across Nori's lips.

'It's ok, I understand.' Her hand reached out sympathetically and patted Joshua on the shoulder.

'I have to hurry, bye.' Nori waved at them and hurried off up the lane.

Joshua watched her disappear into the distance.

'Well, first crush, and on a fairy, wait till I tell Mum,' Milly giggled uncontrollably.

His look quelled her.

'Sorry, but a fairy!' Milly laughed again, she ran away from him, her laughter drifting back to him.

'Yes, only I could be attracted to a fairy!' He thrust his hands in his pockets, and walked home, head down dejectedly.

CHAPTER 6
A POTTER'S SURPRISE

Grandad Rose sat at his potter's wheel, his foot tapped at the peddle, and the head of wheel spun around. His hand slipped over the clay expertly, his fingers pulling the clay higher and higher, with a twist of his fingers, the clay took shape and a bowl sat proudly on the wheel. He took a wire and deftly cut it off the wheel and placed it on alongside thirty-eight other bowls which sat on wooden boards. He examined the bowls he had made that morning, happy with them he got up from his wheel and stretched. He needed to deliver them in two weeks to the café in town. A clock chimed eleven thirty.

'They'll be here soon, better be getting the kettle on.' He washed his hands in a big brown bowl, put water into a kettle and set it on a small oil stove to boil.

He bent down and opened a dark varnished wooden cupboard door and felt his lower back twinge. A jolt of pain spurred its way down his back and thigh.

'I can tell winters here, can feel rheumatism rising in my bones.'

He rubbed his back and eyed the cupboard accusingly for being so low down. His hand rummaged in a cupboard and pulled out three mugs and set them on the side. Into a teapot he spooned out tea from a tea caddy with little roses on it. He smiled; it had been a present from his daughter for his birthday. The kettle whistled joyfully announcing that the water was boiling. He grabbed the kettle with a tea towel and poured the water into the teapot, a fragrant aroma floated up. No sooner than he had put the lid on the pot, Joshua, Milly, and Mathew burst through the door. Prudence pranced in behind. Not being magical, Grandad Rose couldn't see her.

'Hang your coats up, don't want them to get dirty.' He waved towards the pegs.

'Now lad,' looking at Mathew. 'I think it's your time to work at the wheel. You look tired and it's only mid-morning!'

'So would you with the nightmares I've been having!'

Grandad Rose threw Joshua a quick look, he raised his eyebrows giving him a warning. Joshua looked away, he wanted to tell his friend what the nightmares meant, but he knew it was forbidden. He caught Milly's look and knew what she was thinking, he shook his head a fraction. They had to keep quiet on the subject. He saw Prudence sniffing at the freshly made bowls, it was an accident waiting to happen with Prudence.

Prudence, get away from those bowls. Grandad will go spare if you knock them over!

The blue hare jumped back alarmed, bumped into a stool, and sent if flying.

Grandad Rose blinked, 'If you are in here Prudence, I suggest you go and lie down in the corner. I have a lot of work today; it can't be damaged!'

Prudence ears fell and she trembled crossly at the rebuke, looked at Joshua disgruntled.

In that case, I will go, you can have my news later! With that she jumped onto a cupboard under an open window. It rocked dangerously beneath her. She looked at Joshua, cleaned her face with her paws, gave a final 'Humph,' and leapt through the open window.

'Oh dear, upset her, did I?' Grandad Rose shrugged.

'While I give Mathew his lesson, you pour the tea out Joshua, there might be some biscuits in the tin.' He nodded in the direction of the cupboard.

'Milly, have a look at page four.' Grandad Rose pointed to a newspaper.

He watched Milly unfold the newspaper and turn the pages.

'Oh, are we going to see it?' Milly looked over the top of the newspaper.

'What do you think.' He laughed handing Mathew some rich red clay.

Mathew stood with the clay in his hand.

'Well get on with it. We don't have all day!' He watched Mathew wander over to the kick wheel and start the hypnotic rhythm that started the wheel.

Grandad Rose was impressed as Mathew quickly made a bowl. He handed him the wire to cut it off the wheel.

'Watch out!' He shouted as Mathew slices the bowl before the wheel had stopped and watch the clay fly off the wheel and onto the floor.

'Sorry,' Mathew got up from the stool and scooped the clay of the floor and put it into the bin.

'You're too tired for this today. Come and sit with us and have your tea.' He threw a towel over to Mathew so he could clean his hands. He was worried about Mathew. He looked very pale, and his movements were lethargic as he cleaned his hands.

'Well Milly,' he held his mug up towards her, 'tell us all where we are going.'

Milly folded the newspaper neatly. 'We are going to visit Overhill Hall. There is an exhibition of a Ruby Dragon.' She showed them a picture in the newspaper.

'Bet that's worth a lot of money!' Mathew had perked up.

'What's special about it?' Joshua asked, knowing his Grandad was bursting to tell them.

'That statue has a long history.' Grandad Rose took a sip of his hot tea, 'It goes back centuries. No one really knows absolutely where it came from, but many think from the design and carving it's from Peru.'

'Peru, that sounds exciting,' Milly's looking dreamily into the distance.

'Yes, but why is it important?' Joshua put his mug down on the rickety table beside him.

'That dragon has passed through many hands. It is thought to have mystical properties. Unfortunately, it's supposed to be cursed. Everyone who has owned it has had an unfortunate ending.' He looked around at their upturned faces. Milly's pinched face made him change what he was about to say, not wanting to upset his granddaughter.

'Now, that's all in the past. The owners of Overhill Hall have owned it for years, and all has been fine. They are having an exhibition to collect money for charity, so I thought we could go and have some lunch after.'

'That sounds good to me,' Mathew cheered.

'You always think with your stomach!' Milly teased him.

A voice behind made them jump, 'And why is Mathew thinking with his stomach?' all heads swiveled around. Alana Appleby stood in the doorway, eyebrow arched, hand on hip.

'Bet you're here just for a cup of tea!'

'Can't I drop in to see you Dad just because I fancy.' She grinned back, 'actually, Bill and Maurice are here. Maurice was walking over, so we gave him a lift.'

Grandad Rose nodded his head at newspaper on the table.

'And what's this?' She picked up the newspaper and looked at the page.

'You'll be wanting to see that, I know you, bit of history and you're off!'

She laid the newspaper back on the table, 'just remember not to get into to trouble with the children!'

'Bet Maurice will be going to that as well!'

'Did someone mention my name?' Maurice Priddy stepped through the door.

'Ah, Maurice, you've come for your mugs.' Grandad Rose got up out of his seat and went over to a pile of boxes in the corner of his studio.

He handed them to Maurice Priddy who took one out and inspected in.

'Lovely shape, great coloured glaze.' He beamed admiringly.

'Grandad Rose is taking us to see The Ruby Dragon.' Mathew rubbed his hands excitedly.

'You want to come along Maurice, I know you would enjoy it.'

'History lessons aren't the same at our new school. It was much more fun with Mr Priddy!' Mathew puckered up his lips.

'Well, you know Mathew, I stayed when Miss Mooremarsh went. Being the head teacher has been a good move for me. I am sure you will get on with your new teacher soon.' Mr Priddy set down his box and took the mug of tea that Grandad Rose had just poured him.

'Well, Dad. I would be happier with Maurice with you. It means that the children won't wander into danger again!' Alana smiled; her eyes showed a little concern.

Bill came in and rubbing his hands. 'Have you told them yet?' he looked at Alana.

'No,' she giggled, 'I thought I would let you give them the news!'

He snatched off his cap and waved it with a flourish.

'The circus is in town!'

Joshua punched the air with his fist, 'Brilliant!'

Milly looked at Joshua and raised her eyebrows at him. A thought flitted through her mind.

'You know a new girl, called Nori, started our class this week. She said her family travelled a lot but didn't go into details. Do you think she is from the circus?'

'Could be. Do you think she would show us around?' Joshua forehead creased as he thought about the circus.

'Well, I guess the circus beats the Ruby Dragon!' laughed Grandad Rose.

Milly reached over and took his hand, 'No, history is always fun with you.'

'So, when are we going?' Joshua asked impatiently.

Bill looked around the room, keeping them in suspense.

'There is a parade in Tetbury this afternoon, so maybe we can go to see a show tomorrow.'

'That means we will visit Overhill Hall next weekend. That OK with you Maurice?' Grandad Rose had a gleam in his eye, 'Being a headmaster an all.'

'I will make the time. But I have to say, circus parade, I will be there!'

'Why don't we watch the parade together, followed by lunch at the cafe?' Suggested Alana.

'Sounds like a great idea. Maurice, you can go in Bill's car, and the children can come in mine.' Grandad Rose took his coat off the peg and pulled his cap onto his head. 'Haven't seen a circus parade in years'

It was a short drive to Tetbury, however, when they arrived it would seem everyone had the same idea.

'We're going to have to do a bit of a walk.' Grandad Rose rubbed his hip, thinking about his rheumatism.

'Well, we are early enough, the parade doesn't start for a while.' Joshua piped up.

Milly was looking at the excited people standing along the sides of the roads in the high street. She saw a woman in a bright blue sari, and beside her stood, Clarke Sharma. Milly gulped, he had stared right at her, a sickening grin on his face, his fingers reached his temple, and he screwed one finger at her as the car went by them.

'That boy needs to learn some manners,' Grandad Rose gave a dismissive sniff. He hated for Milly to be upset, she had been through so much already.

'Don't worry, I can stick up for myself, but to be honest, he's not worth it.' Came Milly's subdued reply.

Grandad Rose caught Milly's eye in the rear-view mirror and winked at her. 'That's my girl, there are more than enough fools in the world. I understand his mother wanting to protect him from what happened. Being rude to you, that's not acceptable.'

Milly turned away from Grandad Rose's gaze and continued to look out the window. She felt a little less enthusiastic.

'Mathew, get your nose off the window! We will be out of the car soon enough,' Grandad Rose chirped, pulling the car into a small road and parking up.

'Come on, out you get. I can see your father behind me.' He switched off the engine and followed the children to their parents.

The group walked back to the high street, and Mathew darted through the crowd looking for a perfect spot. As they passed a toy shop, a red-haired stumpy man popped out and waved. 'Jethro, Jethro!'

Grandad Rose turned to the calling of his name.

'Donald, this is exciting isn't it!'

'Why don't you bring the family in, go upstairs and watch the procession from my parlour window.'

'Great, the kids would appreciate that.' He called to the others, and they followed Donald into the shop and upstairs to his parlour.

'Can I open the windows Donald?' Asked Grandad Rose, he felt as excited as the children.

'Yes, yes. Get the best view you can.'

Grandad Rose opened the windows, Mathew leaned forward and pushed his legs out over the ledge, Joshua and Milly followed suit.

Milly felt her grandfather rest his hands on her shoulders, she looked up and smiled at him.

Grandad Rose heard the beating of a drum in the distance.

'Here they come everyone, get ready.'

In no time the circus precession began.

Boom, Boom, Boom! Joshua felt the vibration of the drum beat on his chest. Three short fat men, with drums as big as they were, marched at the front. Loosely hanging bright coloured red trousers and tops, they held big sticks and beat a steady walking beat on the drum skins for the procession to follow. A man with symbols walked with them, clashing them together every now and then. A group of clowns followed, they were all sorts of shapes and sizes. Their makeup vibrant, some with smiling faces, some with tears drawn on their cheeks, and brightly coloured wigs, with vibrant coloured clothes. Some clowns ran to the crowd and threw confetti over them from buckets, some had large yellow flowers on their lapels, they lent over and got people to smell their flower's, which squirted them with water, there were shrieks of laughter from the crowd.

A loud sound erupted and split the air.

'Would you look at that,' Grandad Rose pointed at a wondrous sight.

'Wow!' both boys exclaimed together.

Six grey elephants walked side by side down the road, their huge bodies waddled from side to side. In front of each elephant walked a woman dressed in a red uniform and a black cap, holding a silver chain, which was linked onto a silver jeweled headdress on the elephant's head.

On the back of each elephant was a rider, also dressed in red. One elephant stopped, raised its front leg, and raised its body up onto its two back hind legs. The rider raised her arm gracefully and called out.

'Good Marko, good.'

Joshua's cheeks and ears went red, he felt butterflies in his stomach.

'What's wrong with you?' Grandad Rose teased him.

'Nothing.' Joshua replied tersely.

Alana and Bill smiled at each other at the back of his head.

Milly looked at the person on the back of the elephants back and clapped her hands.

'That's, Nori, told you she was in the circus!' Milly furiously waved to her new friend.

Nori saw her but only nodded her head a fraction.

'Down, Marko.' Nori touched the elephants head with her hand.

The road shook as the elephant crashed both its feet down onto the tarmac.

'Move on, Marko.' Nori touched the Elephants back, all the elephants moved off.

Nori looked up at Milly and waved. Laughing, she blew Joshua a kiss.

Milly looked at her brother, who was now turning puce.

'For goodness sake, she only blew you a kiss!' Milly scoffed at him.

Joshua sat unusually silent. His stomach wouldn't stop fluttering, his mouth felt dry. He watched Nori disappear around the corner and sighed to himself.

There followed acrobats, in blue silk trousers and waistcoats. They jumped, did cartwheels, and made a human pyramid, before they went on.

'Now, they are beautiful.' Bill nodded towards some big powerful animals. Glaring at the crowds from their gold gilt cages were tigers.

Large golden eyes peered out, occasionally, they let out a roar and bared white teeth with two long fangs. A smattering of screams came from the crowd, and mothers pulled their children away from the front. Milly leant forward, she felt sorry for the caged animals. They had very little space to walk around in. Her thoughts were interrupted by the clatter of hooves. Six black Arabian stallions, their manes platted with purple and gold ribbons, their coats glistened in the sun. They stood tall, muscles rippling under their rider's touch. Their nostrils snorted loudly, as they pranced down the high street in perfect unison. On their backs sat dark men with green turbans, matching green waistcoats and trousers. On their feet dangled leather Ali Baba shoes with little turned up toes.

Lastly, following at the rear, was the ring master. He was covered top to toe in purple. Waving his black top hat at the crowd, cracking a long whip in front of him. Three women ran behind him, their purple clothes matched the ringmaster. They gave out pamphlets to bystanders inviting them to the show.

'I don't believe it!' Joshua elbowed Milly in the side, he was reward with, 'Ouch.'

'Look, look.' He waved his finger at the back of the procession.

'No, way! Mum, look at this!' Milly's finger tremble.

Alana followed her daughters pointing hand.

Following the procession was Sylvester Bluesky and Prudence.

'Well, I never!' gasped Alana.

What are you doing there! Joshua said to Prudence.

I did try and tell you earlier! Prudence shot back and jumped nimbly in the air, clicking her hind legs together.

Milly bit her lip, above the wolf's head flying in circles, was Miskunn! She didn't send any thoughts to her firebird, worrying that her mother or Joshua would hear her and think her mad.

The procession passes out of sight, they all stood there breathless.

'Awesome, but I am hungry now!' Mathew called out, 'bye the way, the wolf and hare were a nice touch at the back, thought the golden bird was gorgeous too.' Milly rested her eyes on Mathew, aghast.

'Well, better than me lad. I couldn't see anything after the ringmaster!' Grandad Rose turned to Donald, 'Thank you, you've made the children's day. And mine come to think of it. Let's meet one evening for a drink.' He pulled Milly off the ledge; the boys jumped down behind her. 'We'd better get off for some lunch, before Mathew here faints away with hunger,' he ruffled Mathew's hair to show he was jesting.

'Yes, let's do that. Are you going to see them, the circus that is?' Donald asked.

'Yes, tomorrow if we can get tickets!' He watched the expression on the children's faces fall.

'Dad, stop teasing them!' Alana pinched his arm gently. 'Come on, let's go back to the café in Malmesbury, there won't be such a crowd there.'

CHAPTER 7
NIGHT STRUGGLE - NOX CERTAMEN

It was late afternoon; the kitchen was gloomy even though the sun was shining. Mathew snacked on a biscuit; crumbs scattered on the floor leaving evidence from his attack on the biscuit tin. He was still hungry, even after lunch an hour ago. The sound of his mother's light steps warned him of her arrival from the yard. He pushed the last of the biscuit into his mouth, chewed a few times and swallowed. He winced as it scratched his throat.

'Don't be thinking of going out until you have collected the eggs.' His mother launched at him as she came through the door, 'You've been out all morning, your dad also needs some help later this afternoon, so you'd better be at seven acres field by four.' She stood washing her hands.

'I'll get on it right now, Mum,' he grabbed a huge wicker basket and made his way to the door.

'By the way, Joshua, invited me to the circus tomorrow afternoon, can I go?' He looked back at his mother.

His mum stood drying her hands, examining them carefully.

'Well?' he tried not to sound impatient.

A smile twitched at her lips; Mathew knew she loved to tease him.

'Will Alana and Bill be going too?' She joked and laughed at his expression. 'Yes, of course you can, get some money from the tin.'

Mathew rushed over and gave her a hug, 'Thanks Mum'

'Get out there and collect those eggs if you want to thank me,' she laughed and shooed him out the kitchen.

Mathew looked in all the usual hiding places where the hens laid their eggs. Hens clucked at him as he entered the barn. He felt in the hay for eggs, and his hands touch the bounty he was looking for. Thirty-eight little treasures sat in his basket.

'Mum will be pleased!' he grinned walking back to the house.

The familiar afternoon smell of bread in the oven hit him as he entered. He loved the taste of his mother's bread, no one made it as she did. In the kitchen he placed the laden basket of eggs onto the kitchen table, making sure he did not knock over a vase of flowers his mother had picked earlier from the woods.

'Mum, the eggs are on the table,' he hollered, 'I'll be back before four!'

He grabbed his jumper from where he had left it earlier, scrunched up on the back of a chair, and pulled it on over his head. He reached up and muzzled his hair into some sort of tidiness, grabbed his coat and left the house. Two dark brown and white dogs approached him, tails wagging wildly.

'Sit,' he put his hand up, both dogs sat down in unison, 'guess you want to come for a walk with me?'

Tails wagged even faster as an answer.

'Better get the whistle.' He walked back and retrieved the dog whistle from a bowl on the windowsill. 'Come on.' He nodded towards the gate.

Both dogs got up and ran to the gate, one dog jumped up and pawed at it.

'Get down, Spanner!' Spanner got down and waited impatiently for Mathew. He reached over the dog's heads and undid the gate latch. The dog's squashed by him and flew out into the track. Mathew called out, 'right,' and held his hand out to the right. The dogs knew the walk he was taking them on and automatically ran off to the right, through a gap in the hedge. Mathew closed a gate behind him, which had a newly painted sign on it. Anderson Farm.

'Freedom, at last,' he called out as he squeezed through the hedge and raced down to a narrow river at the edge of one of the farms' fields. When he arrived, the dogs were sniffing along the river's edge. It was their favourite place to explore. They looked over at him every now and then.

'Go on.' He encouraged them to explore, the dogs wandered on a little way. He wanted peace and quiet to think. He had had some very strange dreams lately. Strange happenings. Mathew bent down and examined the pebbles close to the water's edge and chose three. He stood up and flicked his wrist and watched a pebble skip across the water, counting the bounces it made on the surface.

'That's not great! Nine skips!' he grumbled. He placed another pebble and weighed it in his hand. Turned his body and flicked it at the water again. He grunted, sixteen skips. He had never reached his record of twenty-one skips again. He yawned and stretched out. The smell of the woods which surrounded the river relaxed him. He sat down and watched the river gently flowing past. The lids of his eyes became heavy.

'I'll lie down just for a moment.' Mathew yawned at the dogs.

The grass supported him like a soft cradle. Trickles of sunlight broke through the overhead branches; the flowing river added its melody. Mathew fell into a fitful dream.

His boots were sinking into the ground. He willed his muscles to lift his feet, the more he tried, the more they sank. Each time he tried to move his foot; a 'slurp' issued from the green slimy marsh. A wave of panic rose in the pit of his stomach.

'I can't stay here,' the words came out as a squeak.

A foul smell irradiated from the marsh. An odour of rotten meat and vegetable, mixed with the tang of sulphur tickled his nostrils. He trembled; the smell always proceeded the voice. A terrible voice that cut him cold.

So, you want to leave me so soon? The odious voice slithered around in his mind.

'I just want to get out of this marsh. I don't want to be sucked under and die here.' Mathew shouted.

You will be with me. Just let yourself go, relax. I can show you how to be powerful. It cooed to him.

'I don't need to be powerful.'

You want to be better than Joshua, don't you? Think of how everyone will like you? It's Joshua they all want to follow. Think of what he did to Clarke. Now Clarke hates him! It pushed smoothly against his mind.

'That wasn't Joshua's fault. He tried to protect him. Magic was new to him. Anyway, it was Mooremarsh who hurt Clarke, not Joshua.' Mathew looked around wildly.

As usual, there was no one there, only that hideous voice. A low laugh reached him; he covered his ears. Mathew tried to hide his fear. He couldn't turn around; the marsh had nearly sucked his boots down to the top. Out the corner of his eye, he could see something, but he couldn't make out what it was, stone maybe.

Come now boy, you know you would have much more fun with me. Think about it. Do you really want to always be in the shadow of Joshua? What about Milly? She really is dark you know. You could both have fun using the power I offer you. The voice was silky.

'No, now go away!' Mathew screamed into the air.

As you wish, we will meet again. If I, was you, I would relax and enjoy what I have to offer you? The voice scraped its way out of Mathew's mind, he flinched from the pain.

'Now to get out of here,' he cried out loud to give himself some courage. In front of him was a large boulder covered in a blanket of purple and green moss.

'I never noticed that there before!' He leaned his body towards the rock and stretched out his arms. The moss felt cool under his fingers, he grabbed a handful and gave a small pull. It took his weight, he sucked in his cheeks and concentrated. With painstaking small moments, he slipped his feet out of his socks, out of the boots and hauled himself onto the rock. His chest felt tight, and he was panting from the effort, he raised to his knees and caught his breath. Dirt stained his face, his fingers wiped some of the dirt off. Sitting up he got a measure of where he was. A grey granite wall loomed above him, from his vantage, the top was not in sight. To his right were ragged stone steps that had been cut into the side of the wall.

'Well, I'm not climbing up there!' his eyes traced the steps up the wall. He stood up; the stone felt cold under his bare feet. There was a small gap between the boulder and the land beneath the wall. He jumped the gap, he saw the marsh reach up wet marsh shaped fingers and try to snatch him back, he twisted to get out of its grasp and landed heavily. His ankle hurt a little from the jolt of the landing. Wind from behind him chilled his back and ruffled his hair, turning in its direction, he surveyed the wet marsh he had just escaped. Scattered over the ground were rock animals. Their bodies contorted in different ways. All telling the same story. They had stuck in the marsh and been petrified to rock. Within touching distance was a lion, its large mane flying back from his noble face. The sight of such a magnificent animal changed in this way disturbed him.

He stretched out his hand to touch the lions face in sympathy. Mathew snatched back his hand in terror, a little scream dribbled from his throat. The lions' eyes creaked open, the salts from the bog falling away from the lids. Two black glistening orbs looked out at him. Mathew was rooted to the spot. A crack split the air, the lion opened its mouth, some of the stone falling away from its cheeks. Roar! The dreadful sound spurred Mathew into action. He ran to the stone steps and ascended them. Cold granite cut into his feet, but Mathew did not feel the pain, he needed to get away from the roaring lion. With a little courage, he peeped down at the lion and stopped. The lion was still in the marsh, stone covered most of its body, only its mouth and eyes were free of the stone. It wasn't following him; he could slow down and catch his breath. His feet felt wet and looking down at them he felt nauseous. Blood was oozing out of the soles of his feet. He rested his body against the wall, the stone beneath his fingers felt smooth and warm. He frowned, why were the steps so cold. He felt something prickle his feet, he looked down, his gaze was met with horror. A crimson stain of congealed blood oozing from his feet was turning to ice, splinters of ice spread out on the stone step. He pulled his foot away from the step and placed it on the next one. Each step he took, his feet froze a little to the stone. He was tired of trying to reach the top, he was tired and wanted to sit down.

Sit down, you will freeze, it will feel like you are falling asleep, but you will be with me! The voice coaxed him.

'No, I will get to the top!' He screamed, it sounded loud in his ears. Mathew pulled his body up each step. He looked up to see if he could see the end. Instead, he saw a light from a small opening a little way ahead. The light spurred him on, he found new energy in his step. The last distance of the climb seemed to go quickly, and he soon found himself at the entrance of a cave. It was lit with a low glow from within. He could see a door in the stone wall within the cave. He walked towards the door; a gentle warmth cocooned him. A beautiful sound of bells caught his attention. He saw an old silver key hanging on a chain on the wall. Mathew walked over and felt the metal of the chain in his fingers. It was hooked onto a large stone hook. Mathew started to take the chain off the hook. Incredulously, he watched as the stone hook turned into a hand. Mathew tugged the chain, and it broke, he thrust out his hand to catch the key. The stone hand turned into the writhing head of a snake.

You are mine; I will not let you go through the door!

Mathew stood petrified, too scared to move, acid burned in his stomach, he was going to be sick. The key hanging loosely in his hand, it felt warmer, in the coldness of the cave. The key vibrated against his skin and played a melody, soothing him. Another voice, softer, sweeter touch his mind.

Mathew, believe in Earth Magic. Believe!

'I don't have Earth Magic.' He screamed in terror as the snake's head turned into a mighty serpent.

Say it and mean it. You believe in Earth Magic!

Mathew looked at the hideous form starting to slither out of the wall towards him. He ran to the door in the cave wall and fumbled with the key and pushed it in the lock.

That won't help. You must realize now you belong to me! Hissed the voice.

Mathew felt the serpent's breath on his neck. His hand trembled, trying to turn the lock.

Believe in Earth Magic, Sang the voice again. The serpents' split tongue brushed his neck.

He trembled and his mouth was dry.

'I do believe in earth magic,' he screamed hysterically, 'I have seen it, Earth Magic is real!'.

His fingers held the metal tighter, and he felt the lock give way as the key turned, the door slowly opened. A river of gold light flowed out; it was so bright he had to shield his eyes. The light issued forth from the open door, wrapping itself around him and irradiating warmth.

Look at me, called the sweet voice. Mathew let down his hand, his mouth gawped open.

My name is Gertie. I am your magical creature. A gold majestic bird stood in the doorway. The gold vision faded away replaced by a black and purple crow hopped forward.

A deep voice spoke to him, *Mathew, you have Earth Magic. A very rare type of Earth Magic.*

'You!' Mathew gasped, 'Sylvester Bluesky, I remember you. I never thought I would see you again.'

The wolf shone like a burning golden flame. Peeking out from behind him, Prudence poked out her head, radiating the same gold light.

Hello Mathew. Her soft touch felt like butterfly wings, she held up a paw shyly.

Mathew, we have much to talk about and very little time. You will need Gertie's help on your journey with Earth Magic. Mathew looked at the wolf.

'Did Joshua and Milly have these nightmares?' Mathew bent over double; the shock was too much for him.

Yes, all with Earth Magic must go through the Night Struggle, it is where you decided to follow Earth Magic or Dark Magic. Sylvester Bluesky answered.

'Why didn't Joshua or Milly tell me about it? Even more so, why didn't my parents tell me?' Mathew sounded cross and tired.

Earth Magic law forbids them. Now wake up, you have much to learn. Came the stern reply. Mathew felt a tug at his trouser leg.

He looked down into the sapphire blue eyes of the crow.

I will meet you this evening. Now, wake up!

A loud barking beside him and he felt a wet tongue licking his face. He opened his eyes and looked up at Spanner towering over him.

'Well, that was one heck of a dream.' He laughed at the dog, 'better get up to Seven Acres, or dad will have my hide!'

Mathew reached the farmhouse and opened the door; he threw the whistle back into the bowl on the windowsill. His mother was absent, so he made his way up to Seven Acres field. He was surprised to see his mother there talking to his father.

'Sorry if I'm a little late,' he looked at his father, waiting for a rebuke. Mathew knew something was up, his parents had that 'look'.

His father scratched his head and put his arm around his wife.

'You understand the meaning of the nightmares now?' his father looked away from him.

'What do you mean,' babbled Mathew back.

'Mathew, you know our family history. You must be aware that our family is different from others?' His mother looked directly at him.

'Yes, I know.' Swallowing hard.

His father sighed. 'Sylvester Bluesky has been to see us. I will get your books when I have time. We have stored them in the attic.'

His mother clapped her hands, 'well, dinner won't make itself, and dad needs your help in this field.' His mother turned to go.

'Wait, I was told I had a rare type of magic, what did he mean?' Mathew crossed his arms; he was not happy his parents had kept the saga of the nightmares from him.

'Well, Mathew. Both your father and I come from families who occasionally are born with Earth Magic. Our family on my side are weak in the ways of Earth Magic.' Mathew looked crestfallen, 'However, we have a rare magic'

Mathew brightened up at this news. 'Yes, well what is it?' He swayed from side to side in anticipation.

'When our family has Earth Magic, we can do this magic, manipulate the elements, but we can hide all magic.' His mother looked across to his father. 'You have a title.'

'Oh?' he looked at her expectantly.

'We are called the Doorkeepers, the Ostiarius Magicae.'

'That's enough for today. Let's get on and finish this field.' His father said gruffly and walked away.

Mathew was about to say something, but his mother caught his eye.

'Tomorrow, Mathew, leave it till tomorrow.'

CHAPTER 8
THE HOUSE ON THE HILL

Mooremarsh was thrown forward as the bus driver braked heavily for the umpteenth time. She had loudly muttered the whole journey from Bristol to Malmesbury, holding court to an empty bus.

'Idiots being let loose on public transport,', and 'Is that dimwit driver blind?', or 'a snail can shuffle faster than this.' Had been the vein of her comments during the whole bus ride. She looked out the window and the darkness of the countryside changed as the bus entered the streets of Malmesbury. A soft glow from shop windows lit the streets.

'Thank goodness we are here. At least I won't be battered and bruised anymore.' She raised her voice.

The conductor had not missed the disgruntled remarks during the journey.

'Last stop!' the conductors west country drawl called out to the only passenger on the bus.

Mooremarsh shook her head in anger, she had been jostled from pillar to post, and she felt sore and bruised. Standing up, she wobbled down the bus isle, orange handbag in one hand, a bag of a few new clothes she had 'procured' in the other. Reaching the door to alight, she gave the bus conductor a stinging glance, rose her nose a fraction and gave him a dismissive sniff.

'We look forward to you riding with us again.' He took off his cap, doffed it and smiled cheekily at her.

Her step stopped, she turned to the conductor, and gave him an icy stare. It pierced his humour and he turned away. Standing for a moment longer, daring him to look at her.

Coward! She smiled knowingly.

Stepping off the bus she found herself in the dark streets of Malmesbury. She walked away from the bus stop making a journey she had made for many years before.

The high street lit her path, and she pulled the little jacket tighter against the cold of the evening. A large clock hung above the jewellery shop, and proudly announced, with florescent hands, the time was ten thirty. Automatically, she looked at the time on the watch she had taken off her victim's body.

'Humph, at least it keeps good time,' she flicked the jacket sleeve back over her bared wrist.

Before her was a hill, at the top of that hill was the house she had lived in for many years. An expanse of grass was to one side.

'Now, if ever there was a stupid man it was Ankleridge,'

Memories of finding Ankleridge, the school caretaker, and the tunnel they had found leading to the Abbey, and the priceless bounty they had stolen. She clutched the bags in her hands tighter.

'Joshua Appleby, and his nosy family. They will pay for what they did to me.' Her teeth gnashed together. 'There will be time for revenge, you will see, all of you!'

Stamping her feet in her new shoes to ward of the cold, she made the last of her journey quickly, and finally stood outside her old home. In the distance she could hear music playing from a nearby house, a owl calling from the nearby woods. Her car stood outside her home, forlornly waiting for her after months of sitting stationary and alone. Her eyes darted around once more, her home looked deserted, she pushed the gate open and walked to the door. She scratched at the door, not wanting to use the knocker and arouse nosy neighbours. Waiting for what seemed an age, she rummaged in her pocket and drew out a key. The key felt cold and familiar in the palm of her hand, her fingers deftly pushed it into the lock. Turning the lock and the door slid open. She let out a sigh, not realising she had been holding her breath. Darting quickly through the door, the toe of her foot closed it behind her. Resting her back against it, she listened for any disturbance outside or within. There was only the sound of the neighbour's music wafting in from the street.

Her eyes adjusted to the darkness, she was sure the electricity would have been switch off months ago, and she did not want to attract attention. Fumbling along she made her way along the dark narrow passage and into the kitchen. The moonlight lit up the kitchen well, she could find what she wanted in its light. She drew out a plate, found a knife in the drawer, and a glass which she filled with water. Out of her bag she took out a teacake and some butter she had purchased.

'Thank you for your donation, Miss Moss,' she whispered into the night.

Quickly, she made her supper of cold teacake, butter, and a glass of water. Scoffing them at the table, licking her finger for any leftover crumbs. Her mind raced as she sat in the loneliness of the house.

She needed two things. The first give a reason for her presence at the house. She had a plan for that. The second was to pursuance police constable Marcus Harrow to get back her books of spells from the evidence room at the police station. Firstly through, she needed to sleep.

Morning came too quickly for Mooremarsh. She stretched under the blankets, and stuck one foot out from their cosy abode, her toes wiggled in the crisp air.

'No time to lie here, too much to do today.' She threw back the bed covers and sat bolt upright. A glimmer of moon light lit the room from under the closed curtains.

'Better open those back up before someone notices they are closed,' she grumbled.

In the distance she could hear the clink of milk bottles as the milkman made his rounds.

She grimaced as her feet touched the cold floorboards. She grabbed a blanket and wrapped it around herself, wandered over to the window and opened the curtains. The creamy white moon was stark in a midnight blue sky. She examined the road outside, it was empty.

'Must be early, everyone's curtains are closed,' she murmured to herself. Her eyes rested on a table, she had left her box with spell books there, months ago. As she thought, the box was gone.

'It would be the first thing police would have taken.' She sniffed.

Her nose wrinkled at the clothes which lay in a crumpled heap on the floor, she had thrown them down, unceremoniously, last night. She hated disorder, but then again, she thought to herself, she did get ready for bed in the dark. At the foot of the drawers, she spied a large brown carrier bag. Tip toeing over to it she scooped it up and emptied the contents onto the bed. Her fingers touched the fine fabric of the clothes while she thought about what to wear.

'Sunday best I think,' She grabbed a green skirt, floral shirt and marched into the bathroom to wash and dress.

'First, I need to see if any of my spell books are still here and find money.' She put lipstick on her lips, turned her face side to side, checking it in the bathroom mirror.

'Well, Delvera, you are ready,'

Another idea rankled, 'I need to change my name, can't go about as Delvera Mooremarsh!'

Several ideas presented themselves, but she settled with one.

'Petula Greensborough. Has a nice ring to it.' She sang to herself.

Mooremarsh left the bathroom and eyed the floor. She grabbed a nail file from a drawer and went to the middle of the room. The floorboards all looked the same, a small mat lay neatly on the floor. She got down on her knees, pulled back the mat, and touched one floorboard. Holding the file tightly, she used it to unscrew the board. Soon enough it was loose, and she prized it from its position. In a gap between the floor joists was a large silver box. She reached in and pulled it out and rested the box on the floor in front of her. She ran her finger over the lid, holding it firmly, she wrenched it open. The corners of her lips twitched as she looked inside it at the contents.

'Well, that's a life saver.' Her hand reached in and touched the crisp notes within.

Her fingers separated the bundle of money and she spread a quarter of the money on the floor. Placing the lid on the box she put it back in its hiding place. Taking up the remaining money, the notes crackled in her clutching hand. She got up and stuffed it into the handbag.

Padding down the stairs, handbag rhythmically banging on her hip, a thought struck her. She would not only have to change her name but hide her magic too.

'Let's see if I can find that meddlesome busy body police Constable Harrow.' Shoving her feet into brown shoes.

She grabbed her jacket off its peg and put it on hurriedly. She glanced at her watch, seven thirty.

'Good, the cafe will be open, and I am starving!' she grunted.

Opening the front door gingerly, she heard the Milkman put out milk bottles across the street. She quickly closed the door and waited until she could hear the milk van's electric engine passing away down the road. Soon the whirling sound of the van went past her door, the noise faded as it went down the hill. Once again Mooremarsh opened the door. All was quiet in the street. Across the road a light flicked on in an upstairs window. Mooremarsh quietly closed the door and tiptoed out into the street.

CHAPTER 9
CARS, VANS, AND MAGIC

Milly opened the curtains; the morning darkness still held court. She ran over the cold wooden floorboards, felt around the wall by the door and flicked on the light. Her eye strayed to a book which lay on the floor. *Elements of Fire Magic. Advanced techniques with Earth Magic.* Rutger had given it to her after their last tutorial on Earth Magic.

'Read it slowly, savour each page, listen to the wisdom beneath the pages.' Rutger had advised her as he handed her the red leather book.

Of course, she got home, stayed up for as long as she could in her bedroom, devouring the books contents. She skipped some pages which were full of mathematical calculations, discussions on cubic capacity, she wanted the nuts and bolts of the book, she wasn't interested in the nitty gritty.

Opening the book to the first chapter, she began to re-read the book, just in case Rutger quizzes me on some of the finer points she thought to herself.

He will quiz you, read it slowly so you don't forget anything. Miskunn stood beside her bed.

'Ok, let me have some peace.' Milly replied grumpily, pulled the book in front of her face so Miskunn was out of view.

Hmph! I was only trying to be helpful! Milly felt guilty, looked over the top of the book, the eagle had disappeared in a huff from her bedroom.

Snuggling down into bed, she began to read. She didn't get far, the telephone started ringing sending out its shrill sound. Mumbling, she got out of bed, slipped her slippers on, and yanked open the bedroom door. She had taken three steps down the hall when her father erupted bleary eyed from her parents' bedroom. He looked at her shivering on the landing, he wiped his bleary eyes, nodded for her to return to bed. He went down the stairs grumbling about the time, he screamed when his bare foot stood on something.

'Put your stuff away you two or else I will bin it!' He shouted grumpily.

The ringing phone came to an abrupt stop.

'Bill Appleby.' He was not in a good mood, no cheery hello this morning.

'I see. I will be over once I have got dressed, about eight.' He slammed down the phone and ran up the stairs. He eyed Milly standing outside her room.

'I am getting another half hour in bed, it was the police station,' his hand touched the doorknob. 'They have a car I have to tow to the garage; they could have waited another hour!'

'Can I come with you?' Milly whispered.

'Of course, you can, I leave at eight, be ready.' He ruffled her hair, 'nice to have the company! Now get a little bit more sleep.' He disappeared into his bedroom.

Milly turned and saw her brother leaning against the door post.

'Are you going back to bed?' he asked her.

Milly felt wide awake. 'No, getting dressed and going downstairs.'

Joshua smiled at her. 'Fancy a bit of practice, it's light enough outside now. Air against fire? Bet you've read the book Rutger gave you. I just finished advanced air magic.' He raised his eyebrows in way of a challenge.

'You are on, meet you in 5 minutes.' She grinned; her brother knew she could not resist a challenge.

Soon they were in the garden, shivering.

'No words, just thoughts to control the elements.' Joshua raised the stakes.

'Done, the loser has to wash up and do the drying after dinner tonight.' Milly threw down the challenge.

'Agreed.' Joshua nodded and looked at the gutter above his sister's head.

Water flooded out of the gutter towards Milly, 'Ha!' she swung her head to one side and the water evaporated.

Milly's hands dangled at her sides. She watched her brother's face, as Sophia had taught her.

'You can tell a lot by a person's face, it gives them away every time,' Sophia had demonstrated on Jasper, much to the glee of Milly and Joshua.

Joshua's eyes slid to a bucket of water. Large fist sized snowballs flew at Milly. She put up her hand and a stream of spiral flames attacked the snowballs. Whilst Joshua was enjoying himself commanding air, he did not see the metal spade behind him moving his way. Wham, it struck him on his calf. The metal was warm enough to sting, but not burn.

'I believe it's my game!' Milly laughed, 'You are washing up tonight.'

'I didn't see that coming!' he chortled, 'You win fair and square, we will have to have a rematch tomorrow.'

They heard the swish of curtains being drawn back, both pairs of eyes went up to their parents' bedroom window.

'Better get in, and don't you dare argue about doing the washing up tonight!' Milly walked back inside.

It was nice to get in from the cold. The morning sun hadn't taken the chill off the night air. Milly put the kettle on and got the teapot ready. She heard the light tread of her mother on the stairs.

'Thank you, your dad will be down in a few seconds.' Her mother gave her a kiss on the cheek.

'Grandad Rose said he wants to take you to see the Ruby Dragon next weekend.'

'Great, I do love his history talks, he brings everything to life, not like school, it is just books and copying off the board!' Joshua grabbed the offered cup, briming with hot tea.

'Your grandad does love his history,' Their mother took a sip of her tea. 'Mind you, no adventures this time please. Your dad and I have only just got over the last one!'

'Too true!' Bill came through the door and grabbed a mug of tea from the kitchen side. 'Maurice Priddy is going with you too, so that should keep you out of trouble!'

Milly watched her dad down the scolding hot tea, how he didn't burn his mouth she could not make out. He slammed down the mug and smacked his lips in satisfaction.

'Are you coming with us this morning Joshua?' His dad asked, reaching for his jacket and cap.

'No, I want to read air magic again.' He raised his eyebrows at Milly.

'Let's go Milly,' he gave Alana a quick kiss on the cheek and headed outside.

Milly grabbed her duffle coat, scrunched a bobble hat on her head and followed in his trail. Outside the sun had risen a little higher, cobwebs on bushes glistened bathing in its light. Her dad was revving up the car, he leaned over and opened the passenger door.

'Better get in quick, I need you to wipe the condensation off the window.' He handed her a rag.

She nimbly got in and closed the door and buffed the misty windscreen.

'That's better. We'll go to the garage, put the stove on to warm the garage up a bit, the tow this car.' He grinned down at her, 'ridiculous time to ask for a tow when it's sitting there! I won't work on it till Monday!' he revved the engine again, 'reckon Harrow is having a laugh at my expense!'

The car shot forward, frightening a pigeon from its morning rummage on the grass. They sat in companionable silence during the journey.

'Out you get, open the garage doors, and light up the stove.'

Milly made light work of opening the door, the stove was another matter. It was an old paraffin stove, there was a knack to lighting it. The sound of a 'pop', the little blue pilot flame boomed as the paraffin combusted in the chamber. She was surprised she had lit it so quickly. Her father was rummaging about in the small kitchen, he came out carrying a coffee pot and plonked it on the stove top, grabbed two stools and set them close to the stove.

'Not doing anything until we've had a coffee and biscuit.' He patted the stool for her to sit on. 'Brain is all fogged up this time of the morning!' they both laughed.

'Really looking forward to the circus this afternoon. Haven't been to one for years!' He got up and found some biscuits in a tin, grabbed three metal cups, milk, and set them down on a workbench. Into one cup he poured some milk and set in on the stove by the pot.

'It's true to say, your coffee will be hot milk with a dash of coffee, your mum wouldn't be too pleased if I gave you strong coffee!' He found a tea towel and wrapped it around the handle of the now boiling coffee pot.

'I love the smell of coffee, dad.' She sniffed the air.

She watched the thick black liquid pouring into her father's cup, he leaned over and put a dash of coffee into hers. He topped both cups up with hot milk.

'Cheers!' he held up his cup and drank. Laughing as Milly took small sips of her drink.

A chill went down her spine, she shuddered, spilling her drink.

'Watch out, girl,' Milly's dad rebuked her.

There it was again, making her bones turn to ice. She felt pale, she had felt that once before.

Dark Magic. Had Delvera Mooremarsh returned? Her hands trembled at the thought.

'Milly, what is it? You look terrible.' Her dad put down his cup and held her icy hand. 'Your hand is frozen!' he rubbed them vigorously in his, 'this should warm them up a little.

'It's ok. I'm just a little cold.' She replied not wanting to share her feelings.

'You're not going down with anything are you?' he tilted his head and examined her face.

'No dad, stop worrying!' she pulled her hand out of his.

'Finish your drink. We need to be off.' He raised his cup and drank the last of his hot coffee.

Milly looked at him over the top of his cup. She held her cup, her hand trembled. She took a deep breath. Was Dark Magic and Mooremarsh back in Malmesbury? Or did she imagine the coldness she had just felt? She touched the charm which hung around her neck.

'Drink up, we need to get over to the police station and collect that car.' He stood up and took his cup to the sink.

'Dad, do you still wear your charm that Mum made you?' Milly asked, washing her mug up.

'Yes, your mother told us we must wear them all the time.' He pulled out a chain with a silver teardrop shaped vial.

Milly pulled out of her jumper an identical silver vial. 'I always wear it.'

CHAPTER 10
MOOREMARSH CLAIMS HER HERITAGE

The smell of toast and fried food hit Mooremarsh as she opened the door to the café. Only one table was taken, so she sat down at a table on the opposite side of the room. She picked up a paper menu and gave it a cursory glance. A woman with a light blue uniform with a white apron bounced over to her table.

'Tea or coffee?' The waitresses voice boomed around the room.

Mooremarsh shuddered. 'I will have tea, two slices of toast and honey.' Throwing down the menu onto the table.

The waitress scribbled onto to her pad and waited, 'Anything else?'

Mooremarsh took in the waitresses tightly fitting uniform and raised an eyebrow, intime to see the women blush.

'I do think the food here agrees with you,' looking pointedly at her well-rounded stomach. 'I have ordered enough for me, thank you.'

'I see,' the waitress replied stiffly and walked away to the kitchen.

The door opened and cold air wafted in.

'Hello, where's my tea!' called out a man's voice behind her.

The waitress came out from the kitchen looking flustered and pulled a note pad out of her apron pocket.

'Marcus Harrow you can sit down and wait your turn,' the waitress giggled and pulled back a chair from the table in front of hers. 'How is that girlfriend of yours, still at her mother's?' she looked at him with sympathy.

'Yes, Amanda is still with her mum in Torquay. She will be with her till well after the new year.' Harrow's mouth set into a grim line.

'Well, pneumonia is a bad thing. Took my aunt months to recover! You sit down and I will be back.' She tapped the chair and walked away.

The hair on the back of Mooremarsh's neck rose, her quarry was here! She watched Harrow sit down opposite her. He looked at her, she felt the enquiring eyes of the police officer.

'Morning,' he waved his hand courteously.

Mooremarsh merely nodded her head a fraction. The waitress arrived with her tea, toast, and honey, plonking them down loudly in front of her.

'There you are, let me know if you need anything else.' The waitress sniffed.

'No, nothing else. I'd imagine this would be a mere snack for you,' Mooremarsh smiled sweetly, looking pointedly at the waitresses well-padded stomach.

'Huh,' the waitress left in a flurry.

Mooremarsh sipped her tea. It was strong and fragrant.

'What are you doing in Malmesbury?' Asked Harrow quickly looking her up and down, appraising her.

Mooremarsh looked over the top of her cup at him.

'Staying at my cousins house, actually, she is a distant cousin. I understand she was in a bit of trouble here. Her name is Delvera Mooremarsh.' She watched as he blinked struggling for composure, 'She was renting my mother's house, and I needed somewhere to stay, the house is empty, so here I am' she shrugged her shoulders.

Harrow stroked his chin, listening to the news.

'How well did you know Delvera Mooremarsh, the police are still looking for her?' Harrow rested his chin on his hand, his eyes narrowed suspiciously, 'we didn't think she had any living family.'

Taking her time sipping her tea, she placed the cup carefully in the saucer.

'Never met her. She was a stranger to my side of the family,' she held back a snigger.

'Now you know about me, what about you?' knifing butter onto a piece of toast.

'He is Sargent Harrow, promoted in the spring he was.' The waitress plonked a cup of tea in front of him followed by a heavily laden plate of bacon, sausages, and eggs, with two slices of toast hanging precariously on the side of the plate.

'Get that down you,' the waitress put a hand on her hip and held Mooremarsh's stare.

'That does look delicious, I think I will join you.' She smiled sweetly at Harrow, looking up at the waitress, 'Could I have the same please.'

Mooremarsh got up from her seat, 'Do you mind if I join you, I am a stranger here, and you could tell me about Malmesbury.' She took the seat opposite him.

Harrow looked surprise but recovered quickly.

'Yes, of course, but I only have another thirty minutes left.'

'Well, it would be nice to know I have made a friend.' She reached across the table and tapped his hand.

The waitress just stood, biting her lip, wanting to say something to the rude woman. Instead, she walked off to give Mooremarsh's order to the chef.

'My name is Petula Greensborough, it is nice to meet you Sergeant Harrow.' She tapped his hand and held his gaze.

Mooremarsh watched Harrow's eyes cloud, she murmured her spell repeatedly. A spell of suggestion, he would do whatever she commanded. She let go of his hand. He jolted.

'Sorry, what did you say?' his eyes focused on her.

'I said your food is getting cold,' looking over his shoulder at the fast-approaching waitress, 'and that looks like my breakfast.'

The plate was set down and Mooremarsh began to tuck into the food. She was hungry and ate quickly. Sargent Harrow just picked at his food, he looked around him bemused.

'Is something the matter, Sargent Harrow?' Mooremarsh patted the corners of her mouth with a serviette.

'Er, no, no.' He looked startled by the question.

'It's time to go to the police station, you will go to the evidence room and retrieve a black box full of spell books that belonged to Delvera Mooremarsh.' She touched his hand again. He nodded back at her. She spied the waitress bearing down on them with two bills.

'Good, I will wait outside, and you will pay for my breakfast,' she quipped at him.

'Yes, of course.'

Mooremarsh got up, the waitress walked quicker.

'Thank you, Sergeant Harrow has kindly offered to pay my bill too!' she took in the look on the waitress's face and left the cafe smiling.

Outside, the sun had risen, and shops were opening. It must be getting close to nine o'clock. She would soon have her spell books and be able to cast a charm spell. Best of all, she will have all the spells she needs to get her revenge. The squeak of a door behind her. She could feel Harrow's presence behind her.

'This way Petula, we will have your black box soon.' Harrow looked down at the pavement.

'Good, off you go, I will follow behind you,' Mooremarsh watched Harrow walk stiffly away.

She looked back at the window of the café. The waitress was looking down at her with her small squinting eyes.

'I might come back for lunch, don't eat it all,' she was rewarded in return with a withering look from the waitress.

Mooremarsh held up a hand, waved, and followed Harrow up the street. She quickly caught him up and soon they stood on the corner of the street. The sun was higher in the sky, its light reflected off nearby windows. The pavement still shone from the early morning dew. Her eyes darted around, studying the road which led to the police station, making sure it was safe. The street was quiet, except for the occasional bird song. She would not be noticed. She watched Harrow, he straightened up and his stride became less stiff.

'I think I need to enforce the spell of obedience on him,' she whispered to herself.

She wasn't sure how strong her magic was, how long it would last. Her magical source came from the life force she had taken from the librarian. She needed her books; generations of spells and incantations were in them. Different coloured ink decorated the pages, over one hundred years of experience poured into the pages. They were beautiful, she had spent years talking to each book, like they were members of her family.

'Get my beautiful books.' Mooremarsh sang to Harrow.

She caressed his face and gently pulled it, so he faced her. Harrow peered down at her; a stupid grin spread across his face. Her eyes drew him into her world of magic, the world of Dark Magic.

'You are the most beautiful woman I have ever seen.' He stared at her. 'Will you always sing that song to me,' he put his hands in his pockets and looked down at his shiny black boots, 'I don't ever want to be without that song.' He sounded frightened; his eyes turned to the police station.

'Go inside the police station and retrieve Delvera Mooremarsh's box of books, it would please me.' She raised her eyes in exasperation, it was like talking to an idiot, she couldn't raise her voice, she had to be careful not to break the spell. 'The song will always be with you.'

'And you, will you stay here, with me?' Harrow swayed, his hand reached out and grabbed at her shoulder to steady himself.

Mooremarsh stepped away from his grasp, 'Yes, if you get my books, I will stay with you forever,' she lied, keeping her voice calm, she squashed the impatience exploding inside her. She squashed the inclination to snap at him.

Harrow nodded, a blood vessel burst in his eye, he rubbed it absent-mindedly.

'Retrieve books,' he agreed, a single strand of dribble slid down the corner of his mouth. Her eyes narrowed, had she pushed his mind too far? Mooremarsh reached out and took the cuff of his jacket, raised it up to his mouth and wiped the saliva away. She inspected him again.

'Go now, meet me in the small park over there, bring my prize to me' she commanded pointing to a small green with a sprinkling of bushes.

Harrow put two fingers to his temple and gave her a salute.

'I will find your books,' his voice was vague, far away, he stumbled towards the police station, his hands grabbed at the stone wall which surrounded the police station to steady himself. He looked back at her with sad eyes. She waved him on irritated. Harrow stepped through the royal blue door.

Mooremarsh watched him enter with bated breath. Her foot tapped on the pavement as she waited outside the police station. It had been a surprise to her how easy it was to cast a spell of obedience over Marcus Harrow. He had been compliant to all her suggestions, she manipulated him with her spell like a conductor conducts an orchestra. It was a good morning to cast the spell, she thought to herself, and she would be reunited with her magic books soon, they had been gone too long. The idea made her heady, Dark Magic was a parasitic relationship, but she didn't care, the power she felt when she wielded her spells. Her heartbeat excitedly making her catch her breath. Wiping her sweaty palms on the edge of her jacket, they had become sticky. Cupping her hand to her forehead to shield her eyes from the sun, she licked her dry lips and looked around, making sure she was still alone. Satisfied, she crossed the road, dodging the occasional horse dung from the early traffic of horse carts. The small seat midway down a grass bank gave her a good view of the police station. She got out a handkerchief and wiped the dew from the seat, throwing the sodden mass to one side when she had finished. Content that it was no longer wet, she sat down, crossed her legs, and waited. She became impatient; time stood still, it seemed like an eternity even though it was only a matter of minutes; maybe Harrow had been caught? She glanced around to make sure there was a way to escape from her position. A sudden movement of the door caught her attention. She sat forward on the seat; every muscle fibre ready to pounce on her prey. Harrow came out carrying one of her books. He marched stiffly, like he was counting his steps, a book dangling at his side. Her eyes snapped. Why did he only have one book? What an imbecile, he only had one job, couldn't he get that right? she quietly fumed.

'Where is the box with all my book?' she snatched the book from his hands. It was small, black leather with carved symbols on its binding. She shoved it in her pocket.

'I er, hum, I couldn't remember what I was looking for,' Harrow had started to come out of his groggy stupor and looked at her befuddled.

Her eyes narrowed. The spell did not last long enough. She had borrowed the living energy from another, it maybe that her magic was not strong enough.

'Who are you?' he asked her, his eyes unclouded.

'Gosh, you have a short memory, and you bought me breakfast!' Mooremarsh gushed, 'You told me you would show me Malmesbury.' She tried to hide her disappointment at not getting her books.

'Oh, did I?' Harrow stood a little straighter, taking in deep breaths, trying to clear his head.

'Yes, you did!' she smiled at him coyly.

Before she could continue a voice called behind her. A voice she recognized too well; her blood froze in her veins.

'Marcus, where is that car you want me to tow away to my garage and fix? I want to get back to my breakfast!' The cheerful voice of Bill Appleby grated on her.

'Morning, Sargent Harrow,' a female voice had sung.

The perfume of Earth Magic stung her nostrils, Mooremarsh clutched her stomach, she felt sick. The girl was here, Milly Appleby was within her grasp, the girl who had defeated her magic. An ugly smile touched her lips, a lightning bolt of an idea struck her. She could use her Energy Vampire spell to bleed Milly Appleby of her magic. If the spell worked, she would have great magic. An expression crept up her face, distorting its shape as she thought about the feat. She wondered if that bit of Dark Magic had ever been performed. It would be stupid to snatch her here. She needed all her books if she was to bleed Milly Appleby of her magic.

'Well, you going to show me which car it is?' Bill sounded a bit impatient, 'I haven't had breakfast yet!'

Harrow's expression was vague, brushing his hands over his eyes, he focused on Bill, his mind cleared a little.

'What's wrong with you, up late?' Bill sounded jovial.

Mooremarsh shuddered, Bill's voice scraped at the back of her eyeballs. She took a few steps towards Harrow. If she didn't cast a spell now, she would lose all hope of getting her books back. She reached out, took Harrow's arm, and gave it a soft squeeze.

'Thank you for showing me around, Sargent Harrow. I had better leave you two to sort out a car,' she gushed, sounding grateful for the benefit of the Appleby's.

Harrow looked into the dark pools of Mooremarsh's eyes, they sucked him in, he was trapped the whirlpool of her magic, he never wanted to leave. He heard her voice, singing to him, it made one more suggestive spell, he would do anything for the voice to keep singing, he heard her wishes.

'Get Mooremarsh's books and meet her at the woods.' The voice sang, only he could hear it and he loved it. He would do anything to hear it.

'Meet you later for dinner, bye.' Mooremarsh let go of his arm and walked past him.

'Yes, yes of course, I finish at four thirty. I will see you then.' He had chanted back to her.

Mooremarsh started to walk away quickly, in her haste, she lost her footing and slipped on the wet grass. The cold mud hit her knees as she landed on them, a searing pain shot up her thigh. The heal of her hands scuffed on the ground, they smarted from the hard contact. Harrow stepped a few steps and bent down and helped her up.

'Thank you, that won't be necessary,' she snapped waspishly, she saw his hurt look, and quickly recovered, replacing her stern look for that of a woman who needed his help. She held out her hand and let him raise her from the ground.

'Thank you, Harrow, that was generous of you,' she brushed down her clothes, inspected her knee, 'I'm fine, see you at dinner.' patted his hand.

She felt Bills and Milly's eyes boring in her back as she made her escape, reaching the pavement, it felt solid under foot. She gave Harrow a final salute and quickened her step, swinging her arms as she went.

'Sergeant Harrow, you need to sit down, you don't look well,' Mooremarsh grimaced at the concerned voice of the girl. She sang to Harrow again, Strengthening her bond with him. He would not be able to resist her magic, or so she hoped.

'Who's that then?' she heard Bill ask Harrow.

'That is Petula.' Harrow replied dreamily. 'She sings a beautiful song you know.'

CHAPTER 11
MILLY FINDS DARK MAGIC

'Is Sergeant Harrow alright, he looks sick, dad,' Milly walked closer to Harrow.

'Marcus are you, ok?' her dad took the police sergeants arm, 'You need to go back to the station, put your weight on me,' Bill stepped a little closer to Harrow.

'No, Bill, it's alright.' Harrow pushed Bill's arm away, straightened his Jacket and tried to stand taller, he wobbled, but steadied himself, 'I can go back on my own thank you, don't you worry,' Harrow's monotone voice gave Milly a chill.

Dark Magic has touched him. Milly felt Miskunn's head nudging her hip.

'Sergeant Harrow, who was that woman?' Milly asked cautiously.

'None of your business, do you hear me, none of your business,' Harrow's harsh voice startled Bill, who instinctively stepped between him and Milly.

Miskunn huddled closer to her, *I am here to protect you against Dark Magic.* She spread her wings about Milly.

Milly felt the warmth of Earth Magic and was grateful for Miskunn's protection.

'Hold on Marcus, no need to be like that with Milly, she is just a little worried about you.' Bill tried to sooth his friend.

'I don't need a child to nose about in my business,' Harrow's jaw clenched, he stabbed a finger at Milly.

'Ok Marcus, calm down,' Bill put his hands out palm upwards, like you would calm a frightened animal. 'let's go back to the station, you can show me which car I need to tow.'

Harrow shook his head like a bull. Milly felt Miskunn's wings tighten.

'I am here to collect a car, do you remember?' Bill put his hands on his hips, thinking what to do to help his friend.

Harrow's vacant stared made the hair on the back of Milly's neck stand up on end. There was something very wrong here, a thought was scratching at the back of Milly's mind. A memory, she couldn't quite grasp it.

'I am fine Bill. Come on, I will show you the car that needs fixing.' Harrow walked away back towards the police station.

'Don't know what's wrong with him,' Bill stood scratching his head, he searched in his pocket, a jangle proceeded a large bunch of keys. He handed them to Milly and nodded towards the cream and green recovery lorry parked to one side of the police station.

'Wait for me in the lorry, I shouldn't be too long,' he called over his shoulder and followed Harrow.

He has been touched by Dark Magic and cannot be trusted. A spell of obedience shrouds him. Be careful. Miskunn relaxed her wings, they fell to her side.

'Who was that woman?' Milly began to walk to the lorry, 'Is she the one who cast the spell?'

I don't know, but you should tell your mother and Sylvester Bluesky. She opened her wings wide to release the cramp in them.

Milly fumbled with the keys looking for the one which opened the cab of the lorry. Her foot struck something, a small thud sounded, and the object slid in the grass.

'Oh,' she let the keys fall to her side. In the grass lay a small black book, wet, and smeared with mud. It was in the spot where the woman had slipped. Milly stooped and picked it up.

'Ouch,' she dropped it, it was ice cold, the coldness burnt her skin. Milly wrapped the cuff of her jacket around her hand, and gingerly picked up the book again. There was an unpleasant aroma coming from the leather cover.

'Well, what do I have here?' she asked herself.

Bad, Bad, Bad! Miskunn flew in circles about her head.

'I think it must belong to the woman who slipped. I will give it back!' Milly looked at the golden eagle.

Bad Magic, put it back on the ground! Miskunn jutted her head out.

Milly held the book in the palm of her hand. Its coldness stinging her hand through the fabric of her coat.

'Mum will know what to do with this.' She quickly walked to the lorry.

Reaching the confines of the lorry's cab, she found an old newspaper. Placing the book on the paper, she got a pencil from the glove compartment and started to inspect the small book. The leather had symbols carved into it and the pages were gilded with gold. She thumbed the spine and turned it over to look at the back.

DO NOT OPEN THAT BOOK Miskunn screamed so loud Milly thought her eardrums would explode.

'OK, OK. Don't scream at me, you're hurting me. I will give it to Mum when I get home.' Milly screamed at the bird.

Dangerous, very dangerous. Tell Sylvester Bluesky about the book. He will know what to do with it. Miskunn disappeared.

Milly wrapped the book up in the newspaper, and placed it into the glove compartment, just as her father came out of the police station. He caught her gaze and shrugged his shoulders as he walked to the lorry. The door opened with a creak, and he hauled himself into the driving seat.

'He finally showed me which car needs towing back to the garage.' Bill stared through the window screen, 'he's not himself. Told another officer, they said they would keep an eye on him. Anyway, we will drive around the back and hitch up the car.'

Milly thought about the book, it was calling to her.

It's our little secret. They don't have to know. It chanted to her.

She threw her dad a look from the corners of her eyes to see if he could hear it to. He was fiddling with the key and pressing the petrol peddle. The engine revved and Bill gave a small cheer under his breath. The lorry coasted past the police station, her dad turned the steering wheel and expertly swung the lorry into the police yard. He stopped the engine and pointed at a duck blue and white car in the corner of the yard.

'Sooner we get this to the garage, the sooner we get home for breakfast!'

Tell Him! Miskunn's voice stabbed accusingly.

Bill worked quickly and had the car hitched onto his lorry. They arrived back at the garage; her dad waved towards his car.

'Come on, let's get home, we can fix it later.' Bill wiped his hands on a rag.

'You really want that breakfast!' Milly laughed.

'You bet, it's the weekend and your mum will cook all the trimmings!' he threw over his shoulder as he walked to the car.

Milly watched her dad walking away. Gingerly took the book out of the glove compartment and slipped it her pocket.

They drove into the driveway of Chestnut Cottage, Milly looked around for Miskunn, she felt a guilty wave of relief. She waited for her dad to get out of the car.

'Come on, Joshua will eat all the sausages!' Bill moved quickly to the front door.

Milly slid her hand into her pocket and touched the book. Her heart raced wildly; her forehead was cold and clammy. She drew out the book and exhaled. A faint stench reached her nostrils and she wiped it with one hand. It was a few steps to the door, opening it as quietly as she could she popped her head around it. Voices wafted from the kitchen; the smell of breakfast reminded her she was hungry.

Taking the stairs two at a time, she tiptoed down the landing to her bedroom, put her back on the door. On her bed was a magic book. The principles and laws of using Earth Magic. She grabbed a pencil from a drawer and threw down the newspaper package. Carefully she knelt on the floor beside her bed. With a trembling hand she peeled back the newspaper to reveal the black book. Would it help her to fight Dark Magic if she knew what spells were being used?

Open me, find out your power! The book sang to her.

'I don't need your power.' Milly got up off her knees. A terrible feeling of panic choked her airways, she felt trapped, she couldn't breathe.

You will only find out how powerful you are if you read me. Dark Magic is your way to powerful magic. You know you are nothing without it.

Milly stood there, paralysed, her hands hung aimlessly at her sides. A single tear fell from her eyelashes. A stench floated up from the book.

You want to know how powerful Dark Magic is, you want to read the book.

'I don't want your magic.' She screamed, she had made a mistake bringing the book here, she should have gone straight to her mother with it.

'Go away,'

You have hidden this book from your mother, why did you do that? You have been deceitful; you have the mark of Dark Magic.

'I do not. I was just curious,'

Curiosity killed that cat; you are not a cat. The voice laughed low, slow.

Milly took a step away from her bed. She had made a mistake and needed to fetch her mother. Her eyes opened a fraction.

Milly, follow me, and you will always have family and happiness. The voice of Dark Magic whispered.

'No! it is not true!' Sophia's voice cried behind her; her words echoed around the room.

Confused Milly looked wildly around; she saw Sophia through a mist, she was standing by a river. 'It is not true!'

A warm flush of courage sliced away Milly's doubts. She backed up to the door, her fingers searched behind her back for the doorknob. She found it, cold under her fingers. She twisted the doorknob, and slowly the door opened.

You belong to us!

'No, I belong to Earth Magic.'

She pushed her body through the opening, and slammed the door shut. Her mouth felt dry, she ran her tongue over her lips. She needed to tell her mum about the Dark Magic book. She hung her head; she would also have to explain how she tried to read the book.

'Milly, come and get breakfast, before it gets cold!' Alana's voice called to her.

Making her way downstairs and walking into the kitchen. Her father was explaining his worries about Harrow. Milly sat down and picked at her breakfast, listening to her parents discuss Harrow. She absent-mindedly fiddled with the spoon in the marmalade jar. She wasn't going to enjoy telling her mother about the book.

'It's really cold.' Joshua sat rubbing his arms.

'Yes, felt it just as you both walked in.' Alana shivered.

Milly hung her head guiltily. They had both felt the arrival of Dark Magic.

'Milly, when you have finished attacking the marmalade with the spoon, could you pass it to me?' her mother broke her thoughts. 'Is there something on your mind?'

Milly looked at her mother and felt ashamed. She had broken a sacred vow. Never dabble with Dark Magic. She had failed her mother; she had failed Earth Magic. The truth stuck in her throat.

You are mine!

Milly felt her chest tighten. She knew Dark Magic could not approach her here, the house was protected with charms laid down by her mother and the Elders.

You brought me into the house. You have broken the charm! A cruel laugh croaked in the distance.

'Mum, can I talk to you in private.' Her eyes widened; she pushed the voice out of her mind. *Miskunn, where are you, help me!* Her mind called out to the eagle.

'I need your help in the garage this morning if we are going to the Circus this afternoon.' Her dad slapped thick butter onto his toast.

'Ok, after the circus.' She smiled weakly at her mother.

The smell of rose petals permeated the room. She felt the heavy wing of Miskunn on her shoulder. *I will protect you so long as you stay with Earth Magic. If you choose to play with the darkness of Dark Magic, I cannot be with you. Fortunately, you did not open the book and your saving grace is that you feel guilty about even bringing it into your home. Tell your mother before you leave the house.* The eagle touched the charmed necklace about her neck. *You are protected once more. Do not touch the book. I think you have learnt a lesson on the power of Dark Magic. You must tell your mother, you must face the consequences, have courage.*

Milly nodded over her toast. She felt her mother's eyes resting on her, but she did not look up to meet them worried she would start to cry. Instead, she took a gulp of hot tea and a bit off a piece of toast, it was tasteless in her mouth. The scrape of a chair announced her father had finished his breakfast,

'Come on, we need to get that car fixed,' He bent over and kissed Alana on the top of her head, 'Great breakfast love.' He looked at Joshua, 'Help your mum with the compost heap while I'm out. We should be back for lunch. After we will be off to the circus' He beamed at Alana, who prodded him playfully in the stomach.

'I want a quick word with Milly before you go,'

'No time, it will have to wait until we get back,' he went out to the hall and grabbed his jacket, 'Come on Milly, we haven't got all day!'

Alana opened her mouth to say something, but Milly stood up.

'It's ok Mum, it will wait until lunchtime,' she smiled weakly at her mother and left after her father.

You should have told her! Miskunn's wing brushed against her face, if Milly didn't know any better, she would have believed it was meant to be a slap with the rebuke.

'I will tell her after lunch.' Milly walked quickly after her father, knowing Miskunn was disappointed with her.

CHAPTER 12
THE DOORKEEPER OF MAGIC

When are they going to get here? wings fluttered as Gertie set herself on a small rock beside Sylvester Bluesky. Prudence came out from the undergrowth and preened her paws.

They will get here when they get here! Prudence chided loftily, eyeing up the very large crow.

The wolf raised his nose to the air, his head turning to and fro.

They are near. Not much longer.

It didn't take long, seven people in odd clothes, walked around the bend in the little lane.

Here they come, they are here! Gertie flapped her wings, purple glitter puffed around them.

Gertie, control yourself. Sylvester Bluesky growled at the excited crow.

She ruffled her feathers and steadied her perch on the rock.

A tall woman approached them; the long skirt of her midnight blue dress swished as she walked. A cat followed behind her.

'Sylvester Bluesky, it is good to see you,' she looked at Prudence and smiled.

Light of winter, Sophia, the wolf nodded his head solemnly.

The crow caught her attention because of her colours. A thick down of black feathers with the occasional purple ones covered her chest, her wings gleamed in the sunlight, with the occasional purple tipped feather here and there. What struck her was the colour of the crows' eyes. Vivid sapphire blue eyes stared up at her.

Its rude to stare! Gertie put her head to one side.

The cat which had remained silent until now, pounced forward.

You will not address Sophia like that, she is a member of the High Council of Elders. The cat hissed at Gertie, he lifted his tail and unsheathed his claws.

'Hush Feles, she is young.' Sophia reproached her magical cat.

She has no manners, Feles retorted, he sat down and licked his paw.

Gertie, Sophia is the high elder of the seven. You cannot be rude to her, Prudence gasped.

Sophia laughed her tinkering laugh. 'I do apologise, Gertie, but I have never seen such a deep blue in one of your fellow crows. Quite stunning.'

The crow preened her feathers in appreciation.

'Come on you slow coaches!' Sophia looked at Sylvester Bluesky, 'You are sure Mathew is a Doorkeeper of Magic?'

Yes, I believe he is Ostiarius Magicae. You will have to test him.

A voice behind them chipped in, 'Three children in a year, with Earth Magic. This may be an omen; we need to be on our guard and watch over them all.' Rutger lent heavily on the eagle head silver handle of his cherry wood walking cane. The journey from the town had been longer that he remembered, his feet ached, and it made him grumpy.

'I have not seen a Doorkeeper before, what are we going to give Mathew to hide?' Morag Lacorr stood behind Rutger; long red hair ran down her back in rivulets.

'What about the crow,' Morag laughed at the crow.

Just make sure he does not lose me! Gertie turned her back on them, stretched out her wings.

Gertie, stop being so rude! Prudence stared at Gertie's back.

It might be best for us all, a crow with an attitude like that. Feles stared at Gertie.

It's not you that is being asked to vanish into oblivion! Gertie shook her feathers and an explosion of red gauze like mist surrounded them.

Gertie, behave. You are old enough to know how to conduct yourself! Sylvester Bluesky's voice boomed.

The crow turned around and bobbed her head up and down apologetically.

Well, you have better come and find me if Mathew loses me. She grumbled.

I will look for you, don't worry. Prudence tapped the floor with her hind foot.

Sophia clapped her hands, 'Well, that is all sorted. Let's get on.'

'Crows are always difficult to deal with,' whispered Morag to Rutger.

He raised his eyebrows in reply.

Sylvester Bluesky looked hard at Gertie. She ignored him and took flight from the rock and was soon out of sight.

Did Gertie not train with you? Prudence tried to make out where the crow was.

The Wolf was silent, he scanned the sky, his ears pricked up.

She is full of fire that one. She will be good for Mathew. I have made the right choice. He looked back at Prudence, *Remember, those first few months were difficult for you too. Joshua is not an easy human. You have done well.* He smiled at the hare, her ears were twitching, and her back foot banged the ground excitedly. *Come on, let's see if we can beat her to Mathew's door.*

Gertie landed on Mathew's Kitchen windowsill. She could see Mathew had his head in his hand. He was sleeping. She pecked at the glass. He didn't move.

Get up, you lazy human! She hopped on the windowsill, laughing. Mathew jumped awake at her voice. *I am here, open the window!*

Mathew looked around the kitchen.

Over here, you cannot have forgotten me so soon! Her feathers lifted in the gentle breeze.

'You! I thought it was a dream.'

Yes, and no. I am Gertie, your magical animal. Sylvester Bluesky must formally introduce us. She put her head to one side.

'My magical creature. I have not been tested by the Earth Magic elders yet.

'Mathew stretched and yawned. Pushing the chair back with his legs, he got up and wiped his eyes with the back of his hand. Groggily, he wondered over to the window.

The crow hopped onto the kitchen counter. Mathew looked at her.

The elders are on their way now. You need to tell your parents. Don't want them surprised!

'They are coming now! Shouldn't they have sent a message or something?' Mathew babbled.

For goodness' sake, pull yourself together. They want to test your magic, that's all. Her head twisted around as she looked around the kitchen.

'What sort of magic?'

You must hide my magic; you will make me invisible to others. Her sapphire eyes rested on him.

Make sure you bring me back quickly. I don't want to be hanging around in limbo!

'Let me get this right. I have never done magic, and you want me to make you disappear,' he waved his hands around exasperated.

Mathew, its Earth Magic, not just any magic. Earth Magic, she interrupted him.

'You're really bossy aren't you!' he brushed his fingers through his hair. 'Your bigger than normal crows. Why is that?'

You must have noticed; all magical creatures are bigger. You're not dim, are you? That would really be frustrating!

'I have only just come into Earth Magic; only vaguely seen a wolf and a blue hare before. You should know that if you are so bright. I hope you're not the dimmest of the crows, they are supposed to be really clever.' He sniped back.

The crow and Mathew glared at each other. They were interrupted by Mathew's mother tapping open the door with her foot. In her arms she carried a wicker basket laden with dry tablecloths and tea towels.

'Mathew, Sylvester Bluesky came over last night when you were in bed.' His mother put the basket into the scullery and came back.

'How can you see him if you don't have Earth Magic,' grumbled Mathew.

His mother pulled out a chair and sat down at the table. She rested her chin on her hands.

'I have never said that I did not possess Earth Magic. The truth is I am very weak, I can make out magical creatures, have the occasional premonition, but that's all really. Not like your uncle Trim, now he was skilled, he could feel if something was happening. Always admired him, even though most of the family thought he was a little strange,' She took an apple out of a fruit bowl and smelt it, then rolled it between her fingers,' 'no, Trim wasn't strange, he was just eccentric.'

'What about Dad?' Mathew looked out the window.

'You have to ask him. He comes from a family that has a powerful kind of magic. Unusual Earth Magic.' Her head tilted to one side.

A loud knock at the door made Mathew jump, his heart was beating wildly in his chest.

'You two need to get on, could hear your raised voices from outside.' His mother put her hands on her hip and glared at them.

The door opened and Mathew's father came in followed by seven strangers, and Sylvester Bluesky padded behind them. The wolf looked at Gertie, his eyes narrowed. She had the grace to lower her head ashamed.

'Found these folk outside.' Mathew's father did not look pleased, 'There's a lot of work to do.' He grumbled under his breath.

'Thank you for letting us come today. I know how busy you are at this time of the year on the farm.' Rutger held out his hand and Mathew's father took it graciously. The elder peered at Sylvester Bluesky, 'Sylvester, could you reveal yourself so that Mr Anderson can see and hear you?'

The wolf walked to Mr Anderson's side and pushed his nose under his hand. Mr Anderson's eyes opened in astonishment as the wolf materialized at his side.

You must always keep your hand on me if you are to see me and hear my voice.

Mathew's dad looked into his amber eyes and nodded.

Sophia stepped forward. 'We are here to see if Mathew has Earth Magic,' she paused and waited for any questions. 'Mathew,' she said solemnly, 'standing before you are the seven, we sit on the Earth Magic Council of the south. It is our duty to make sure that each young person who exhibits Earth Magic is judged to be true.'

Mathew looked as if he was about to say something but was quelled by a look from his mother.

He watched a man in a jaunty turquoise suit leaning on his walking cane. The cane had a silver handle in the shape of flame, a large rose quartz stone peeping out within its gaps.

'I hope you remember me. I am Jasper Wooton. We are not only here to see if you bear Earth Magic, but also, if you are a Doorkeeper,' he looked across at Sylvester Bluesky, 'magical creatures detect this type of magic better than us.'

'The Anderson's have always been strong in *Ostiarius Magicae*, I sadly am not very strong in Earth Magic,' his mother sighed.

'Well, shall we go into the living room? I think we will be comfortable in there.' Geraldine had been quiet so far, she caught Morag's look, 'My corns are hurting, I told you I should have worn my old shoes!'

'No, its fine, we can go in. I will get the kettle on and bring in some tea and cake,' Mathew's mother gestured to her husband to take the elders into the living room.

'Tea and cake, that sounds splendid,' Jasper banged his cane on the stone floor.

'This way then,' Mathew's father went in the direction of the living room leaving Mathew to follow in their wake, he thrust his hands deeply into his pockets. He was not looking forward to being interrogate.

'You need to bring in three more chairs, Mathew,' his father called.

Mathew stopped and took two kitchen chairs from the table and dragged them to the sitting room. The elders had already taken up position on the comfortable sofas and armchairs. Gertie stood beside Sylvester Bluesky looking very solemn. He went back to the kitchen to retrieve the last chair.

'Watch where you're going son, nearly had me over with this tray,' his mother held a tray with a large teapot, sugar bowl, milk jug, and several teacups.

'Can you fetch the plate with the lemon cake on it please,' his mother winked at him and smiled.

'It's not going to be that bad Mathew. Just do what you feel comes naturally to you.'

Mathew nodded grimly, convinced he was not going to pass the test.

Hobbling back with a chair in one hand, a plate with slices of lemon cake in the other, a silence fell in the room as he entered it. He set the chair down and handed the plate to Sophia. Once tea and cake were served, Rutger stood up from his chair.

'Now we can begin.'

All eyes turned to Mathew; he wiped his sweaty hands down his trousers.

'You have had the nightmares and have shown, you would follow the light and repulsed by darkness.'

'It is the beginning of your journey with Earth Magic.' Rutger sat down and leaned forward. 'We are here to guide you,' before he could finish, Gertie ruffled her feathers.

I will be the one you will talk with most though, Gertie stopped mid-sentence.

A deep growl came as a warning.

Well, it's true. She turned her back, huffed.

Rutger cast an amused glance at the crow.

'You are very eager. But you must learn courtesy. Don't be in such a rush to demonstrate your magic. You still have much to learn from Sylvester Bluesky.'

Ruffling feathers, Gertie turned back to the group, her head hung a little lower. She did not want to meet the wolf's stare.

'Now, let's get on. Mathew, have you found odd things happening? Maybe an object come to you when you think about it,' Sophia asked soothingly.

'No,' Mathew shrugged.

'Maybe, you had a premonition?' Sophia looked at him hopefully.

'No,' The knot in his stomach got tighter.

'You could see the magical creatures in this room?'

'Yes, I thought I saw glimpses of them after Christmas,' Mathew sat up straight, pleased he could answer one question at least.

The next hour Mathew was quizzed by the Elders of Earth Magic. They questioned his parents as well, which he found a little unsettling.

'There is one more task to perform.' Jasper stood up and looked at the crow. 'Mathew, look at Gertie. What do you see,'

'Who's coming to get me if he loses me?' The crow hopped from talon to talon.

I will Gertie! offered Prudence.

Are you a Doorkeeper? Gertie looked the blue hare up and down.

Prudence looked down at her feet.

Prudence may not be a Doorkeeper, but she is of good heart. I will find you, but maybe I will leave you there for a while to teach you a lesson! The wolf scowled at the crow.

Mr Anderson nearly fell off his chair, the booming voice of Sylvester Bluesky sent his senses reeling. He made sure his hand stayed on the wolf.

Now keep still! I have taught you better than this! He finished with a growl.

OK, OK. Just making sure! She hopped over to Mathew and stood in front of him.

Well, get on with it, don't hang around! Sapphire eyes bored into his.

Mathew cleared his throat. 'I don't know what you want me to do.'

Jasper walked over to Mathew and put his hand on his shoulder.

'Look into Gertie's eyes. Can you see her aura of Earth Magic?' Jasper encouraged him.

Mathew took a deep breath and looked at Gertie.

Nothing happened. He screwed up his eyes and concentrated on the crow.

'Where is your aura, where is your Earth Magic.' He whispered under his breath.

'Gertie, show me your aura, show me your Earth Magic,' he uttered his words louder, almost singing, repeating the same sentence.

Then it happened. Mathew saw Gertie's shape as shimmering gold. Sapphire eyes sparkled.

'I see the magic which binds you to the earth. Earth Magic will be hidden, from human, animal, and earth. You are bound away, no one can see your magic. Gertie, be gone.'

Mathew heard a shrill scream; it was his scream. he was thrown back against his chair.

Gertie was gone.

'Oh my,' Morag broke the astonished silence. 'Well, I never,' she looked at Mathew.

'I don't know how I did that!' Mathew's words came out stilted, he started to tremble uncontrollably.

'Drink the sweet tea. It will calm you. You've had a bit of a shock!'

Jasper started clapping, 'I never thought I would meet a Doorkeeper in my time!'

Sophia poured out a fresh cup of tea and put four teaspoons of sugar in.

'Here, drink this.' Sophia looked around for Gertie. 'You will need to bring Gertie back.' She handed Mathew the cup.

Mathew slurped the tea; his hand still shook and some of it went down his jumper.

Sophia took a biscuit and handed him that too.

'For your strength,' she smiled and looked across at Rutger.

Silent minutes passed; the Elders looked at each other.

Well, I think you need to try and get her back. Prudence looked up at Sylvester Bluesky.

No, Mathew must get her back. He is powerful with this magic. It's in his blood. Resting his eyes on Mathew.

'I don't know how.' Mathew looked shocked. He really didn't know how he had made Gertie disappear!

'Mathew, you have old magic within you. Earth Magic, which is not often given to many, it is a rare form of Earth Magic. Now, you will close your eyes and think of the crow. Think of her aura, her Earth Magic. Call her to you.' Rutger banged his cane on the floor to bring Mathew out of his stupor. 'Close your eyes!'

'You can do this. Earth Magic blood flows through your veins. You are the Doorkeeper, believe in yourself.' Morag whispered.

Mathew grabbed the bottom of his jumper and closed his eyes.

Your mind needs to feel her magic. Sylvester Bluesky nudged Mathew.

'Where are you, Gertie? Come to me.' Mathew willed the crow.

See her in your mind. The wolf coaxed.

Mathew twisted his jumper in his fingers.

Control your fear. Look for her. Sylvester willed him.

Mathew blew out air from his lungs. All he could see was blackness.

'Where are you?' he called out. 'Come to me Gertie, show yourself.'

'I summon you to me, bring your magic to me,' Mathew saw a glimmer of gold in the darkness. His mind moved towards it. The closer he got to the shimmer, the warmer it felt.

Well, you took your time didn't you! Gertie grumbled.

Mathew looked around. They stood in a sunny meadow.

'Well, it's not dark and gloomy like you said,' Mathew countered, 'are you ready to go back?'

Of course not, do you always state the obvious? The crow preened her wing, she looked at him snapped her beak at him, *get on with it!*

Mathew screwed up his eyes. A golden haze surrounded Gertie; the meadow became a blur.

'Come back to me, Gertie. I can see your magic, come back to me.' He thrust out his hands, 'come back, now!'

Mathew opened his eyes. Gertie was perched on his wrist, he tried not to let his arm down under her heavy weight.

I'm not volunteering for that again! She pecked Mathew's thumb.

'Oww,' he pushed the crow off his hand.

Sophia clapped, 'Brilliant, this is fabulous!'

A cough stopped her clapping. Rutger raised an eyebrow; she mirrored the action.

'Mathew, you did well, more practice is needed. You are a Doorkeeper.' Rutger turned to Mathew's parents. 'You have books on Earth Magic stored away for him to read?'

Mathew's mother nodded.

'Yes, he can read mine. The book of the Doorkeeper is hidden in the attic. She turned to her husband expectantly.

He looked out the window, not wanting to admit it had been a long time since there was Earth Magic in his family.

'Yes, I have my grandfather's books. I have read them, but they were of no use to me. I do not have Earth Magic.' He clarified. 'I was surprised Mathew was born with the gift.'

Mathew looked on, questions bubbling inside.

Don't worry, I am here to help you. I can answer some of your questions. She pecked his thumb again and flew off his wrist and onto the floor.

The clock struck one o clock and Mathew thought about the circus. His friends would arrive soon.

'Can I tell Joshua and Milly, I mean about me having Earth Magic, and the Doorkeeper thing.'

Sophia laughed at him. 'Yes, you can tell them. I will ask Alana to make you a charm pendant so that no one can detect your magic.'

Outside the dogs were barking, the grating noise of the gate opening and a car revving up along the drive.

'Great, they are here.' Mathew hollered.

Mathew, you are with the Elders, have a little respect!

Mathew felt a chill at the bellow of the wolf's voice in his head.

'Thank you, Sylvester Bluesky. Mathew, there is a final part to this meeting.'

Mathew nodded stupidly, not really understanding what Rutger was saying.

'Mathew, you have to make an oath.' His mother whispered to him.

'Do you promise to keep to the law of Earth Magic?' Rutger's voice filled the room.

'Yes,' Mathew squeaked.

'Do you promise not to use Earth Magic on others except against Dark Magic.'

'I do,' another squeak.

'Do you promise not to discuss Earth Magic with anyone who does not have Earth Magic, except in the case of your father, although he does not have Earth Magic, some of his ancestors were gifted with it.'

'Yes, I promise,' his eyes levelled with Rutgers.

'These promises are a solemn oath to the Earth Magic Council. We the Seven Elders of the Southwest hear your promise.'

'Go on lad, see your friends. We have made our judgment. Leave us to talk with your parents now.'

Mathew looked at his mother.

'Off you go. Ask Bill to drop you at the gate after the circus.' His mother waved a hand towards the door.

Mathew was about to dash off, instead he turned to the Elders and gave a bow with his head. 'Thank you for coming and showing me the way of magic.' He turned on his heal and left the room.

'Well, I suppose you'll be wanting another cup of tea while we discuss Mathews Earth Magic lessons.' Mrs Anderson got out of her chair and collected the tea tray.

'Any chance of more of that delicious cake?' Jasper asked.

'Of course.' Mrs Anderson's lips pulled into a smile at the side of her mouth.

'When you get back, we will discuss Mathew's tuition. How to help him through the difficulties he will have ahead being a Doorkeeper.' Sophia smiled encouragingly at Mrs Anderson.

'One more thing, make sure Mathew makes his offering to Earth Magic before the morning.' Rutger reminded them, 'It is important he understands how important it is.'

Mr Anderson smiled wryly, 'He can plant out the broad beans then!'

'Yes, that will do it!' Rutger laughed.

CHAPTER 13

THE MYSTICAL WORLD OF FORREST'S CIRCUS

Milly got out of the car to the sound of Joshua and Mathew grumbling how squashed they had been on the journey. She caught her mother's look and rolled her eyes. Sometimes she found Mathew's grumbling tedious. Her mother's eyes crinkled at the edges and Milly knew she was going to quell the moaning boys.

'I can always get dad to take you both home,' Alana Appleby raised an eyebrow at the two moaning individuals.

Milly watched Joshua flick a glance at his mother, she raised her chin which was always a sign she was not pleased with him.

'Sorry, Mum,' he gulped apologetically.

'Where is Grandad Rose?' Asked Milly.

'He is coming later with Donald, the toy shop owner.' Alana replied, she waved her hand towards the big-top.

In front of them stood a red and white candy floss striped big-top. Red and white lights flashed the words:

Mysterious world of Forrest's Circus.

'Wow, that is huge!' Milly clapped her hands; she felt her father's hand on her shoulder.

Can't wait to see inside! Gertie pecked at Mathew's ankle.

'Hey, you can't come with us!' Mathew snatched his ankle away from her beak.

And why not? Gertie huffed, feathers rippling.

'Because it's a place for humans!' Mathew threw out his arms exasperated.

Well, why has Sylvester Bluesky and Prudence gone in. Tell me that. It's favouritism, that's what it is!

'Really, what are they doing here?' Mathew scratched his head.

Humph, as if you didn't know!

She stood taller, wafted her wings, and took flight. A trail of red glitter followed her.

Joshua patted Mathew on the back, 'Glad she's your magical creature.'

Mathew shrugged his shoulders in reply.

'You will get use to her.' Joshua smiled encouragingly.

'You and Milly have the best ones,' Mathew hunched his shoulders, 'I've been landed with a dud!'

'Mathew, Gertie has a lot to learn. Be patient with her.' Alana chided him.

Mathew gave her a mutinous look and looked as if he was about to say something.

'Come on Mathew, we're here to have fun, and you have just passed your interview with the Elders,' Milly raised her eyes up at the sky searching for Gertie, she smiled at him and continued, 'and you are a Doorkeeper, it's a very rare type of magic. Cheer up!'

'Right let's get the tickets so we can get some good seats.' Bill Appleby marched ahead of the group in the direction of a bright yellow booth, lights flashed 'Tickets' on the side.

Milly walked quickly and caught up with her dad. They stood in a short line waiting their turn.

'How many?' A clown peered down at them from his lofty position in the booth, he grinned exposing his yellowing teeth.

'Three children and two adults please.' Bill said courteously, he turned and laughed down at Milly, 'you should never annoy a clown, you know, they are always playing tricks,' his lips gave a quirky smile to the side of his face.

'That will be six shillings,' the clown smiled, his ruby painted cheeks rose to his eyes.

Milly stood back a little, the sight made a hollow in her stomach. The clown threw back his head and chuckled, a deep belly laugh. His yellow wig was in danger of dislodging off his head.

'Come now child, everyone likes clowns!' He handed five green tickets to her dad.

Milly bit her lip; in fact, she found the clown quite frightening. Discoloured teeth gleaming out from behind his painted lips. Black glistening eyebrows stood out from a face covered with white powder. She shuddered again. No, clowns were not for her!

'Let's go, don't want to miss anything do we.' Her dad waved the tickets in the air and walked away towards the circus.

The clown caught Milly's eye, 'I know what you are. You should enjoy the evening.' He gave her a dismissive salute, and looked over her shoulder at the next customer, 'Next please,'

Milly felt stung, what could the clown mean. She looked at him a little closer, there was something a little odd about him. His eyebrows twitched and he put up a white gloved hand and waved her away, his laugh smacked against her eardrums, and she put her hands across her ears. The clown poked his tongue out at Milly and carried on laughing.

'We're going in, you had better hurry up!' Mathew's voice floated across from the small queue outside the entrance.

She dragged her eyes away from the laughing clown and made her way quickly to her family.

'Now when we get inside, we are all sitting together.' Bill handed out tickets to everyone.

A sweet smell pricked at Milly's nostrils.

'Cor, candy floss, could we have some?' Joshua looked at his dad, 'Please,' he chortled as an afterthought.

Bill sniffed the air, 'Now that is a smell that makes my belly grumble, hot dogs!'

Alana laughed. 'Milly and I will get some snacks; you go in and save us some seats.' She slipped her arm through Milly's, took the food orders, and pulled her in the direction of a food stall.

Milly watched her dad take the others into the circus and walked reluctantly in the opposite direction with her mother. The queue was short, Milly was thankful as she didn't want to miss anything. A tall woman in a blue suit with gold braid stepped up to the counter to serve them. Her hair was puffed up and came to a cone at the back of her head in a flamboyant beehive hair style. Milly watched in fascination as pink candy floss whirled around in a metal basin.

'Well?' the question threw Milly out of her daydream. 'Well, do you want candy floss or a hotdog?'

'Candy floss, please,' she licked her lips imagining the sweet taste.

The woman grabbed a stick and began to collect the sugared concoction on to it, soon enough she presented them with three tall puffs of candy floss.

'Onions on the dogs?' Milly giggled at the reference to dogs. A stillness made her look up. The woman glared down at her with cat like eyes.

'Yes, that would be great,' Alana smiled sweetly at the woman.

Hot dogs were prepared with the occasional utterance of 'Children today,' and 'Where have all the manners gone.' Milly knew her mother did not want to catch her eye; they would break out laughing and offend the woman even more.

Two hot dogs in white napkins were thrust into Alana's waiting hands. The woman's hands briefly touched her mothers, when they did, both women flinched.

'Oh, I didn't know.' The woman in blue looked startled.

'Nor did I.' Alana held her stare.

Confused Milly looked from one to the other.

'Come on Milly, we will be late.'

Milly watched her mother march ahead of her, hot dogs held at a distance to avoid spilling onions.

'Mum, what was that about?' she asked her mother excitedly.

'You will find out at the end of the performance.' Her mother threw back cryptically as she stepped through the doorway, flashing her ticket in the other hand at the clown waiting on the door.

Milly gingerly held out her ticket to the clown and skipped on after her mother. She could not see in the gloominess, she followed the voice of her father calling, 'Over here!'

She made her way up the wooden step after her mother. The smell of earth intermingled with food was heady.

'Quick, sit down, before the show starts,' Joshua's voice floated over to her above the excited dins of the audience. She handed out the candy floss and sat down and settled in for the show.

She didn't have to wait long. It got dimmer if that was possible. A spotlight made a bright circle in the middle of the area. The light was broken by the form of a tall dark exotic man, dressed from top to toe in purple. On his head he wore a shiny top hat, a magnificent black handlebar moustache adorned his top lip, a pointed beard which had a small braid with amethyst jewels at the end fell from his chin. In his hand he held a whip, he raised his hand above his head and brought it down suddenly.

Crack!

The loud sound boomed around the space as he lashed the floor with a whip.

'Ladies, gentlemen, boys and girls.' He rolled up the whip and raised it in the air.

'Welcome to Forrest's circus.' He twirled and the tails of his coat flashed out, the silk material shining, catching the light of the spotlight.

Milly could not believe someone so tall could move so fast on the balls of his feet. The crowd roared and clapped furiously.

'You will be amazed, mystified and entertained this afternoon. Horses that gleam, people who will fly through the air, balancing acts which defy gravity, animals with grace and lastly, the comic of clowns.' Opening his arms wide, the crowd clapped, and some stamped their feet in excitement.

'First, the human cannon ball. I introduce,' he placed a finger to his lips, the crowd hushed, 'the Lady of Flight, Tori Magnificence,' he waved his arm towards a curtain which opened wide.

The brass band in the corner played a cheery tune, and a small woman in a green leotard skipped out from behind the curtain. Four clowns pushing a huge cannon followed in her wake. More clowns came out, doing cartwheels and jostling each other. They grabbed thick ropes and pulled on them, a safety mesh arose from the floor, higher and higher. After tightening off the ropes, the clowns ran out of the arena leaving the woman alone. The music stopped, a drum beat a forlorn rhythm, the woman walked slowly to the cannon. She climbed up a ladder and slipped inside the cannon.

'Ouch!' Milly jumped as she felt a weight on her hand. She whipped around and Miskunn was at her side.

I love the circus! I bet Sylvester Bluesky is here! The golden eagle wagged her head side to side.

Milly looked at her family and Mathew to make sure they had not noticed her outburst. They were all transfixed on the cannon. Milly ignored Miskunn and watched the cannon, waiting with bated breath for it to fire. She didn't have to wait long; a loud explosion announced the firing of the human cannon ball. Through a haze of smoke, a green vision flew into the arena. At the same time Miskunn screamed in fright and began to fly around in circles above the safety net. Milly held her breath and squeezed her eyes shut waiting for the green image of the woman and Miskunn to collide in the air. A chorus of cheers and clapping, Milly opened her eyes. On the safety net bounced the woman, and above her, nearly touching the roof of the circus big-top was Miskunn, flying in graceful circles.

'That was amazing, especially when that bird started flying around her!' Mathew called out, clapping and hooting.

'Bird, what bird?' Joshua asked above the din.

Milly closed her eyes; the truth was about to come out. Mathew was a Doorkeeper and could see all Earth Magic. They would all find out about Miskunn.

The human cannon ball took her bows and left the arena in darkness. The noise settled down to a silence. A dragging sound echoed, something very heavy was being pulled on the earth. A white blaze of light cut through the inky darkness to a point on the ground in the arena. The whisper of padding of feet, and then silence. A man entered the spotlight and his bald head shone in the light. He made a flourishing bow, and the lights went on. Everyone gasped. Three very large, orange, and black tigers sat behind him. White twitching whiskers protruded from their cheeks. One tiger stood up and crept slowly up behind the man. A woman's scream cut the silence. Milly realised she had been holding her breath.

'Watch out!' someone cried out a warning.

The man merely held up his hand. The tiger came closer, and stuck its head forward and pushed it under his limp hand.

'This is Jade. She is beautiful is she not?' The bald man called to the audience.

Jade promptly placed a paw in the air and looked at everyone staring at her. She looked as if she was seeking someone. Miskunn landed on the safety net above the tiger's head, the tiger looked up and growled. Milly gulped. Mathew lent forward, she heard his excited whisper to Joshua, 'That golden bird is going to be for it before long!' he leaned forward and called to Milly, 'do you think it's part of the act?'

'What are you talking about?' Alana whispered back to him.

Yes, what are you talking about? Sylvester Bluesky's voice boomed at them.

'Mum, I need to talk to you.' Milly grabbed her mother's hand.

'Milly, its ok, Mathew is pulling your leg. Let's enjoy the rest of the performance.' Her mother motioned in the direction of the arena with her head.

Milly sat back in her seat, the rest of the afternoon a blur. Until the trapeze artists came on. They were dressed in white and silver climbing the ropes to high swings.

'Isn't that…' Joshua began turning red.

'Hey, that's Nori at the end.' Mathew furiously waved to her, but she ignored him.

The troupe did impossible acrobatics in the air, spinning and catching each other mid-flight. The audience was in wonder. Milly was in awe for another reason. She looked at her mother and exclaimed, 'Did you know Nori is a fairy?'

'Yes Milly, the trapeze artists are fairies.'

'I can see their wings, they are magnificent!' Joshua sighed.

The act ended and the audience stood up and clapped, their appreciation radiated around, the canvas walls vibrated with all the energy. The trapeze artists waved to the audience from their lofty swings, with a flourish of their legs and arms, slid gracefully down the ropes and left the arena. The ringmaster came out, took off his top hat and waved to the audience. Everyone calmed down and listened to him.

'Thank you for coming, we hope you enjoyed the mystical adventure. Goodbye, will hope we will see you next year!' He spun on his heels, a puff of smoke and he vanished. Everyone clapped wildly and stood up. Bill beamed at his wife and shouted, 'Bravo!'

We have been invited to meet the circus members, come on follow me. Sylvester Bluesky beckoned them all to follow him.

'You're going to enjoy this Bill, we are meeting the circus performers,' she called to him, giggling at his excited expression.

'Mum, I need to talk to you.' Milly pleaded desperately to her mother.

'When we get home, it would be rude to keep Sylvester Bluesky waiting,' and moved down the stairs.

Milly took a deep breath hoping Mathew had forgotten about seeing Miskunn. The crowd was hard to push through, but finally they all stood near the curtained opening. Sylvester Bluesky materialised at Alana's side.

There are people I would like you to meet. This is a very rare occurrence. Follow me. The wolf padded behind the curtain. Alana pushed the children forward and grabbed Bill's hand.

'Well, this is going to be an experience.'

'I will follow your lead, so not to embarrass you all.' Bill gushed. Alana laughed and pulled him behind her.

Milly stood apart from Joshua and Mathew, she found herself in front of an empty elephant's cage. In fact, as she looked around the glittering cages, they were all empty!

'Joshua,' she hissed alarmed.

He turned around and followed the direction of her pointing finger.

'Where are the animals?' he asked her.

'I have no idea!' she replied in a shrill voice. 'That means they are loose!'

'Yes, we are.' A silky voice purred behind her.

Milly swung around. The tall woman from the food stall stood there, cat like eyes boring down at her, hair no longer in the puffed-up style, but hung down past her shoulders.

'I don't understand.' Milly stammered and took a few steps back.

'Well, you don't think a mystical circus would have real animals?' The booming voice came from the ringmaster. Milly swallowed hard.

Let me introduce the ringmaster, this is Forrest. Sylvester Bluesky stood beside Alana, looking across at Milly with his big amber eyes.

'The animals are shape shifters.' Forrest explained affably. 'The clowns are dwarfs, and as you have no doubt guessed, the trapeze artists are...'

'Fairies,' shouted Mathew, he felt Prudence butt his leg at being rude and shouting at the ringmaster, he ignored her, 'but what about the golden bird, who is she?' he giggled pleased with himself.

Forrest looked confused. 'No golden bird in the act.'

'Yes, there was, a huge golden bird. I saw it talking to Milly.' Mathew sounded affronted.

Milly felt all eyes turn on her. Her voice caught in her throat.

'Well Milly?' Her mother's gentle voice broke down her secret.

'Yes, Mum. It's true, there is a golden eagle. Her name is Miskunn. I have known her forever.' Milly hung her head; she didn't want to meet the hurt look of her mother.

MISKUNN, IT CANNOT BE, SHE IS DEAD! The howl of the wolf hurt her, she watched everyone except her father put their hands to their ears against the pain of his cry.

Her spirit is with Earth Magic. The wolf wailed and pawed the ground. It was a frightening sight; He lost control of his feelings and they all felt the onslaught of his pain.

Her spirit is with Earth Magic. I have made a mistake, if you see a dead animal spirit, I have judged badly. I must call the elders, Milly, your magic must be bound, you have followed dark magic. The wolf disappeared leaving Prudence shivering by Joshua's side.

Her mother's next words hurt her, branding her heart.

'Milly, what have you done,' Her mother lifted both hands to her mouth just staring at her.

CHAPTER 14
THE REVELATION OF HAZIM SHARMA

Forrest changed out of his purple ringmaster's costume and into a pair of comfortable old jeans, he grabbed a thick polo neck jumper hanging on the arm of a chair and struggled to pull it over his head. His hair was ruffled after the battle with his jumper, he grabbed a thick braid from the back of his head. With nimble fingers he re-braided it, took a checker cap off his bed, and pushed his hair under the cap and fixed it firmly on his head. Looking at his wrist he pulled up the sleeve of his jumper and looked at his gold antique watch. Four o' clock. He had three hours before the next show started.

'More than enough time,' he murmured to himself. 'I don't want to ride back in the dark.'

He looked in the mirror to make sure he had removed all the stage makeup. His rich skin glowed in the late afternoon light. He tugged his beard, stroked his moustache, his large hand grabbed a leather jacket and headed out of the caravan.

A black Arabian stallion scuffed the ground with its hoof as Forrest approached its corral.

'Ready to go out, Hurricane?' he spoke gently to the horse.

Hurricane tossed his head loftily in the air. Forrest stretched out his hand, and the horse sniffed it. Reaching up to the horse he stroked it neck, the hair was smooth under his hand. A leather and silver saddle sat on the corral gate.

'Calm down, we have a journey to make,' he took the saddle off the gate, opened the gate, and came through into the corral.

The horse shied away playfully.

'I haven't got time to play today. Stay still,' Hurricane gave him a baleful stare.

Forrest placed the saddle on the horses back, pulling and tightened the strap under the horse's belly before trying to mount him. The horse raised his head and nudged him.

'No, I won't use a bridle, I know you will behave,' he held the horses muzzle close to his face and nuzzled it.

Grabbing a tuft of the horse's mane, he thrust his foot into the saddles stirrup and swung his other leg over Hurricane's back.

'Let's go,' he held the horse's mane and coaxed him forward.

Forrest felt the thrill of riding the stallion across the fields towards Tetbury town. Hurricane jumped across hedges and fences effortlessly. Too soon the exhilarating ride came to an end, and they stood outside a small terrace cottage. He dismounted his steed and whispered in his ear.

'Stay here, I won't be long.' Patting the horses rump

Forrest received a low neigh and a gentle butt on the shoulder. He looked across the road at the line of cottages, all the same stone design. Each cottage had a different coloured door. Forrest smiled, everyone must have their stamp of individuality, it was a quirk of human nature, he mused to himself. Taking a deep breath, long strides soon had him standing outside a cottage door. He was just about to knock on the blue door when it swung open, and a startled boy stood in front of him. His skin the same hue as his, his hair a little lighter. The face looked back at him quizzically. The boy juggled two milk bottles and they clattered as he placed them down on the pavement.

Forrest took off his cap, the braid escaped from under it and fell casually over one of his shoulders.

'Does the Sharma family live here?' He gave a little bow of his head.

'Yes, why?' the boy asked suspiciously.

'I am Hazim Sharma, also known as, Forrest. Please tell your father that I am here.'

An awkward moments silence passed between them.

The boy turned and called over his shoulder.

'Dad, there is someone at the door.'

'What is your name may I ask?' Forrest looked down at the boy, certain he knew who he was.

'Clarke, Clarke Sharma.' He looked the man up and down.

The sound of slippers slapping the floor sounded behind Clarke. They came to an abrupt halt.

'You!' A choked whisper sounded behind Clarke, the boy turned and looked at his father. 'Why now?'

Clarke's father's face blanched, he stood, a granite statue, looking up at the man on the pavement.

'Erik, it is good to see you.' Forrest's taught voice broke the space between them. 'You have grown tall, you look well.'

'It is not safe,' Erik gasped, he moved Clarke to one side and looked up and down the street.

'Walk with me.' Commanded Forrest, as an afterthought he asked, 'do they know?'

'No, I always felt it would be too dangerous. There has already been an episode with a dark magic practitioner.' Erik put his hands behind his back and glanced sideways at Clarke.

'I see,' Forrest stroked his beard slowly, 'I have things I need to tell you. I will wait by my horse. Be quick.' He threw Clarke a look, 'I am your grandfather Clarke, Erik is my son.'

Clarke gaped at him, 'Is that true?' he turned to his father, his skin flushed, 'Well?'

Forrest turned and walked back to Hurricane, when he got closer, he stroked his mane comfortingly. Over his shoulder Erik's voice floated to him.

'Go in Clarke. Tell your mother I will be back soon.'

Forrest got back onto Hurricane's back, steadied himself, and put out his hand for Erik to catch. He felt Erik's cold hand slide into his and tightened his grip in his.

'Ready?' Forrest looked down at Erik and pulled him onto the back of the stallion behind him. 'We won't be long. I have much to tell you.'

Forrest felt Erik adjust himself on the back of the horse, once he was settled, he squeezed his knees onto the ribs of the horse, letting Hurricane know it was time to go.

Twenty minutes riding found them in a small wood on the edge of Malmesbury. They dismounted and stood in a clearing facing each other.

'Hurricane don't go far,' he called to his horse, he was reward with a neigh as a reply.

'I thought we would never meet again.' Erik choked voice cut with emotion.

A terrible memory flitted through Erik's mind, the night his father had left him, alone in the world, bereaved without parents.

'I am sorry Erik.' Forrest sucked in air, 'I had to leave you when my beloved Jasmine died.' Forrest's eyes clouded, his fists clenched up and his knuckles became white. 'I loved your mother very much.'

'I know. Father, you explained, I understood. You hid me well, they never found me.' Erik kicked the leaves with his boot. 'Not that I have your power, I don't have magic.'

'My kind of magic cannot be passed down. It is what it is.' Forrest looked around the clearing, feeling weary. 'I hid you to make sure they would not do to you what they did to your mother.'

'I still remember that night. It is as clear as today.' Forrest swallowed hard. 'One moment Jasmine and you were holding my hand, then poof, Jasmine was dead. They not only took your mother from me, but they also took you.'

'Dad, the people who hid me with were kind. They treated me like a son. They understood.' Erik came forward and put his hand on his dad's arm. 'Why are you here. I haven't seen you for over thirty years?'

Hurricane whinnied in the distance, as if she could understand their conversation.

'I am here for two reasons.' He put his hand over his son's. 'Both are not good.'

'Over the years I have watched you grow up from afar. I never contacted you in case they were still watching.'

'I understand. If they caught you, they would have imprisoned you for that one *wish* you would have to grant them.' Erik looked at the ground trying to hide the pain he was feeling at the memories that were being stirred up.

'I would have gladly given up my freedom for you and your mother. They didn't give me the chance.' His grip tightened on Erik's arm, 'They killed her and hoped that the shock would allow them to have me as captive. Instead, I used my magic to transport you to friends in Deli. They could not track us there.'

Forrest crushed Erik in a hug, his throat ragged at the memory.

'This time, I will get it right,' he whispered.

He held Erik at arm's length. 'You look well.'

'You don't look a year older!' snorted Erik.

'Let's sit down on that log over there. There is much to tell you and very little time.' Forrest walked over to a felled tree and kicked it with his boot. A low tone hummed back and showed him the log was not rotten to sit on. He sat down and waited for Erik to join him.

They sat in silence, listening to the birds, watching the gentle breeze tickle the fallen leaves.

'I have run a circus these last thirty years. Never open in the same place. It has been a place of sanctuary for many magical beings.'

Forrest unconsciously stroked his beard. It was an action which brought back memories to Erik of a happy childhood before the dark robed men had burst into their house and killed his mother.

'They wanted your power. A power that no human or those with dark magic should acquire. Mother knew this, she knew the danger when she married you. Your power had to be hidden, from this world.' Erik watched his father's face harden as he talked of the wretched night.

'I have been happy dad, it was hard at first, but there was a lot of love from my adoptive parents.'

Forrest hit the log with his fist. He remembered that night like it was this morning. The night which had stolen his happiness. Jasmine, he had never loved like that in his lifetime. He passed a hand over his eyes as he remembered. A night filled with so much blood. Three bull like men, in dark robes had broken into their home and given him an ultimatum. Jasmine's life for his power. He was to wear the bangles of slavery to their master and grant him his wish. Jasmine told him to flee, she knew the consequence if he was enslaved. His silence had been her death sentence. Forrest felt the rawness of the night still, he looked at his feet. An ant climbed his booted toe and scuttled about. He had killed three men that night, not slowly, but a death that would take an eternity. With only a thought he had pushed them through the veil of this world, into a world so terrifying they would never know a moments peace, forever tormented, an eternity of pain. He had snapped out of his rage to the feeling of Erik's hand in his and the cold body of his wife in his arms. Forrest rasped in a lung full of air; he was suffocating in the memory.

'I met with a magical wolf, Sylvester Bluesky, and he told me what had happened to Clarke. Of course, I had to find out for myself if my grandson had been touched by dark magic. When I met him earlier, he had the aura of one who is in league with dark magic.' He let his words sink in.

'I can't believe it, we would have noticed, surely!' Erik sounded panicked.

'He has not gone far down the dark path, there is still hope for him.'

'And the second thing you wanted to tell me?' Erik pulled him back to the present.

Forrest rested a sad gaze on his son. 'I have reached the age of death. I will be two and a half thousand years old soon. I must return to realm of the Djinn, my own realm to die.'

The news was a heavy blow, Erik felt its crush, he felt lightheaded. His father had just come back into his life and was to be torn away from him again!

'You cannot die, you are a Djinn.' Shouted Erik.

'Sorry son, the veil of death is near me.' Forrest replied, he blew out his cheeks.

'We must talk about Clarke. He must be shown the destructive nature of dark magic. He needs to know what happened to his grandmother.'

'I will bring Clarke to you tomorrow; we will talk to him about our history.' Erik stood up from the log, and went on, 'Dad, I have missed you.'

'Me too son, I have a few weeks left, I want to spend them with you.' Forrest stood up and hugged Erik in a quick crushing embrace.

'I need to get you home, and get back for tonight's performance,' he slid his hand in his pocket, took out three green tickets and held them out, 'Come and see the circus, Clarke will enjoy it.' He pushed them into Erik's hands and walked back to his horse. He whistled to Hurricane who trotted over. Forrest got onto his back and held out his hand for Erik.

'He is stunning dad.' Erik looked at Hurricane admiringly and took his father's hand. He felt the horse shiver as he sat behind his father.

'Home to Erik's' Forrest commanded the horse.

Hurricane moved swiftly out of the wood and back towards Tetbury.

As they left the wood neither of them noticed the woman squatting behind a holly bush. She stood up slowly when they had galloped off. A cold smile played on her lips.

'Well, well. A Djinn, here in Malmesbury. Now that is helpful.' Mooremarsh looked after them with calculating eyes. Her fingers touched the talisman at her neck. It protected dark magic from discovery.

CHAPTER 15
WHO IS MISKUNN?

A lonely howl filled the wood. The afternoon light reflected in his eyes, turning them to two flaming orbs. He lifted his head, opened his mouth, a howl like scream ripped from his chest, pouring out his emotions

It is not Miskunn. She is dead. He muttered repeatedly.

Sylvester Bluesky felt his heart twisting in his chest. He remembered a past long ago when he had been brought to this land from Norway. It had been so long ago he had almost forgotten the country of his birth.

As a cub, his mother had pointed out repeatedly that he was very different from the others in his litter, that he was in some way special. He had been happy, until the fateful day his father arrived back from a long hunt. His father had inspected the loud noisy litter, baying for his attention. When his father saw him, he had lowered his head and bared his teeth and growled menacingly.

'Fenrir!' his father had growled, 'A wolf of the evil gods.'

'No, he is not Fenrir, I think he belongs to Earth Magic.' His mother had jumped in front of Sylvester Bluesky and defended him from the deadly snapping jaws of his father.

'Get him out of this Den in the morning. He cannot stay here.' He had growled at Sylvester Bluesky and turned his back on him.

Early in the morning, his mother had woken him even before there was light.

'Come Sylvester, we have a long journey today.' She had gazed at him forlornly. Licking his fur clean, she inspected him, sniffed his neck, and nudged him forward.

'We leave now, keep close to my flank,' she gave a belligerent look at his father, and made her way to the entrance of the den.

Sylvester looked at his brothers and sisters, a mass of entwined paws. His white coat and amber eyes set him apart from them, he was twice their size, his stature thick set and strong.

'Come Sylvester, we must hurry.' His mother's voice whispered down from the mouth of the den.

Sylvester took a final look at his siblings and walked after his mother.

They had walked for several hours in crisp snow, and Sylvester was hungry.

'Can we eat?' Sylvester called to his mother; his stomach hurt with hunger.

She stopped and raised her head, sniffed the air. She didn't like being out in the open alone with the cub.

'We will be there soon. We can't stop.' Her tail swished and she walked on.

In the distance, Sylvester Bluesky smelt the acrid smoke before he saw it wafting up through trees.

'We are near.' She ran ahead and Sylvester Bluesky followed her.

They entered a small clearing where a fire burnt. In one corner stood a small hut with a wooden door.

'The Earth Magic human lives here.' She licked Sylvester Bluesky's fur, washing away mud splatters from their journey.

'He will know what to do with you.' She wailed sadly.

The door of the hut creaked open, and a man stepped out. In one hand he held an axe, the other a staff. Sylvester Bluesky jumped back in alarm; a small growl erupted from his throat.

'Calm Sylvester, calm.' His mother chided him.

'Mother wolf you bring magic here. We thank you.' The man called; Sylvester Bluesky's mother could not understand his human words.

'Do you understand what he is saying?' she asked her cub.

Sylvester Bluesky blinked. 'Yes, I can understand a few of his words.'

'I cannot, he does not speak in the wolf tongue. Your understanding is a sign you have Earth Magic. I am proud of your gift Sylvester. Very proud. My heart will always be with you. There has not been a magical wolf in the family for three hundred years.' She licked his face, 'Sadly, we will not meet again.' He felt his mother's warm muzzle on his back coaxing him forward.

'Go child, this man will help you. You cannot come back with me. You have magic and this human can help you.' His mother gazed into his eyes. He sniffed her scent, never wanting to forget it. His heart was breaking.

'I want to stay with you all. I am a wolf.' He stammered; his throat hurt.

'No Sylvester, I cannot teach you what you need to know.'

She touched her cheek against his, 'go, be proud of your heritage, be strong in your conviction, remember my love for you,'

He wanted that moment to last forever, but it didn't. His mother had nudged him forward and backed away. He threw the man an accusing stare, turned back to his mother. Only her tracks indication she had stood there. He had howled, willing her to come back to him.

Can you hear me? Sylvester Bluesky jumped, alarmed at the voice in his head.

It's me. The human. Sylvester Bluesky looked at the human, his head on one side. *Sit down and paw the ground.*

Sylvester Bluesky stood still, his heart thumped wildly in his chest, his tail whipped the air. He backed away from the human.

Sit down and paw the ground, the voice commanded him, *there is nowhere to go.*

Sylvester Bluesky had slowly sat down and pawed the snow.

Good, good. Now we shall have breakfast. Stay seated. The human went inside his hut and Sylvester Bluesky sat where he had been told.

The man came out with two bowls. Sylvester Bluesky sniffed the air. The scent of roots and meat filled his nostrils. A bowl was set down on the ground and the human walked away, sat on a rock, and began to eat from his bowl.

My name is Bo, you must be hungry. You had better eat that before the rats take it from you. The voice coaxed him.

Sylvester Bluesky waited. The man scraped his bowl with his finger. He stood up and walked down to a stream and washed it. Flicking the bowl dry he made his way back to his hut. He gave Sylvester Bluesky a look and pointed at the bowl on the ground.

'Eat.' Bo called and vanished into his hut.

Sylvester Bluesky sat sniffing the air. He was hungry, his stomach growled loudly. He got up and took a few tentative steps towards the bowl, never taking his eyes off the hut. He reached the bowl and gingerly licked the meat inside. He devoured its contents and spent ages licking the bowl.

I am glad you enjoyed it, Sylvester Bluesky jumped at the sound of Bo's voice, *a simple thank you would suffice.* He felt humour in Bo's voice.

I must go and find some roots to make into a soup. Come with me if you want. Bo encouraged him.

He had a leather bag hung over his shoulder. He waited for the cub to move from the spot where he sat.

I will be back when the sun reaches high day. He marched into the wood without a backward glance at the cub. *When I get back, I will introduce you to Miskunn.*

Bo returned at high day as he had promised. He put a black pot onto the fire and poured some water from an earthenware jug into it. Cleaning the roots with his hands he threw them into the pot.

Well, that's done, now to introduce you to Miskunn, it is still light outside. Bo stood in the doorway, *Miskunn, come and meet Sylvester Bluesky.*

He followed Bo outside and gasped. A huge golden eagle stood in the clearing. She stretched out her wings, they shone like liquid gold in the sun.

Hello, my name is Miskunn. The eagle bowed her head at him. *Well, are you not going to reply?*

Sylvester was tongue tied, he managed a weak, *Sylvester Bluesky. Hello.*

We will be spending a lot of time together. There is a lot to learn, and so little time to teach you. I will see you in the morning. She looked at Bo, *the sun will go down behind the mountain soon, bye Bo.* She flew off towards the highest mountain.

'We need to get inside the hut to keep warm. You have a lot to learn in the morning.'

He lived with Bo for three years, learning the eloquence of language. The important lessons were the ways of Earth Magic. His greatest surprise was when he was told that he was to be a magical animal to a magical human.

But don't they have their own kind to guide them? He had pranced from side to side in front of Miskunn. *Surely, they understand how to use Earth Magic and the laws which govern it?*

We do not police them, we guide them. They rely on our friendship and our wisdom, and sometimes our protection. She pushed her chest out; *I do wonder if you will ever acquire wisdom. You are so boisterous!* She laughed at his crest fallen face. *Sylvester, we learn with experience, this is where our wisdom comes from. We help our companion stay away from Dark Magic; we try to protect them from the terrible consequences of using magic badly.*

Sylvester Bluesky looked her in the eye, he was now a good head taller than her.

Autumn arrived, cold and brutal. Bo introduced him to his first magical companion, Toke.

'Sylvester Bluesky, Toke is important to our people, he is a seer, it is a rare gift.' Bo stroked the wolf's head.

'Toke will be here this evening. You will be introduced, you will leave with him, I have taught you everything you need to know.' Bo looked sadly at Sylvester Bluesky, 'I have trained you and taught you everything you need to know. You have done well. Keep good council Sylvester Bluesky. Be strong in Earth Magic. Guide your Earth Magic human well.' Bo placed his arms around the wolf's neck and gave him an affectionate squeeze. 'I think your mother will be proud.'

Miskunn flew by and settled in front of them.

We will keep in contact my young wolf. Magical creatures have a way of communicating with each other over distances which Humans do not share. Her wings raised above her head, *if you need my help, I am always here. Goodbye, my friend.* She took to flight, flying on the pockets of air. She circled in the sky above, getting higher and higher, finally, she let out a screech, the sound echoed eerily. Sylvester Bluesky watched her glide into the mountains, with a last screech, she disappeared into the mountains.

The afternoon came too quickly. A tall man, his face hidden by his cloaks large hood arrived. A large silver broach held the cloak closed at his neck.

'My name is Toke, The Seer. I am here to stand the test.'

His slim hands reached up and removed his hood. It fell away to reveal thick blonde hair, falling in its wake down his back.

'My years are young; my mind is older.' He planted his staff in the earth in front of him. 'It is time for me to take a magical animal as my guide and friend. You are here, will you accept me?' His voice was strong, Sylvester Bluesky looked up from his sleeping place beside Bo. He stretched out and waited for Bo to instruct him.

'Sylvester Bluesky, go to Toke, you will know if he is the one for you.' Bo stood up, and winced at his arthritic pain, he leant heavily on his staff. 'Go.' Unceremoniously, pushing the butt of the staff against the wolf's leg. 'I have raised you for this.'

Sylvester Bluesky raised his nose a little. He caught the salty tang of Toke's skin. Begrudgingly, he got up from his warm spot, padded to the silent man and sniffed his outstretched hand.

'Decide if I am wanting. If we are destined to a great future.' Toke said.

Why do you want me? Are you worthy of the protection and guidance as such a one as I? Sylvester Bluesky recited the words he was taught for the greeting.

Toke flinched, his hazel eyes looked surprised, he smiled quizzically at the wolf. 'I beg your pardon; It was a strange sensation when you touch my mind.' He touched Sylvester Bluesky's muzzle, 'I want you because it is lonely when you are few with Earth Magic. A magical companion who is not afraid to tell me when he thinks I am straying from the path of goodness, one who will keep me out of the shadow of darkness.' Toke put his head to one side, 'Will it be you?'

My name is Sylvester Bluesky, he rubbed his head against Toke's hand.

'Come Toke, stay this night with us, make your way home in the morning.' Bo waved to his hut.

'Thank you. I must leave early in the morning. My chief, Arvid, asks me to come to him in two moons.'

That evening, Sylvester Bluesky had stood outside the hut, calling for Miskunn.

'Miskunn will not say goodbye twice. Her heart is heavy at your leaving. Get inside and get some sleep, you have a long journey before you tomorrow.' Bo turned to go into the hut, the wolf followed him. 'Sylvester, sleep beside Toke tonight, understand him through his dreams.'

Toke had risen early and bid goodbye to Bo. Sylvester Bluesky had stood for a long time without saying anything. Words choked in his throat, they seemed inadequate for goodbye.

'I understand Sylvester. Good and long life.' Bo stroked Sylvester Bluesky's chin.

He looked once more to the sky to see if Miskunn had returned. She had not. With a heavy heart at leaving his two friends he followed Toke to the East.

Over the years, Sylvester Bluesky travelled many lands with Toke. He heard Miskunn sometimes in his dreams, but she was gone when he woke up. Toke had become his friend by day and Miskunn by night. After seventy-four years he stopped seeing Miskunn in his dreams, her silence a dark chasm, he was lonely without her. He knew the only reason for her silence, she had died. Tragedy struck Sylvester Bluesky a year later, Toke died on British shores.

I am alone, in his despair he lay down in the same spot without food or drink for three days.

On the fourth day he awoke to a woman sitting beside him. He found her words difficult to understand, but he felt the intention behind them.

'Earth Magic has guided you to me. I am the chief Elder of the Southwest.' She spoke with great kindness, 'my name is Mynthel.'

Mynthel spoke the ancient language of the celts infused with Latin and old English. Sylvester Bluesky spoke Old Norse.

'We will have time to discover our words,' she laughed, 'come with me, be safe.'

He spent six seasons learning her languages, tempering his Earth Magic skills under Mynthel's guidance. Until the day arrived for him to share his knowledge with another.

Mynthel sat beside a fire tapping a tune on her knees.

'Sylvester, it is time for you to leave.' She stopped tapping, and looked at him earnestly, 'a child has been found with Earth Magic, Rufus Roisin. He has great power and needs a magical animal who will give temperance to his magic.'

I see, you think I should give that guidance. Sylvester Bluesky asked.

Mynthel felt his reluctance.

'Yes, I do. You have had experience with a powerful Seer. You would be an ideal choice.' She stood up and brushed leaves off her girdle. 'You do not have to accept; it will be your choice. I think you will find him interesting.'

'Earth Magic has carved out a destiny for me. I shall accept.' Sylvester Bluesky shook his fur and stood up. 'Introduce us.'

Rufus Roisin had been the second Earth Magic human, out of thirteen he had been a companion to.

Sylvester Bluesky brought his thoughts to the present. Now, Miskunn, his friend and mentor of old was here. But it could not be her, she was dead!

Only Dark Magic could raise the dead.

CHAPTER 16
THE CHALLENGE

Rutger briskly walked up the garden from the adjoining paddock. He was returning from his evening ritual walk around the field with his two donkey's, sisters Gwyn and Bonbon. Gwyn was his magical animal and best friend. Rutger smiled at the memory of being introduced to Gwyn. The magnificent brown and white donkey had stamped her hoof and demanded that Bonbon stay with her. Rutger accepted the bond between the sisters, arrangement was made by the Elders for a field to be rented for the two donkeys. Rutger's mouth twisted into a grim line. He thought about the previous months, Dark Magic had nearly cost the lives of so many. He should have been better prepared.

The past is the past, don't dwell on it. Gwyn's stubborn voice filled his mind.

The memories still plagued me. He bit his lip and looked back down the field at the pair.

Gwyn brown and white, Bonbon black as night.

You have done well. Be focused on the children, their magic is important, they must be taught how to use it well. I feel it in my bones, there is a great battle ahead. Gwyn counselled him, baying loudly, her sister joined in the chorus.

He walked into the cottage and was glad of the warmth after the chilly afternoon. Taking off his boots, he took a bristled brushed from its place on the windowsill and vigorously brushed off his boots. His hand hesitated, he thought of his home in a small village outside of Oxford. He missed the comfort of home, but he was here for a good reason. He rented the small cottage he was staying in Malmesbury. Sophia and Jasper had joined him, they had decided to live nearer to the Appleby's with everything that was going on. They wanted to take advantage at the closeness so they could teach the children Earth Magic.

A flash of red caught his eye. Mr Witherington the robin darted from branches to the fence. Gwyn's head bounced up and down as they started a conversation, Bonbon moved away disgruntled she could not join in, she had no idea what the robin was saying to Gwyn.

A message, Rutger Sweets-Patrick, Elder of the Southwest. His song trilled from the fence.

He is up at the house. Hope it's not bad news! Gwyn turned to her sister, *stop moping, the robin might have bad news for Rutger,* she neighed loudly, walked over to Bonbon, and nudged her in the side.

Rutger opened the window and beckoned Mr Witherington, the robin skipped along the ground, black glistening eyes looked around, satisfied it was safe, he flew up and perched on the windowsill.

A message for Rutger Sweets-Patrick and the Elders of the Southwest. The robin stood a little taller and cleared his mind to deliver the message.

Come immediately. You are needed at Chestnut cottage. It is of the upmost urgency. Something shocking has happened. We have made a mistake. I will keep guard in the woods opposite the Appleby's cottage. Come as soon as you can.

Your humble servant,

Sylvester Bluesky

Rutger blanched; the robin was talking about Milly Appleby. Could they have been mistaken in their judgement, after everything which happened?

Do you require me to repeat the message? Came the trill voice.

Yes. The reply is: We will be there within the hour. Rutger went to the kitchen and found sunflower seeds. His hand reached into the bag and scrapped a few seeds out. Returned to the robin and placed them on the sill in front of him.

Thank you. Rutger turned on his heal to find the others.

Rushing into the kitchen he was glad that Sophia and Jasper were still there. He slumped down into a chair. His hands banged on the table; the sound vibrated around the room.

'Mr Witherington has been sent by Sylvester Bluesky.' He looked at each of them, 'Milly has Dark Magic.'

'No,' screamed Sophia, her hands wrung together agitatedly. She felt Feles nudge against her calf, trying to comfort her.

Careful, you used Time magic to see the child. All may not be as it seems. Tread carefully Sophia before you decide. Feles whined.

'We must go to the Appleby's now and bind her magic.' Rutger sat back in his chair, not wanting to meet Sophia's eyes.

He heard the scrape of a chair, he looked unseeingly at the wall.

'We have to judge her first, the Challenge must be performed. We cannot barge in there and perform a binding spell.' Sophia's anger stung him.

'Well of course we will have to perform the Challenge, we will hear what Milly has to say.' He turned a hurt look at Sophia, 'we must be prepared.'

'I don't believe Milly has turned to Dark Magic. There must be an explanation why Sylvester Bluesky asked for the judgement. I think we will find he has maybe jumped to the wrong conclusion.' Jasper tried to calm the situation. 'Let's get over there now and get the facts.'

'True Jasper, but just in case, Sophia bring the herbs needed to perform the binding.' His eyebrows knitted together, half expecting her to refuse.

'Of course, I will bring them with me.' She snapped and started to walk to the door, her hand held the doorknob, 'I cannot believe the girl who fought Mooremarsh last year is full of Dark Magic.'

Rutger watched Sophia's stiff back as she left the room.

'She will find this difficult,' Jasper began.

Rutger cut him off, 'we will all find this difficult if it is true.' He sighed, shaking his head, 'we made a pact after what happened in the barn, Mooremarsh's Dark Magic, Joshua and his friends nearly getting killed, Milly's display of powerful Earth Magic.'

'Well, let's make sure that we don't make a mistake then.' Jasper got up and picked up his jacket. 'Let's go.'

The trio walked to Chestnut Cottage in silence, each wrapped up in their own thoughts. Soon they stood in front of the gate. Outside the door stood Sylvester Bluesky.

Sophia banged her staff into the ground, a brilliant purple light shone from the amethyst perched on top of it, she stepped forward, 'We are here to make judgement. We are here for the Challenge.'

The door swung open, Alana stood pale and wide eyed.

'Welcome, light of Winter to you all,' she stood back and stiffly waved them into the cottage.

'Light of Winter Alana, sorry we meet under such circumstances.' Rutger took hold of her hands; they were limp and cold. He gave them a squeeze and passed into the cottage.

All three Elders entered a warm kitchen. Bill sat gazing at burning logs in the fireplace.

'Bill, it is time.' Alana called softly over Jasper's shoulder.

Bill looked startled, jumped out of his seat. 'I see. I will call the children down.'

'We will be thorough with the Challenge. It has not been decided yet that she has Dark Magic.' Rutger put a hand on his shoulder.

'The house feels cold, have you not noticed?' Sophia quizzed Alana.

'Yes, but I thought it was the time of year.' Alana looked defensively at Sophia.

Bill stepped out of the room and called to Joshua and Milly.

You must stand firm. Sylvester Bluesky sat in the corner.

'We know what we must do!' Sophia replied waspishly.

'Well, this is just a mistake, I know there will be.' Rutger did not finish his sentence.

Milly walked into the kitchen carrying the book of Dark Magic wrapped in newspaper.

All three Elders took a step back.

'No!' Sophia shouted, Feles hissed and jumped protectively in front of her.

'You brought that into this house?' Rutger asked, his cane out in front of him, waving her away. 'Put it on the table.'

Milly put the book down and slid it into the center of the table.

'I haven't opened it,' her face was pinched, 'I found it.'

'Milly, sit down. We will start the Challenge. If we judge you to have Dark Magic, we will bind your magic.' Rutger rested his gaze on her. 'Do you understand?'

'Yes,' her soft whisper replied.

'Milly does not do Dark Magic. I would know, she is my twin sister.' Joshua stuck his chin out defiantly.

'Joshua, you may stay, but you will be silent.' Rutger threw him a stern look.

'Joshua is right, I do not perform Dark Magic.' Milly faltered under the Elders stare.

'Milly, you said you found the book, how?' Sophia asked gently.

Milly swallowed hard.

'We were talking to Sargent Harrow, I kicked it in the grass and picked it up,' she looked across at her mother, 'sorry Mum.'

'Did you not notice if felt strange, cold or different?' Rutger barked at Milly.

'Don't talk to Milly like that!' Alana raised her voice.

Rutger's lips held a grim line. 'Alana, if you are to stay during the Challenge, you must keep quiet.'

Bill took her arm and guided her to a chair and sat next to her.

'Thank you,' Rutger bowed his head slightly. 'We will continue.'

'Did you not feel anything strange about the book?' he asked his question again.

'Yes, I noticed it was different. I wrapped it in newspaper.' She whispered.

'Why didn't you tell your mother?' Jasper interceded.

Milly thought about the question. 'I was curious. I didn't open it. I was going to tell Mum.'

'Curious? You knew this book was Dark Magic. Yet you held onto it.' Rutger accused her.

'I know. I should not have brought it into the house. I should have told dad in the car. I don't know why I didn't, I really don't. I don't want to do Dark Magic. I thought if I understood the spells, I could fight it better.' She looked pleadingly at Sophia.

'You knew what you were doing was wrong. That is why you took the book to your bedroom. Secrecy. A clandestine action like that does not look good, how can we believe you?' Rutger wrapped up the book and placed a silk scarf about it. Sophia sprinkled herbs over the top.

'It is safe for the moment.' Sophia put back the bottle of herbs into her bag.

All eyes looked at the book.

'Can't we put it outside of the boundary of the house?' Bill asked.

Don't touch it, you need to destroy it! Sylvester Bluesky shouted; his tail beat loudly on the floor.

'We will. First we finish the challenge.' Rutger replied, he looked at Milly and continued, 'Sophia will need to touch your hands.'

Milly held out her hands and Sophia took them in hers. Milly's hands felt cold and clammy. Sophia closed her eyes and let Milly's aura pass over her. It was warm, but there was a vague coldness.

'We continue with the Challenge. Milly's aura is not pure enough.' Sophia's hand slipped off Milly's.

'I hate Dark Magic!' Milly screamed at Sophia.

Yet, you used Dark Magic to summon up Miskunn. She is dead. Why did you do that? Sylvester growled at her.

Milly's hands balled up in anger.

'I have always seen Miskunn. She has been with me forever.' She breathed hard; her body trembled angrily.

'If Miskunn has already been with you, why did you not mention this when we tested your magic last year?' Rutger asked. 'What is she?'

'Miskunn is a magical eagle, gold and beautiful.' Milly looked across to her mother, 'sorry Mum, when you couldn't see her, I was worried.'

'When you say, Miskunn has always been with you, why can't we see her?' Jasper asked gently, he wanted to give her every chance to explain herself.

Milly thought about the question. She had no answer for him.

'I don't know, I can't ever remember being without her,' Milly held her hands wide in front of her.

'I see.' Jasper shook his head.

'Milly, we need an explanation. You have a Dark Magic book, an animal no one can see. You never went through the Nox Certamen, which side would you have chosen in the dream? This makes this challenge difficult.'

Remember Mathew. Miskunn whispered to her.

Milly's eyebrows screwed up together, a recollection, a small gleam of hope.

'Mathew can see Miskunn.' She shouted.

The room was electric.

'How, if we cannot see her, why can he?' Asked Rutger.

Sylvester Bluesky took a few steps towards Milly.

Mathew is a Doorkeeper. He sees all Earth Magic. The wolf looked at Milly.

Your father has Earth Magic in his blood. Ask your mother to hold his hand, Miskunn nudged Milly. *Hold my wing.*

'Mum, Miskunn asked if you could hold dad's hand.' Milly took hold of the eagles' wing, trying not to crush her feathers. A brilliant gold light irradiated the room.

'Wow!' exclaimed Bill, he put his hand in front of his eyes against the glare of the light.

Everyone could see Miskunn standing tall, her wings feathered out.

Miskunn, my old friend! Sylvester Bluesky lowered his head and rasped; *I don't understand!*

Sylvester, you do not need to understand, only believe. I was sent by Earth Magic. I have been with Milly since she was born. It is sad that you all did not believe her. She is pure of heart.

'I could see darkness in her aura.' Sophia stammered.

Milly is a teenager. Of course, she has the occasional dark thought. I think I know the difference between a dark thought and Dark Magic after all these years! Miskunn retorted. *The only thing Milly is guilty of is the stupidity of the youthful folly. Youthful arrogance wanting to know everything too soon.* Miskunn looked at Milly, her stern features softened. *I believe Milly has learnt her lesson about truth.*

Milly hung her head and looked across at her mother.

'Really sorry Mum.'

Alana crossed the room and threw her arms around her daughter, 'No, I am sorry that you did not feel you could talk to me.'

Miskunn looked at Sylvester Bluesky, *I believe the truth has come out. The Challenge is now over.*

'Milly, we had to do this,' Rutger looked at Sophia and Jasper in turn.

'You don't trust me. You didn't ask me about Miskunn.' She turned her back on them, 'Instead, you went straight to the Challenge. Do you think fighting Dark Magic was easy for me?'

'Milly, Sophia had a vision about you, it may have had some bearing on our decision.' Rutger spread his hands out.

'How could you believe I would perform Dark Magic? You of all the magical animals, how could you doubt me?' She glared at Sylvester Bluesky.

Be humble Milly, anger is not our way. Miskunn chided her.

Sophia stepped forward; something had crossed her mind.

'Milly, may I ask, did anything else happen when you were in your room with the Dark Magic book.'

Milly looked away. Could she tell them about the vision she had of Sophia and not give them more reasons not to the trust her?

Truth is the way forward. Miskunn encouraged her.

Milly looked Sophia directly in the eye.

'I saw you, in a vision.' She got the satisfaction of seeing Sophia blanch, 'you were standing by a river. Sophia, you were looking at me; when Dark Magic spoke to me.'

'Dark Magic spoke to you!' Rutger growled, 'You never revealed anything about that during the Challenge.' He glared at her.

'Would you have believed me if I told you what happened next? Or would you have condemned me?' Milly lifted her chin and sent him a challenging look.

'Let her finish.' Alana's voice broke the silence.

'Sophia looked upset, her voice called out repeatedly to me through a haze' she blinked, 'she called out *It is not true!*'

'Sophia, you performed the Seer's ritual with Time,' Jasper whispered.

I told you! Feles preened his paw in a 'told you so' way.

'Yes, I did see Milly, I did call out to her.' She grasped her staff a little tighter. 'I did not know that Milly could see me in her future from my past.'

Now you know how special she is, maybe you understand that you need greater trust in her. Her Earth Magic is unique. That is why I have been sent here. Miskunn ruffled her feathers and left the room leaving them with their thoughts.

CHAPTER 17
MOOREMARSH IN THE WOODS

Mooremarsh rummaged about in a cupboard, her fingers touched a box of English breakfast tea. Putting three teaspoons of tea into the awaiting teapot, she poured hot water from the kettle into the pot, her nose twitched at the aroma. She slid into a chair and waited for the tea to brew.

'How did that happen. My magic book is in the hands of that girl, Milly Appleby?' she kicked the leg of the kitchen table, 'all that effort and to lose it in the snow and hear that girl pick it up.'

Mooremarsh sat for a moment seething over the wasted effort of using Dark Magic on Harrow to retrieve her spell book.'.

Her face lit up as a thought slid into her mind.

'Maybe Milly will read the book, and seeing its power,' she banged the table with her fist, 'she will become a follower of Dark Magic.' She threw back her head and laughed.

'Two of them under my spell, more than enough to steal the Ruby Dragon.'

Mooremarsh dabbed a few loose tea leaves onto her fingers from the table, 'Gormlessly Harrow and that stupid boy Clarke, they were easy to ensnare with my magic,' she scoffed to the empty house. 'Eternity will be mine soon!' she clapped her hands.

Dragging a crumpled newspaper out of her pocket, she smoothed it out on the table. Boney fingers traced the picture of the Ruby Dragon.

'You are quite delicious,' she growled. 'You will be back with my family; we will once more share the same history.'

Delicate rose buds decorated the teacup which stood on its saucer. It was one of a pair. The other one was in the office she used as the Headmistress of the local primary school. Until she had been discovered stealing the Flaming Sword of Edward the Elder and a chalice.

'Must retrieve that at some point,' she spat at the memory.

She poured the fragrant tea to the cup and stirred the liquid vigorously with a silver teaspoon. It adorned an intricate monogram on the handle, it had been in her family for generations.

'Now, why didn't father sell you, he sold most of the other heirlooms.' Musing she put the spoon at the side of the saucer.

'Not a mistake I will make. I intend to be rich, and very powerful.'

The black and white image on newspaper enticed her again, she contemplated the Ruby Dragon's history. It had been fashioned in the bowels of the earth, discovered by Htun a wandering mystic, three hundred years ago who lived in Burma. Over the years his spells became famous in Dark Magic circles. Spells on changing time were prohibited by Dark Magic law, the consequences of bending time, had catastrophic consequences. Htun had found a way around this law. To stop the ravishing of time on his aging body and keep his youth. Htun had fashioned the ruby into the shape of a dragon and used the ruby as a receptacle for his magic, giving him eternal life. Each day he performed an incantation to the Ruby Dragon, the daily spell kept time at bay and his youth. After two hundred and ninety-eight years, the dragon was stolen. Htun died three days later.

Mooremarsh stabbed the newspaper with her forefinger and picked up her cup of tea.

'Htun, you should have looked after it better, you'd still would have been alive today!' she cackled into her tea. 'My grandfather would have had eternal life, if he had kept his wits about him, and not sold it!' she took a long sip of her tea, 'I will not make the same mistake!' an inaudible hiss escaped her lips.

The small grandfather clock in the hallway struck four, her train of thought broken, the teacup jangled as she slammed it down into its saucer.

'Time to meet Harrow, he better have my books this time.' Prizing herself up from the table, 'If he hasn't, I won't have any use for him.' Her mouth curved into a spiteful smile. 'But then again,' a long fingernail scratched her incisor, 'I could top up my life energy!'

A loaf of bread stood forlornly on the kitchen side. She hacked off some slices with a breadknife and stuffed a few slices of ham inside.

'That'll do for a picnic. Not that he will notice, if my spell is still working.' Her lip curled.

The sandwich was tossed unceremoniously into a basket and covered it with a check cloth. Grabbing a jacket from the coat stand, she put it on and buttoned it up quickly. A gilt mirror at the door caught her attention. She stopped and inspected her face in the mirror for signs of ageing. Her fingers stroked her newfound smooth skin.

'Not bad given I have been using Dark Magic,' she murmured, aware that the cost of using it usually damaged her body, seeping away some of her life force. Inspecting both sides of her face.

'Interesting,' she purred, satisfied the life force she had taken from the librarian was keeping her sustained.

It didn't take her long to arrive at the small wood. Sitting down behind a holly tree she awaited the arrival of Harrow. The crunch of footsteps behind her sounded, she sat up in anticipation, her prize was being delivered. She flinched in disappointment, two men had entered the woods, she recognised one of the men, Clarke Sharm's father. Irritated she cocked her head to listen to the urgent tones of their conversation. It was difficult to hear them. One sentence did reach her.

'I must return to the realm of the Djinn,'

Her eyes narrowed at the information she overheard. Clarke Sharma's grandfather was a Djinn! Not any type of Djinn, but a Djinn who could grant wishes! It was all she could do, to stop herself screaming out with excitement. She was glad she had a charm around her neck to stop the Djinn from detecting her dark magic. The two did not stay long, but from their conversation she had discovered where the Djinn lived and what his Achille's Heel would be. Clarke. The Djinn would do anything for his grandson, and she started to formulate a daring plan.

Steal the Ruby Dragon with Harrow, Enslave the Djinn with the help of Clarke. Two daring plans, one great opportunity. Eternal life and all the power she could ever have to practice Dark Magic.

'It's all mine!' she cheered into the empty wood.

'What is all yours?' A man's voice startled her.

She stood up and swung around into Harrow's blank stare.

'Your late, I have been waiting for an hour!' she snapped at him.

He looked as if she had slapped him, he opened his mouth to say something. Her glance took in the box he was carrying.

'You have it sweetest.' She clapped her hands, 'Sit down. I have made a picnic.' Mooremarsh sat down and Harrow quickly followed suit.

'Well?' she looked at the box.

Harrow held out the brown cardboard box to her, his mouth was slack, giving it a simpleton's grin.

Mooremarsh snatched the box out of his tightly clenched fingers and laid it in her lap.

'Eat the sandwich in the basket, I made it for you dearest.' Her lip curled as she kicked the basket in his direction with her toe.

She watched Harrow grab the basket, tear away the cloth and pull away the paper from the sandwich. Mooremarsh turned her attention to the box, tentatively she opened the lid. Inside were eight books of different sizes, all in immaculate condition, her breath caught in her chest, air exploded from her lungs.

'Thank you, Harrow, thank you very much.' She patted his shoulder condescendingly.

'Will you sing to me?' Harrow looked vacant; his words were slurred.

'Yes,' she snapped, 'you will help me with these back to my house, we can finish tea there, and I can sing to you while you rest,' crushing the lid on the box.

'Yes, anything for you,' he gushed.

'Where is your car?'

'It's at the end of the path.' He pointed in the direction of his car.

Mooremarsh stood up and handed the box back to him.

'Carry them for me.' Mooremarsh got up, passed him the box, and walked towards his car.

She could hear Harrow lumbering after her. Her mind calculating a plan on the way.

'You would like to go to Overhill Hall to see the Ruby Dragon. Maybe next Saturday?' she cooed.

'Yes, sounds good. Anything for you.'

'We will meet here at one o clock. Wear your uniform as well.'

Harrow was silent, his vacant face took on a conflicted expression.

'Not allowed to wear my police uniform when I am off duty,' his lower lip stuck out.

'But you look so fine in that uniform. Wear it when we meet.' She sang to him.

He sucked in his cheeks, 'Yes, will wear it, for you.'

'Good,' She wagged a finger up at him, continued coyly, 'I can't sing to you if you are not in uniform.'

'I will be in uniform.' He slurred.

Mooremarsh walked around the car, sat in the passenger seat.

'Put the books in the boot.' She ordered, directing him with her thumb.

Harrow put the books in the boot and softly shut it. Soon he had the car in gear and was driving towards Mooremarsh's house. As they drew up outside her house, she looked around the street. It was empty.

'No busy bodies watching.' Opening the car door, she swung her legs out, 'Fetch the books with you.' casually throwing the command over her shoulder as she pulled her jacket back into shape.

Walking to the door without a backward glance, she was satisfied when she heard Harrow shutting the car door. Her hands trembled with anticipation, she pushed the key into the door, feeling the lock spring open. In a few moments she would have her Dark Magic books.

'Where would you like me to put these?' Harrow's monosyllabic voice floated to her.

She stood to one side; her bony finger pointed down the hall.

'Put them on the kitchen table, then go.' She waved in the direction of the kitchen.

'What about the song?' he wailed.

'You will hear it every day until Saturday. We meet at two.'

Harrow huffed; his bloodshot eyes had dark circles under them. Stomping up the hall he laid the box on the table. He wrinkled his nose; the room had an unpleasant smell.

'Thank you, Harrow.' She looked into his eyes, 'You will forget this afternoon, you will forget taking the books.' Her hand touched his arm, 'We will meet at the woods on Saturday.' She sang the sentence over and over, until she was satisfied the spell had worked, 'You can go Harrow.' She let go of his arm.

Harrow lumbered along the hall, the song in his head. Mooremarsh watched the door shut slowly, it clicked shut, she sat down and looked at the box. Her hands trembled in her lap in anticipation.

'Alone at last, that fool has no idea,' she cackled, 'if he is caught, he won't remember taking the box of books.'

Ripping off the lid, she took out the first book, caressed the cover, and put it to one side. She examined each book putting them in a pile in the center of the table, the largest she pulled towards her.

'You are all back where you belong.' Her finger felt the spine, 'Let's find the spells I need.' She crowed. Taking the book up to her nose, running her nostrils over the cover, inhaling deeply, enjoying the fettered smell.

'The bouquet of Dark Magic, there is no thrill like it,' placing the book reverently back on the table, she threw up her arms, and shouted with glee, 'I have a Ruby Dragon to steal and a Djinn to trap, the biggest adventure ever!'

Flicking through the pages, her finger stopped at a heading. Her body trembled, the words jumped up out at her and she felt terrified.

Energy Vampires. Why Dark Magic is never used.

She breathed heavily. She recognised the chapter from when she was a child and her father had made her read it. She slapped closed the book.

'Well, I am an Energy Vampire, there is no going back, so there is no need to read that chapter.' Her voice sounded uncertain in her ears. Mooremarsh pushed the fear out of her mind and focused on the days ahead.

CHAPTER 18
TRIBULATION

Clarke leaned against the brick wall and watched Joshua crossing the playground. Like a cat seeing its prey his body became alert. An unexpected wave of venomous rage caroused through his veins. Heat swept through his body; he began to tremble with uncontrollable rage. He wiped sweat away from his cheek and scratched his heat prickled skin. Joshua's laugh speared his ears, grating on his eardrums like nails scratching down a board. Clarke clenched his fists, he wanted to lash out, his fists shook. His rapid breath ripped air painfully from his lungs. He turned his attention to the floor; the focus would keep him calm. Voices became clearer, he could hear the occasional word, for no reason other than he hated them all, his anger grew stronger.

They hate you, they are laughing at you, the voice of Mooremarsh sang in his head.

'Did you follow all those calculations Allcart was writing all over the board?" Mathew shook his head at Milly, 'she then had the cheek to look at the class and ask, are there any questions?'

'I did take a brief look around the classroom while Allcart was scribbling on the board, nothing but blank expressions, except Nori that is. I don't think anyone understood a thing!' Joshua sympathetically patted Mathew on the back.

'Well, I thought the percentage calculations were fun.' Nori pushed her hair behind her ears.

'You're a showoff Nori!' giggled Milly and put her arm through hers.

'No, it's true, I just get math's. It's just puzzles and language.' Nori looked at Milly sideways and grinned.

'I'd better be getting on. Got to help dad on the farm this evening.' Mathew stuck his hands in his pockets, shrugged his shoulders.

'I can walk with you part of the way.' Nori offered.

'You could come to ours and listen to a new record album I have got, well, dad found it in a junk shop, but I think it's great.' Joshua got excited.

'He hasn't stopped playing it. It's a wonder dad hasn't hidden the record player!' Milly jested, secretly she really liked the music, 'it's called *Please Please me*, by the Beatles, heard of them?'

'Oh, love them!' Nori exclaimed, her wings peeped out and fluttered wildly.

'Hey, Joshua, what's wrong with your face,' Mathew teased.

Joshua looked away, 'Nothing, are you coming or not?' he always felt shy when Nori was around.

Mathew didn't get a chance to answer, a sneer from behind cut across his reply.

'Nori, fancy going over to Lavinia's, her parents have just bought her a Portable Record Player, some cool records too. Heard of the Rolling Stones?' Clarke walked over to Nori smiling.

Nori looked at Clarke, her mouth hardened.

'No thank you, just off to Joshua's to listen to some music with Joshua.'

'Well, expect a little weirdness from Milly.' Clarke sneered.

Joshua stepped forward and squared up to him.

'What did you say about my sister?' Joshua challenged him; his heart was beating wildly in his chest.

'You heard what I said.' Clarke snorted derisory at Milly, 'she is really strange, I am sure Nori has started to pick up on that,' he looked at Nori, 'haven't you Nori,' he threw her a knowing wink.

Don't use Earth Magic, especially when you are angry. Prudence warned him, he saw her sitting behind Clarke. Joshua bit the side of his cheek he was so angry.

'Clarke, get lost, go back to whatever hole you have just crawled out of.' He nodded his head at Mathew, 'Come on let's go.'

Clarke shook at Joshua's response, a veil of red mist crossed his vision, before he knew it, he released all his anger and landed a punch squarely on the side of Joshua's cheek. Blood pounded in Clarke's ears; adrenaline pumped in his veins and made him stronger. Joshua turned a stunned look on Clarke, then screamed as rushed at him. Clarke didn't feel any of the blows Joshua struck at him, or the screams of his friends. All he wanted to do was listen to the song singing in his mind and give in to the terrible anger and pain he felt towards Joshua. He had been his best friend and had lied to him, fracturing their friendship. Fingers bit into his arm, he swung his face around and came eyeball to eyeball with Miss Atwell.

'What are you both doing?' her voice screeched as she towered over him.

'Clarke started it Miss.' Mathew shouted.

'You can keep your voice down for a start.' She snapped and placed a stony glare on Mathew.

She pushed Clarke away from her and turned to the girls.

'Well, what happened?' she barked her hands rested on her hips.

Milly stood opened mouthed, shocked at Clarkes unprovoked assault on her brother. Nori untangled her arm from Milly's and stepped forward.

'Clarke passed a rude comment about Milly and threw the first punch Miss Atwell. Joshua was defending himself.'

'I see.' She held out her hand and pulled Joshua's face side to side, examining it, 'no harm done, you four get home,' she nodded towards the gate and turned an iron gaze on Clarke. He stood fists by his side shaking.

'You follow me.' Her nose tilted up like there was a smell under it.

Clarke watched Milly pull Joshua away and the group walked away in shocked silence. Mathew turned to face him but thought better of saying anything under Atwell's gaze.

'What are you looking at?' Clarke sneered at Mathew.

'That is enough, you're in enough trouble as it is!' snapped Atwell, 'get move on to the heads room!'

You were right, they were wrong! The song sang to Clarke.

Yet why do I feel I have lost? He asked himself.

An hour had passed, Clarke sat slumped in a corner playing the fight repeatedly in his head. A knock on the office door caught his attention. The door opened and his mother stepped into the office. Her face was pinched, she threw a quick glance at Clarke and proceeded to the desk. She was wearing her hospital uniform instead of the classical sari's she wore at home. Clarke felt an electric stab of guilt and sat up smartly.

'I am here to see the headmaster please.' The heads secretary looked up over her ledger, stood up and went to a large oak door and knocked at it.

'Come in,' a low voice behind the door called out.

The secretary opened it and peeped her head around it.

'Mrs Sharma for you. About the fight'

Clarke watched his mother straighten her back; the sight of his mother going before the headteacher made him instantly regret his actions.

'Yes, bring her in.' A low authoritative voice floated out into the office.

His mother slipped passed the secretary, into the headmaster's room, leaving Clarke alone. He could hear mumbling behind the door. What seemed like an eternity the door flew open, his mother stepped over the threshold, walked past him and out of the office.

'You can leave now.' The headmaster looked down at him, shushing him away with his hand, 'Go!'

Clarke stood up; his legs felt like jelly. He tidied his clothes then followed in his mother's wake. When he came through the doors leading to the playground, she was standing outside waiting for him. She spun away from him and made her way to the awaiting car. Got in and slammed the door a little harder than usual. Clarke got into the passenger seat and waited for a stern telling off.

'I have never been so disappointed with you.' She whispered and started up the car.

Those eight words stabbed his heart, he stared out of the window screen, choking to make an apology, he said nothing.

The journey back to Tetbury seemed eternal. The car eventually came to a stop. His mother slid around to him. 'When we get in go to your room. I do not want to talk to you.' She got out the car bristling disappointment.

Clarke sat looking at the road ahead lost in thought. The sound of the car door slamming cut into his thoughts and startled him. They had arrived home and he hadn't noticed. The jangle of keys broke the silence as his mother opened the front door. Sliding out of the car he leaned against it, he shook his head, his thoughts felt sticky and muddled. He sucked in the cold evening air; his nostrils flayed under its crispness. The air cleared his mind and made his way to the door. As he entered the house, he heard his mother's voice on the phone. Cocking his head, he could tell by her tone she was talking to his father. Clarke made his way quietly up the stairs, threw his school satchel on the floor and flounced onto his bed.

Why had he attacked Joshua? Sure, they weren't friends any more after what happened last year. He had lost his best friend, and to be honest he missed the friendship. Joshua had kept him in the dark about Mooremarsh, about his hidden world of magic, and he had paid the price. He could hear his mother downstairs moving about. Clarke had a sinking feeling. She had always been there for him, and he had let her down. Clarke fell into a miserable uneasy sleep.

The bang of a door woke him up, daylight had gone, and his room was in darkness. He blinked at the ceiling and lay waiting for his father to call him downstairs. His eyes scrunched up; he could hear three voices.

'Clarke, come down.' His father's voice wandered up to his room.

He got off his bed, switched on the light, combed his hair, and uneasily made his way down to his parents. The door opened before he got a chance to touch the doorknob. His father looked down at him, his eyes sparking with anger.

'Inside.' His father stood back.

Clarke walked into the small sitting room and hesitated. His mother sat in a chair, in the corner was a man he recognized, Hazim Sharma or Forrest, he didn't know why he had two names. Worst of it all, this man, whom he had never seen, he claimed to be his grandfather.

'Clarke, there is much to talk about. Come in.' Forrest flourished his hand to command his entrance.

'Not sure why I have to listen to you.' He heard his mother's intake of breath.

'It is alright. The boy has a point,' Forrest looked at his mother, 'I have been an absent grandparent in Clarke's mind,' he looked back at Clarke.

'Sit down. Do not be rude to my father again.' There was menace in his father's words, Clarke flinched, sat down quickly and waited.

Forrest paced the room, he looked like he was trying to find the right words.

'Clarke, what I am about to say to you is the history of this family, it is a past I cannot change, but a future I can share with you all for a time.' Forrest looked hard at Clarke.

'Let me start with your grandmother, Jasmine. She was the most beautiful woman I had ever met, both in looks and character. The wisest of women. A gentle spirit, wonderful mind. Her laughter warmed any room.' Forrest was quiet for a moment, lost in another world.

'I am a Djinn.' Forrest let the news strike home for a moment.

'A Djinn?' Clarke questioned.

'Yes, sometimes referred to as a Genie, not a term I like personally.' Forrest replied. 'Djinn's have walked the earth throughout time. We are not supposed to marry humans. But you had never met a woman like your grandmother.'

'What's this got to do with me?' Clarke burst out glaring at his father. His father's sad stare stopped him saying anymore.

'True Clarke, what has this got to do with you. I will tell you the story of Jasmine, your father and a promise.' He looked down at his feet, 'Hopefully, you might understand. Did you know Djinn are invisible to this world? I saw Jasmine and that changed. I took this form so she could see me.' Forrest raised his eyes to Clarkes. His breath caught in his throat. Two golden orbs sat in Forrest's eye socket; he was drowning in Forrest's world. His grandfather's fear for his wife and child, the pain at her savage death, the despair of losing his son. Yet, through it all, Clarke felt the power of love which bound Forrest to his family. When it was over, Clarke put his face in his hands.

'You should have told us, dad.'

'He couldn't, he swore not to. You understand, you were all spared this knowledge to protect you. Your lives were at stake, they would use you to capture me, that single wish is a great alure to humans.' Forrest walked over and rested his hand on Clarke's shoulder.

'You must now make a decision Clarke. Do you wish to walk the path of Dark Magic?' Clarke pulled his shoulder away from Forrest's touch.

'Everyone around here has magic it would seem. The Appleby's with their Earth Magic, some with Dark Magic, and you, what is your magic?' Clarke felt wretched as he spat the words out.

The room became electric, dangerous.

'My magic is from another realm. It is not the same as here. That is all you need to know.'

'Does my father have this magic, do I?'

'No, the power of the Djinn cannot be passed down to humans.'

'I see.' Clarke looked away disappointed. The memories Forrest had shared with him made him ashamed of his envy.

'Clarke, I cannot choose what choice you wish to make with following Dark Magic. I can say however, your parents were unwise to make you give up your friendship with Joshua and his sister. They would have been powerful allies.'

'Well, that's all very well telling us now. Where were you when was Clarke was attacked by Mooremarsh?' Clarke's mother stood up and spoke for the first time. She wandered over to Erik.

'He could not interfere. It would have attracted more danger for our family.' Erik spread out his hands, wanting his wife to understand.

'I have to go; I will see you all again in a day or two. You have Jasmine's look about you Clarke.'

'Goodbye Forrest,' His mother woodenly offered out her hand to Forrest. Forrest took her hand and held it to his forehead.

'Continue as the jewel beside my son's side.' He hugged Erik, cast Clarke a quick look and was gone.

'You need to go upstairs. I will bring your supper up to your bedroom.' His mother swished past him.

'Go Clarke, I will come up later.' His father sounded sad, sadder than he ever remembered.

Clarke left the room and climbed the stairs to his bedroom. He felt alone, very alone.

But you're not alone. You have me!

CHAPTER 19
A FAIRY'S ADVICE

'We need to get to dad's garage.' Milly looked at Joshua's bruised face, 'you need a lift home after the pounding Clarke gave you.' Milly caught his elbow and directed him down the hill.

'Dad can drop you off at the farm Mathew and Nori to the circus.'

'No, there is something I want to do first. Something isn't right about Clarke. I want to go to the grass outside Mooremarsh's old house.' Joshua's jaw thrust out stubbornly, his head was throbbing.

'Why would you want to go there?' Mathew blanched.

'I want to make sure she has not come back.' He replied.

'How would you know?' Milly stammered.

'There is a way, come on.' Joshua walked away towards the high street.

'Better follow him. I think I know what he is going to do.' Nori watched his back as he walked away.

Nori pulled her coat tighter about herself and strolled after Joshua.

'Guess we're following him!' Milly grabbed Mathew's arm, 'let's go then.'

Daylight was fading and the high streetlights had started to light up as they trundled along. They passed the café and saw a woman in a bright orange jacket sitting inside. Milly felt her neck tingle, she looked at the woman. There was something familiar about her, she couldn't put her finger on it.

'Come on Milly,' hissed Mathew nodding towards Joshua and Nori as they disappeared into the crowd.

Milly turned from the window and followed Mathew. Not before the woman in the orange jacket turned and caught a glimpse of her. The woman put her hand up to her neck and touched the charm she wore and turned back to her beverage.

Joshua looked up at Mooremarsh's house.

'Are you there, I need you.' He called out to Prudence.

Mathew caught him up. An explosion of purple smacked him.

What are you doing here? Asking for trouble if you ask me. Why would you be so stupid to be standing in front of the Dark Magic human's home? Thick are you! Gertie burst into Mathew's mind. *Well, quite stupid I would say. They had to give me the dim human!* She landed just outside of Mathew's reach.

'You don't know me enough to speak to me like that.' He stabbed a finger in the air at her.

Why are you here then?

Mathew looked up the hill, he was not happy to be here.

Heard that! Gertie scoffed; her head wagged from side to side.

'Ok, you asked. Do you sense Dark Magic?' waving away the purple smoke oozing around her.

Gertie stood still, raised her head, jigged it from side to side.

What are you doing? Prudence asked Gertie watching her with astonishment.

Gertie jigged her head a little more. *Nope, can't detect Dark Magic here.*

'Phew!' Mathew sighed; his relief didn't last long.

Just because I cannot feel it, doesn't mean it's not here. They could have a charm to hide it. Gertie stopped jigging her head and hopped onto Mathew's shoulder instead.

He adjusted his body to accommodate her weight. She nibbled the crown of his head.

'Stop that, it hurts.' Mathew slapped her beak away.

'Do you agree Prudence?' Joshua a little irritated at the competition between the two magical animals.

Prudence stamped her foot a few times, closed her eyes. Her eyes flicked wide open a few moments later.

No Dark Magic here now. But there has been recently. I feel the magic of Mooremarsh. We must tell the Elders. She stamped her foot, she was frightened. *I will find Sylvester Bluesky; you must find the Elders. Go!*

Milly looked back at the high street and thought about the feeling she had had.

Come Milly, I will stay with you all alongside Gertie. We must go from this place. Miskunn had arrived sensing that Milly was in danger.

'We go to dad; he can come with us to the Elders.' Joshua marched ahead so there could be no argument.

'Guess we follow him,' Nori shrugged her shoulders and walked back down the hill after Joshua.

As they passed the café, the woman in orange was no longer inside. Milly looked about but could not see her.

What is wrong? Miskunn asked.

'There was a woman with Harrow, well, I didn't see her face, but she had an orange jacket on. She was there when I found the Dark Magic book. Is it a coincidence?'

I don't believe in coincidences like that. I will see if I can find her, so the Elders know where she is. First, I will escort you to your father. Miskunn touched Milly's mind reassuringly.

They walked in silence watching the shadows as they went. The sound of an engine reviving up roared down the road from the garage. Mathew ran on ahead to warn Bill about Joshua's fight with Clarke.

'What!' Joshua heard his father's voice boom from within the garage.

Joshua pushed open the door to the garage and smiled weakly at his father.

'Hi Dad.'

His father walked over and looked at the bruises on Joshua's face.

'Well, what happened?' Bill put his arm around Joshua and led him to a seat.

'I was in a fight with Clarke.' Joshua swallowed hard.

'I see. What was the fight about?'

'Clarke started it. He was saying awful things about me, out of the blue he hit Joshua. It was unprovoked Dad.' Milly held her hand up defending Joshua.

'I see. Is that right Joshua.' Bill rubbed his chin, shocked at seeing the bruises start to form on Joshua's face.

Joshua nodded, his face still throbbing from Clarke's punches.

'I invited Nori and Mathew to listen to some music after school, then Clarke went mental.'

Bill looked at Nori, a small smile turned at the corner of his mouth.

'I'll get my coat and run you all home.' Bill marched to the back of the garage and took his coat off the peg.

Rummaging around his pocket he held up his car keys.

'Let's go.' He jangled the keys and headed for the door.

'We are not sure dad, but we think Mooremarsh might be back.' Joshua babbled.

His father's step faltered.

'How?' That one word held a lot of meaning.

Joshua felt the prickle of guilt in his stomach. He had promised to stay out of trouble, especially after last year.

'We were on the green. Mathew asked Gertie to see if she could feel Dark Magic, after Milly finding that book. She replied that she could not, Prudence said she also could not feel Dark Magic, but she felt Mooremarsh had been here. We thought we should come to you first then the Elders.' Joshua looked at his dad.

'I see.' Bill bit his lower lip, a disappointed look flited over his face, 'You should have asked us first before you went snooping about.' Bill shook his head, 'I think we will go and get your mother first.' He went to the back of the garage and put on his cap and jacket.

'Outside all of you. Joshua, lock up the garage, then into the car.' Bill threw him the keys to the garage door, walked past him to a large car parked outside the garage. Opening all the doors he called, 'Everyone in.'

Branches looked spooky in the headlights as they drove down the lane. Joshua thought something would be jumping out at them in a minute. The cars bright lights shone on the nameplate on the cottage gate.

'Go and fetch Mum.' He nodded towards the cottage.

As soon as Joshua got out of the car, he felt fear, pins and needles crept up his arm

Was Mooremarsh here? He ran to the door and opened it.

'Mum, you have to come right away. We need to see the Elders, now.' Joshua called out.

'I am in here,' her voice floated from the kitchen.

Joshua ran the few steps to the kitchen and yanked open the door.

His mother was taking off her apron. 'What is this all about?'

'We think Mooremarsh might be back. We need to warn the Elders.' Joshua's pupils were dilated with the shock of the news his arch enemy may be close.

'What happened to your face?' she gasped inspecting Joshua's bruises.

'Had a fight with Clarke, but I will tell you about that in the car.'

Grabbing her handbag, she grabbed a bottle with clear liquid from a drawer.

'Open your mouth.' She unscrewed the two little bottles and took out their stoppers. 'Don't argue.'

Joshua opened his mouth, and she dispensed some drops under his tongue.

'Chamomile, it will soothe you,' she examined his face, 'arnica for the bruises. come on, let's go.'

A small journey brought them outside a tidy cottage on the edge of town. Sylvester Bluesky stood in the driveway waiting for them, Sophia came out waving them into the cottage. Soon everyone was settled down with Sophia's tradition of tea and cakes.

'What has happened?' Jasper asked leaning forward his hand hovered over a piece of cake. He caught Rutger's eye and thought better of it and sat back huffily in his chair.

'Prudence says she has detected Mooremarsh.' Joshua licked his lips; they were dry from shock at the discovery.

Rutger put his fingertips together. 'What about the other animals?'

'Gertie said she couldn't sense Dark Magic, but they may have hidden it.' Mathew jabbered.

'The first thing is to be calm. She may be here she may not.' Sophia encouraged them.

'We will be defensive this time. The children may not go anywhere without an adult with Earth Magic.' Rutger looked at the children, 'Understood!'

All heads nodded at once.

'Good.' He turned to Sophia, 'Could you draw up a timetable, so we know who is protecting which child.

Sophia exhaled patiently, 'I think we can say three children, three Elders, one elder needs to stay with one child. I will stay with Milly, Rutger, you can watch Joshua and Jasper, that leaves you with Mathew. Everyone agree with the simplicity of this plan?' She raised an eyebrow at Rutger.

Sometimes I wonder about you Elders. Feles shook his head in dismay.

Sophia ignored the cat and waited for Rutger to reply.

'Yes, yes, sounds practical.' He replied gruffly.

'Alana, you can put us both up?'

'Yes, no problem. I just wonder though, if Mathew should stay with us, given the circumstances.' Alana replied. 'Strength in numbers?'

'Dad needs me on the farm.' Mathew stated.

'In that case, I will help on the farm, but I think it's a good idea to stay here in the evenings.' Jasper scratched his beard.

'What about Nori?' Joshua blurted out.

Rutger looked at Nori and seemed to notice her for the first time.

'If you don't mind me asking. Are you a fairy?' He quizzed her.

'Yes, that I am.' Nori spread her wings open.

There were lots of oohs and aahs at the sight of them.

'I do not need your protection,' she smiled sweetly at Bill, 'just a lift home would be nice.'

'No problem, Nori, we will drop you off first.' Bill lifted his keys.

'There is something you should know. Charms do not work on fairies. I have detected darkness in the town. You are right to be careful. It is powerful, but worse still, I have detected an Energy Vampire, here in Malmesbury.'

With that shocking announcement Rutger grabbed his cane.

'We had better be prepared.' He looked at Bill, 'your cars too small to take us all, we will go in two groups.'

'Alana, and family go first, Bill will collect us next.'

The journey home seemed quicker. Joshua kept watch as his mother opened the door and went inside and lit up the house. Milly and Mathew helped carrying some pillows and blankets which Sophia had stuffed into the car. Nori came up behind them with tins of cakes and biscuits as Sophia didn't want them to all starve! Once they were all safely inside, Bill drove off to collect the Elders.

'I need to talk to you.' Joshua felt Nori standing behind him as he watched his father go from the living room window.

Joshua turned and looked into the greenest eyes he had ever seen. He felt his heart thumping in his chest.

'You see, that is the problem. Humans fall in love with fairies too easily.' Nori looked over his shoulder at the ever-darkening evening.

'I don't understand,' blustered Joshua, she had caught him off guard.

'Fairies are strange creatures. Like humans we come with all sorts of personalities. Sadly, love with humans is very complicated. Humans can be ensnared easily by a fairy.' Her eyes looked into his, 'Joshua, we will be friends, good friends. Push any ideas out of your head that there would be anything else between us. Your feelings for me are just like fools' gold. It's not real. You will find something stronger, like the bond your parents have.' Nori put a hand on his shoulder.

Joshua felt he was falling, his breath caught, and his chest crushed tight.

'But Nori, it may be different.' He began, his face draining of blood.

Nori shook her head, a smile played at her lips.

'Humans are, very predictable. What you feel is not real, it's a gossamer, a veil of the real thing. You will understand in the future. I am saving you from a lot of pain.'

'I don't understand, if this is what I want, it's my choice.' He pleaded with her.

'You, do not know what you want in these matters.' She poked him on the shoulder, 'you will want to be with me forever, once you have dined at my table, you will never leave.' She stepped back; her wings opened in a full display of beauty. 'I on the other hand, will find love here there and everywhere, never faithful to you, just enjoying the vanity of the world. I would hurt you deeply, it is in my nature.'

'Please Nori, I will take that chance.' He begged, he felt she had punched him in the stomach.

'I will not.' Her wings opened and shook angrily. 'You and Milly are good friends. I want to keep it that way. Your friendship is important to me,' her lips drew into a fine line, she would not discuss the matter further.

'Joshua, come and help lay the table, Nori, if you could help Milly make up the bedroom and fashion a bed in Milly's room for Sophia.' His mother's voice broke the moment.

'Better go help Milly.' Nori smiled sadly at Joshua, 'Maybe if I had been human things would have been different.' She walked away without a backwards glance, left him alone with his thoughts and a gnawing feeling in the pit of his stomach.

CHAPTER 20
SCOUTING

Harrow stood scuffing the front of his boot on the back of his trouser leg. He had noticed a small splatter of mud on the toe and that would not do. He paced the small alley and thought about who he was meeting tomorrow. Petula. He couldn't wait. But something didn't feel right. Her perfection seemed to fade after not seeing her for many days. But he would meet her tomorrow. And they were going out on a trip, a surprise she had said. He hated surprises, he liked things neat and in order.

Harrow, have you tired of me so soon? Do I have to find another to take my hand? The song sang in his head and felt it dreamily take him away.

His radio crackled in the vanilla morning, he snapped awake, raised his fingers to try and tune it in to the right radio frequency, he had no success, it still crackled. No one wanted to talk to him, that meant all was well with the world. He carried on his walk; his toes hurt in his new boots, he wiggled them to make more room within his boots. A small grimace passed his lips, they still hurt. He pulled up his sleeve and looked at his black strapped wristwatch, eight o clock in the morning, his night shift would be over soon, and he would be off for the weekend. Harrow stamped his feet; he liked the sharp sound they made in the alley. Time to finish off his rounds and check the shop doors. He swaggered to the end of the alley, turned into the high street and rattled shop doors, making sure they were still locked.

'Time for a cup of tea at the station.' He turned up the high street towards the station. A gate creaked under his hand and bounced back into its latch. He gave a cursory gaze at the police station, its sandstone bricks looked grey in the morning light. His boots clipped on the path, and he put his hand out to open the door. He stepped inside and nodded at the uniformed man sitting behind the counter.

'Morning Michael, having a cup of tea before I go off duty.' Harrow nodded.

'Right you are, Marcus.' Replied the officer.

Harrow found the kettle in the small sitting room and threw tea into a teapot. His eyes felt heavy, he had been tired all week, he sat down in a plump chair and closed his eyes. Images flashed up under his lids, some he recognized, some not. A memory lurked just out of reach.

'Hey, Marcus, Inspector Stone is looking for you.' He was snapped out of his nap.

'Do you know what about? Hope he's not wanting me to work over the weekend!' Harrow stood up, tidied his uniform, and made his way to Inspector Stone's office.

A blue door with a neat sign presented itself at the end of a corridor. Harrow knocked on the door.

'Come.' A soft voice commanded.

Harrow walked up to the desk where a greying man sat scribbling into a book.

'You wanted to see me, sir?' Harrow coughed.

The hand stopped scribbling and put down the pen. Dark eyes inspected Harrow.

'We have a problem Harrow.' Inspector Stone sat back in his creaky chair.

Harrow felt the hair on his neck rise.

'Oh?' Harrow's eyebrows knotted together.

The inspector took up the pen and began tapping on the desk.

'There was a box of books in the evidence room.'

'Yes.' Harrow felt uneasy.

'They have gone. It has been taken. Wondered if you knew anything about it?'

'No, I have no idea.' Harrow shook his head. There it was again; the prickle ran down his neck and shoulders. He wanted to scratch it but refrained from the relief it would bring him. Harrow put his hands behind his back. 'What would you like me to do?'

'Nothing, nothing. I will give it a few days to turn up. This has never happened at this station,' His eyes caught Harrow's, 'Dismissed.' Inspector Stone nodded towards the door.

'Right sir,' Harrow left the office, something was scratching at his memory, but he could not see it. He walked quickly to his locker and took out his coat.

Tomorrow, Harrow, tomorrow. The song filled his mind. He threw on his coat and marched out to the street thinking no more about the box which had disappeared. He was unaware of the figure which watched him from across the road, controlling his thoughts.

Mooremarsh hid behind a statue and watched Harrow walk away from the station. She sent her song to him, singing into the wind. Tomorrow they would steal the Ruby Dragon and one part of her plan would be in place. She took out her watch from her bag, glanced at the time, the early bus to Cirencester would be here soon.

'I think it might be a good idea to visit the Ruby Dragon exhibition by myself.' Mooremarsh tapped her front tooth.

Pushing the watch back into the handbag, she rushed to the bus stop to catch the bus.

The countryside was a blur to Mooremarsh as the bus whizzed along country roads. The reality was she hated the countryside, the early bird chorus, all that high pitched squawking and bouncing from branch to branch. She found the sound jarring and strangely antisocial. The only thing going on in her mind was how to steal the Ruby Dragon and get the last reward, eternal life! The bus bumped to a stop and the bus conductor called out. 'Last stop, all alight here please.'

She blinked and looked around. A large market square stood in front of a church. Rummaging around in her handbag she found a map. She made her way down the aisle and off the bus. A cafe was across the road, Mooremarsh decided to have a drink and examine her map. As she passed through the door, a little bell chimed overhead. A small woman, dressed in black came bustling towards her. 'Would madam please follow me.'

A cruel smile warmed Mooremarsh's face as she followed the waitress. She sat down and pushed aside the menu she was offered.

'Just coffee made with milk please.' Mooremarsh glanced at the waitress.

'Thank you, madam.' The waitress took the menu and slid away from the table.

Mooremarsh once more got out her map and spread it across the table. She found Cirencester; her fingers traced the map trying to find Overhill Hall. She grunted unsatisfied with the situation. The clinking of saucer and cup hailed the arrival of her drink. The waitress deftly set the cup and saucer with its steaming contents in front of Mooremarsh.

'Anything else I can get you?' The waitress pulled a stray hair back behind her ear.

'Not unless you know where Overhill Hall is!' Mooremarsh snapped waspishly.

The waitress blinked at the rebuff. 'Well, actually, yes I do.'

Mooremarsh seemed to notice the waitress for the first time. Her head cocked to one side; a slow smile spread across her face.

'And where on this map would it be? If possible, could you direct me?'

The waitress fidgeted under Mooremarsh's stare.

'If you turn your map around, I will show you where Overhill Hall is. It has a famous jewel being shown there.' The waitress pointed to a spot on the map. 'That's where you want to go. Out of here. Keep going down the lane, then you will get to a little bridge, go over that and Overhill Hall is on your right.'

'Thank you. You can go.' Mooremarsh was indifferent to the waitress expression.

Sipping her drink, the hot liquid scolded her throat, she didn't mind, she was on her way to the Ruby Dragon, eternal life, all hers for the taking. Folding the map up and tucking it neatly into her pocket, she threw some coins on the table and left the café.

The walk to Overhill Hall was in fact quite short. She passed through large iron gates; a drive lined with horse chestnut trees. A loud noise she recognized clipped the air. Children, a large class she guessed from the sound. Turning the corner of the large Victorian mansion, Mooremarsh bumped into a group of school children, their teacher looked flustered as she tried to keep order of the group.

'St Victorious School?' A man in a navy uniform stepped out of the house and looked at the tormented teacher.

'Yes, yes that's us.' She replied, 'I am their teacher, Miss Stead.'

'I see. I am Mr Wilks.' He looked down his nose at the teacher, 'The children are not to touch the exhibits, they are not to make a noise in the house, they are to remain with you.' He looked at the teacher, his expression condescending at her lack of ability to control the young group. He met Mooremarsh's cold gaze. Miss Stead had gone after an escapee. Mooremarsh screwed up her eyes, an opportunity had presented itself to her. Miss Steads returned with her errant student.

'This way then,' Mr Wilks waved the children and Miss Stead ahead.

Mooremarsh walked beside the group, pretending to be their teacher too. As she came up beside Mr Wilks, she patted a girl on the back, 'Come on, Mr Wilks hasn't got all day!' the girl looked at her in surprise, Mooremarsh raised an eyebrow daring her to answer her back. Turning a look on Mr Wilks she commented, 'I will make sure they behave.'

'I'm sure you will, not like the other one.' Mr Wilks winked at Mooremarsh, followed the group in with Mooremarsh at the rear.

Once inside, Mooremarsh admired the large hall. The walls were decked with paintings, colour was everywhere.

Mr Wilks cleared his throat. The party of children and adults quieted down.

'This is the Mills Hall, Sir Edward Mills acquired thirty-eight paintings during his life here at Overhill Hall. Sir Edward had a liking for contemporary art. You will see that Jackson Pollock hangs with a newly acquired painting by Paul Nash depicting the second world war.' Mr Wilks went on in that vein and Mooremarsh turned her attention to the hall itself.

'Mr Wilks, I am sure the children would like to know about how these wonderful paintings are kept safe?' Mooremarsh simpered.

Mr Wilks through her an irritated look, his speech had been interrupted. 'Yes, of course.' He put his thumbs under dark green braces on his chest.

'Overhill Hall is protected by the latest intruder alarm system, and each evening a keeper of the watch stands on guard. In the library is the newest Tanner Edwards safe. So, all these valuable artworks are well protected.' Mr Wilks replied smugly and let his braces lightly smack his chest. 'Any more questions, or should we proceed?'

'Thank You, so informative.' Mooremarsh bowed her head.

Now she wanted to see the Ruby Dragon. After half an hour of the Monotonous drone of Mr Wilks historic tit bits, her mind focused on the new information he had to offer. They stood in the library, row after row of books lined the large room.

'This is used mainly by her ladyship, Lady Anna Mills. The books have been collected by various family members since the early 18th century.'

'And where is that splendid safe you were telling us all about?' Mooremarsh interrupted.

Mr Wilks looked put out at being interrupted again. He looked around the room, cleared his throat, and asked conspiratorially to the upturned faces of the children.

'Can you see it?' he waited for a response, 'no? then sadly, I cannot disclose its whereabouts.' Mr Wilks smiled slyly at Mooremarsh.

'And now, the final part of the tour. The Ruby Dragon,' he flourished his hand in the direction of the door and the group trundled out of it.

Irritated, Mooremarsh tapped a small utility table with her toe, a bud vase rocked dangerously but didn't fall. She sniffed dismissively and followed the crowd. She placed her hand over her eyes, after the dimness of the library, the room they had entered was very bright. She felt her eyes acclimatize to the light and slowly removed her hands. She peered around the room. It was spartan, except for two armchairs and a large glass case in the middle of the room, red rope acted as a barrier to stop anyone getting too close to the glass. Mooremarsh gasped at the brilliance of the stone. She leant over the rope cordon and almost pushed her nose against the glass. She was mesmerized by the Ruby's colour, she had never expected it to be so red. Light shone from above onto it exposing the fine carving of the ruby.

'The Ruby Dragon.' A small sigh escaped her lips.

'Actually, the title is The Ruby Dragon of Craig Hall.' Mr Wilks smirked at correcting Mooremarsh.

Mooremarsh stood taller, bristling with anger, her eyes snapped at Mr Wilks.

'You insignificant little man. You know the name of this jewel, but you have no idea of its significance.' She hissed in his ear. She was rewarded with a wide-eyed look from him.

'You will forget I was ever here.' She sang her spell to him.

'Never here.' He whispered back.

'You will meet me here at two-thirty tomorrow.' Her spell cast, she gave one more craving look at the Ruby Dragon and left Overhill Hall.

CHAPTER 21
GAMES WITH THE DJINN

Joshua awoke from a broken night of sleep. His body felt stiff, he rubbed his neck, his mouth was dry, and his tongue felt like cardboard, he licked his dry lips and pulled his blanket up over his chin. He lay still, eyes closed, enjoying the start of the day. A noise he didn't recognize echoed down the hall. Snoring, the loud vibrating sound jarred against his skull. His hand shot out and he patted the side table to find his watch. His fingers touched the cold face of the watch and he slid it out of its place. Six-thirty in the morning, he groaned, he wouldn't be able to catch a few more minutes with that incessant noise in the background. He decided he would get up; no sleep was better than listening to that noise. He sat up and rolled back the blankets and put his feet on the floor, his toes touched something soft and warm.

'Hey!' A groggy voice he recognized came up from the floor.

He had forgotten that Mathew was staying in his room. He pushed his foot to one side and stood up.

'Sorry, forgot you were there.'

'Great!' he heard him roll over, 'Did you hear that snoring, kept me up all night!' Mathew scratched his chin disgruntled.

The door opened and Milly popped her head around the door.

'Mum say's you'd better get downstairs if you want breakfast.' She threw a bag into the room, it landed with a thud on top of Mathew. 'Here are your clothes, your dad brought them up this morning.'

'Right. If you get out and I can get dressed.' Mathew's muffled retort came back.

Joshua went to the bathroom to wash, he reached out for the door handle when the door opened.

'Morning Joshua,' flinched a startled Rutger.

Rutgers wore eye-popping purple tartan pyjamas; Joshua swallowed a smile. Rutger looked down and grinned ruefully.

'Yes, they are rather bright,' he brushed down one side. 'See you at breakfast.' He slid past Joshua leaving the slightly spicy scent of his aftershave after him.

Joshua quickly went into the bathroom and washed and pulled on his school uniform. He peered into the mirror; with quick movements he combed his hair.

A light knock at the door was followed by Mathew's bleary voice. 'Can I use the bathroom, been waiting a bit.'

He opened the door to Mathew standing there balancing from toe to toe.

'I'll see you downstairs then.' Joshua left the door open and raced downstairs.

The kitchen table was filled with buttered toast and bowls of porridge.

'You'd better sit down quick before all the spaces are taken,' Milly laughed at him.

'You two will be polite and offer your seats to the Elders!' Alana came in with another mound of toast.

Milly raised an eyebrow at Joshua and pulled a slice of toast onto a plate.

'Mum, the Elders aren't going to come into school with us surely?' Joshua slapped marmalade onto his toast just as Mathew burst through the door.

'No, this is going to be difficult to manage. You lot will fill out the car once you're in. I think maybe I will drive you to school and pick you up afterwards.' Alana's forehead creased as she thought it through.

'Sounds like a plan to me.' Bill came in from outside. His clothes smelt of oil. 'Just made sure the car was ready.'

'Ok, finish quickly, your dad needs to get to work as early as he can this morning.'

The kitchen door opened, and three Elders stood there. Joshua nearly choked on his porridge. Jasper wore a fluffy dressing gown with little blue birds printed on it. Rutger wore a matching purple tartan dressing gown with purple patterned Moroccan slippers. Sophia looked at each of the Elders and shook her head, she was dressed immaculately.

'Alana is driving them to school. I will take you back to town and pick you up again later.' Bill poured them cups of tea.

'Do you think we should stay at the school gates?' Jasper said.

Jasper took a cup of steam of tea and nodded his thanks. He grinned slyly as Joshua turned a look of horror in his direction.

'Well, that would look silly. No, if Mooremarsh attacks it's when she thinks there is no one around to help them. We stick with the plan of staying close to them when they are not at school.' Sophia slapped thick honey onto her toast, 'We have to go over to Forrest and make some arrangements.'

Joshua felt his stomach drop at the mention of the circus. Rutger placed a kind hand on his shoulder.

'It's for the best,' he whispered, 'fairies are flighty creatures.'

The day passed quickly for Joshua and soon he was waiting outside the school gate with Milly and Mathew.

We are all here! Prudence called out.

Joshua saw the blue hare sitting up right at the corner of the road. In the air above them Gertie glided in circles.

'Can you see Miskunn?' Asked Joshua.

'Yes, she is sat on the Abbey steeple.' Her sentence was cut off short, a large lorry driving down the road came to a standstill beside them.

The door shot open, 'Get in.' Bill jerked a thumb to the back of the lorry.

Everyone ran to the back and clambered in.

'Afternoon, we are off to Forrest to use his circus for training.' Alana leant forward from a box she was sitting on.

'Your dad did come up with this marvelous suggestion, we can now all travel together,' she clapped her hands.

Mathew noticed Sophia's hem was caked in mud.

'Went to your farm, helped with some of the chores you had to miss. Really interesting birds' chickens!' Sophia laughed.

'It's alright for you. I had to load stone into a lorry, and then unload it where Mr Anderson was building his wall. Of course, Jasper got off lightly, helping making cakes, what can I say!'

'Mathew's father was grateful for the help, given Mathew cannot help him now!'

'All right for you, we have to sit on the floor and be jostled about!' Rutger grumbled from a sack he was sitting on.

Joshua banged the side of the lorry, and hollered, 'Ready!'

The lorry jerked forwards and they were on their way to Forrest Circus.

'Thought we would take advantage of the circus folk. You can practice the magic we have taught you over the last few months,' Rutger held up a hand to Mathew, 'Yes, I know it's only been a matter of weeks for you, I am sure we can come up with something.'

You better think hard for Mathew, he is a bit slow learning Earth Magic. Scoffed Gertie, purple glitter sprinkled over Mathew, he brushed it off angrily.

'If you don't want to help me, you can always go!' Mathew chewed into Gertie. He was surprised as she looked a little hurt.

As you wish! Gertie retorted.

Stay where you are. Stop arguing, after the last confrontation with Mooremarsh, the children are not to be left unprotected. Sylvester Bluesky's growl blasted at them from outside the lorry, they both jumped in unison.

Ok, ok, snapped Gertie and perched in a corner of the lorry staring at Mathew belligerently. *Last time I will waste my protection aura on you.* She placed her wings around her head.

'Protection Aura?' Mathew stuttered.

'Yes, the colours she pours over you, she is sharing her protection with you,' Sophia sucked in her lips, 'she does it at great expense to herself. When she protects you, she is unprotected from evils harm. She is being selfless.'

Mathew recognized the admonishment in Sophia's voice. The back of his neck grew hot, he felt guilty.

'I didn't know. Gertie, come and sit with me. You might be more comfortable here.' He encouraged her.

A wing moved slightly; an eye peered out.

Joshua could have sworn he saw a tear about the Crow's eye.

'Go on Gertie, Mathew is sorry.' Joshua called to Gertie.

Gertie made much of opening her wings and jostled over to Mathew.

The lorry came to a halt. A familiar voice called out to them.

'Welcome, welcome to Forrest circus!'

Well, let's see what you can do! Gertie gave Mathew a bruising peck on the arm and flew out of the lorry.

Mathew rubbed his arm, 'I don't think I will ever get used to that crow!'

Joshua jumped out the back of the lorry and was surprised it was an empty field.

The circus has moved on, a few circus folk have kept behind to help Forrest train you this evening. Prudence padded her foot impatiently.

Joshua noticed Nori and turned away. She laughed her bright tinkering laugh, stepped forward and slipped her arm through Joshua's. He couldn't help himself, his face beamed, his stomach had butterflies.

'Now, you asked for a magical obstacle course, here it is,' Forrest waved at the field.

'Maybe I am missing something, what are we supposed to practice against?' Joshua whispered to Nori.

'You will find out!' she untangled her arm from his.

'Now, Joshua, you will practice fire magic and defense.' Rutger shooed him towards a spot in the field. 'Off you go.' He banged his cane into the soil.

'I suggest you remove your coat.' Sophia called.

'Let's sit down and enjoy this little battle.' Forrest pointed at some hay bales covered in luscious blankets he had placed on them earlier.

Once everyone was comfortable, Joshua removed his coat and walked into the field.

'Use your senses Joshua,' called Rutger.

Joshua looked around; the field was still empty. He walked one step at a time. The hair on his wrist lifted away from his skin. Pressure built up on his left side, against his chest. Before he knew what was happening, Prudence had materialized in front of him and hit him square in the chest and knocked him on his rear.

'That's not fair, you made yourself invisible.' Joshua shouted stabbing a finger at her. He felt guilty as Prudence looked down at her feet dejectedly.

'This training is for you to use your sense and your magic,' rebuked Rutger.

Joshua got up. He walked a little way and felt the pressure on his right side of his chest. Before he could use fire magic to defend himself, whoosh, he was covered in water.

Nori materialized laughing. 'You need to be quicker than that!'

'Great,' he grumbled.

After six attacks, Joshua got into the stride of defending himself with fire magic. A singed clown, one slightly blistered lion trainer. Rutger called time. 'Two out of eight, it's a start.' He waved Joshua to him, 'Right, your turn Milly.'

Milly looked apprehensively at Rutger and Sophia.

'Go on Milly, you can do this,' she heard her mother call at her back.

Milly walked tentatively forward and stood still. She looked at one blade of grass. suddenly, she felt the pressure, straight in front of her. Without thinking she brought her hands up with lightning speed. The hair on her forearms raised and quivered as she used magic and forced air forward, a dull crashing sound followed. A clown sat on the floor; his face grimaced and he stuck out his tongue.

'You're no fun!' he blew a raspberry at her and walked away.

Before she could answer, she felt the attack again and again, each one she deftly fought off.

'Well done, Milly, six out of six.' Sophia clapped her hands and waved at her.

All eyes turned on Mathew. He got up, a grim line of determination on his lips. He limbs felt wooden as he started to walk.

You point to where you feel them, I will deal with them. Gertie called to him

'I will get pulverized,' He whispered to her.

Just have a little confidence in me if you please! Gertie lightly nipped his shin. *Keep alert and point!*

Mathew wandered into the field. He decided where to stand and waited.

A dark shadow came towards him, he shrieked, he was knocked over. A clown leered over him. Mathew got up again.

You need to tell me where they are! Gertie flashed her wings at him.

Mathew saw another dark smudge coming towards him, he pointed at it. Gertie swiftly took off from the ground, and released a haze of red.

'What do you think you are doing!' Two clowns materialized patting flames out of their clothes.

Two more smudges loomed towards Mathew, and he quickly pointed at them. Gertie poured down a haze of blue.

The lion tamer and an acrobat, came forward coughing, soaked by water.

Mathew was laughing, when, a smack in the back tipped him over. Nori laughed down at him.

'Never, ever, stop being on guard!' she held out her hand.

Idiot! Gertie squawked in the background.

'Well done, Mathew, four out of six,' Jasper clapped.

Would have been six out of six if you had paid attention! Gertie grumbled.

Mathew looked at the Crow, 'You are amazing, absolutely spectacular.'

Crow primmed her feathers. *Listen and learn.* She quipped back.

'Well, time for some tea and cakes before you go.' Forrest clapped his hands together.

'That went better than expected.' Rutger drawled to Sophia.

'They did very well, given it was their first time.' Alana murmured as she walked past Rutger, 'before we have tea, we will give a sacrifice for the Earth Magic used, I have brought snowdrop bulbs for us to plant.'

'Let's plant those bulbs and give thanks.' Jasper winked at Mathew, and handed him some bulbs, 'then it's time for tea and cakes I think!'

CHAPTER 22
THE RUBY DRAGON OF OVERHILL HALL

Joshua sat at the kitchen table finishing a handful of walnuts. He idly flicked over the date on the calendar. Seventh of December. Only a few more weeks till the Christmas holidays. He popped the last nut into his mouth just as the front door opened.

'Ready to go out?' The voice of Grandad Rose floated through to the kitchen.

'Grandad,' Joshua opened the kitchen door, 'would you like a cup of tea?'

'No, Mr Priddy is in the car ready for our outing to Overhill Hall, it's going to be an interesting trip. Can't wait to see the Ruby Dragon.'

'That sounds good, looking forward to going with you.' Rutger unfolded a newspaper he was reading by the fire.

'Well, it was supposed to be a family outing really.' Grandad Rose sounded disappointed.

'You understand we are here to protect the children.' Rutger irritated ruffled the pages of his newspaper.

'Now Rutger, we are here to protect, not interfere,' Sophia came into the kitchen carrying a mug of ginger tea. She sat down at the kitchen table.

'Jethro, I understand you will be going to see the Ruby Dragon?' She sipped her tea, wrinkling her nose, the strong fragrance wafted about her.

'If the legend is true, there are many replicas of the statue,' she took a quick sip of her tea, 'it is supposed to hold the power of eternal life. Dark Magic was used to fashion the Ruby Dragon. Many copies have been carved of the original. Thankfully, the original carving was lost many hundreds of years ago.' Rutger commented in a matter-of-fact manner.

'Yes, yes, I know. It's just it would be nice to have some normality at the weekend.' Grandad Rose grumbled.

'Hello Dad, I will get Milly down, Mathew is in the garden practicing Earth Magic with Gertie.' Alana turned a gaze on Rutger, 'I was thinking how to keep the children safe. I made up seven charms last night. We can place them around Overhill Hall whilst they enjoy the morning there. We go with Bill in the other car and enjoy the gardens, we can create an Earth Magic web of protection using our staffs. I have my great grandfather's staff upstairs, it chose me when he died; it has the Emerald of Brylan, he used to call it Brylan!' She pointed at Sophia's staff leaning idly against the wall, 'Sophia has the Amethyst of Eunice in her staff, Rutger, the eagle head, I believe hides the Diamond of Henrik?'

Rutger nodded. Alana clapped her hands together.

'Jasper's cane holds the Ruby of Winter,' she nodded, 'it is settled. Grandad, Mr Priddy and the children will enjoy their day out. We will enjoy the gardens.'

'I suppose that is acceptable.' Rutger put his paper down.

'Joshua, go get Mathew from the garden, and get into grandad's car. I will call Milly down; we will see you at Overhill Hall.'

She turned and gave her father a hug, guess we meet at the café for a bit of lunch, say one o'clock?'

Joshua grabbed his coat and went out of the back door into the garden.

I told you, think and point! If you don't do both quick enough, I will miss the target! Gertie snapped her beak at him, *you understand don't you, think and point!* She displayed her wings crossly.

'I am trying!' Mathew replied huffily, pushing his fingers through his hair.

Joshua watched the pair for a moment. Gertie shook a bush, leaves would fly off, Mathew would point at the leaf she needed to hit with her power.

She missed the target again.

'Mathew, we are leaving for Overhill Hall now.' Joshua caught Mathew's the look of relief.

'Gertie, been good practicing with you.' Mathew jabbered; it was clear he wanted to get away.

Don't forget to make your offering.

'Yes, of course, will do it right now.' Mathew felt into his pocket and pulled out the last of the snowdrop bulbs.

Joshua pointed to a patch of mud and Mathew quickly heeled them in.

'Thank you for Earth Magic.' Mathew said and raced over to Joshua.

Joshua heard Milly before he could see her as he swung around the corner of the cottage.

'Who's sitting in the middle then?' Mathew asked.

Joshua didn't answer, he raced to the car and opened the back passenger door and said, 'After you!'

'Morning everyone.' Priddy turned around in his seat, 'hurry up or else it will be lunch time before we get in.' he laughed.

Grandad Rose slid into his seat, turned the ignition, the engine roared into life.

'See you there, we won't be far behind!' Alana stood in the doorway, the staff of Brylan in her hand.

'What are they going to say at Overhill Hall, two women with staffs!' Joshua laughed watching his mother out of the back window climbing into the car his dad had just driven up in.

'Am I missing something?' Priddy asked confused.

'It's like this Maurice, after last year and what happened to you and the children. They aren't taking any chances. They think Mooremarsh might be back.' Grandad Rose recounted.

Joshua wished his grandfather hadn't mentioned anything, from where he sat, he could see Priddy was distressed.

'Did you know about all this Earth Magic stuff before last year Mr Priddy?' Mathew asked conversationally. He received a glare from Joshua, hunched his shoulders.

'You know, I didn't know much about it.' His fingers tapped on his thigh, 'but I did know there was some sort of mystical connection in our family. Obviously, it all clicked when Alana brought me out of the Sleep of the Dead.' He shivered, 'I guess we will have to be on the lookout.'

'Mr Priddy, I forgot, Mum made this for you,' Milly handed him a silver vial filled with herbs, 'she said it will protect you from Mooremarsh, you must have it on you at all times.'

Priddy put the vile of herbs up to his nose, 'Well, it smells nice!' and popped it into his pocket.

'Most importantly, who do you think will win the football this weekend!'

Grandad Rose caught Milly's raised eyebrows and smiled at her.

'We will be there soon!' he laughed gruffly at her.

The car pulled up outside the regency mansion of Overhill Hall. Milly got out the car and looked up at the magnificent building, its large windows, and cream stone walls. Joshua squeezed out of the back seat, he had cramp in his legs, stamping on the spot, he tried to get the blood in his legs, and back to life.

Got here first! Gertie cheered to herself.

Actually. I have been waiting for you all! Sylvester Bluesky drawled humourously. *We are here to keep watch!* He said more seriously.

Joshua looked around, there was a gardener sweeping up leaves, a man in a blue suit standing outside the door with a large group of people.

'This tour is about to start, make sure you have your tickets please.' The man in blue called to them.

Joshua spied a small wooden shack with someone sitting inside it.

'I think we get the tickets over there,' he pointed.

Mr Priddy looked over at the rickety shack and started to walk towards it.

'Wait Maurice, I need to get some tickets too.' Grandad Rose held out his wallet.

'No, you drove us here, you can buy me lunch,' Priddy walked away a little faster.

'Get us two guides!' Grandad Rose chuckled back.

Joshua watched the group of people file into the house.

'It's all right lad, Maurice and I will give you a grand tour of the house. We've been reading up on it.'

'Your tours are always the best.' Cheered Joshua, pleased to see his grandfather looking happy.

A loud splutter of an exhaust announced the arrival of their parents and the Elders.

'This is going to be embarrassing,' groaned Mathew.

'Young man, my daughter and her friends are here to make sure you are safe. Never take that for granted. Don't forget what happened last year. Be grateful!' Grandad Rose gave a low rebuke.

Yes, don't be ungrateful. Gertie called from a nearby branch.

Mathew mumbled, 'Sorry, didn't mean it.'

Mean what you say, never say what you don't mean. It's just too confusing. Gertie darted her head side to side.

Mathew threw her a stern look.

'Ok, break it up.' Joshua shook his head; will they ever get on? He was glad Prudence was his magical animal, they had grown very close over the year.

'Here they are!' Priddy marched up and gave Grandad Rose some tickets and a guide, which had large red letters.

The Ruby Dragon of Overhill Hall.

Priddy looked over to Bill.

'Are you and Alana coming in?' Priddy called out to them.

Bill waved back, 'No, we are going on a walk with Alana and friends.'

Alana looked at Sophia, her face was pale, she looked tired.

'Sophia, are you ok?' Alana walked towards her.

'I am not sleeping well,' Sophia closed her eyes, 'not since the mention of Mooremarsh,' her eyes flicked open, she glanced over to the house, 'the Ruby Dragon,' she shook her head, 'I think we should keep our thoughts on the task ahead.'

Something is wrong here Feles his fur stood up on end, he nuzzled closer to Sophia.

'Keep close Feles, we will join the others in the garden.' Sophia marched over to the others and they walked into the garden.

Joshua caught Milly's eye, she ran towards the mansion, Joshua grabbed Mathew making his way towards the grand door. Two huge carved iron studded oak doors were overlooked by winged gargoyles. Their massive bodies hung each side staring down at them, daring them to enter the house.

'Imposing aren't they.' Grandad Rose looked up at the gargoyles, 'they were put up in churches in medieval times to ward off evil and stave off rainwater from the foundations of the building. I think these were added during the Victorian times as a gothic feature.' He peered at them a little longer.

'Positively good looking compared to ones on churches,' Joked Priddy, 'in fact, they look like they are laughing at us!'

Grandad Rose moved into the house and into the room called Edward's Hall.

'Wow,' Joshua was hit by the riot of colour from the paintings.

Grandad Rose got out his guide, put on his spectacles and started to talk about the paintings, bringing them alive.

'Let's move on then, there's lots to see.'

Each room was a treasure trove of antiques and curios. They reached the library and Milly strode up to the shelves to examine the books. A red rope sectioned of a space between the books and her. She was dying to touch and smell the old aroma of the leather covers.

'I knew you would like this room. I bet you would devour these books very quickly!' Grandad Rose stood behind her.

'It's amazing, you could spend months in here and never need to leave,' Milly whispered.

'Not me, need my food!' Mathew laughed in the corner.

Joshua was engrossed in some bookshelves. Priddy walked over to see what he was looking at.

'What can you see?' Priddy asked.

'Well, you see that line of books.' Joshua pointed to a line of dark leather books, 'They don't look real, do they.'

Priddy leant as close as the red rope would allow him.

'I see what you mean.' Priddy stretched out his hand and pressed a green book.

The bookcase moved; a door swung open.

Joshua and Priddy looked at each other and said, 'Oh!'

'Now you've done it!' Milly called, looked at the door expecting someone to run into the room.

'What can you see in there?' Mathew asked excited, walked over to examine the discovery.

'I can see a safe!' Joshua smacked Mathew's shoulder.

'Wonder what they keep in there?' Priddy whispered in a conspiratorial tone.

'Just a few documents,' Everyone jumped at this unexpected voice, they turned in unison to be faced with a man in a blue suit.

'I am Mr Wilks, the guide of Overhill Hall.' He held his hand out to Grandad Rose and pumped his hand, 'I think we might have met at few times at the Cirencester History lectures in the library.'

'Yes, I do believe we have.' Grandad Rose beamed across at Mr Wilks.

'The next room houses the Ruby Dragon. I will show you around.' Mr Wilks waved the way,' He leant across the rope and clicked shut the bookcase door, 'You're the first to find that, well done!'

They entered a room, and Mr Wilks walked over to a wall with a row of light switches. Everyone stood around the glass cabinet which housed the Ruby Dragon.

'This is the Ruby Dragon.' Wilks exploded with showmanship.

'Goodness!' Priddy exclaimed struck with awe at the sight of the stone.

Joshua stood with an open mouth, its brilliance made him feel drawn to it, he heard it calling to him, *look at me!*

Joshua felt the muzzle of Prudence on his calf.

Look away, this is bad magic, look away! Her head butted him harder.

'Bet that's worth a bob or two,' Mathew sighed. An eerie sound hit him.

'Can you hear that, the sound of a beating heart?' Mathew looked around the room, the sound was louder, ringing in his ears.

Milly stared into the heart of the stone. Her iris widened in horror. She felt ice cold, a wave of nausea washed over her. She held out her hands to the Ruby Dragon.

Look away, Milly, Look away! Miskunn flew around her wildly. *You will not touch it!*

Milly felt the impact of Miskunn's body on hers.

You will look away. The eagle screamed at her.

They are jealous, just recite the incantation and eternal life will be yours.

The Ruby Dragon looked like it was pulsing brilliant red light.

'Joshua, it harbours Dark Magic.' She felt the coldness of Dark Magic trying to wrap its tendrils around her. Her hand felt sweaty, she wiped them down her coat, her breath became shallow, she was fighting to breath.

'Joshua, help me!' Milly screamed a blood curdling scream, she felt lightheaded, her legs melted like jelly, she gave a terrified stare at her brother. 'Help me!'

'We need to get Milly outside,' Joshua held his sister's arm to steady her.

Grandad Rose took one look at Milly's mottled pallor and helped Joshua guide her to the door.

'Maurice, fetch Mathew, Milly isn't feeling well.' Grandad Rose called to them.

Mathew gazed into the Ruby Dragon. A slap smacked his head, it snapped back, he felt pain in his neck, but he ignored it, he just wanted to look at the Ruby Dragon. Inside the brilliance, something dark moved. It called his name.

Mathew, do you know the incantation, you can have eternal life, just say the spell.

Mathew flinched at the sound of the voice, he felt he was being sucked into a decaying, moldy dream. It made him wretch.

You can stay with me; Eternal life is yours.

'Mr Priddy, Mathew must come too.' Joshua demanded; he nodded his head at Mathew.

Mathew shuffled along shakily, terrified at the dark drowning power he had witness.

Once outside, they stopped for Milly. She doubled up and started to vomit. Wave after wave she retched, finally, she stopped, and they found a bench for her to sit on.

'What's happened is Milly alright?' Sophia came running to the group. She put her staff down to rest against the bench.

Milly looked weakly at Sophia, 'The Ruby Dragon possess Dark Magic.' Milly sat up right. 'I felt it, Dark Magic, trying to get out. Trying to possess me.'

Sophia's eyes narrowed; she took a quick glance at the house. Over the top of Milly's head, she waved to Alana and Bill who were running towards them.

I told you I felt something was wrong. Feles hissed, his fur raised across his spine.

'You are not helping.' Sophia nodded a rebuke at the cat.

'There were stories that the Ruby Dragon had been used for

Dark Magic. There are so many replicas of the original.' Sophia mused, 'it would seem the owners of Overhill Hall own the original. I must report this to the high council. The artifact cannot be left here, they will know what to do.' Sophia waved to Rutger and Jasper who were walking towards them at a quick pace. 'Alana, while we are here, sink your staff into the ground, we will make a ring of protection around the children.'

Rutger reached them and hit his cane into the soft ground. There was a hum, Joshua felt his hair reach out with static.

'We must be diligent. The Ruby Dragon will attract those who hold Darkest of Magic, powerful Dark Magic. We need to get the children away from here.' Sophia pressed a hand to her temple, only now feeling presence of Dark Magic.

'Milly is right. I saw a darkness, something living and evil within the ruby.' Mathew shivered at the ordeal.

'Of course, you are a Doorkeeper, you see all magic.' Joshua mused, 'Come on, let's get going.' He strode off towards the car.

'Wait Joshua, you will walk within the circle of three whilst we are so near Dark Magic.' Sophia lifted her staff out of the soil and slithered it across the ground.

'I think it's time for lunch, some sweet cake is just what we all need.' Jasper smacked his cane at the ground as he walked with Mathew, discussing the different types of cake at the café, as a way of taking his mind away from the Dark Magic he had just encountered.

Sophia watched Milly walk to the car, turned to Rutger, and placed a hand on his elbow to stop his pace.

'That was close, too close. I should have listened to Feles. He detected something.' She looked at the children, 'They need more training. They need to be able to protect themselves when we are not here.'

'They need to fashion their own staffs. We need to see which stone will give them the most strength.' Rutger started to walk away, he paused.

'As you say, they need to be able to protect themselves when we are not here.' Rutger said sagely.

CHAPTER 23
CLARKE CHOOSES HIS PATH

Clarke flicked over the page of his latest superhero comic. He was supposed to be meeting Forrest this morning, he was not looking forward to it, and he knew the reason why. Forrest saw right through him. The old man knew what he was thinking and why he was thinking it. That made him uncomfortable.

'Come on, get a move on. We will be cutting it fine if we are going to meet Forrest on time.' His father's voice called up to him from downstairs.

Clarke swung his feet over the side of his bed, grabbed his walking boots and pulled them on. He stood up and stamped his feet to get a good fit. Looked in the mirror and tussled his hair. He knew the look would annoy his father, but he was in no mood to please him. He grabbed a thick striped jumper and pulled it over his head.

'Clarke!' His father's high pitched exasperated tone made him smile.

Clarke came down the stairs more casually than he felt. His father stood at the bottom of them stabbing his watch with his index finger.

'We will be back after lunch. Do you need me to collect anything?' Erik called to his wife.

'No, just come home safe.' Her voice floated down the hall.

Clarkes mothers soft reply melted his heart a little.

'Come on, let's get going.' His father walked out of the house and to the car.

Clarke deliberated if he should drag his feet, just to irritate his father even more. He was still angry the truth had been hidden from him. The truth of another world, a real world of magic. He decided against it and marched to the car and got inside. They drove for some time in silence, each to their thoughts.

'We're here.' Clarke's dad pointed excitedly in the distance.

Clarke looked in the direction of his father's finger was jabbing; his jaw fell at the sight facing him. In a field was a huge circus, red and white colours gleamed in the distance.

'Forrest wants us to have our own private show.' His father sounded like an excited child.

Clarke cringed at his father's excitement.

'Why now, after all these years?' Clarke sneered churlishly; he regretted the words as soon as he said them.

'You will find out.' His father replied cryptically.

'Welcome to Forrest Circus.' A clown cheered at a gate and waved them in.

Forrest stood outside the big-top and waved to them. His hair hung down his back in a thick ponytail, held at the base of his neck with a purple ribbon. His beard platted with small jewels; a large pearl hung at its tip. In his hand he held his black top hat. He lifted his hat up in the air, and waved to them, summoning them to him.

His father looked across at him.

'Clarke, let him help you understand.' His gaze looked at the spectacular site in front of them. 'We only will get this chance.' He opened the door and left Clarke alone in the car.

Clarke watched his father walk into Forrest's wide embrace and felt a stab of envy.

Your father has never hugged you like that since Forrest has been here. The insidious song sang, *Forrest is your enemy, do not trust him.*

Clarke got out the car, he felt cold, a different type of cold from the weather, a bone gripping cold.

'Come Clarke, be with family, enjoy the show.' Forrest waved him over.

Beware of Forrest, he is not good for you. The song clawed at his ears, wanting him to only listen to it. *He is the reason you nearly died. He is your enemy.*

A girl came out of the big-top, she was dressed in a sea green body suit with a gossamer cape. He recognized her. Nori. She marched up to him, hand on hip.

'Well, show some appreciation. The whole circus is doing this to show gratitude to Forrest.'

Clarke snorted derisory. Nori squared up to him, her eyes blazing.

'There is a lot you don't know about Forrest. So be respectful when you are here.' Nori turned her back on him, her shoulders squared and marched back into the big-top.

Clarke stood still, flabbergasted by Nori's behaviour. What could his grandfather, the man who had neglected his son, to protect him so he said, have done to gain the trust of the circus people? Clarke walked a little quicker and entered the darkness of the circus.

'I will sit in between you, occasionally, I will let you see what I see.' Forrest said cryptically, 'Follow me, its best if we sit a few rows up to get the best views.'

Once settled, a clown came along, overloaded with popcorn and hot dogs. He passed them along and the last hotdog he handed to Forrest, 'Lots of mustard, easy on the onions. Just the way you like them.'

'Thank you, Mortimer.' Forrest smiled at the clown.

The lights were dimmed, a voice announced the beginning of the show. Out of the darkness a brilliant light shone up towards the ceiling. Nori stood alone on a beam with a swing bar in her hand.

'It is with thanks to Forrest, my family were able to leave the slavery of the terrible queen fairy, Tibianna. We are forever thankful; this act is for you.'

Nori proceeded to do twirls and death-defying acrobatics in the air, occasionally, Clarke covered his eyes, thinking she was going to plummet to the ground. She had the grace of a ballerina in the air. The music stopped and Nori threw herself across space onto the ropes hanging down to the ground. Nimbly, she swung down, and landed on her toes. Bowed at Forrest and skipped across the ring and dipped behind a curtain.

Clarke looked at Forrest and was aghast to see one single tear fall down his cheek. He looked away from his grandfather embarrassed he had seen something so intimate.

Six clowns solemnly entered the ring. They bowed at Forrest.

'We are thankful to you Forrest. You hid us from the world, allowed us to live in this family. This act is for you.'

Clarke's eyebrows knitted together. Why had Forrest done so much for so many, yet left his son alone in the world?

Forrest touched Clarke and he flinched from his grandfather's touch. Forrest nodded towards the clowns. Clarke recoiled from the faces of the clowns; they were hideous. His toes scrunched up and scratch the soles of his boots.

'Dark Magic did that to them. They refused to side with a Dark Magic family, so they cursed them. For a time, my magic can protect them from the discrimination of the world, the world judges by what we look like.' He let go of Clarke, 'I cannot protect them for much longer.' He sounded weary.

The clowns juggled, did acrobatics, told a few jokes, bowed, and left the ring.

Each act was the same, an outpouring of gratitude, followed by a performance. They were all brilliant. Clarke could not choose which he liked the best.

The end of the show was spectacular fireworks within the big-top. How they don't burn down the circus with all the sparks, Clarke's mind spun with thoughts on this matter.

'Let's go outside, I want to introduce you to some more of my circus family.' Forrest clapped his hands together. He stood up and walked away not waiting for them to follow.

The sun had hit the midday sky, low and sharp, the brightness hurt Clarke's eyes. Forrest stopped walking and waited for them to catch up.

'Did you enjoy that?' he asked them both, he looked earnest in his desire to impress them with the circus.

'It was great.' Clarke enthused.

'That was amazing.' His father beamed.

'Come and meet some of the family who didn't perform,' Forrest chuckled.

Over the next hour they were introduced to 'people' as Clarke later found out, they were all magical creatures of different realms.

'I don't understand. Why were they paying you so much homage?' Clarke asked.

Forrest stood still and looked away. Clarke thought he looked embarrassed.

'We give homage because of what Forrest has done for us. We are refugees from our magical families for all sorts of reasons. Forrest has given us a home and a purpose.' Nori put her hand in Forrest's, 'now it is time for Forrest to go. It is his time.' She kissed his hand affectionately and left them.

Clarke looked at Forrest quizzically, 'Where are you going?'

Forrest turned a sad gaze on Erik, 'You understand?'

Erik nodded, 'Yes, father.'

'Then explain to Clarke. I am weary now.' Forrest hugged Erik, 'We will meet tomorrow.' He put his hand to his forehead, bowed and left them.

Erik watched his father go. He was bone tired, and now had to deal with Clarke. He had to broach some difficult subjects.

'Come on son, let's get lunch, and have a chat.' Clarke watched his father walk to the car.

'You need to listen to them both.' Nori's voice advised him from behind.

'And what would you know!' Clarke balled his hands into fists in anger.

Nori stood her ground. 'I know two things. You need to forgive, or you will lose all. Dark Magic will destroy you; it is a void of darkness, consuming you without giving anything back, destroying those who love you in the aftermath.'

'You know nothing of us, shut up and go away!' Clarke hissed at her.

'I know Forrest put his life in jeopardy by coming here when he heard you were hurt last year.' She saw the shocked look on his face. 'Yes, you didn't know that did you,' her chin lifted a little higher, 'we hid in Bristol whilst Forrest watched you. He saw the evil woman come to you, but it was too late for him to help you. He sat by your bed when you were alone, he tried to undo the spell she cast upon you.' Nori shook her head, she ran her fingers through her hair, trying to grasp at the words which would make Clarke understand.

'His magic is not the same as Dark or Earth magic. His only hope was to help you walk the right path. A path that is not Dark Magic.' Nori touched his arm, Clarke went to yank it away, but he stopped. He could see Nori in her beauty, her wings spread out, a glow shone around her, she was magnificent, a glorious fairy.

'Make the right choice Clarke.' Nori turned away, 'bye Clarke, we will probably not meet again,' she threw over her shoulder and marched away.

Clarke's mind swam with a jigsaw of news. He didn't know who to believe. He walked slowly to the car, and once again sat in thoughtful silence as his dad drove them to a small café outside of Tetbury.

Sandwiches and lemonade sat on the table in front of Clarke. He watched his dad stir a cup of tea.

'So, Forrest is leaving, when and why?' Clarke asked abruptly.

His father looked up from his cup, 'He is dying. His time has come, he will go back to the realm of the Djinn, when he comes to the end of his days.' His father looked at his cup broodily.

'His realm? I really don't understand. He can't be with you, but he can be with a circus? He leaves you with foster parents but doesn't raise you himself? How does that work?' Clarke said scathingly, felt anger tugging at his insides.

His father sighed. 'Clarke, my life was in danger. He had to hide me, so I would be safe. If at any time it was found out I was the child of a djinn, I would have been kidnapped, and tortured so that my father would appear to save me. They would have enslaved him, to grant them that one wish. My life and his would have been finished.' He took a sip of his tea, 'I am not going to repeat this, or justify his actions anymore.' He met his father's steely gaze, 'What he did, he did for love.'

His father stared into his cup, collecting his thoughts.

'Clarke, you must not get involved with Dark Magic. It tried to destroy our family. We are strong, Dark Magic makes you weak,' he reached out and took a hold of Clarke's hand, 'do you understand? Will you promise not to go down that path?'

Clarke looked down at his father's hand, it was strong, an image of Mooremarsh's frail hand flittered through his mind. He quickly pushed it away.

'I will think it all over. I cannot make a promise that I may break.'

His father let go of his hand as if he had been scorched.

'You have listened to nothing. I cannot help you if you choose that path. No one can help you.' His father got up and went to pay for their food.

Yes, but you do have help. You have my help. Dark Magic will make you powerful, strong, and invincible. The song cut into his thoughts.

'Yes, but you weren't powerful enough for Milly Appleby, she defeated you, so why should I believe you!'

Insolence, you have much to learn. I will teach you in your dreams tonight. You will learn the power of Dark Magic.

Clarke ate the last of his sandwich and washed it down with his drink. Dark Magic was enticing, but he had started to question everything he had been told. His mind was conflicted, he wanted to sit somewhere quiet, so he could sort his thoughts. Did Dark Magic destroy you if you used it? Was the magic of the Djinn not passed down to their children? Why did he feel so much anger when he was in the presence of Joshua Appleby, did his old friend really fail him?

'Come on Clarke, let's go home,' His father looked tired.

Clarke felt guilty. Maybe it was time to forgive his father. For the first time in months, he felt a little warmth in his heart.

There is no forgiveness in Dark Magic, forgiveness is weakness, Dark Magic will give you power. The song sang to him, and he listened.

CHAPTER 24
THE STONES

Joshua watched as Mathew licked the last crumb of cake from his fork.

'Two cakes, three cups of tea, and a pancake, how do you fit it all in?' Joshua shook his head at Mathew.

'Now, Mathew has had a shock, nothing better for a shock than sweet tea and cake!' Jasper waved his lemon drizzle cake expansively.

'Milly isn't stuffing herself like that, and she had and even bigger a shock!'

Milly clutched her hot milk with sweet cinnamon closer to her. Her eyes grew wide, the memory of the Ruby Dragon slipping her defense, she shuddered at the memory and felt cold. A hand touched hers, warm, strong. Her mother's hand.

'Drink up Milly.' Her mother encouraged her.

A bell chimed and Sophia entered the café. She sat down at the table with the others.

'I have dispatched Mr Witherington with a message for the Council of Elders. We will wait to see what they say about the Ruby Dragon.' Rutger pushed a cup of tea her way.

'I have to say, we are impressed that you recognized Dark Magic. We need to keep up you're training so you detect it even faster.' Sophia looked at Milly and took a sip of her tea.

'They have had enough training today. They can start again next week.' Bill held Alana's steady gaze.

'Yes, tomorrow we will have a family day, us, grandad and Maurice if you would like to come over?' Priddy shook his head, 'Mathew will go home, I am sure Jasper that the Anderson's won't mind putting you up if you feel you need to stay with Mathew.' Jasper hunched his shoulders in reply. 'Good, we will all meet after school at Chestnut Cottage on Monday.'

'And if Mooremarsh pays you a visit, and we are not with you?' Sophia spilt the question.

'She will woe the day she comes after my children again. The gloves are off. I will be on the offensive instead of a defensive.' Alana's eyes shone brittle and hard. 'Earth Magic will help defend us, we believe in its power; we will ask Sylvester Bluesky and Prudence to stay in the garden as a precaution.'

Sophia sipped her tea. 'Then, so be it. I will be at our cottage if you need me.'

Rutger scrapped back his chair a little.

'There is one more task for today,' he held a hand up seeing the expression on Bill's face, 'The Choosing of Stones will take place today.'

'Oh, so soon?' Alana's forehead creased, 'I did not choose until I was sixteen.'

'Choosing of the Stones?' Priddy asked.

'You are not of magic; this does not concern you.' Rutger dismissed Priddy.

Priddy sat back in his chair, taken aback at Rutgers response.

'Rutger don't be a rude old fuddy duddy! Maurice Priddy has been involved with the children and the magic surrounding them since they came into magic.' Jasper raised his eyebrows. 'The Choosing of Stones is where the power of Earth Magic chooses a stone with magical properties for a human who has magic. There is no reason for him not to be involved.'

'That sounds interesting.' Joshua said excited.

'You have the box of stone?' Jasper asked Sophia.

Yes, I brought them with me, just in case.' She glanced at Rutger, 'It seemed the right thing to do.'

'Let's get to it. Anything which will help them is a step in the right direction.' Bill stood up and paid the bill for their lunch.

'The Choosing will take place at Chestnut Cottage. Sophia and I will fetch the box of stones from our cottage.' Rutger stood up and left the café.

They arrived at Chestnut Cottage and Joshua looked at the box Sophia was carrying.

'When you have chosen your stone, come into the garden with your stone and choose your branch.'

Alana led them into the house. It felt chilly, the fire stove had cooled. In the living room the coals in the fire grate were dim, she threw a few wood logs onto top to warm the room up. She scuttled into the kitchen and put a log into the fire stove.

'It will be warm in no time.' Alana said and started to rummage around in a drawer and withdrew three bees wax candles.

'Those will do.' Sophia called from the door. 'I think we will use the living room.'

Alana walked through to the living room, lit the candles, and placed them about the room. Sophia followed with a rosewood box and set it onto a low table. Out of her pocket she took a silk scarf, opened the box, and placed the scarf over the box. Milly stood in the doorway watching Sophia.

'Come Milly.' Sophia ordered her.

Milly came to the table, looked at her mother enquiringly. Miskunn sat quietly in the corner.

'How do I choose?' Milly asked.

'The stone will choose you. Put your hand under the silk, touch each stone, choose the stone which feels warm to the touch. It will be the one choosing you.' Sophia instructed; her hand waved to the box.

'It helps if you close your eyes.' She added encouragingly.

Milly tentatively put her hand under the silk, closed her eyes, and focused on the feeling. Some stones felt rough to the touch, some smooth. Slowly her fingers slipped over the stones. Her eyes flicked open. There it was, a stone felt warm, tingling under her fingers. She wrapped her fingers around it and withdrew it from under the silk. A large green stone nestled in the palm of her hand.

'Peridot. This is the stone of Adel the Noble. Its power is legendary amongst the Earth Magic community. It has healing properties.' Sophia whispered. 'Find a branch to make your staff.'

'Shouldn't it go to Joshua; he has more interest in the healing of herbs than me?'

Sophia smiled, 'The stones never lie. There is more than one type of healing Milly.'

Milly left the room, the stone pulsated warmly in her hand.

Mathew poked his head around the door. Sophia waved him in and pointed to a spot on the floor by the table.

Mathew placed his hand under the silk and withdrew it immediately.

'What is wrong?' Sophia asked, her hand touched the amethyst stone which hung about her neck.

'There was an explosion, under the silk.' Mathew grimaced at the sensation.

'I see. Put your hand in and leave it there. Wait for the stone to choose you.'

Do as you are told. Keep your hand there! Gertie swayed by the table. *I can't wait to see which stone chooses you, numbskull!*

Mathew grimaced at Gertie and slid his hand under the silk once more. He closed his eyes, a stone exploded under his fingers, simmered as he turned it in his fingers. He dropped the stone and let his fingers touch the other stones. They lay cold and dormant. His fingers found the lively stone and grasped it. It vibrated in his hand with a tingle which was not unpleasant. Slowly he withdrew his hand, and he turned it over to show Sophia.

'Light of the Universe. That fits given you are a Doorkeeper. The stone is Labradorite, be careful with it.' Sophia whispered.

Mathew marched into the garden to find Milly, clutching the blue green simmering stone.

'It's called the Light of the Universe, it's Labradorite. Pretty really. Apparently, it will give me intuition and illumination.' He looked down at the stone in Milly's hand, 'What about yours?'

Milly looked down dully at the stone in her hand.

'Apparently it has healing properties. It's Peridot, Adel the Noble is its name. Can't see me using it, I am no healer.' She hunched her shoulders.

'You're not noble either!' Mathew scoffed at her.

Joshua entered the room and looked at the silk cloth covering the box. He walked up to the box and pushed his hand expectantly under the cloth, his fingers touched the stones. They were cold. His eyebrows scrunched together, and he looked at Sophia questioningly.

'Sorry Joshua,' she rested a hand on his shoulder, 'there is not a stone here for you.'

Joshua looked away from her hiding his disappointment and jealousy. Why hadn't a stone chosen him?

He felt Prudence at his side, he opened his empty hand showing her a stone had not chosen him.

The stones do not choose everyone. Maybe the stone that has chosen you is not there. Sophia does not have all the stones in that box. She stood in front of him. *You must not be cross.*

'Sophia explained that the stones in that box were the most powerful stones in Earth Magic. It is obvious that I am not worthy of being chosen.' Joshua sulked.

They are not all the most important stones. There are five others. The people who own them are still alive. You will have to wait. Stop sulking it does not become you. Prudence gave a little kick to Joshua's shin, and left Joshua, disappointed with his behavior.

Joshua walked into the garden and hunched his shoulders.

'None of the stones chose me.'

Milly placed the stone in her pocket, 'Why?'

'Sophia said the time was not right for me. Not sure what that means?' He said gruffly, a stinging sensation ripped at his throat, he looked away from her feeling despondent.

'Anyway, they are leaving now. Mathew, dad said to get the things you want to take back, he is driving everyone home.'

Mathew looked sideways at Joshua. 'Ok, won't be long.' He felt awkward, he could see Joshua's disappointment and he didn't know what to say.

Joshua watched Mathew go into the house. Milly stepped forward, he held up his hand. 'It doesn't feel great that a stone didn't pick me, can't say I'm not jealous of not being picked, but I guess there is a reason.' He turned to go back in the house, 'You don't have to hide Adel the Nobel from me.' He grinned at her, 'Anyway, I think dad want's the Elders to go, he is itching to pick up his guitar and sing a few songs.'

CHAPTER 25
HARROW'S END

Mooremarsh pulled on a grey raincoat. The clouds looked heavy with rain, and she did not want to get wet. She grabbed an umbrella from an iron umbrella stand for good measure. Striding into the kitchen, a potion she had made earlier in the day sat on a counter, she grabbed it and slipped it into her pocket.

'A little something for Marcus Harrow,' she laughed to herself and patted the pocket.

She closed the door softly as she left her house. Whisps of white vapour escaped her mouth into the cold winter afternoon. She walked quickly across town and to the small, wooded area where she had told Harrow they would meet. When she arrived, Harrow stood rocking on his toes. She cast an unpleasant look at him. He was not in uniform; she would have to adjust her plan. Her foot trod on a small branch on the floor. It snapped and Harrow turned around to the noise.

'You have not worn your uniform dearest,' She cooed.

Harrow looked confused.

'Not allowed to wear it outside of duties,' he whispered to her; his chin thrust out stubbornly.

'Never mind, you look handsome,' she slipped her hand into his, and noticed he recoiled a little.

'I want to tell you something, but you will have to lean your ear to me.'

Harrow did as he was asked, bent over a little bringing his ear near to her mouth. Mooremarsh sang a spell, Harrow's eyes clouded, and his lips set into a smile.

'Now Marcus, where is your car?'

Marcus lumbered towards his car and opened the door for Mooremarsh to get in.

'Thank you, Marcus.'

They sat in silence on their journey to Overhill Hall. They were soon turning through the large gothic gates into the grounds of Overhill Hall. Mooremarsh stroked her chin. Most visitors had left, a few cars smattered about the carpark.

'Right Marcus, I want the Ruby Dragon. You will steal it for me.' She touched his hand and sang a spell.

'What have you got to do for me?' she stroked his hand, smiling as she watched the hairs on the back of his hand rise.

'I will steal the Ruby Dragon for you.' He smiled at her, intoxicated by her magic.

Harrow lumbered along beside Mooremarsh to the wooden shack and bought them tickets. He stood looking around, the tickets dancing in the wind between his fingers.

'Come on this way.' Mooremarsh walked ahead of him.

Wilks stood at the entrance leaning against the door post. As they approached, he stood up.

'Hello, my name is Wilks. I will guide you around the hall, tell you wonders, explain the fantastic.' He waved his hands theatrically.

'Listen, be a dear, just take us to the room with the Ruby Dragon.' Mooremarsh gave a sarcastic jerky flourish with her hand.

'Yes, yes.' He peered at Mooremarsh a moment, shook his head and nodded in the direction they needed to take.

Wilks led the way to the room where the statue was being exhibited. He stood to one side and let Harrow and Mooremarsh enter.

'Have you never seen anything so magnificent?' Wilks sighed. Mooremarsh gasped as she stood in front of the Jewel.

'I knew it was beautiful, but nothing like this.' She put out her hand to touch the glass, her hand was suspended as it was suddenly wrapped in a vice like hold.

'Pressure pads,' he waved at the cabinet, 'if you touch the glass the alarm goes off.' Mr Wilks beamed proudly.

'So how do you get to touch it if the glass is alarmed' She glared down at Mr Wilks.

'I go to the security cupboard and turn off the alarm.' Mr Wilks monotone voice echoed around the room.

'Go on then. Switch off the alarm.' Mooremarsh sang her spell of obedience to him.

Mr Wilks swayed to and fro. Mooremarsh's eyes narrowed. Wilks was resisting her magic. She needed to press him further.

'I said, you need to switch off the alarm!' She gazed into his eyes, pouring her magic out, slicing through his resistance.

'Go with him, make sure he switches off the alarm.'

Harrow dogged Mr Wilks steps. He watched him flick a switch, as Mr Wilks turned around, Harrow hit him and watch him crumple unconscious to the ground. He returned to Mooremarsh's side.

She handed him a pair of gloves.

'Put these on,' she commanded, 'now smash the glass and retrieve the Ruby Dragon,' she ordered, picking up a small chair and handing it to him.

Harrow looked at the chair, stupefied. He lifted it mechanically and slammed it into the glass. The sound of smashing glass crashed around the room. Harrow stood limp with the chair in his hands, he dropped it with a thud. Reaching in he took the Ruby Dragon off its pedestal and gave it to Mooremarsh.

'Thank you.' She purred, she withdrew a handkerchief from her pocket and brushed glass fragments from her prize.

Raising her hand, she let the light captured it.

'You are coming home with me,' she sighed, 'come Harrow, we must finish our afternoon. We need to drive to your house, there is some unfinished business we need to finish.'

'What is that?' Harrow looked down at her, a stupid grin on his face.

Mooremarsh placed the artifact into her bag and marched to the door. Harrow looked after her waiting for an answer to his question.

'Come on Harrow don't keep me waiting!' her voice echoed down the hall.

Mooremarsh marched out into the open as if nothing had just happened. No one was in sight, she continued casually to Harrow's car. She looked back and watched him walk stiffly towards her. Her toe kicked the snow impatiently into a small mound in front of her.

'Well, your part is paid, now for your reward.' She gloated as Harrow came closer.

'Open the door, we need to hurry!'

Harrow fished around in his pockets, the jangling sound of keys, announced he had found his car keys. Automatically he opened the passenger side, then the driver's side and looked at Mooremarsh across the top of the car.

'Thank you dearest, I really enjoyed that. Now let's go to your house for a late lunch.' She swung herself into the seat and waited for Harrow.

The car coasted its way to a stop in front of a small stone brick house. Mooremarsh lent forward and wrinkled her nose. Not much for a policeman she thought. Turning in her seat, she took in the road. All was quiet, she smiled, no one would see her go into Harrow's house.

'Let's go in then.' She murmured.

Harrow got out of the car and opened the door. He stood to one side as Mooremarsh passed him. Mooremarsh looked around the tidy house, a little spartan for her taste.

'You want some tea?' Harrow asked her. He shook his head again, like he was trying to remember something just out of his reach.

Mooremarsh's eyes narrowed. The spell was weakening. She needed to perform the Sleep of the dead now. She slipped her hand into her pocket and felt the crisp paper and withdrew it.

'Yes, be a dear and make us a pot of tea.' She cooed to him.

Harrow turned and filled a kettle and placed it on a stove. Mooremarsh undid the folded paper and brought it to her lips.

'Harrow,' she whispered.

He turned around and she stepped closer.

'This is for you,' she blew the contents of the paper and muttered a spell under her breath.

Harrow screamed a blood curdling scream; it was loud and guttural.

Mooremarsh kept saying her spell. Harrow fell to the ground, a heavy silence followed. He was still, apart from his eyes which moved restlessly under his eyelids. She kicked him with her toe.

'Good, you will sleep the sleep of the dead forever. Nice meeting you Harrow.' Mooremarsh turned off the heat on the stove and moved the kettle to one side. She examined the room, satisfied she had left nothing behind, she left Harrow to his fate.

Mooremarsh stepped into the street; the sun was low; it was starting to get dark. She walked hurriedly towards the High Street. She would have something to eat at the café, it would be good to have an alibi she thought. A smirk wiped her face she could enjoy the secrets of the Ruby Dragon after she had eaten. As she turned into the high street and saw the Appleby's and the Elders getting into cars. She shrank back a little into a doorway.

'Don't want to meet them, not when victory is mine!' she hissed into the air.

Mooremarsh's hand caressed the Ruby Dragon in her bag, her hand shook uncontrollably with anticipation. Her predatory eyes gleamed, waiting for her prey to spring its trap.

'Soon we will meet, and I will savor the moment when I destroy you all.'

Her fingers reached up and stroked an old silver locket hanging about her neck, it held a charm within it. She chanted a spell to make sure they would not detect her dark magic. The sound of engines rattling to a start, grey exhaust fumes, and she watched two cars drive away from the café. Once they turned a corner, she left her hiding place and walked up the small hill. The cafés windows were steamy, and she couldn't see in clearly. She pushed the door, and a small bell rang announcing the arrival of a customer. Taking off her raincoat she hung it on an awaiting peg and sat down at a table. There were two people eating, she chewed the side of her mouth, well, maybe two people would remember her instead of a packed room. The waitress from the other day approached her table. Mooremarsh smiled to herself. Now she would remember me!

'What pie's do you have?' Mooremarsh asked, she did indeed feel hungry after the excitement of stealing the jewel.

'Apple or blackberry,' the waitress replied surly.

'I think Apple, lots of cream, some of us can take cream without gaining a large girth,' she gave a cursory glance at the waitress's stomach, raised an eyebrow, and went on, 'also, a cheese and pickle sandwich, and a large pot of tea.'

'That all?' sneered the waitress waspishly.

Mooremarsh looked at the watch on her wrist.

'It's too early for anything else.' She saw the waitress look at the clock on the wall. 'That will be all thank you.'

Mooremarsh watched the waitress walk away, she placed her fingers into a pyramid. 'Alibi achieved I think.'

She spent a long time eating, issuing the odd stinging remark for everyone to hear. The waitress came to her table and slapped down the bill.

'We close in ten minutes,' She gave Mooremarsh a mocking smile, turned and walked away.

Mooremarsh examined the bill, threw down the right amount of money and left the café into the new blanket of snow coating the street. She took in a deep breath, sucking in the crisp air. Now she could settle in and enjoy the Ruby Dragon she smiled to herself.

Her breathing was heavy after walking at a pace to get home. Opening the gate, she ran up to the front door. Her keys were already waiting impatiently in her fingers. The door seemed to take an eternity to open. Pushing it closed behind her, she strode into the kitchen, and she set her bag on the table. She threw off her leather boots and smiled as they clanked on the floor. Her feet had been released from the torment of ill-fitting boots. She squeezed her frozen toes, so the blood would freely flow in them after the tight confines of her boots. She gave them a wiggle, satisfied at the feeling as they warmed up. Pushing herself away from the table she walked out of the kitchen and ran upstairs to her bedroom. Slipping open a floorboard, she took out a red bound book. Mooremarsh flicked the pages between her fingers and stopped at the back of the book. She went over to her drawers, and rummaged through the contents, her fingers found what she was looking for, the cold steel of a knife. She took it out of the drawer and judged its sharp edge against her thumb.

'Feels good enough,' her hand trembled in anticipation.

She slid the blade down the edge of the paper binding and watched it peel away. A piece of yellowed parchment was exposed.

'There you are, told you we would meet again.' She lifted the thin parchment from its hiding place. 'Glad I hid you from prying eyes! I have the Ruby Dragon, it's with our family once again. I will not be so tardy with you.'

She walked carefully downstairs; making sure the delicate parchment was not damaged. Entering the kitchen a light draft caught the edges of the paper, Mooremarsh held her breath worried it would tear. The parchment fluttered still in her hand, she exhaled realising she had been holding her breath. She continued into the room and set the delicate paper down on to the table next to the Ruby Dragon. Sitting down on a wooden chair she reached out and pulled the jewel closer to her. The light was too dim to examine it properly, she got up and switched on the kitchen light, strode over to the window, and pulled the curtains shut.

'Don't want anyone to see us!' she crept up to the red shining Dragon. Lifting it up to the light, the air caught in her throat. She could hear it talking to her, it felt hot in her hand.

Delvera, do you know the incantation, you can have eternal life, just say the spell.

Mooremarsh gasped in excitement, it knew her name!

'Yes, I have the incantation.' She whispered feverishly.

You have something more than that. You have another force energy, the energy of another soul?

'Yes, I do, but I will not need another's energy now that I have you.' Mooremarsh picked up the parchment, her hands were sweaty with anticipation.

Wait! The Ruby Dragon screamed at her, it's blood red whirled within it. *Wait!*

'No, you are mine. You will give me eternal life!' she screamed at it hysterically.

She shouted out the incantation at the Ruby Dragon, saliva dripped down her chin.

'You are mine; eternal life is mine; you cannot undo this now.' She laughed and rocked on her chair. 'I have done it!' she tore the silence with her wretched scream.

She panted hard, her hands trembled, she had achieved her feat. Putting the parchment on the table, her heart was thudding wildly in her chest, her vision became blurry.

Delvera. The Ruby Dragon called to her. *Delvera.*

Mooremarsh rested her hands against the table.

'I have eternal life; I have a lifetime to master Dark Magic.' She sang to the room, her arms splayed apart, then she drew them close and hugged her body tightly.

Delvera, you must hear me, I have something to tell you.

Mooremarsh wiped her chin, sat back, and studied the Ruby Dragon. It no longer shone with a deep red, there was a speck of black in its core. She pulled it closer, her eyes squinting to see what was within it. The darkness slid around in the jewel, it felt cold in her hands. Mooremarsh shook it but the darkness did not move, it seem to solidify into a mass.

Delvera, I tried to tell you.

Mooremarsh felt a cold sweat on her brow. Her breath came in rasps.

'Tell me what?'

I cannot give you what you wish for. I cannot give you eternal life.

'No, that's not true, I repeated the incantation, you must obey and give me eternal life.'

Mooremarsh grabbed the Ruby Dragon and shook it violently.

I cannot give you eternal life because you carry two souls. You are not of this life now. Another realm owns you. They will come for you when it is time. You can never possess me or force me to give you what you want.

'It's not true!' she screamed, her fingers curled tighter on the Ruby Dragon, 'you are lying.'

She smashed the jewel against the table, 'you are trying to deceive me!'

No, you have become an Energy Vampire. The magic within will not help you. You are not worthy. You have deceived yourself; you did not read the conditions Htun left. If you had, you would know that what you have done has changed you.

Mooremarsh threw the jewel at the wall.

You cannot have this magic! The jewel goaded her.

Mooremarsh rushed to a cupboard and threw open the doors. She dragged out a hammer.

'If I can't have your power, then no one else will.'

She brought the hammer down on the jewel and kept pulverizing it till nothing was left. Sitting back on the floor, she watched the fragments of ruby turn to dust. She had broken the spell. The Ruby Dragon was no more. It could not give her eternal life.

'No, no, no!' She cried rocking her body.

She stopped rocking and sat deadly still. A thought crossed her mind, a terrible grin wrecked her face.

'I know someone who can give me eternal life,' her fingernails scratched the floor, 'and I will have the power, no one can stop me!'

CHAPTER 26
HARROW'S HELP

Gertie sat on top of the Abbey enjoying the late afternoon wind. She needed to be on her own after the events at Overhill Hall. She lifted her wings and allowed the cold air to ruffle her feathers. A car driving through the street caught her attention. Its headlights shone out in the dusk of the early evening, lighting up the white snow and the black tracks in the road in front of it. Gertie pushed off the steeple feeling the air beneath her wings and followed the car. The car stopped and she came to a rest on the roof on a house on the opposite side of the street. Two people got out of the car, a man, and a woman. The man's gait was strange, wooden, he proceeded to a house. He drew out some keys from his pocket and opened a blue front door. The woman stood behind him, looking impatient, she followed him into the house.

Now that looks interesting, being an inquisitive crow, she decided to investigate.

Gertie flew down to the pavement, hopped up onto the windowsill, and smelt the air. Nothing seemed to be happening in the front room. Curious, she flew to the back of the house and peeped through the kitchen. A woman stood sideways to her; she couldn't see her face. The man turned around, and the woman blew something into the man's eyes. Gertie felt a tidal wave of ice-cold air hit her. She recognized it immediately and hopped from foot to foot. The man was in danger. The women started to whisper into the man's ear. Gertie came closer to the window, trying to hear what the woman was whispering, but she couldn't make out the words. The man crumpled to the floor, and the woman kicked the man. Gertie flapped her wings in alarm, mesmerized by the scene she continued watching. The woman spoke louder, and this time Gertie could make out the words.

'Good, you will sleep the sleep of the dead forever. Nice meeting you Harrow.' The sickening shrill voice split the air.

Her feathers stood away from her body, the static of Dark Magic electrified her, she bowed her head in pain. Gertie shrieked and flew back to the rooftop; she lost her footing as she landed and slipped down a few roof tiles. She still felt the smack of Dark Magic. She was terrified, for a moment she could not move.

I must tell Mathew and the Elders.

Gertie pushed off the roof and her wings beat hard against the air. Chestnut Cottage came into view, she was glad Joshua and Milly were in the garden, but she really wanted Mathew and hoped he had not already left. Unlike her usual graceful landing, she landed with a thump and fell onto her chest. Struggling to get up, she beat her wings to help herself.

'Hello Gertie, we have just got home.' Milly called out to the crow.

Is Mathew here? I need to see him, Gertie gabbled, *Get the Elders, I must talk to the Elders, hurry.* She became hysterical, beating her wings frantically. *Something terrible, terrible! I want Mathew!* She sobbed.

Jasper came out of the house, the others following on his heals. 'We heard a commotion.' Jasper stopped, seeing the distress of the crow.

Dark Magic. The woman performed Dark Magic; the man has fallen into the sleep of the dead.

Mathew came forward and stroked Gertie's wing.

'Be calm Gertie. Can you show us where the man is?'

Gertie squawked several times and placed her other wing over her head. Prudence arrived at her side.

Gertie, think of your responsibility. You must show them where the man is. Prudence stamped her foot.

Gertie huddled against Mathew. He stroked the back of her head.

'We do not have time for this!' Rutger banged his cane into the ground, sparks went flying.

'She is scared.' Alana stepped forward, gently she touched the crow, 'Gertie, show Mathew where you saw the man. He may need our help.'

Gertie took her wing away from her face. *Follow me.*

Mathew felt her tremble. 'Gertie, be brave, they will all be with you.'

Sophia turned to Bill, 'Would you drive us, please.' Sophia looked at Joshua and Milly, 'Alana, I think its best if you and the children stay here,' she rested her gaze on Mathew, 'Mathew, you will stay here too, safety in numbers.'

Joshua looked mutinously at Sophia. 'It is for the best, go inside Joshua with your mother.'

'Come on Joshua. We can set up some more charms around the place.' Milly grabbed his arm and pulled him towards the house.

Prudence and I will stand guard in the garden. The deep growl of Sylvester Bluesky gave Alana some comfort that her friend was here with them.

I assume Miskunn is here too? The wolf rested his gaze on Milly.

'Yes, Miskunn is here. She is staying in the house with us.' Milly answered.

Bill and the Elders got into the car, and Mathew bent down to the crow. 'You will be safe; the Elders will look after you.' He ruffled her neck, 'I know how fast you fly, keep an eye on them so they don't lose you.'

Mathew was rewarded with a gentle peck on his thumb from the crow. Gertie waved her wings and took to flight. Bill kept an eye on her, which was quite difficult when he was also driving.

Gertie landed on a roof and pointed her beak towards the house with Dark Magic.

Bill got out the car and took off his hat.

'This is Marcus's house. He doesn't practice Dark Magic.' Bill scratched his head.

'You stay here. We will go across and investigate.' Rutger pushed Bill to one side. Bill pursed his lips not liking Rutgers dominating attitude, but he knew he was not equipped to deal with magic.

The Elders approached the house cautiously. At the window Jasper quickly peered in. No one was in the living room.

'What now?' He asked.

'We knock at the door, see who answers our call,' Sophia tapped on the door with her staff.

Sophia, Dark Magic has been here. Feles meowed at her.

There was no answer. She closed her eyes to detect Dark Magic. She felt the sour taste of its distant presence. She spat out the taste.

'Feles is right. It has been here. Try the door, Rutger.'

Rutger gingerly put his hand on the doorknob and turned it. The door swung open.

'Hello, anyone in?' He called out. There was no reply, so he stepped inside. 'Come on, follow me.'

Once inside they walked down the tiny corridor and into the kitchen.

'No!' Sophia gulped as she looked down at Maurice Harrow's still body.

'Well, is he alive?' Rutger asked, his eyebrows anxiously knitted together.

Sophia examined him; It was the eyes which gave it away, the terrible movement of his eyeballs under their lids. She felt cold and sick, she knew Harrow was suffering the Sleep of the Dead.

'He is alive, but we have a problem.' She looked up from Harrows still body, 'He is suffering the Sleep of the Dead, he needs a magical relative to undo the spell.'

Jasper held out his hand, Sophia took it gratefully and stood up.

'I will need to consult with the family trees to see if he has any relatives alive who can help him.' She turned as Bill entered the room. He pushed passed them and dropped to his knees and shook Harrow's arm.

'Wake up Marcus.' He moaned. 'What is wrong with him.'

The silence was painful, he looked at Sophia.

'He has the Sleep of the Dead. If we cannot find a magical relative blood line, we will never wake him. He will eventually die.' Sophia looked past Bill at the still body on the floor.

'We can do nothing here. It is best we leave and not be discovered here.' Rutger looked around the room. 'The question is, what has he been involved in?'

Bill looked up at Rutger, 'He was with a woman, Milly found the spell book after the woman left. I assume it is her?'

Rutger leaned on his cane, 'Maybe.'

Bill got up and went to the telephone. 'I am phoning for an ambulance, you had better all go. He is my friend, and I will not leave him here alone.' He picked up the receiver, dialed 999 and heard the quick response of the operator.

'We will walk back to Alana and tell her what has happened.' Rutger suggested.

Sophia looked once more at Harrow.

'No, I will not go with you. I will go right away to Salisbury; the family trees of all Earth Magic families are in my study at home.' She drew her cloak about her.

Bill put down the receiver. 'You need to go; I'd imagine they might send out a policeman seeing as Marcus is a police sergeant.' He pulled a chair away from the table and sat down. 'I will come home as soon as I am finished here.'

'Be careful Bill, she may still be close.' Jasper looked concerned. 'I will stay here just in case she comes back. Bill, you will need some protection.'

Rutger thought about the plan, to split up was dangerous, the power of three was strong. There was no other way to go on.

'Sophia, I will walk to the bus stop with you and wait for the bus.'

Sophia interrupted him, 'No, go straight to Alana, it is there that you are needed, I appreciate your offer.' She touched his arm, 'You know that I am right.'

Rutger nodded and looked her in the eyes.

'Keep safe, Light of Winter, Sophia'

She placed her hand on his, 'Light of Winter, Rutger.'

In the distance they heard the shrill of a bell.

'Go now, they will be here soon.' Bill urged them.

Jasper sat down at the table with Bill as Sophia softly closed the door behind her and Rutger.

'I will say if we are questioned that I am here visiting Alana, my cousin. We came to town to meet Harrow as you had to collect a book from him. We found him in this state.' Jasper turned to a pecking on the window.

Gertie sat trembling on the windowsill. *I am going back to Mathew.*

'No Gertie, you must be brave. I need you to stay just in case I need to send a message to Alana. Go sit on the roof across the road.' Jasper replied.

I don't want to! Her head gigged side to side.

'You will do as you are told!' Jasper's voice thundered around the room.

You are not my magical human, she replied huffily.

'No, but I am your Elder, if you don't go and keep watch now, I will ask Sylvester Bluesky to deal with you. Now go onto the roof!' Jasper sounded dangerous.

Bully! Gertie stuck out her beak and flew up to the rooftop.

A banging at the door announced the arrival of the ambulance. Bill got up and threw Harrow a look. He hated seeing his friend in this state. With quick strides he walked down the hall and threw open the door.

A nurse stood on the pavement along with a member of the ambulance crew.

'Come in, this way.' Bill turned on his heels and led them to the kitchen.

He heard a sharp intake of breath from the nurse. Harrow's mottled skin, flickering eyelids was a frightening sight.

'What happened?' The nurse asked with clipped professionalism.

'We found him on the floor like this.' Bill kept the explanation short.

The nurse reached down and took Harrows pulse, felt his brow.

'Fetch a stretcher, we need to get him to hospital.' The nurse stood up.

'Do you know what's wrong with him?' Bill asked, feeling a little foolish as he did know the answer to that question.

'No, but the doctor will examine him. What is his name?'

Bill spent the next few minutes giving the nurse Harrows details.

'Let me through please.' Demanded a gruff voice in the hall.

A man entered the kitchen. He didn't notice Harrow on the floor but followed the nurse's stare.

'Harrow! What has happened?' His eyes flicked around the room and rested on Bill. 'Well?'

'We have no idea what has happened. We were supposed to meet Marcus here. The door was open, we knocked, when there wasn't an answer, we came in and found him on the floor. I immediately phoned for an ambulance.' Bill answered Stone.

'Was there anyone in the street when you arrived?' Stone glanced at Harrow and looked away. The sight of one of his officers in such distress made him uneasy.

'No, we didn't see anyone.' Bill replied.

'I see.' Stone turned his gaze to Jasper. 'Who are you?'

'I am visiting Bill, and wanted to see Malmesbury, so I came along with him.' Jasper answered coolly.

'I see. Thank you for your help.'

'I really do need to get Mr Harrow to the hospital.' The nurse demanded, she turned to the ambulance men in the hall, 'Get him on the stretcher,' when they hesitated, her voice raised, 'Now!'

Stone nodded, Harrow was carefully put onto the stretcher and into the ambulance.

'You can both go now. I will lock up.' Stone nodded dismissively.

Bill and Jasper left the house and got into the car.

'Let's get going, we might meet Rutger on the way,' Bill started the car. 'Glad Maurice Priddy wasn't here. He went through this last year.'

Bill revved the engine and pulled away, leaving Inspector Stone looking after them as they drove up the road.

CHAPTER 27
SOME THINGS ARE NOT AS THEY SEEM

Joshua walked ahead of his sister and Rutger. He held a brown paper bag in his hand, it contained a preparation of herbs he had to deliver for his mother. He came to the lane which led up to Anderson farm and run up the short lane to the gate. Mathew was just coming out of the house and waved to him.

'Come on Jasper, Joshua is here.' Mathew called into the house.

Milly and Rutger finally arrived; Joshua could hear the elder grumbling with each step.

'Why couldn't Bill have run the herbs over in his car? I know Alana had to finish some orders making soaps and other herb teas, so she had very little time.' Rutger huffed.

'The telephone call to Mum asking for the herb tea didn't come until Dad had left for the garage. The lady is not at all well. Bit of an emergency order for Mum.' He looked slyly at Milly and grinned, 'Anyway, we can all do with the exercise.'

'You wait till you get to my age!' Rutger grumbled back.

Joshua sighed. He found it hard to have his moments restricted and dogged by the elders, even if it was for his safety. Mathew marched across to him, wrapped his scarf tight about his neck.

'Too cold to be out,' Jasper called, wrapping his coat tightly about himself, 'I was sitting in front of a nice fire!' he stamped his feet to warm them.

Mathew raised his eyebrows; Milly caught his look and shrugged her shoulders back at him.

'Dad got an early call, Mr Green needs his van tomorrow for deliveries. We usually make the deliveries for Mum.' Milly quipped.

'Hmph!' Rutger grunted.

Mathew opened the gate and let Jasper go on ahead.

'I think after we deliver that little package of yours, we will need a hot chocolate at that lovely café to fortify ourselves for the journey back.' Jasper laughed jovially.

'I think we will pop in on Bill first, find out when he is finished so we can get a lift back!' Rutger grumbled.

The walk to town was quiet, apart from Rutgers complaining about his feet, and Jasper making observations about the countryside. Joshua and Milly didn't look at each other, they knew they were bound to laugh. Soon they passed Bill's garage and Rutger went inside.

'Bill?' Rutger called.

Bill came out the back with a dirty rag in his hands.

'Rutger, is there anything wrong?' Bill sounded a little alarmed at Rutgers presence.

'No, no. Joshua is delivering this herbal preparation for Alana.' He pointed at the package in Joshua's hand with his cane, 'I just wondered how long you will be.' Rutger looked over his shoulder at the yellow van, with the words Mr Green, fresher groceries delivered to you, painted in green on the side.

Bill scratched his head. 'I guess I will be another hour. I could collect you or you could all wait here while I finish.'

'We will be in the café, should we wait for you there?' Rutger was hopeful, his feet were playing up today, the walk back would cripple him he thought.

Bill saw a moment of pain pass over Rutger's face.

'I should be with you in an hour. I will press the horn when I am outside.' Bill smiled.

'I am really grateful, Bill.' Rutger lifted his cane and walked back outside to the group.

'Let's carry on then.' Jasper walked on.

In the high street Milly looked at Joshua. 'What is the address?'

'It's at the top of the hill out the other side of Malmesbury.' Joshua eyes widened with dawning realisation.

Milly stopped dead still. 'Not Mooremarsh's street, surely?'

Joshua looked down the High Street and up at the hill where Mooremarsh's house sat. He read the label again.

'Afraid we have to walk past it. We could go the long way around,' Joshua cast a glance at Rutgers feet, 'Do you want to stay here?' Joshua looked concerned for his sister.

'No, if we have to walk past it, we walk past it.' Stuttered Milly, she rubbed her arms, memories from the past flittered through her mind.

'Can you summon Miskunn. She might make you feel a little more confident.' Joshua suggested.

I am here. Never worry, I am never far away. The eagle flew past her and perched on a nearby roof top.

Coward, I will go and see if there is Dark Magic about. Gertie jumped up and down on the spot.

'No Gertie, you will stay with us.' Mathew commanded.

Scaredy cat! Gertie flew up to the roof and sat there in a huff.

'I will walk in front, Jasper to the rear. We believe Mooremarsh maybe around, so it's best if we proceed with caution when we are near her house.' Rutger became alert.

Walking up the hill Rutger held out his cane, he could detect no Dark Magic.

'Do you feel anything Milly,' He rested his gaze on her.

Milly closed her eyes. She felt the cold air on her skin, but other than that, nothing.

'No, I don't feel anything.' She replied shakily.'

'Good, we proceed.' Rutger decided.

'That's her house.' Joshua pointed at a house. He shivered remembering the power of the Dark Magic she wielded.

'Well, I'm walking on the opposite side of the street, just looking at her house gives me the creeps.' Mathew shivered.

Coward! Gertie crowed from a rooftop.

Mathew looked up at the crow and shook his head, 'No, not a coward, just cautious.' He whispered under his breath.

Joshua paled; his breath caught in his throat. Mooremarsh's door opened slowly, a young woman stepped out. She closed the door behind her, turned and blinked seeing them for the first time. Jasper stood in front of Mathew, Rutger walked casually in front of Milly and Joshua. The woman opened the gate and stepped onto the street.

'Good morning. I am new round here. Name is Petula, Petula Greensborough.' She cocked her head, 'I don't believe we have met.' She waited expectantly for an answer.

Rutger looked at her, summing her up.

'Nice to meet you Petula, how come you are in Delvera Mooremarsh's house?' he was direct in his questioning.

Her eyes widened, Rutger thought he detected irritation behind her veiled eyes.

'This is my mother's house, Delvera Mooremarsh was her tenant and left, poof, just like that. I needed somewhere to stay, so I am here for a while.' Her nose rose a fraction, 'I have to say you are rather nosey.' She sniffed rudely.

'Not nosey, inquisitive. Nice to have met you. Good day. Petula.' Rutger walked away, pushing Joshua and Milly along in front of him.

Mathew stood in a trance. He saw a different scene from the others. He trembled, across the road stood a young woman, behind her hovered a hideous, frightening creature. He clutched his stomach, it ached with fear, his throat closed, and he gasped for air, he felt Jasper's hand on his shoulder.

'Come on Mathew, we have to get going if we are to have that hot chocolate.'

Mathew heard Gertie squawking overhead, he took his eyes off the creature and walked in the direction Jasper was pushing him. Mathew turned back and there stood a young woman. He screwed his eyes up, not believing what he had just seen. What was the creature? His mother would have probably called it a hag. He walked faster after Milly and caught up with her.

'Did you feel it?' He asked her, he was sweating even though it was cold.

'I didn't feel anything.' Milly looked at Mathew's drawn face, her eyes widened, scared she had not detected Dark Magic.

Joshua turned into another street and stopped in front of a green door. A gleaming brass knocker sat proudly on the door. Hand on a brass knocker Josher gave three polite knocks.

'This is it.' He noticed Mathew's pallor, 'What's wrong with you?'

Mathew was about to reply when the door opened. A woman in a tweed suit stepped forward. Her red rimmed eyes darted to the small brown parcel Joshua was holding.

'Ah, you must be Alana's boy. Just a moment.' Her voice was hoarse. 'I'll just get your mother's money.' She walked down the hall coughing, and soon returned with her purse.

'Two shillings, I believe.' She placed the money in Joshua's hand. 'An extra thruppence for you. Thank you, your mum's remedies are the only thing which touches my coughs. Thank you.' The woman briskly shut the door.

Joshua stuffed the money in his pocket.

'Now, what's wrong with you.' He turned to Mathew concerned.

Mathew remained silent, words stuck in his throat, he just shook.

'It's the magic of the Doorkeeper, it's not easy to control. He has seen magic we have not detected.' Jasper took Mathew's elbow.

'The woman, Petula Greensborough, she wasn't on her own, there was a hideous creature, in the form of a woman behind her. The creature had the magic of an old hag!' Mathew shrugged off Jaspers hold on him, 'Don't ask me how I know it was a hag, I've never seen one before, I just know it was.' He rubbed his mouth horrified at the vision he had just seen.

'Is it Mooremarsh?' Milly whispered, looking around.

Mathew turned his gaze on her. 'No, not Mooremarsh something even more terrible.'

'Well, she did say she was related to Mooremarsh.' Joshua stroked his chin. 'Maybe, she is a different branch of the family with some sort of terrible magic.'

'No, there is only Earth Magic and Dark Magic amongst us humans. If she has neither, she is from another realm. This area of Malmesbury is off limits now.' Rutger held his hand up, 'Don't ask me about it, that is Sophia's knowledge. In the meantime, we forgo the hot chocolate and make our way back to the garage. For the moment, it is better for us to wait there.' Ruger noticed Jasper's fallen face. 'I am sure Alana will make us all hot chocolate at her house!'

'Don't you think we should tell the police, if she is the woman who was with Sargent Harrow when I found the book, the police should know.' Milly remarked.

'You're right Milly. Unfortunately, I don't think they can help.' Rutger thinking it over, 'we don't want anyone else to get hurt by magic. We will keep this to ourselves.' He tapped his cane on the ground. 'Is there another way back so we don't pass Mooremarsh's house?'

Joshua scratched his head, thinking of an easier route.

'Yes, follow me.' Joshua looked at Mathew, worried by his pallor, his hands were shaking.

'I'm ok, it was just a bit of a shock.' Mathew shuddered; Milly placed a protective arm through his. He gave her a smile, appreciating the gesture.

'I think we should go to the café; Dad is expecting to meet us there.' Milly kept an eye on Mathews drawn face, 'Like Jasper says, something sweet is good for a shock,' she nodded at Mathew.

'Let's see how it goes. This way back takes a little longer, doesn't it?' Rutger looked down the hill.

The new route did take longer, by the time they reached the café, Bill was waiting for them. As they drew nearer, he knew by the look on their faces something had happened. He opened all car doors.

Rutger held up his hand, 'Not now Bill, wait till we get home.'

Bill clenched his teeth together; he hated the way Rutger addressed him. Jasper squashes in the back with the others. Bill got into the car and looked in the rear-view mirror at Joshua and Milly.

'You both OK?' he asked them.

'Yes, Dad, no harm done, it's Mathew, we need to get him home to mum.' Milly said quietly.

'I see.' Bill turned on the ignition, 'We'll be home soon, then you can tell what this is all about.'

Joshua and Milly nodded silently in the back, each to their own thoughts.

'Of course, I will make hot chocolate for everyone, the sweetness will do Mathew good.' Jasper offered.

Rutger grunted at the elder and kept his own council.

'Sounds like a good idea.' Milly gave Mathews arm a reassuring squeeze.

CHAPTER 28
MATHEW'S GIFT

Joshua felt the smack of a snowball in his back.

'Four nil,' hollered Mathew punching the air with his fist, he moved away from his position by the barn.

Joshua spun around, annoyed he had yet to land an icy mass on either Mathew or his sister.

Splat. A lighter ball landed on his thigh.

'Six two to me I think,' Milly ducked a flying ball from Mathew. 'You'll have to do better than that' she chuckled.

'Mathew, could I talk to you?' a quiet voice caught their attention.

Nori stood at the gate. She looked pale.

'Sure, come into the house.' Mathew looked across at Joshua. 'We need a cup of tea to warm us all up!'

Joshua looked away; it didn't hurt quite as much being near her. He brushed off the snow from his clothes.

'Actually, I need to speak to you alone.' She closed the gate behind her.

'Don't mind us, we will go and see if we can collect any eggs, that is the reason we came out here.' Joshua walked up to the barn door and grabbed a basket they had left there before they got involved in their snow fight.

'Come on Milly, give me a hand.' Joshua opened the door and stepped in.

Milly looked across at Nori, shrugged her shoulders and followed her brother into the barn.

'What do you think she wants with Mathew,' he huffed jealously.

Milly fished around in the hay for eggs.

'Not sure, must be important, the circus has moved from Tetbury, I think it's over the other side of Cirencester now.' Her fingers touched a round smooth shell and she scooped three eggs out. She placed them gently in the basket. They spent the next half an hour looking in all the usual places for eggs, Milly even found a few new places the hens had discovered to lay their eggs.

'What do we do now, go into the house and disturb their cosy discussion?' Joshua moaned sarcastically.

Milly looked across at him, he felt uncomfortable under her scrutiny.

'Nori was honest with you Joshua. She didn't lead you on, and she explained how fairies behave in relationships. She must have had real feelings for you if she didn't want to hurt you.' Milly said simply.

Joshua whipped around. 'What would you know, the only relationship you have had is with your books!' he was sorry as soon as he uttered the words, Milly looked pained.

'You did not have a relationship with Nori other than friendship.' She replied quietly, 'You wanted more from the relationship, you wanted her as your girlfriend, Nori said no.'

'Yeah, but it still hurts.' Joshua picked up the basket.

'You were enchanted, fairies don't love the same way as us. She saved you from yourself.'

'Sorry, I shouldn't have lashed out like that.' Joshua offered by way of an apology, 'not sure what came over me.'

'No, you shouldn't.' She walked to the barn door and pushed it, the door was now wedged, she pushed harder, and it flew open.

'It's starting to come down a bit thick now.' Milly looked at the snow collecting in front of the barn door.

They walked back to the house in silence. Milly still smarted from Joshua's attack. Mrs Anderson opened the door and waved them in.

'You too look frozen! Get in front of the fire and I will get you a cup of tea.' She took the basket of eggs from Milly, 'You can tell its winter, those hens aren't laying as many eggs as usual.'

Jasper and Mr Anderson were engrossed in a game of Draughts at the kitchen table. Joshua took off his coat and laid it on the back of a chair and stood by the kitchen fire.

Clip, clip, clip! Mr Andersons handheld a black draught and removed three of Jasper's red ones from the board.

'I think you are in danger Jasper.' Mr Anderson's gentle voice held a hint of victory.

'Maybe,' Jasper studied the board and stroked his beard.

'Pull up a chair by the fire you two.' Mrs Anderson walked over with two steaming mugs of sweet tea.

Joshua grabbed a chair from the table and set it down near the fire. A cup was thrust into his hands, it was so hot he nearly dropped it.

'Where's Mathew?' Joshua asked, trying to sound casual.

'In the living room with Nori. I better see if they would like some tea too.' Just as the words left Mrs Anderson's mouth, Nori and Mathew walked into the Kitchen.

'Nice to meet you Mrs Anderson,' Nori waved to Milly, 'Bye then.'

She turned at the door and looked at Mathew.

'Thank you. He will be here at five.' With that she stepped out into the snow.

Joshua looked at Mathew. His friend turned away and walked over to a large cupboard. He took out a white box.

'Want a game of dominos' before you go?' Mathew asked, aware Joshua would want to know what Nori wanted

'What's happening at five?' Joshua asked casually.

Mathew swallowed. 'I can't discuss it.' He looked away from Joshua.

'Why?' Joshua snapped, irritated at Mathews secrecy

'I promised Nori.' Mathew set the game down on the floor. 'A promise is a promise,' he replied simply.

Joshua felt a stab of jealousy. 'I see,' he raised his eyebrows a fraction.

Mind your own business! Mathew has a secret! Gertie laughed, sitting by Jasper.

Milly shook her head at Joshua warning him to leave it alone.

'I think we had better get home, it's snowing again.' Milly watched the snow building up around the window.

'Your right.' Mrs Anderson stood at the kitchen window, 'the road will soon be thickly covered, way too deep to walk in if you don't get a move on now.' Mrs Anderson walked to the front door and peered out at the fluffy snowflakes falling thick and fast. 'You better get your boots on and make a start. Phone us when you get home, want to make sure you don't get stuck in that snow.'

Joshua handed Milly her coat and slipped on his own.

'Thank you for having us, Mrs Anderson.' Milly thanked her politely.

'Give these to your mum, we aren't going to make it to Mr Green's today with these eggs, not with all that snow!' Mrs Anderson handed Joshua a bag with four boxes of eggs.

'Thank you Mrs Anderson, I will bring the boxes back when they are empty.' Joshua took the bag. 'See you later,' he called quietly to Mathew.

'I think we should walk you home, Rutger wouldn't be too pleased if I let you walk home alone, I know it's been a few days since Harrow was attacked, but with everything that's been going on, I think it would be safest.' Jasper got up and reached down to the draught board and moved a piece. 'I do believe I have a king in the game now, we can finish this game when I get back.'

'Huh!' Mr Anderson grunted, having been taken by surprise.

'Come on Mathew, grab your coat, Gertie, you can do with some exercise too!'

Joshua stepped outside and regretted having to do the walk home. It was deathly cold, the snow reached his calf, it was going to be a slow journey home.

'You know, we could practice air magic and make a path!' Milly sounded excited.

'You know you should use Magic sparingly.' Jasper admonished her, 'Making a path because there is an emergency it one thing, just because you don't want to make your way through it is quite another. I do have to say though, the idea is tempting,' he laughed to take the sting out of his admonishment.

Mathew looked back at the house; the dogs were looking at them through the window.

'Think the dogs have the right idea!' Mathew joked.

With the heavy snowfall they found it was difficult to see very far in front of themselves. They hadn't got far when they heard an engine roaring towards them.

'Stand to the side, whoever that is they might not see you.' Jasper waved them up onto the bank of snow.

Joshua recognized the car immediately.

'It's Dad!'

The car came to a slow crunching stop. Joshua jumped down from the bank, raced to the car, whipped open the door. And jumped into the warm interior.

'Just finished at the garage. Thought you might still be at Mathew's.' Bill smiled.

'Great Dad, wasn't looking forward to that walk!' Milly climbed in the back seat.

Bill looked out at Jasper and Mathew. He noticed Mathew's depressed expression. He wound down his window.

'Did you hear, the Ruby Dragon was stolen. They're not sure how it happened yet. Do you both want a lift to the farm?' he called to them.

'No, you get going, don't want you stranded in this! I will send a robin to Sophia to let her know about the disappearance of the Jewel. The Elders won't be pleased, it is a dangerous artifact of Dark Magic. Very powerful if the person who possess it knows the spell to make it work. You go on home, keep a look out.' Jasper waved to them and pulled Mathew back up along the track.

Bill reversed the car all the way down the track and was soon on the way back home. He hummed a tune and turned to Joshua.

'So, what's up with you and Mathew?'

'Nothing.' Joshua sulked and looked out the side window.

'I see.' Bill continued humming, 'Just remember, he is a good friend.'

'Joshua is upset because Nori wanted to talk to Mathew, and he wouldn't tell Joshua what it was about.' Milly explained.

Joshua turned in his seat, screwed up his eyes and looked at Milly with dagger eyes.

'Mathew must have had a reason.' Bill bent a little closer to the window screen so he could see the road.

Mathew heard a knock at the door. Jasper pulled himself out of the armchair and went to answer the door.

'Oh, it's you,' he heard Jasper say.

Long footsteps were followed by the door swinging open. Forrest entered the room, his dark eyes crinkled when he saw Mathew.

'I want you to know how thankful I am.' He bowed.

'What is going on?' asked Jasper.

Forrest turned his gaze on Jasper.

'I would have thought that was obvious.' Forrest looked at Mathew, 'He is going to hide my magic.'

'Can he hide your magic? You are a Djinn,' Jasper's eyebrow knitted together, 'is that possible?'

'Well, there is only one way to find out. He attempts to hide my magic.' Forrest looked around the room. 'Do you mind?' He pointed to a chair and sat down.

'Why do you want to hide your magic?' Jasper asked, suspicious of the Djinn.

Forrest looked long and hard at Jasper.

'I believe I can trust you.' His hands opened in front of him. 'I will die soon. I want to spend Christmas with my family before I cross to my realm. I do enjoy human customs; it's been enlightening to have experienced so many of them. To keep my family safe, I want Mathew to hide my magic, hide me.' Forrest directed his gaze at Mathew. 'When it is time, Mathew will bring me back. I will be able to spend three days with my family.' He stretched out his leg and tapped the fire grate with his boot.

'And if Mathew cannot hide your magic?' Jasper looked at Mathew.

'I will say goodbye and cross over today.' Forrest looked at his hands.

I think it's Mathew you should be asking, he is the Doorkeeper, it is his decision. Gertie interrupted.

Jasper threw Gertie a withering look.

What do you think Mathew? Gertie ignored Jaspers look.

Mathew blinked, not wanting to be the center of attention.

'If Forrest needs my help, I will try and hide him.' Mathew whispered slowly. 'I have to warn you, I have only ever hidden Gertie.'

That was scary, He hasn't got control of his power yet! Sure, you want to trust him? Gertie bobbed up and down at the memory.

'I put my life in his hands, my feathered friend.' Forrest raised his hand to his forehead and waved a salute.

Mathew got up and walked over to Forrest. He looked at Jasper for guidance.

'I think it might be an idea if you put your hands on his temples, make a connection with him.'

Mathew nodded and reached out and touched Forrest's temples.

'Don't be alarmed if my eyes become flames, it is the energy from which I draw my power.' Forrest warned Mathew.

Mathew nodded.

'Now concentrate on Forrest's magic, seek it out, then hide it.' Jasper whispered.

Mathew looked into Forrest's eyes, drawn into their depths.

Where is your magic? He called to him, his mind touching his.

Nothing happened. Mathew remembered why he was doing this; Forrest was about to die and wanted time with his family.

Where is your magic? He screamed at Forrest, commanding him to show him his magic.

Then it happened. Mathew made connection with Forrest's magic. Forrest's eyes turned to flaming orbs, flames licked his body.

Mathew tried to step back but the joining was too strong.

I hide you Forrest, I hide your magic. Mathew felt different, he was in command of Forrest's magic. *I hide you safely, until Christmas Eve when I will release you. Hide in the safety of the Doorkeeper. Rest Safe Forrest.*

Mathew was wrapped up in the warmth of his magic. Forrest smiled at him. Mathew watched in awe as he evaporated.

Forrest was gone.

I never thought you had that sort of power. Gertie stuttered in awe.

'Neither did I.' Mathew stared at the chair where Forrest had sat.

'I just hope I can get him back and have not doomed him too oblivion.' Mathew whispered.

CHAPTER 29
MOOREMARSH ON THE HUNT

Mooremarsh examined her face in the mirror looking for the ravages of using Dark Magic. A fine line furrowed her eyebrow, tiny but she noticed it. She thought about the Ruby Dragon and shivered at its warning.

You are not of this life now. Another realm owns you.

What had it meant by that? She brushed the memory to one side and thought about what she had to do now.

Capture the Djinn for a wish. It was the only way to gain eternal life. She had to come up with a plan and that would involve the boy, Clarke. A thin smile cracked her mouth. She had been feeding his dreams for months with Dark Magic. Wrapping him in a cocoon of paranoia. Distrust of his father, hatred for the Appleby's, suspicious of everyone's actions. Soon, he would only trust her.

She grabbed a hairbrush, roughly brushed her hair.

'Today we will meet, and a plan will be hatched.' Mooremarsh studied her face in the mirror once more.

She looked at the tiny clock on the mantelpiece.

Closing her eyes, she called to Clarke. Hoping her magic was strong enough to control him while he was awake.

Clarke. It is time to commit to your training. Mooremarsh closed her eyes. *Now we will meet. You hold the key to great power. Do you hear me?*

Mooremarsh licked her lips in anticipation. Never doubting Clarke would want to meet, hoping to gain the power of Dark Magic. Or so he thought!

I am here.

Mooremarsh clapped her hands in delight. Clarke could hear her.

Meet me in the field where the circus was. One o clock this afternoon. Mooremarsh grinned a toothy grin.

I will be there.

'Now the puzzle starts to fall in place.' She smacked the table and went to the hall, pulled on her boots, put on her coat, and slammed the door behind her.

The drive had taken a little longer on the icy road than Mooremarsh expected. She entered the field; the snow was deep and crisp. She took a few steps feeling it crunch between her booted feet.

'I am here.' Clarke's voice announced his presence behind her.

Mooremarsh turned slowly, not wanted to give away how excited she was.

'I see.' She looked him up and down. 'Do you have what it takes to follow Dark Magic?' she tapped her tooth with a long finger.

'I think so.' He replied, his voice warbled nervously. His eyes examined the young woman before him. Was it really Mooremarsh? His thoughts were interrupted by a callous cackle.

'The answer is yes or no.' her voice lashed at him.

Clarke stood looking at her, uncertain of his answer. How did she change from a grey-haired woman to the youthful woman before him?

'I see I am wasting my time here.' Mooremarsh made to walk away.

'The answer is yes; I will do anything to command Dark Magic.' He covered the space between them and put his hand on her arm. She flinched and looked down at his hand, like an insect on her arm. He removed it quickly.

'Then, we have a good beginning.' She licked her lips. 'Will you give me total obedience.'

Clarke looked uncomfortable, 'Yes.'

An unpleasant smile stretched across her face.

'Good, let us begin.'

Mooremarsh slid her hand into her pocket and took out a small silver knife. She raised her hand palm upwards and slashed the fleshy pad of her hand. Crimson blood flowed out of the wound and stained the white snow under her hand. She handed the knife to Clarke, he looked unsure.

'We will make a blood oath, a binding that will show your allegiance to me and the Dark Magic I am about to teach you.' Her smile twisted her face.

Clarke held the knife still tainted with her blood.

'Come boy, make the oath willingly, or walk away now.'

Clarke held her look and made an incision into his hand with the blade. Mooremarsh stepped forward and swiftly grabbed his hand and held it in hers. Clarke tried to hide his pain as she squeezed his hand.

'You pledge your allegiance to me; you give it freely?' Mooremarsh's breath came in rasps.

Clarke turned his head away a fraction from the smell of her fetid breath.

'I agree.' His voice was but a whisper, he felt the warmth of her blood mingling with his in his hand.

'It is done. You are bonded to me; you will honour my wishes.' She let go of his hand abruptly and stood looking at him.

'Let us begin then.' She pointed over to a dead tree trunk and walked over to it, her steps crunched in the newly fallen snow.

Clarke looked down at the blood sullied snow. Was this the beginning of change, would he walk in the footsteps of Dark Magic forever? His train of thought was interrupted by Mooremarsh's hackling as she brushed away some snow from the dead tree trunk and sat down on it. She beckoned him over. Why did he feel reluctant to join her, they had just shared a bond in blood? Clarke took one more look at the red snow and made his way cautiously to Mooremarsh.

'Your grandfather, Forrest has caused a great deal of trouble.' She watched his face. 'You know he is a Djinn?' Mooremarsh stabbed the question, knowing the answer.

'Yes.' Clarke replied woodenly, the blood dripping from his wound felt cold against his skin, he shivered.

'I require one of his wishes.'

'I see.' His reply was mechanical.

'Do you know how you force a Djinn to give you a wish?' Her question rattled out like a machine gun.

'Yes, you trap the Djinn, enslave them. They have to give you a wish.' Clarke gave a precise answer, he shoved his aching hand into his pocket.

'Then we have to trap Forrest.' Her eyes gleamed like a snake facing its prey. 'How should we do that?'

Clarke stared across the field saying nothing.

'Come now, you must have heard your father and Forrest talking about such things.' She was irritated.

Clarke looked down at his shoes. 'Only thing Forrest talked about was how his wife was killed by people who wanted to enslave him. He hid my father so that he would never be hurt.'

'So where is Forrest now?' she asked in a clipped tone.

'Forrest has disappeared.' Clarke kicked the snow.

'What do you mean he has disappeared?' Mooremarsh stamped her foot, looking at him dangerously.

'Nori came and saw my father. Told him Forrest has disappeared. No one knew where he was. She said Forrest would see us on Christmas eve, spend three days with us then he will go.' Clarke repeated what he had heard.

'Well, if he is coming to you on Christmas eve for three days, we have that time to put a plan into action.' She wrung her hands with glee.

Mooremarsh noticed the uncertainty on Clarke's face.

'Once, I have eternal life, I will be able to grant you the same power. What do you think?' She nudged him with her magic.

'Yes, that would be good.' He replied unconvinced.

'You doubt me?' her voice had an edge to it.

Clarke looked away from her, certain she would be angry if he told her he didn't trust her, or any one for that matter.

'Yes, I trust you.' He lied.

'On the third day after Christmas eve you will tell Forrest you want to go for a walk, just the two of you.' She rubbed her hands together to warm them up, 'You will lead him to this field. I will do the rest.' She turned her gaze on Clarke. 'Well?'

'I will bring Forrest here. You will trap him and force him to give a wish.' Clarke answered monotone.

'You are clever.' She got up from the tree trunk, 'Go home and tell no one our plan.'

Clarke stood, hands dangling lifelessly at his sides.

'I have a question; will you kill the Djinn.' He raised his eyes to hers.

She let out a slow breath. 'I have no reason to kill him. I only want one wish. Once he has granted me that, I will have no more use of him, he is yours.'

'It is the only thing I ask; you do not kill Forrest.' Clarke turned to leave.

'Promise you will keep this plan a secret.' Mooremarsh order.

Clarke stood still, 'I promise not to tell anyone,' He pulled his coat a little closer and walked away towards Tetbury.

Mooremarsh watch Clarke walk away, he never looked back. She was sure she had a strong hold on him, the blood oath helped with that. She sighed contently; everything was falling into place nicely. Brushing the snow off her coat, she thought about the great power she would have once the Djinn had granted her wish. Kicking snow as she went, she made her way back to her car and drove off home.

Sitting in her car outside her house she noticed a police car drawing up in front of her. Mooremarsh got out of her car and started towards her front door.

'Excuse me Miss.' A voice called behind her.

Mooremarsh stopped and turned around.

'Yes,' she simpered sweetly.

'My name is Inspector Stone. Could I ask you a few questions?' The man in a suit came closer.

Mooremarsh hid her irritation. 'Yes, of course. I was just going to make myself a pot of tea. It's a bit cold to talk out here, please come in.' She proceeded to open the door and walked into the kitchen. 'Would you like a cup?'

'I don't want any tea thank you, I am just asking questions about Marcus Harrow.'

Mooremarsh felt a cold chill go down her back. She filled up the kettle with water and placed it on the stove.

'Marcus Harrow?' She placed her head to one side and her eyebrows knitted together. 'How can I help you?' she asked, feigning concern.

Inspector Stone took off his brown trilby hat and set it on the table.

'Do you know Marcus Harrow?' he asked casually.

Mooremarsh looked directly at him.

'Yes, I met him at a café when I first arrived here.' No sense in lying she thought to herself. She turned and put three teaspoons of tea into a teapot.

'When did you see him last?' He walked around the table and examined some ornaments on the dresser, he picked up one and looked at it closely.

'We had a picnic in the woods a few days ago. He was supposed to phone but never did. Thought he had lost interest in me. Why?' She grabbed the kettle and poured the scolding water into the teapot.

'He was attacked and is in hospital.' Stone looked at Mooremarsh.

Mooremarsh slammed down the kettle and spun around feigning shock. 'What happened?'

'He was attacked in his home.' Stone put a figurine back in its place. 'What date did you last see him?'

'It was a few days ago. We met in the late morning, early afternoon, had a picnic, I wasn't very hungry, and Marcus ate most of it. He said he was tired from working late shifts, so I suggested he go home and rest. He dropped me off in the high street.'

'What did you do after that?' Stone looked at her, trying to sum up the truth in her account.

Mooremarsh took her time answering. She bit her lip, pretending she was trying to recall the day.

'I did a bit of shopping; I went to the café and had some food.' She looked Stone in the eye, shrugged her shoulders. 'I went home after that; I can't help you.'

'I see,' Stone replied in a tone that meant that he clearly didn't see.

'Can I visit him?' Mooremarsh asked quietly.

'No, visiting is restricted until he recovers.' Stone picked up his hat, 'Just one more thing, The Ruby Dragon of Overhill Hall has been stolen, did you visit it at all?'

Stone looked at Mooremarsh carefully.

'Yes, we did drop in and see it. Didn't stay long though. It was a fine jewel if a bit ostentatious for my liking.' Mooremarsh decided not to lie.

'If you think of anything else, please get in contact.' He went to the front door and left.

Mooremarsh stared at the front door thinking about Inspector Stone.

'Marcus Harrow won't be waking up anytime soon!'

She took the teapot to the table and sat down.

'No, he will sleep for a long time, and now, I need to plan how to trap the Djinn!'

CHAPTER 30

SOPHIA'S TALE

Sophia stamped her feet; she was bitterly cold standing at the dead of night on the edge of the Abbey graveyard. Her eyes cast over the snowcapped tombstones, light dribbling from the Abbey's stained-glass windows peppering them with colour. The grounds were empty except for Rutger and Jasper standing behind her. They were keeping watch whilst the children went to the Christmas Midnight Mass at the Abbey. Strains of organ music and a chorus of voices trickled out of a slightly open oak door, she smiled it was a pleasing sound.

'Well, all is quiet so far,' Rutger said, his voice trembled a little.

Sophia nodded and closed her eyes. She had had a bad night's sleep the previous evening, and now she needed her bed, she was weary and bone tired. Her eyes flicked open, warm air from her breath turned to white tendrils as she breathed out into the crisp night air. Something had been bothering her all day. It was a nightmare; the same dream had disturbed her sleep for weeks; causing her to toss and turn all night leaving her drained the next day. A strange dream, yet somehow familiar. She had tried all day to remember its essence but had failed, that was until now, standing in the darkness and overshadowed by the Abbey.

Remember!

She closed her eyes and groaned as images exploded into her mind. Memories of the nightmare unfolded, and she trembled. Her father's grim pale face floated behind her eyelids, he pointed at an object on the table.

'Fetch it to me Sophia,' his gravelly voice had ordered her.

She had felt light, only as you can in a dream. She had looked at the object, instinctively she had felt a deep loathing for the shining item. It was always about Dark Magic with her family.

'Sophia, do as you are told,' His dark watery eyes had commanded her.

A fine mist swirled around his body; his eyes had grown frighteningly larger. His gnarled hand slowly raised, and he pointed towards a large dark wooden table. White lank hair bobbed about his face as nodded her onwards in the tabled direction.

Let me wake up, wake up! Her mind had screamed in the dead of night as she thrashed around in her bed.

Her brain had had other ideas and would not obey her wishes. The nightmare had continued. The dreams onslaught her body felt heavy as she approached the table. Standing in front of the ornate polished wooden legs and her fingers reached out to touch the object her father desired, her hand had hesitated, hovering just in front of it.

'I said now!' her father had hissed at her through a grey mist.

She had breathed in deeply, the mist tasted tangy and had stung the back of her throat, she swallowed down the taste in her mouth, and had grabbed the crystal. It felt cold and lifeless in her hand.

'Well, what do you feel?' her fathers voice reached a fever pitch.

Sophia considered the question as she held the crystal. She felt nothing. No dark power or the queasiness she usually felt when she handled Dark Magic items such as her parents Dark Magic spell books when they requested them. After a while of standing and holding the crystal, she found her voice.

'I feel nothing,' she turned to her father, 'It just feels like a crystal.'

Her voice had caught in her throat at the sound of her voice echoing in the mist. She still felt the trembling in her hands as she had turned and seen his murderous look. Her father's face had contorted dangerously, and he whispered something she couldn't make out, the words had been just out of the range of her hearing. She had trembled, waiting for him to speak to her.

'Bring it to me,' he held out his hand to her.

Sophia remembered her limbs feeling heavy in her nightmare. She wanted to run across the room and throw the crystal into her father's hand and make her escape. But she couldn't, she was rooted to the spot.

'What is wrong with you?' her father was scathing, 'twelve years old and you are yet to perform Dark Magic,' he spat the words at her and motioned for her to return to him.

She had struggled making each muscle in her legs work, walking was painfully slow. Her father's low evil laugh whipped at her, scalding her ears. After a lot of effort, she was close enough to throw the crystal at him. His hands stretched out, a looked of surprise at her sudden action.

'Careful, stupid girl!' he hissed at her as he caught the crystal.

Her father caressed and spoke to the crystal form, and then, cried in exasperation at it. 'I will find your secret!'

His dull eyes rested on her, and he held the crystal up towards the light.

'Look at it, have you never seen anything so beautiful?'

Sophia could not move; her father's low mocking laugh caused her breath to catch in her throat.

'This Sophia is The Ruby Dragon, and it is mine, it's dark power will give me eternal life.'

Instinctively, Sophia knew the object her father held did not have any power. Her mouth was dry, and her limbs would not move.

'Did you not feel its power child?' her father moved closer to her.

She had been terrified giving the answer. A truth which would cause her pain.

'No, I felt nothing,' the words left her mouth, there was a stinging pain in her head as she recoiled from the blows from her father's fist.

'You lie you wretch. You are trying to provoke me. This jewel has power!' her father's screams became a mist of sound; she fell into a deep dark hole as the nightmare had claimed her sleep.

Now she remembered as she stood in the cold grounds of the Abbey. A nightmare of her childhood, a time she had locked away into the dark recesses of her mind, trying to forget, obliterating them completely. Sadly, some of the memories surfaced occasionally, escaping the prison she had built for them, taunting her to remember.

Her father had owned a Ruby Dragon.

A replica of the original, she was sure. It had been without power or Dark Magic. She had held a lifeless inert object in her child's hand. She breathed out deeply, trying to wash her body clean from the Dark Magic she had been exposed to as a child. Why had she only just remembered the incident, why not when they had been at Overhill Hall? A memory washed over her and made her stand bolt upright. She had woken violently from a fitful slumber a few nights ago. A wall of coldness had hit her, and she recognised it's foulness. Dark Magic. A faceless grey apparition stood before her. She had reached for the pendant at her neck which carried a protection charm. The amethyst stone felt warm beneath her fingers.

You do not need protection from me. I am free, she destroyed my prison, and has set me free.

Before she could reply, Feles had pounced on the bed and hissed at the unseen foe.

What ever you are, go from here. Hackles crept down Feles back.

I bring you a gift. The grey form sang to her.

GO! Fele's had pushed his body against Sophia's shocked one.

Mooremarsh cannot use the Ruby Dragon. You will both sleep and forget; the memory will surface when it is needed.

Before Sophia could get a grip of her fear, the apparition had gone as quickly as it had appeared. She had fallen asleep with Feles by her side waking the next day without any memory of what had happened.

Until now.

I remember! Feles voice brought her out of her stupor.

'Yes, Feles,' she looked down at him, 'and so do I.'

Jasper looked through the darkness at Sophia and puffed out his cheeks. They stood with Rutger in a huddle within the Abbey grounds.

'I have been thinking about The Ruby Dragon and it's theft.' Jasper glanced over at the Abbey a shaft of light shot out from an open door.

'I had been too. Your message terrified me. I sent Mr Witherington to the Elder's Council with the news,' Sophia shivered; it wasn't from the cold, the shock of the memory of the dream still lingered. Her thoughts were interrupted by Feles.

Do we have to stand out here, why couldn't we be inside that warm Abbey? Feles whined at Sophia, he nudged his way under her cape and snuggled against her calf.

'Do be quiet Feles, you are supposed to be here to help us keep watch!' she felt the cats head butt her calf in protest, 'with all that fur I am surprised you are cold, go and take a walk around the outside of the Abbey and make sure we are alone!' she heard Feles grumble as he pulled himself away from the warmth of her legs.

Rutger wrapped his arms around his body and watched the entrance of the Abbey. There was no movement just a shaft of light from a slightly open door. Sophia pulled her cape a little tighter about her, not wanting to talk about the jewel or the memories which had just surfaced.

'I heard lots of replicas were made, people must have paid a fortune for what they thought was the original Ruby Dragon,' Rutger smacked his arms against his body to warm up, the night air cut into his bones.

Sophia hid her face from him, not wanting him to see her distress at the mention of the Ruby Dragon.

'Wish it had remained lost,' Jasper flicked a glance at Sophia, 'all that power in the hands of someone who can use it. It's not a good thought.'

The pale streetlight reflected against her white skin, giving it a pearlescent quality. Jasper saw gentle lines in her face as she winced at the turn of the conversation. She looked very uncomfortable.

'If Mooremarsh has stolen the Ruby Dragon,' Jasper paused, 'can she use it?'

Sophia looked at the snow glistening in the light, her eyes rested on Jasper, he felt uncomfortable under her gaze.

'My parents owned a Ruby Dragon,' she whispered softly into the darkness, she flinched under Rutger's shocked stare, 'The memory has only just resurfaced,' her head lifted a fraction, 'they couldn't make use of it, you see they didn't have the spell which was needed to unlock the Dark Magic it was supposed to hold within it,' her voice was harsh and brittle in the night air, 'I am not unfamiliar with the history of that gem.'

Old memories of her childhood flooded back. Even after all these years away from the darkness of her family, she still felt the pain of being the only person with Earth Magic amongst all that evil. She clapped her hands together to warm them.

'My father sold the jewel, there was no use for it if he did not have the spell to control it,' she shivered from a memory, 'he made me pick it up and fetch it to him once. I can still remember his sickening smile as he asked me to retrieve the jewel, I think he wanted me to touch it to see if I felt any Dark Magic within it.'

'Did you?' Jasper asked.

Rutger threw him a warning look.

'Sorry, Sophia, its just I am worried that Jewel maybe in the wrong hands,' Jasper shrugged, 'we all know it was the cursed jewel from the way the children reacted to it.'

'What my father had was a fake. I never had a reaction to the Jewel, not the way the children did,' she stopped clapping her hands, 'If Mooremarsh has both the Ruby Dragon and the spell, she could cast the spell and attain eternal life if the legend is true.'

'Well, lets hope that the Council of Elders send us some guidance then. Don't fancy doing battle with her if she is indestructible!' Rutger grumbled.

Sophia looked over at Joshua walking out of the Abbey doorway *alone*. Her eyebrows knitted together, such carelessness.

'I believe she had the Ruby Dragon, but somehow the Dark Magic within it has escaped,' she held up a gloved hand as Rutger was about to ask a question, 'another time for questions, I am certain she no longer has the power of the stone, she has not been able to use it.'

The glance between Rutger and Jasper made her wince.

'Let's focus on the children. They are our priority,' Sophia looked across at the Abbey, she nodded in its direction, 'Joshua is not his usual self, he shouldn't be out on his own, will he never learn.'

Jasper smacked his arms against his body to warm up and watched Joshua make his way to the Abbey railings, he looked over to them and waved.

'He had a bit of a falling out with Mathew,' Jasper waved back at Joshua.

'Mathew has a powerful gift,' Rutger said watching Prudence approach Joshua.

'Joshua will have to be less sensitive,' Sophia murmured, 'his pride will be his undoing if he is not careful,' she watched him walking across the graveyard to the solitary Christmas tree.

'They need each other. It hasn't missed my attention with Mathew coming into Earth Magic they now have the power of three,' Rutger leaned heavily on his cane, 'We need to teach them to respect each other's strengths, envy is a destructive force in itself.'

'Look,' Jasper nodded towards the Abbey.

The Elder's watched Mathew standing in the Abbey doorway. He made his way gingerly through the snow towards the side of the Abbey.

'Where is he going?' Asked Rutger.

'He is fulfilling a promise I think,' Jasper said quietly.

The trio were startled by the crunching of snow behind them, they turned in unison. Two figures walked through a metal gate into the Abbey grounds. Jasper turned away and looked in the direction Mathew had taken earlier.

'They are here, it is time,' Jasper called out to Mathew, 'Release him, now.'

CHAPTER 31
MATHEW'S SECRET IS UNDONE

Joshua stood by the Abbey railings waiting for his family. They had all been to the traditional Christmas Eve service. As always, the Abbey looked wonderful lit up with candles and winter flowers. Grandad Rose had wanted to stay and talk to friends after the service. Joshua made his escape and found a spot to stand and wait for his family. He thought about the festive dinner they had had a few days ago to celebrate the winter solstice. A large bonfire had been lit in the garden to mark the return of the sun; the house was filled with candles glowing during the night. Jasper had spent the evening telling stories of Earth Magic history, everyone had held on to every word. His dad had sung old ballads and they had joined in. A movement caught his attention, he saw Rutger, Sophia and Jasper standing in a corner of the graveyard, huddled in conversation. Jasper was pounding his arms across his chest. Joshua smiled to himself; Jasper hated the cold the most out of the three elders. Jasper noticed Joshua and gave him a wave. Joshua returned the gesture, walked across the graveyard, and stood in front of a Christmas tree; it topped the height of the large Abbey doors. Joshua stamped his feet to get the snow off his boots, the cold was biting through them. Bathed in the twinkling light of the snow laden Christmas tree, he felt festive, now he wanted a hot chocolate and go to bed. The clock struck twelve, heralding the arrival of Christmas day. Joshua let out a solitary whoop.

It's lovely here. Prudence rested against his leg.

He looked back at the Abbey, its windows cast a soft light over the graveyard. Joshua squinted at the Abbey doors; a figure was creeping out into the snow. He cocked his head to one side trying to make out who it was. He stood up with a jolt, it was Mathew leaving the Abbey; Gertie flew down from a branch and hopped along behind him. Joshua was just about to call out to him when Mathew ducked down the side of the Abbey out of view.

'Now, what's he up to?' Joshua mused.

Leave him alone, it is a private matter. Prudence nudged his leg.

Joshua looked over the Elders, they didn't seem interested in what Mathew was up to, although Jasper looked over from time to time. Joshua was just about to leave his place when the squeak of a rusty gate tore the silence of the graveyard. A man stepped through the gap, he stood in the shadows. Joshua couldn't make out his face. The man shut the gate behind him and walked slowly along the path. Jasper left the group of Elders and stood under a streetlamp. The man approached him, and shook his hand, the light fell on his face.

Erik Sharma!

'Well, Mr Sharma, what are you doing here?' whispered Joshua, white vapor followed his breath. 'And what could you be discussing with Jasper?'

Joshua watched the unfolding of events. Mathew poked his head out from around the corner of the Abbey.

'He is here, it is time.' Jasper called to Mathew, 'Release him, now.'

'I have done it. He is here.' Mathew turned and waved.

A dark shadow appeared at the back of the Abbey. A scream caught in Joshua's throat, he thought Mooremarsh had come back. As the dark shadow stepped forward, light from one of the Abbey windows illuminated his face, Joshua recognized the figure. Forrest.

'My son, it is I. Come, help me, I grow weak. I am too close to my time.' Forrest called to Erik.

Erik ran forward and let Forrest rest his weight on him, he placed his arm about his father's shoulders.

'Thank you, Mathew, I am in your debt.' Forrest called to Mathew.

'It's fine, Mr Forrest, enjoy these days with your family,' Mathew stuttered.

Now you understand do you. Prudence stood beside Joshua.

'No, I don't understand.' Joshua mumbled glumly watching Forrest slumped against Mr Shrama, each step was slow, Forrest looked like he was in pain.

Mathew hid Forrest from Dark Magic so he could spend his final days with his family. Clarke Sharma is Forrest's grandson.

'What! Why didn't you tell me?' Joshua stamped his feet.

It was not our place. The deep voice of the wolf admonished him.

Joshua whipped around; he was nosed to nose with Sylvester Bluesky.

Somethings are taken on trust.

The comment made Joshua smart.

'Like when you accused Milly of Dark Magic,' Joshua snapped, 'Where was your trust then? You nearly had my sisters magic bound; it wasn't her fault Miskunn doesn't want to show herself to you.'

Sylvester Bluesky growled at Joshua; his tail cut the air angrily.

'Growl all you like; I nearly lost a friend because of all this stupid secrecy stuff.'

Prudence gulped in shock. *Joshua No!* She rebuked him.

Joshua turned his back on them, angry at being left in the dark. He marched across the graveyard to Mathew. His friend looked away, too tired to talk. Joshua followed Mathew's gaze, Erik Sharma and Forrest disappeared through the gate.

'I'm sorry.' Joshua put out his hand, Mathew took it limply in his.

'I should never have judged you.' Joshua said gruffly.

Mathew looked for a long time at the gate.

'No, you shouldn't have asked me to break a promise.' He rested a hurt gaze on Joshua, 'Never ask that of me again.' Mathew rubbed his hands over his eyes, 'You know this Doorkeeper business is exhausting!' Mathew kicked some snow. 'I know you were angry, you thought Nori was interested in me. Believe me, I have no designs on her.'

The sound of people leaving the Abbey caught their attention.

'Guess we had better get back. Mum said you are all coming over to us for dinner tomorrow. That will be great.' Joshua tried to heal the breach between them.

'Yes, I just want to get some sleep now.' Mathew coughed. 'It was hard bringing Forrest back. I was scared for a moment that he would be trapped.' He turned wide eyes on Joshua. 'I was terrified. I wouldn't give this magic to anyone.'

Joshua patted Mathews back. 'Let's go and find everyone. It's Christmas day now!'

They walked against the crowd into the Abbey. Joshua saw his grandfather talking to Reverend Phillips. His father was talking to Maurice Priddy. His mother beckoned him over.

'Mr Priddy will be over tomorrow, he is staying with Grandad Rose tonight. It's a full house tomorrow.' She looked at Priddy and Bill, 'The pair of them are cooking up what songs to sing to entertain us!' His mother laughed.

'So, it's Grandad Rose, the Andersons, the Elders and Mr Priddy and us. Have we got enough chairs for the dining table?' Joshua was wondering if they would all fit around it.

'We'll manage, don't you worry,' his mother clapped her hands, 'I do love a family get together.'

Milly stood to one side; she bit her bottom lip. She waved him over.

'Miskunn is upset.' She whispered to Joshua. 'You were rude to Sylvester Bluesky.'

'That's between us. Leave it alone.' Joshua's lips drew into a fine line.

'No Joshua, I won't leave it alone. Sylvester Bluesky appeared to me on this night last year. Ever since he has helped and protected me. He always tries to do the right thing.' She held a level stare, 'He was beside himself with guilt when he found out the mistake he had made when he accused me of Dark Magic. If I can forgive him, so should you.'

Joshua gave her a mutinous look.

'Go outside and apologise to the wolf. Now. Or I will tell Mum what an ass you are being.' She stood hand on hips.

Joshua glared at his sister. She pointed at the door. He turned and walked slowly to the door. He braced himself against the cold night air and stepped out into it. The Elders were still standing in a little huddle. He walked further into the graveyard.

You should be ashamed of yourself talking to Sylvester Bluesky like that! Prudence butted his calf none too gently.

'Do you know where he is?' Joshua asked.

I am here. Sylvester Bluesky stood at his side. Eyes wide and sad. *What do you want?*

Joshua looked at the wolf, a wave of overwhelming guilt washed over him. The wolf had guided him, defended him and was his teacher. He flushed ashamed of the outburst. The apology stuck in his throat. His mouth felt dry, and he coughed.

'I shouldn't have said or thought those things. I cannot apologise enough for what I said. Forgive me.' Joshua's voice was hoarse.

The wolf stood a little taller, he placed a paw on Joshua's shoulder.

I forgive you. We will not speak of it again. The wolf's nostrils flayed, *never, ever use your anger in such a way again.*

'I understand,' Joshua replied hoarsely, looked down at the ground not able to meet Sylvester Bluesky's eyes.

Go back to your family, enjoy your festival.

Joshua looked up; the wolf had gone.

He walked back towards the Abbey, still feeling guilty for his harsh words.

So, you should. Sylvester Bluesky is the greatest of us all. Prudence stamped her foot and ran away from him still displeased.

Joshua felt even worse, his feet felt like lead blocks, he trundled back to the Abbey. Grandad Rose came out waving goodbye to friends.

'There you are, wondered where you had got to.' He pulled Joshua's hat down over his eyes playfully.

Joshua pulled his woolen hat back. Milly ran over to him and skidded in the snow. He held up his hand before she could ask.

'Yes, I apologised.'

'Ok, Grandad Rose and I will get the cars, so be ready on the pavement.' His father called out to them.

The elders walked over and stood with them and Alana. They didn't have to wait long for the cars to arrive. Joshua waited for his sister to get into the car and looked around for Prudence, but she was nowhere to be seen.

'She'll come round, don't worry.' Milly slid into the car and Joshua followed her.

The drive home didn't take long. Once inside Alana took orders for hot chocolate and teas, as usual Milly had hot milk with cinnamon.

Joshua looked out the window sipping his hot chocolate. The snow was coming down in a trickle. He had a feeling inside that wouldn't go away. Something bad was on its way, something terrible. He was sure it had something to do with Mooremarsh, he just couldn't figure out what it was.

CHAPTER 32
AN UNEXPECTED GUEST

Joshua stretched blurry eyed, he glanced at the clock, seven thirty, he had been up since six and now he was hungry. They were waiting for Grandad Rose, so they could have Christmas breakfast together. He heard the rattling of a car engine in the distance. He grinned; he could recognize the sound of that engine anywhere. Walking from the kitchen he opened the door and watched his grandfather and Priddy each drag a kitchen chair out of the car. Joshua pulled on his boots and went out to help carry the remaining two chairs into the house.

'Well, that's twelve chairs now, so a seat for everyone!' Alana clapped her hands happily. 'Milly, help your dad get the spare table in from the sitting room.'

Joshua laid the table with plates and cutlery; Alana decorated the center with flowers.

'Well, this looks splendid! Watch out for Rutger, he will be hogging all the food if you're not careful!' Sophia entered the kitchen. In her hands she carried two brown boxes.

'For you.' Sophia handed it to Alana.

'Oh, thank you!' Alana pulling the string off one box. Inside were twenty-four apple pies, each with two perfect pastry leaves. 'They smell delicious!'

'Thought you could serve them with breakfast if you like, but like I said, watch out for Rutger!'

In the other box were gingerbread stars, smattered with white icing and silver sugar balls.

Alana looked at Sophia and laughed, 'Like you said, watch Rutger.'

'Sophia, what have you been saying about me?' His eyes caught sight of the boxes. He stretched out his hand to take an apple pie, Sophia slapped it playfully.

'We wait until everyone is around the table!' Sophia chuckled.

'I had better let them know!' Rutger went out of the kitchen to find the others.

Joshua eyed the table, it was laden with bread, butter, cheeses, honey, sausages, jam, eggs, and a plate of Sophia's apple pies.

Alana put two large tea pots on the table and a jug of creamy milk. Joshua, Priddy and Grandad Rose had hot chocolate and Milly had her usual milk combination. Joshua looked around the table, everyone looked happy, even Rutger had a smile on his usually serious face.

Breakfast over, Joshua washed up, Milly and Rutger dried the crockery. Joshua felt restless, he needed to release some energy.

'Mum, can I walk to Mathews and walk back with them for Dinner?' Joshua asked.

'Firstly, I need help pealing the potatoes, Milly you can sort out the carrots and brussels sprouts. After that, yes, you can walk over to the Andersons. Dinner will be on the table at one-thirty. Don't be late.' Alana handed him a peeling knife, then one to Milly.

Rutger walked into the kitchen, 'Did I hear, go for a walk.' He rubbed his full stomach, 'I could do with the exercise, although I know it won't be at your young pace,' He laughed.

Sophia had dark circles under her eyes, from all the late nights she had stayed up looking for a relative of Harrow's. She looked around him. 'I will come too, Milly bring your stone with you, we will see what you can do with it,' she saw Joshua's crestfallen face. 'Joshua, not everyone is chosen. Don't fret about it.'

'You were so tired when you arrived yesterday afternoon, I didn't want to harass you. Was there a relative in the Earth Magic community that was related to Marcus?' Alana asked Sophia.

'After many days of searching the family trees, I was successful in tracking down a relative.' Sophia sighed, 'Only problem is she would be one hundred and five. No one knows where she lives, she must be a hermit. I have dispatched Feles to look for her. I am not hopeful that she is still alive.'

'I see, Bill will be distraught at the news. Marcus was good friends with Bill and Maurice.' Alana looked through to the living room at her husband. 'I will have to warn him of the bad news.'

'Be patient, the day is not over yet.' Sophia patted Alana's hand.

Adorning her midnight cape, Sophia grabbed her staff and nodded at the front door.

'Well, we had better leave, the sky looks heavy with snow in the distance.'

Joshua stood alone, hands in pockets, his jaw dropped. Rutger came along the hall in the most outlandish multi coloured cape. He smacked his cane on the floor and bowed with a flourish.

'I am ready.'

'There is no way they will miss you in that cape!' Sophia laughed.

Milly stood quietly on the last stair; in her hand she clutched the stone of Adel the Noble. She hid it in her pocket out of Joshua's pained stare.

'Let's get going then,' Rutger nodded towards the door.

'Are you sure you don't want any help with cooking dinner,' Sophia called to Alana, feeling a little guilty she was leaving her to all the preparations.

'No, you enjoy the walk.' Alana's voice came back.

They all left to make the short journey to Mathew's house. There had been more snow the night before. It was difficult to walk through, their steps were sluggish and their pace slow.

'The stone of Adel the Noble has a long history. Adel the Noble was born into aristocracy. She had to hide her Earth Magic from her family, she knew they would try and use it for power. When her family found out about her gift, she fled, with her magical sparrow hawk into the woods.' Sophia flicked a snowflake from her cheek, 'Hiding in a cave, she found the stone. It is said, the stone hid her from her enemies, increased her magic against Dark Magic. Unfortunately, it has never wielded that power again in recorded history' Sophia gazed questioningly at Milly, 'so far that is.' Sophia kicked the snow lost in thought, 'Maybe with time Milly, the stone may find you worthy to share all its power with you.'

'So how do I use it?' Milly asked confused. 'How do I prove I am worthy?'

'That is what we will talk about on the way to Mathew's.' Sophia smiled.

Rutger saw Joshua's down cast face.

'Come here. I have something to tell you.' Rutger beckoned him over with his hand.

Joshua walked beside Rutger, not catching his eye.

'Joshua, I want to tell you about my stone, the Diamond of Henrik.' Rutger held up his cane. 'Did you know when the chosen one of a magical stone die, if the stone has already chosen a successor, it will ask the owner's magical creature to find the successor. This is rare, so most are returned to Sophia to keep for the choosing.' Rutger looked at Sophia walking ahead with Milly. 'The stone did not present itself to me until I had been practicing Earth Magic for six years, I was eighteen, I thought I would never have a stone, most with Earth Magic are never chosen by the stones. It waited for its master to pass beyond the Vale of Death. It knew it was destined for me. I was shocked I can tell you when Sylvester Bluesky dropped it at my feet!' he held up his cane closer to his eyes, 'I had this cane fashioned so it would hold the Diamond of Henrik. I never go anywhere without it.'

Joshua stopped walking and gazed at Rutger's cane. He felt the warmth of hope spread its way through his veins.

'Not everyone knows that. I just thought it would help you to know, if there is a stone out there for you, it is worth waiting for the right one.' Rutgers craggy features softened.

Joshua reflected on what he had just been told.

'Thank you, that helps.' He smiled gratefully, not feeling so envious of his sister and friend.

Rutger walked ahead to catch Sophia and Milly up. Sophia taught Milly to balance the stone in her palm.

'Now we will practice the defense of three. All three stones will work together to protect us against Dark Magic. Joshua, stand in the center. Milly, hold your stone towards Rutgers's cane, which holds the Diamond of Henrik. I will hold my staff with the Stone of Eunice towards your stone. Close your eyes and think the word Protection.'

Joshua stood in the middle of the three and waited. Each stone flickered, he sucked in cold air, it burnt his lungs. Startled at the bright light pulsing from each stone.

'When all three stones light up, protection is in place, Dark Magic cannot force its way through.' She placed her staff upright and the glow stopped. 'That is the first lesson of the stones.' She pointed her staff towards a lane. 'I think this is the turning we take.'

Two dark brown and white dogs announced their arrival at Anderson Farm. Mathew came flying out the door to greet them.

'Happy Christmas!' He called to them all.

After an exchange of greetings, they went inside to get warm by the fire. Jasper was settled comfortably by the fire playing draughts with Mr Anderson.

'Come in and enjoy the warmth.' Mr Anderson waved them in, a sliver of Christmas cake in his hand.

'Thank you,' Rutger pulled up a chair to the fire. 'Enjoyed the walk here, not looking forward to going back on foot though!'

'I tell you what, I was just about to drive us all to Bill's. Be a bit of a squeeze, but I think we could all fit into the car.' Mr Anderson challenged jovially.

'Can't we walk and let you all ride?' Mathew suggested.

'No, you can't, unless Jasper walks back with you.' Rutger shook his head at Mathew.

'Well seems fair to me. We'll carry this game on when we get back, Peter.' Jasper challenged Mr Anderson.

Mr Anderson grunted and gave Jasper a wry smile.

'We'll see who wins, I am one game ahead now.'

'Pride before the fall, Peter!' Jasper laughed, wrapped his scarf around his neck, pulled on his coat and cap.

'Right, ready to brave the cold.' Jasper called to the children. 'Let's get going.'

Joshua thought the journey back seemed quicker than the walk to Mathew's. The Andersons car was already sitting outside Chestnut Cottage when they arrived.

'Hope there are some apple pies left, I know there were a few left after breakfast.' Jasper looked at Joshua and they both laughed.

Alana opened the door, waved to them, and proceeded into the garden.

'Mum's getting some more herbs I'd imagine, how she can find them under all that snow is beyond me!' Milly laughed at Mathew.

Inside the cottage they could hear Bill and Priddy singing a song. The smell of dinner and spices made Joshua's mouth water.

'Go and wash up you three, dinner will be on the table soon.' Joshua turned, saluted his mother, and ran upstairs.

On his return, everyone was sat at the table, excitedly talking. Joshua went over to his red-faced mother. 'Anything I can do to help?'

'Thanks, put those two bowls onto the table.' She pointed to mounds of carrots and roast potatoes.

Once his mother sat down, Rutger stood up and gave thanks for the earth and all it provides for them. They ate, sang, and joked as they enjoyed the feast Alana had set before them.

'This has been one of the best Christmas days I have spent in a long while.' Sophia sighed.

'Yes, normally sardines on toast for me, this was sumptuous!' Jasper laughed mischievously.

'Don't believe him, Rutger and Jasper usually come to me.' Sophia raised an eyebrow, 'and you've guessed it, they eat me out of house and home!' She burst out laughing seeing their crest fallen faces.

Sophia, Sophia! Feles pushed his face against her leg, *Sophia!*

Sophia pushed back her chair. 'What is it Feles?'

Before he could reply, the air split with three loud knocks at the door. Bill got up and answered the door. In front of him stood a woman dressed head to toe in lavender blue. A thick lavender cloak was held at her neck with a large silver broach. On her left chest she had a silver boutonniere, a lapel vase, it had fresh lavender peeping above it. Her wooly knitted hat pulled down over her head, tired blue eyes could just about see out below its rim. In one hand she held a cane with a large azure sapphire and silver head. In the other an old-fashioned carpet bag. Her hands were covered with sheepskin mittens. Bill stared into pale blue eyes, watery from the cold, or maybe age he wasn't sure.

'Well, you going to keep me standing here all day. I have traveled some way with that cat.' She moved Bill out the way with her cane and stepped into the hall. She removed her mittens, deftly unclasped her broach, and gave Bill the garments.

'Where is everyone.' She asked briskly.

'Who are you?' Bill asked.

'I won't repeat myself twice.' Her jaw clenched. 'Out of the way.'

'That way.' Taken aback, Bill nodded towards the kitchen.

The woman strode to the kitchen and shoved open the door. Everyone fell silent. She looked around the room at all the faces. Then she noticed Feles. Her eyes locked onto Sophia.

'I suppose it is you who summon me?' she sniffed at Sophia, 'I am one hundred and five years old. I have never been ordered around by a cat!' she threw Feles a scathing look.

'My name is Ethel De Gallo. I am the great, aunt of Marcus Harrow, although I have only met him once.' Her eyes looked at the food on the table. Her eyes rested on Alana.

'Tea, three sugars, and with this cold, a tot of brandy.' She looked over to the kettle, 'No milk, it tastes sour in tea.'

'Yes, you must be weary from your journey.' Alana went to the kitchen to prepare the drink for their new visitor.

'I understand you wish me to perform the undoing of the Sleep of the Dead on my great nephew.' She moved around the table and sat in Bill's chair, 'I need to eat, and sleep, in that order. After that you will tell me why my nephew who does not have Earth Magic should be saved from the Sleep of the Dead.'

She looked at all the shocked faces around the table and let out a long sigh.

'If Marcus Harrow is worthy, it will be the last time I can perform Earth Magic. My bones will wither and die, which I am happy to do, if the cause is just.' She sat back in the chair; her thin hand pointed to the food on the table. 'Now if you don't mind, could I have some of your dinner.'

CHAPTER 33
ETHEL DE GALLO

'Come this way. You can sleep in Milly's bedroom for a while.' Alana offered.

Ethel De Gallo inspected the room Alana showed her.

'It is adequate.' She sniffed and turned back to Alana, 'I will come down when I have slept.' She shut the door just allowing Alana enough time to get out of the doorway.

'This is going to be interesting.' Alana grumbled crossly at Ethel De Gallo's rudeness. 'But then again, I suppose she is tired after her journey.' She reasoned to herself.

When Alana opened the door to the kitchen everyone stopped talking.

'Well?' Sophia asked.

'She didn't say a thing. Just shut the door and said she will come down when she has slept.'

Sophia turned to Feles. 'You found her, well done!' she tickled his chin, 'where did you find her?' Sophia enquired sitting forward in her seat.

I found her in a pub outside of Ogbourne St George. He licked his paw and continued. *She was not happy when I informed her the Earth Magic Council had found her to be the only relative that could reverse the Sleep of the Dead on Marcus Harrow, her great nephew. She said it wasn't her problem as he did not have Earth Magic! I told her you would come yourself, a member of the High Council. She was not happy about that either. Got really cross with me. Made me wait outside in the snow whilst she finished her pint of Irish Stout!*

'Ogbourne St George, where is that?' Rutger asked.

Outside of Marlborough. Feles jumped up onto Sophia's lap. *Well, I wasn't going to sit out in the cold, so I crept in and sat by the fire and watched her sup her stout. I thought at one moment she had fallen asleep over it. She hadn't she was just lost in thought. By the time she had finished it was nine o'clock, so she suggested we set off in the morning.* Feles stretched out and padded Sophia's knees.

'Don't go to sleep yet, you have to finish what happened!' Sophia pushed him.

Well, her little house wasn't far away, so we stayed the night. In the morning, she led me to a barn, inside was a brown and white horse, she called him Chester. She put a saddle on him, tied her carpet bag onto it, then, she was up on the horse, staff in hand. Thankfully, she let me snuggle into the carpet bag. The journey took us a day and a half. She has left him roaming in the wood's opposite. Now, I want to go to sleep.

'Joshua, get one of the small hay bales we have in the store for Rutgers donkeys, take it out to Chester.' He must be hungry.' Alana.

No need, Chester can look after himself. Feles replied cryptically.

'Thank you, Feles. I will put you in the living room.' Sophia scooped him up, staggering under his weight. Rutger held out his arms and took the sleeping cat.

'I will put him near the fire in the living room.' He disappeared with his heavy burden.

'What do you think, will she perform the reversal? She doesn't seem that keen.' Alana sounded concerned.

'Well, she has come this far.' Bill yawned trying to inject some hope into the room. 'She is one hundred and five, we have messed up her routine.'

'Yes, that's true.' Alana went over and sat on the arm of the chair he was sitting in. 'Sorry but she is sleeping in your room Milly,' she looked at Sophia, 'in the bed you are using Sophia.' Alana shook her shoulders.

'Well, I think we should wash up, get the table ready for some games.' Jasper s looking across at Mr Anderson.

'We accept the challenge!' Mr Anderson's eyes crinkled.

'Well, why you set up the table, Maurice and I will sing a few tunes.' Bill suggested.

Bill grabbed his guitar, strummed a few chords that Priddy would recognize, and they set off in harmony with a song.

Bang! Bang! Bang! The sound came from the ceiling.

'I think we have been sent a message!' Bill put down his guitar. 'Mind you, she has stamina, day and a half riding a horse, she must be tough!'

'She is the only one who can help Marcus, we need her in good spirits.' Alana whispered.

After several games, early evening closed in, the light from the windows reflected on the snow crystal on the window.

'Well, we need to be getting off.' Mumbled Mr Anderson with a slight slur.

'I think its best if you stay here the night Peter.' Bill looked over at Mr Anderson.

'That sounds nice, it's been a while since we stayed away. Peter doesn't need to tend to anything until morning.' She nodded amiably.

'Yes, Ceri, you and Peter can have the pull-out sofa in the living room, Mathew can sleep in Joshua's room.' Alana's forehead creased.

'It's ok, I will sleep on the floor with Rutger and Jasper, we are old friends, sharing a room won't be a problem.' Sophia offered.

Milly, looked at Joshua, 'It's ok Mum, I will sleep in Joshua's room.'

Joshua nodded, he had something else on his mind.

'What happens if Ethel De Gallo does not want to perform the reversal of magic for Sargent Harrow?' Joshua asked.

'There is nothing we can do. Earth Magic cannot be forced; it is given freely.' Rutger reflected, 'I just hope that she realized that even though Marcus Harrow does not have Earth Magic, he is a good man, and comes from a family who have a strong history with Earth Magic.'

'Why has there not been a family member who has been born with Earth Magic more recently?' Joshua enquired.

'Earth Magic is a mystery. Some families like the Applebys, seem to have children every other generation with Earth Magic.' Rutger rested his eye on Alana, 'Some like the Andersons, who pass down the magic of the Doorkeeper, not so frequently. The Harrow family, it is very infrequent, but they are usually very powerful with Earth Magic.'

'I see, so Earth Magic it's self decides who will be born with magic?'

'Yes, like I said, it's a mystery we accept.' Rutger raised his palms upwards and shrugged his shoulders.

'We can debate Earth Magic all night, I usually leave that to you and Sophia. I think under that gruff exterior, Ethel De Gallo will make the right choice.' Jasper encouraged them, 'But now, I think it's time for a spot of supper, any of that excellent ginger cake Alana?' Jasper smiled at Alana, 'Omph!' he felt an elbow in his ribs.

'I think Alana has done enough running around today.' Sophia looked over at Rutger. 'We will make supper,' she smiled at Alana, 'That is if you don't mind.'

'No, no, you go ahead.' Alana laughed.

Mrs Anderson went to get up from her chair.

'No Ceri, you sit back, I know you get little time to do that.' Sophia put up her hand.

Sandwich's, cakes, and drinks were prepared and laid out on the table; Sophia cast a critical eye over the table.

'Looks splendid.' Rutger picked up a plate of sandwich's, held it out for Alana to take one.

Bang! Bang! Bang!

'Ah, it would seem our guest has awoken.' Bill smiled at his wife.

Alana got up from her chair and poked her tongue out cheekily at him.

Bang! Bang! Bang!

Alana blew out her cheeks and left the table and climbed the stairs to Milly's bedroom. She placed her hand on the door handle, took a deep breath, knocked on the door and went in.

Ethel De Gallo was sat up in bed. Her fingers drummed impatiently on the blanket.

'Before I come down, I want a plate of sandwiches, a glass of stout which has had a hot poker plunged in it, and a slice of cake. When I have eaten, I will come down and you can present your case for the reversal of the spell which has been cast on my great nephew.' Her voice sounded like crackling glass.

'Would you like any company while you eat?' out of habit Alana straightened the blanket. 'We could make a space at the table for you.'

'Don't fuss,' Ethel De Gallo pulled the blanket to loosen it from its edges, 'did I say I wanted company? If I wanted company, I would have my horse Chester in here, fancy getting him up the stairs?' her eyebrows raised, she cocked her head to one side.

Alana locked eyes with Ethel. 'If you want a horse in your bed, I can oblige, but I am sure it will not be comfortable.' She walked to the door, 'I will be up soon with a tray.' Alana threw over her shoulder and gently closed the door.

Bill was standing on the bottom of the stairs waiting for Alana. She wrinkled her nose at him and held up her hand.

'Don't ask.' She said as he stood to one side. 'She is an old curmudgeon!'

'Well Mum, what did she say?' Joshua asked Alana as she walked in.

Alana raised her eyes to the ceiling.

'This is not going to be easy.' She replied, 'Rutger, put a poker in the fire, she wants it to be put into her stout to warm it up.'

Alana poured out a glass of stout and gave it to Rutger. On a tray she made several different sandwiches. She heard the hiss as Rutger plunged the white-hot poker into the stout.

'Well, hope she enjoys this!' she stood with the laden tray.

'Remember, this is for Marcus.' Sophia encouraged.

Alana climbed the stairs and tapped the door with her foot. Balancing the tray in one hand she opened the door.

'Well come in quickly, you're letting in a draught!' grumbled De Gallo. She pulled the blankets around her neck.

Alana put the tray on the bed and the stout on the bedside cabinet.

'Hope you enjoy it.' She said simply.

'Where is the horse?' De Gallo quipped.

Alana bit back a reply, instead she went to the door to leave De Gallo to eat.

'I am very tired.' She pushed a sandwich around the plate, 'I will come down at breakfast to talk about Marcus Harrow. Leave me now.' De Gallo nibbled on a sandwich, took a large gulp of her drink and waved Alana out from the room.

CHAPTER 34
TRANSLATIO MAGICAE

Joshua rubbed his elbow; it was sore after he hit it last night on the side of his bed. He crept into the kitchen and put the kettle on, spooned tea into two teapots. He wanted to set up breakfast on the table for everyone. He had just set the table when the ceiling vibrated.

Bang! Bang! Bang!

Joshua gritted his teeth. De Gallo had made her presence known. And probably woken everyone in the household. He wondered if he should go up and see what she wanted but decided to leave it to Mum or Sophia. He heard his parents' door open and shut and his mother's light tread as she went along the landing. The mumbling of voices, a door shutting quietly. His mother coming down the stairs.

'Oh Joshua, you're up!' his mother exclaimed.

'Yes, thought I would set out breakfast and save you a job,' he smiled ruefully at his mother, 'does she want breakfast taken up to her?'

'Yes, porridge and tea. I'll get that going if you want to finish doing breakfast.' She washed her hands and dried them briskly.

The kettle boiled and Joshua filled the teapots with water and put a knitted tea cosy on each of them. Everything was out on the table, and he was pleased at his presentation. A door opened and Mrs Anderson stepped in from the living room.

'Morning Joshua,' Mrs Anderson said, her eyes glanced at the table, 'Oh, that looks smashing. Very considerate of you!'

Joshua ran upstairs to get Milly and Mathew up. He stopped his step when a voice called out to him.

'Be quiet! Its only six thirty in the morning.' De Gallo's voice broke the silence of the house.

'Well, if anyone is not awake, they are now!' he grumbled to himself.

'I'm old, not deaf!' De Gallo called out.

'And really annoying.' He whispered.

Now, don't be rude. Ethel De Gallo is old in Earth Magic; she should be respected. Prudence stood behind him.

Yes, what have you done compared to her? Insolence, that's what I call it. Gertie hopped about.

Rutger popped his head out of the bedroom door.

'Breakfast is ready downstairs when you're ready.' Joshua said.

'Ah, right, we will be down shortly.' He replied blearily.

Joshua opened his bedroom door. Milly was already dressed; Mathew pulled the covers over his head.

'Come on Mathew, breakfast is ready, and your parents are up.' Joshua jovially nudged Mathew with his toe. 'See you downstairs.'

Taking the stairs two at a time he raced Milly downstairs. In the kitchen the Andersons were already seated and pouring out tea.

'We have to get off early to tend to the chickens and other bits around the farm.' Mr Anderson took two sausages and put them in bread. 'Mathew can stay here until tomorrow. I will pick him up in the afternoon.'

'That's great. Thank you.' Joshua grabbed a slice of bread, buttered it and drizzled honey all over it.

Alana entered the kitchen, 'Well she has her breakfast. Now we wait.'

Joshua pushed a cup of tea over to his mother. 'There you go Mum.'

'Now that's what I call breakfast.' Commented Bill as he entered the room followed by Sophia, Rutger and Jasper.

Everyone sat down and delved into the scrumptious breakfast. Mathew opened the door. 'I am sure I could hear Ethel De Gallo talking to someone.' He squeezed in between his parents at the table.

Well of course she is nub skull. She is talking to her horse. He is her magical creature. Gertie pecked Mathew's shin under the table.

'Well, I think Ethel De Gallo might have a sense of humour after all! Bring my horse to my bedroom indeed!' Alana looked across the table at Sophia. 'I'll go up and see if she needs anything else'

'We had better get going, farm won't run itself.' Mr Anderson pushed his chair back, 'Mathew, we will pick you up tomorrow afternoon.'

'Thanks Dad.' Mathew replied with a mouthful of toast.

Alana opened the door and stood back in alarm. In front of her stood Ethel De Gallo.

'Good morning, I was just coming up to see you.' Alana smiled brightly.

'Well, I am here now.' She put her hand up and waved Alana out of the way.

Joshua vacated his seat as it was nearest the door to allow De Gallo to sit down.

'It is nice to see manners in the young.' She promptly sat down.

'We'll be off then. Nice to meet you, Ethel.' Mrs Anderson said.

'It is Miss De Gallo, thank you.' De Gallo responded coolly.

'Right, well, thank you for a lovely day. We'll see you tomorrow.' Mrs Anderson raised an eyebrow at Alana.

'Tsk, hurry up, I don't have all day!' De Gallo brushed an imaginary hair off her forearm.

When the Anderson's had left the room became quiet. De Gallo looked around the table at each of them.

'I will hear your request now.' She sat back and closed her eyes.

Rutger leaned forward. 'A good man, your great nephew,'

De Gallo's eyes snapped open. 'I know who he is, don't take all day telling me. I need the facts.' She closed her eyes again.

'Marcus Harrow is a sergeant Police Officer. He met a woman who unbeknown to him is a practitioner of Dark Magic. She used her Dark Magic and put him under the spell of Sleep of the Dead. Harrow needs a relative with Earth Magic to get him out of the sleep and reverse the magic. You are his only relative who has Earth Magic, you are the only one who can reverse the spell and bring back a good man.' Rutger tapped the table with his hand, he wasn't sure if De Gallo had fallen asleep.

Her eyes opened, bright and intelligent, she brought her fingers into a steeple in front of her.

'Marcus Harrow is without Earth Magic. I cannot help you.' De Gallo looked around the table.

'What just like that, you're not even going to try,' Bill burst out.

'You ask a lot of me for no real gain. I am old, trying to perform this magic would kill me. I will not use up the last of my days on a fool's errand.' De Gallo got up from her chair. 'I cannot help you.' She turned to the door.

'Mooremarsh has won.' Joshua shouted at her.

De Gallo stood dead still, her hands trembled at her sides, she turned slowly to Joshua.

'What did you say,' Her voice was a hoarse whisper.

'I said, then Mooremarsh has won,' Joshua looked at her defiantly, his eyes blazed into hers.

'Do you mean Delvera Mooremarsh?' she grabbed the back of the chair.

'Yes,' Joshua replied confused at her reaction.

'Delvera Mooremarsh, whose grandparents are Alister Amissum and Ana Vicks?' Her mouth drew into a fine line.

'They were the epitome of evil!' she rasped, she turned pale and looked as if she would fall. Her fingers held the back of the chair tightly, her knuckles turned white.

'Yes, that is the lineage of Delvera Mooremarsh,' Sophia got up and helped her sit back in her chair.

De Gallo sat trembling. 'Ana Vicks killed my fiancée on the eve of our wedding.' Her hand fluttered to her chin, lost in thought, 'She killed him for no other reason than he loved me and not her. Jonah was a gentle man; his Earth Magic was beautiful to behold. How could she have ever thought he would have been interested in someone so dark and evil.' She spat the words out, 'She pursued him, knowing he was already taken. Ana Vicks didn't care, she wanted Jonah, coveted him like an object. She couldn't have him, so she told him she would kill him on the eve of his wedding. I told Jonah we should not marry, but he would not have it, he loved me deeply.'

Alana stepped forward and put a hand on her shoulder.

'Thank you, there is no comfort here, the memories of Jonah's slow and painful death, it was a form of torture really. The memories are still raw today.' She sighed deeply, 'I could not retaliate with Earth Magic. I sought her out, I wanted to kill her, but Naïve, my horse stopped me, he kept me sane and in the light. He spoke to me day and night, never leaving me while I was in a frenzy of despair, hovering on the cusp of Dark Magic.'

They all sat in shocked silence.

De Gallo sat back and looked at Rutger.

'I will perform what you ask. It will be some way of honoring Jonah.' She looked at Joshua, 'First I must rest, we will perform the ritual this afternoon. Young man, help me up the stairs.'

Joshua came around the table and took De Gallo's arm and helped her out of the chair. Slowly they climbed the stairs together. He opened the door to Milly's room, it was dim, the curtains had not been drawn. He went to the window and drew them back. In the corner he spied De Gallo's staff. He heard her laugh low behind him.

'That is the stone of Ealdread, it has great power. The stone was found a thousand years ago. It has not been passed down too many. I am honoured it chose me.' She walked over to the staff and picked it up. 'Soon it will have to choose another, for I know my time is near.'

'Here, hold it.' De Gallo went to the corner and took the staff from its position, stretched out her hand to Joshua.

Joshua took it gingerly. The wood was smooth to the touch.

'Grip it properly, don't be afraid of it!' De Gallo pursed her lips.

He placed a tighter grip on the staff. It felt warm in his hand, the blue stone flickered a gentle glow, and burst into a brilliant blue flame. He stood opened mouthed and looked at De Gallo. She was smiling at him.

'I think the stone of Ealdread has chosen well. The staff is yours when I pass the veil of death. Now go. Send Sophia and Alana up to me, there are things I must discuss with them.' She nodded to the door, 'leave the staff in the corner it's not yours yet.'

Midday arrived and De Gallo came down. She wore her hair in a lose braid at the nape of her neck. Her eyes were clear.

'Let us go to my great nephew, Marcus Harrow.' She commanded.

'Jasper, you stay here with Milly and Mathew.' Alana gave him a watery smile.

Joshua held De Gallo's arm as they walked over the slippery snow and helped her into the front seat of the car. Once everyone was squashed in Bill drove them to Malmesbury Hospital. As they drew up, Joshua thought how old the building looked.

'Bill, you stay in the car. Everyone else, let's go in.' Rutger commanded.

Once more Bill felt the hair on the back of his neck bristle at being ordered around by Rutger. Alana put a hand on his cheek before she got out.

They found their way to Harrow's ward quite easily. The noise of their boots on the linoleum amplified in the silent corridor. A nurse came out from a side room.

'Can I help you?' She asked suspiciously, looking at the Elder's strange attire.

Sophia put her hand up and whispered, 'Sleep.'

The nurse started to crumple to the ground, Rutger caught her. He dragged her to the room she had just come from and put her in a chair.

'We have about twenty minutes before she wakes up, we will have to be quick.' Sophia warned them.

Alana walked ahead looking in the small wards. She finally found the one with Harrow. She waved the others to follow her.

'Thankfully he is alone. Joshua, you stand in the doorway and watch for anyone.'

De Gallo walked to his bedside and looked at him.

'He has the Harrow look about him.' She murmured and placed her hands on his temples.

Sophia stretched out her hand to help. De Gallo shook her head.

'You are not of his blood. You cannot help.' She shook her head and waved Sophia's hand away.

De Gallo closed her eyes and called his name.

Marcus! Marcus Harrow, it is I your great aunt, Ethel De Gallo. Seek my voice, you are in danger, you are dying.

All De Gallo could see was darkness. She could not touch his mind. She tried again with more force.

Marcus Harrow, it is I your great aunt, Ethel De Gallo, find me!

Nothing. De Gallo opened her eyes and looked at Sophia.

'You, have it?' she asked.

Sophia nodded, from within her cloak she took out a silver dagger. It gleamed under the ward lights.

'What,' Rutger began, he was silenced by De Gallo raising her hand.

'The only way to help Harrow is Translatio Magicae, the transfer of magic,' De Gallo looked at them calmly, 'our hands must be joined in blood.'

'I won't allow it, it is forbidden.' Rutger folded his arms.

'Yet, I understand one amongst us performed it unwittingly to save a loved one.' Her eyes rested on Alana.

'You waste time, go if you do not want to be here.' She waved him away, she turned her gaze to Sophia and held out her hand.

Sophia placed the dagger into De Gallo's Hand.

'You performed the ritual of cleansing on the dagger?'

Sophia's head nodded a fraction.

'Jonah, I do this for you, my love.' De Gallo whispered and kissed the dagger.

She grabbed Harrow's cold and clammy hand and rested it flat on the side of the bed. She held her staff and kissed the stone.

'Goodbye old friend.' She handed her staff to Sophia.

Placing her hand on top of Harrow's, she plunged the knife through her hand and his, locking their hands together with the blade.

'We are connected by blood. We share my Earth Magic.' De Gallo gritted her teeth, forcing herself not to scream out from the pain. She felt her blood flowing through the wound into Harrows.

'My staff.' She held out her hand.

Sophia placed the staff back into De Gallo's hand and stood back as the stone exploded into a blue flame. She placed her cheek against Harrow's temple.

Marcus Harrow we are connected by the blood of our ancestors, by the blood of one who has Earth Magic. It is I your great aunt, Ethel De Gallo. I am here seek, me out!

Aunt Ethel? Harrow's voice reached her faint but clear.

Yes, nephew, it is I. We don't have much time; I need you to listen. You must touch my hand, you are dying. She stretched out her hand to him.

But I like it here, so calm, so warm. Harrow's stubborn voice came back.

You are from a family who have magic, Dark magic has been used against you. Take my hand. De Gallo implored him, she felt herself growing weak from the loss of blood. *Family and friends await you; this is a lie. Take my hand.*

I am happy here. His reply lacked conviction.

Then why are you alone, when those who love you are waiting for you, she pressed him. *Take my hand Marcus, come home.*

For what seemed an eternity she waited for his answer in the abyss.

I can't see your hand.

De Gallo smiled, she thought of her staff, the abyss lit up with a warm blue light. Marcus Harrow stood with his back to her.

Turn around and take my hand Marcus. She guided him gently.

Marcus Harrow turned and stared at her, astonished at her ancient age. He took a few steps towards her. She flung her arms around him in an embrace. Then stepped back.

You must ask Alana and Bill to explain everything to you. They are true and good friends. Take my hand.

Harrow took De Gallo's hand; he felt his body being sucked away. He opened his eyes to the dead body of Ethel De Gallo, her head resting on his chest.

'Harrow, we don't have time to explain now. You must not tell anyone what happened, they will think you are mad.' Alana looked at him, 'do you understand?'

Harrow nodded weakly at her.

Sophia took the staff from De Gallo's hands and touched her with it, whispering something under her breath.

De Gallo disappeared.

'This will hurt.' She grabbed the knife in his hand and pulled it out. Harrow held in a scream.

'Well done,' she touched Harrows wound with the staff and it healed.

'We must go if we are not to be detected.' Rutger urged.

'Tell no one!' Sophia demanded, 'they will think you mad if you do!' she held his gaze for a moment, turned and headed out the ward with the others.

Outside Sophia called Joshua over.

'Ethel De Gallo is dead.' She lamented quietly, she looked back at the hospital.

'She died saving Harrow.'

She held the staff out towards Joshua.

'She told me the stone recognized you.' She solemnly handed him De Gallo's staff, 'The stone of Ealdread is now yours. Treat it with respect, learn its ways.'

CHAPTER 35
IT DIDN'T END WELL

Mooremarsh sat in her dressing gown, she hadn't bothered to get dressed. She drummed her fingers on the kitchen table. Something was nagging at her, gnawing at her mind. She thought back over the past few days. What was niggling her?

Mathew Anderson, the name came unbidden into her mind. He had stood with the elders and the Appleby children the other day when she was coming out of the house. She rubbed her temples, closed her eyes, and tried to pull the memory into her mind. She had been so caught up with satisfaction that they hadn't recognized her at the time, she had dismissed Mathew Anderson. But he had seen something, and she wondered what it was. She recalled the memory and tried to focus on his face. The way he looked at her. Her forehead crinkled. The boy was not exactly looking at her but threw her. His eyes were wide with revulsion and terror. Her eyes snapped open. What had he seen? She had to find out.

'What is it he saw?' A shiver ran down her back.

The chair scraped against the floor as she stood up.

You are not of this realm The Ruby Dragon had told her. She pushed the memory out of her mind and went to her bedroom to get dressed.

She applied cerise lipstick to her lips and looked carefully at her face. The little fine lines annoyed her, but there was nothing she could do about it. Slipping the lipstick into her handbag she noticed a blotch on her hand.

'No, not yet I thought I would have more time.' Mooremarsh shrieked.

You must find another, before the life force you have is finished. A voice called to her.

Mooremarsh flinched, 'Who are you!'

No reply came, she shook her head. 'Must be talking to myself.'

She looked at her hand, the blotches were getting worse. Her eyes flicked up to the mirror. She sucked in air. The fine lines were deepening.

You need the energy of another!

Without hesitation, Mooremarsh raced down the stairs, donned a coat, grabbed her keys, and left the house. The street was still, empty, only the snow gave it any company. Mooremarsh got in her car and drove carefully on the icy road towards town. As she drove down the high street there were few people. She grimaced; they all hovered around in groups so there was no one to prey on. She drove on slowly so not to skid in the icy road. She decided to turn left and drove past the old hotel, in the window were twinkling lights, behind them were people celebrating.

'Soon you will all be old.' Mooremarsh snorted at their joy.

She screamed out in pain, her vision began to blur, she drove on and took the road that led past Bill Appleby's garage and over the bridge. All was silent and still in the snowy lane. She stopped the car; the windows were starting to mist up. Her hand slipped down to a knob, and she found her fingers were stiff, it was difficult to turn the knob to adjust the heater.

It won't be long, you are dying. The Vale of Death slowly approaches.

She was near the Appleby's cottage, she needed to be careful, she didn't want to be detected. She winced at the beating pain of her ageing hands.

That one. Young and full of life force! The voice urgently pushed against her mind.

Mooremarsh put the break on the car, and gasped as she spotted her next victim. A postman was walking away from her, a bag on his back. She followed him for a few minutes, taking pleasure in the uncomfortable glances he threw back at her.

Quickly, or it will be too late! The voice hissed.

Mooremarsh pushed her foot down on the accelerator and came to a stop just past the postman. She opened the door and got out of the car and waited for him to catch up

'Excuse me, is this the way to the Appleby's' she asked in a croaky voice.

He threw a glance at her, he was smiling, but it left his lips, her appearance startled him.

'Yes, they are just beyond the bend.' He looked at her unsure.

Mooremarsh smiled, he was young, he would have a good supply of lifeforce to give her.

She cupped her hand to her ear, 'Sorry, I can't hear very well.' She shuffled towards him and feigned slipping.

The postman dropped his bag, snow flew up and littered the bag's fabric.

'Wait, I will help you,' he rushed to help her.

He flung his arms out and ran towards her and caught her.

'That was close, you need to be careful.' He smiled goodheartedly. He was so close she could smell his spicy aftershave.

'Thank you, you are doing me a great service.' She said coyly.

His eyes looked at her questioningly. Mooremarsh put her arms around his neck and dug her fingers into the soft flesh. She felt him flinch in pain.

'What are you doing,' he shrieked out, his hands clawed at hers.

Her fingers like talons clung on tighter, digging into the tender flesh, waiting for him to weaken under her spell. She sang her spell, holding him firmly, she felt the pulsating lifeforce pump through her fingers, leaving him, entering, and feeding her.

'Exhilarating,' she sang out ecstatically.

The Postman's struggles became limp beneath her fingers, she chuckled at his weakness. His brown eyes turned white and stared into hers, finding nothing but coldness, the depths of evil. Mooremarsh held his stare and bored into his terrified look; she stripped the last embers of his life force. He let out a blood curdling scream, birds overhead flew out of the trees in fright, leaving behind bare branches. Mooremarsh felt a new lifeforce pounding in her veins, the feeling was exhilarating. She let go of the unfortunate post man and watched his desiccated parchment thin corpse sliver to the ground.

'That was delicious, quite delicious!' her voice intoxicated, it echoed out to the silence.

She tapped the body with her toe. The postman's paper like corpse fragmented into small paper like shards. Mooremarsh looked down quizzically, a nasty smile spread over her face.

'Now this is an interesting way to get rid of a body.' She kicked what remained of the postman, clapping her hands with glee as the corpse fragmented into the air, leaving no trace behind except some smudges of grey ash here and there in the snow. She walked back to the car. A cold breeze touched her face, she closed her eyes enjoying the touch. She examined her hands as they took hold of the car handle. They were smooth and without the ugly blotches. The handle felt hot as the ice stung her skin, she opened the door and slid onto the driver's seat. She laughed as she drove home. Now there was only one more thing to do. Capture the Djinn. For that she needed the help of Clarke. Driving back to her house, the snow was falling again. It covered the bonnet of the car in a thick blanket of snow. She kept the car wheels in the dark tracks in the road, following the icy trail until she got home. She came to a slow halt outside her house. The snow was starting to build up around the door, it had covered the pathway and looked like a white carpet. She sat in the now cooling warmth of the car, reluctant to get out and brave the snowstorm. Her feet were getting cold, and her hands started to feel numb.

'Time to go,' she grimaced to herself. Mooremarsh threw open the car door, slammed it shut behind her, her boots ploughed through the thick snow. Reaching the door, she fiddled in her bag for the house keys. Her numb fingers could barely hold them. Eventually, she crashed through the door and ran to the fireplace. Small embers of coal flashed their orange faces at her. She grabbed some small sticks and started to encourage the embers to set fire to the sticks. Soon she had a roaring fire, she sat with a cup of tea and her toes pointing towards the heat. She eyed the snow which was now increasing the thickness of its fall.

'I think we will change the venue to the circus. It will be a pleasure to see the look on the Djinn's face when we trap him in a cage!'

Mooremarsh pushed herself lazily from her chair and stepped into the living room. It felt cold and the hair on her arm raised up. In the corner was a small cupboard with a veiled object on top. She removed the veil and revealed a large crystal ball balanced on an onyx plinth. Carefully removing the ball from its place, she took it back to the warm kitchen.

'Not sure if it's too soon to use Dark Magic to contact Clarke. This should amplify my magic.'

She set the ball on the table and sat in front of it. Placing her hands around it, she stared into the middle of the glass orb. It was clear, the occasional shard of light shone through it. She closed her eyes and steadied her breathing, feeling the beat of her heart in her breast. Clearing her mind, she brought Clarke's image to the front of her mind, seeing only his face. Her fingers felt the ball growing colder, a bone chilling coldness, she shivered, but controlled her thoughts.

Clarke. She called to him; her fingers felt the blistering coldness of Dark Magic as she used it to amplify her thoughts.

Clarke! She screamed his name.

The silence was like a chasm, it frightened her, had she lost her power? Then she felt it, his presence.

Clarke, I need to talk to you. He was ignoring her!

Clarke, answer me now! You bound yourself to obedience! She screamed, hoping the force of her voice would hurt him.

I am here. Don't be so violent! Clarke's voice sounded upset.

Always answer me when I call you. Mooremarsh smiled, at least he learnt a lesson.

I thought we were to meet tomorrow. He replied surly.

We do. I want you to bring the Djinn to the circus tomorrow. She ordered.

Are you mad? There is thick snow out there, Forrest can hardly walk now. How are we to get to Cirencester from here in this snow! Clarke sounded desperate.

That is for you to sort out. We will meet there late morning. Make sure you do not fail me. She warned him.

And if I can't get Forrest there. Then what? Clarke asked.

Do not disappoint me. Mooremarsh hissed. She felt his uncertainty.

Yes, but what if I can't get him there? Clarke babbled.

She laughed a slow, evil laugh.

You love your family, don't you? She issued the veiled threat.

Yes, of course, why? He sounded scared.

Do I have to spell it out for you? Her acid laced voice threw the question to him.

Clarke was silent, she felt his insecurity across the distance. A cruel smile played on her lips.

It's not my fault if I can't get him there. Why don't you come here? Maybe in the back garden? He offered.

Don't be stupid. Bring him to the circus or face the consequence. She let the sentence sink in. *I will not be trifled with.*

Yes but- Clarke started but Mooremarsh cut him off.

ENOUGH. No more if's, but's or maybes. Make sure he is there, or your family dies a torturous death. Do I make myself clear? You are to obey; you entered into a pact with me of your own free will. I require your total obedience, or you will pay the consequences for disobedience. Do we understand each other now? She felt him recoil from the sting of her words.

Yes, I understand. We will be there mid-morning, as you command. Clarke sounded stunned; he only now realized the price of his alliance with her.

Mooremarsh took her smarting fingers off the orb and put them under her armpits to warm them. Everything was falling into place. Tomorrow the Djinn would be enslaved, and she would have eternal life.

CHAPTER 36
HARROW IS REVEALED

Rat-tat-tat

The knock at the front door was all too familiar to Joshua. He rushed and opened it. Grandad Rose stood in front of him, he turned and waved Priddy and Harrow into the warmth of the house.

'No, I am not here just for a spot of breakfast, but I am sure that would not go amiss.' Grandad Rose gave Joshua a hug.

'Get your parents could you.' He pointed to the kitchen, 'This way Marcus.' Harrow limped after Priddy.

Before Joshua could call out, Alana came into the kitchen from the living room, she held a bushel of dried basil in her hand.

'Marcus, you are up soon. Thought they would have got you to rest for at least a week.' Alana sounded uncertain.

Harrow rested a painful gaze on her.

'I am here to hear the truth. I want to know what has been going on. Everything.' Harrow sat down heavily at the table, 'and I mean everything. Or else our friendship has meant nothing.' He looked over at Priddy.

'Yes, you deserve that, even though I am sworn to secrecy, you have entered my world, I will not lie to you.' Alana sat opposite him.

'We are stone cold. Joshua, cups of tea all around please.' Grandad Rose asked rubbing his hands in front of the hot stove.

Milly and Mathew entered the room having heard voices they recognized.

'Mr Priddy, hello,' Milly gave him a hug, 'Hello Sergeant Harrow. Are you feeling better?'

Harrow grunted and looked over at Alana.

'Milly, is there any cake?' Grandad rose enquired; his eyes glanced at the pantry.

'Yes, Mums made some seed cake and there is Christmas cake left over.' Milly went to the pantry, grabbed two cake tins, and took them to the kitchen counter.

'I will phone Bill; he is at the Andersons helping Peter converting the tractor into a snow plough.' Alana got up and went to the phone.

Mathew put out plates and forks, then sat down next to Grandad Rose, not sure what to say, he took time adjusting his chair, and straightening the tablecloth. Alana came back to the table and took a teapot from Joshua.

'Bill will be here soon.' She started pouring tea and paused, 'it would be better Marcus if Bill was here too. He can explain somewhat the experience you have gone through.'

The door burst open, and Jasper stood there.

'I see you have recovered then.' He eyed the table, 'ah, tea and cake, don't mind if I do.' He grabbed a cup and plate from the cupboard and sat down with them. He tapped his cup towards Alana and hacked off a large piece of Christmas cake. 'It's the cherries and ginger, can't resist them.' He rubbed his hands together in glee.

Sophia and Rutger came in from the garden. Sophia kicked off her boots in the hall, Rutger sat down on the stairs and struggled to get his off.

'Good to see you in good form Marcus.' Sophia said gently.

Mathew got up and retrieved some more cups and plates, leaving a spare setting for Bill.

'This must have been traumatic for you.' Sophia sat down opposite Harrow, 'Everything you once knew has been turned upside down. On top of that, to have your life hanging on a thread.' She took the cup Mathew offered her, 'Yes, I can understand why you are here.'

Rutger sat down, leaning heavily on his cane.

'Our laws forbid any discussion on this matter.' Rutger's face set like stone.

Harrow looked as if he was going to say something. Sophia held up her hand.

'Rutger, Harrow is of an Earth Magic bloodline.' Sophia started.

'Earth Magic bloodline?' Harrow interjected, his face a picture of confusion.

'Yes, Marcus, Earth Magic,' Sophia turned back to Rutger, 'I know magic has not been seen in his family for generations, but it is still there.' She stirred her tea. 'He has been exposed to our world, like Bill and Maurice, truth will keep our world protected.' She sipped her tea, 'very nice, thank you.' Putting the cup down in its saucer she continued. 'It is our duty to do what is right, not live by the letter of the law, but by its spirit.' She raised her chin challenging him to defy her.

Rutger breathed a heavy sigh. 'I bow once again to your wisdom Sophia. You really should have held the position the Highest of the Elders.'

'All that paperwork, surrounded by a narrow-minded vision. I don't think so, I would be stifled.' She made a pushing away motion as she replied.

A key rattled in the front door and Bill came in. Stamping snow off his boots, he kicked them off and walked into the kitchen in his wet socks.

'Welcome to the club Marcus.' Bill patted Marcus on the back solemnly.

Milly made a new pot of tea and poured her dad a cup, cut him a few slices of seed cake, and passed it to him. As he drank his tea, he slid the wet clammy socks off his feet under the table.

'Where do we start.' Alana began.

'The beginning would be good.' Harrow sat forward. 'And don't leave anything out.'

'Yes. My family, Maurice and yours are from an ancient line of people who are born with Earth Magic.' She began.

'Don't forget mine,' Mathew spluttered as he chewed off a piece of cake. He felt Milly's kick under the table. 'Sorry.'

'Our magic is hidden from the world by secrecy. That vow of secrecy we all take, protects us from dangerous people who want to use our magic for bad. Those who practice Earth Magic are governed by laws, and a regional council called the Elders of the Southwest. The elders of these councils make up the High council. We cannot use Earth Magic to harm others unless in self-defense or protecting the defenseless against Dark Magic. We live for the earth, caring for it, nurturing it.' Alana stopped waiting for Harrow to ask a question. He stared back at her intensely.

'On the opposite side of Earth Magic is Dark Magic.' She glanced at Sophia. 'Dark Magic has no rules, the magic they practice feeds off them, turning them evil or insane.'

'Sadly, you were attacked by someone who practices Dark Magic.' Sophia interjected.

'Why did that woman, Ethel De Gallo, put a knife threw our hands? Where did she go and how did you heal the wound in my hand?' Harrow's questions came abruptly.

'I think you should answer these questions, Sophia.' Alana suggested.

Sophia nodded slowly, she held Harrow's confused gaze.

'The first, why did Ethel De Gallo tie your hands together with a knife? She tried to save you just using Earth Magic, the spell which had been cast on you could only be undone by someone who carries your bloodline. She was the only living blood relative with Earth Magic.'

'What do you mean was?' Harrow sat back in his chair.

'Hear me out first, Marcus, everything will make some sense at the end,' Sophia took a breath, 'When just using Earth magic did not work, she used her lifeblood and performed *Translatio Magicae*, translates the transference of magic. This magic is forbidden under Earth Magic law, but she knew it was the only way to save you.' Sophia was parched and took a sip of tea. 'She performed the magic again and she found you in the darkness of your mind,' she tapped her temple, 'Do you remember her?' Sophia looked at him expectantly.

'Yes, I vaguely remember as bright blue light, her talking to me, asking me to take her hand. I opened my eyes,' Harrow stopped remembering the scene, 'there was a dead woman on my chest.' Harrow looked at her with haunted eyes.

'She gave her life to save yours.' She reached across the table and touched his cold hand. 'She did it to save you, and to honour her lost love.'

Everyone sat in silence, waiting for Sophia to continue.

'Now to your second question. The staff Ethel De Gallo had is powerful. It was able to send her body back to Earth Magic. I do not expect you to understand, it is something that is debated even amongst those with Earth Magic, there is no conclusion, it just happens.' Sophia waited for a question from Harrow.

'Does that mean she can come back like Miskunn?' Asked Milly.

Sophia raised an eyebrow at Milly. The message was loud and clear, it was not a question Sophia wanted to talk about.

'Miskunn is a magical creature, it is the first time I have heard of Earth Magic sending back someone from the dead. Magical creatures are one thing, humans are another.' Sophia put her head to one side.

'So can you raise the dead?' asked Harrow.

'No, we cannot. It is forbidden to even try. That would be in the realms of Dark Magic.' Sophia snapped at him; her eyes grew narrow.

'Sorry, didn't mean to offend you, just trying to understand.' Harrow sat back in his chair.

'No offence taken,' Sophia bowed her head. 'In exceptional circumstances, we can perform a healing, we had the staff, so I used it to heal you. Before you ask, no, I could not bring Ethel De Gallo back once she had passed over the Veil of Death.' Sophia finished.

Harrow looked at Bill. 'So have you gone through this?'

Bill looked uncomfortable talking about something he had kept secret for so long. Alana put her hand over his.

'Yes, Alana saved my life during the war. Her blood type was the only one compatible with mine. I don't have magic like she does. I can feel her moods, even when I am not around her. I can feel the energy in nature. That's all really,' he explained.

'I see.' He turned to Priddy. 'What about you?'

'I was put under the same spell last year.' Priddy shuddered. 'Alana is a distant relative. I was fortunate, she along with Joshua performed the same ritual that Ethel De Gallo did on you and managed to save me. Can't lie, I still have the occasional nightmare about it all.'

Harrow sat in silence, digesting what he had heard.

'This is going to take some time to take in.' He thought about what they had disclosed to him. A light flickered in his mind. 'Last year, all that business with Mooremarsh. Was she involved in all this magic stuff?'

Alana and Bill exchanged looks.

'Yes,' Rutger confirmed, he looked at Sophia and Jasper, shrugged his shoulders, 'In for a penny, in for a pound as they say. Delvera Mooremarsh is a practitioner of Dark Magic. Listen carefully, this may be difficult for you to understand. Delvera Mooremarsh has what we term in the Earth Magic community become an Energy Vampire, she steals the life force of others to keep her own going.'

'No.' Harrow was getting past his ability to take on new information.

'There is one thing you must understand. Petula Greensborough may practice Dark Magic.'

'There is something not right about that woman. Remember when we saw her outside Mooremarsh's house. I saw that Hag in her shadow.' Mathew's hands trembled under the table.

Milly saw them shaking and put a hand over his. He gave a thankful look.

'We are not sure what Petula Greensborough is, but good she is not.'

Harrow felt memories trying to surface, they were just out of reach. He pursed his lips trying to retrieve them.

Sophia saw his frustrated look. 'Sorry Marcus, if she has put a spell on you to stop you remembering, those memories are gone. It maybe for the best.'

'That's easy for you to say.' Harrow brushed his fringe back with his fingers.

Outside there was the blast of a horn. Bill went to the kitchen window and waved at someone.

'Peter has got the snow plough going, he is clearing the road now.' Bill came and sat down at the table.

'Why is that stone glowing on the sideboard,' Harrow pointed at Mathews stone.

Mathew got up from the table.

Don't touch it, it won't be nice. Gertie jumped up and down.

'Be quiet!' Mathew spoke sharply.

'Who's he talking too?' Harrow asked Bill.

'They each have a magical creature. We can't see them, but they can.' Bill answered.

'This gets more and more bizarre.' Harrow whispered back.

Mathew picked up the stone and winced. He was being dragged through a tunnel; his stomach felt hollow. Mathew could see Forrest sat in a cage, the woman from Mooremarsh's house stood there, then he saw Nori's face.

'Forrest is in danger, help him.'

Then the image was gone. Mathew dropped the stone on the sideboard.

'Did you see that, it dragged me down a corridor!' Mathew shouted.

'No, it did not. Your mind followed the stone, your body did not.' Rutger sighed, 'What did it show you?'

Mathew looked at all the faces around the table. 'You're not going to like it.'

CHAPTER 37
FORREST GOES HOME

Clarke stood watching Forrest rocking in the rocking chair, his eyes were closed as he rocked to the soft music of the cello playing on the record player. Forrest's hair fell in a white braid down the side of his chest. Clarke had been shocked at how quickly Forrest was ageing. His skin had turned sallow, his movements were slow and jerky. Clarke was brought out of revere by Forrest's voice. Clarke felt a stab of hatred for the Djinn. Forrest's eyes opened and he looked directed at Clarke.

'Elgar is one of my favorite composers,' he confided in Clarke.

'Prefer the Rolling Stones myself.' Clarke replied.

Forrest laughed and demanded to listen to one of Clarkes records.

'Punchy,' was Forrest's verdict when the album had finished.

. 'If you don't like it, you just have to say so.' Clarke turned a shade of salmon and took his album off the turntable.

'I do believe your father wanted to go for a walk. Go and fetch him please, I will just get on my coat.'

'It would be nice to see the circus one more time.' Clarke threw out casually, 'but I guess there is no way to get there in all this snow.'

Forrest's eyes looked away dreamily. He felt a coldness in Clarke, he had chosen to follow darkness, and there was nothing he could do about it. Too many years had passed by for him to make any relationship with the boy.

'There is a way.' Forrest said abruptly.

Forrest grabbed the side of the rocking chair and struggled to get up. His time was coming to an end, he was glad he could spend it with his son, Erik. He heard the characteristic slap of feet on the floor. He recognized his son's walk anywhere.

'Okay Dad, where would you like to go for that walk?' Erik smiled at his father.

He tries to hide his sadness well thought Forrest.

'Clarke would like to see the circus; it would be nice to see them before I go.' He suggested.

'It's about three feet of snow out there, no way can we get to the circus.'

'I can get us there. Don't forget I am a Djinn.' Forrest smiled wryly at his son. 'It will be a good ending.'

Forrest watched the conflicting emotions cross Erik's face.

'How are we going to get there?' Clarke asked feverishly.

Forrest put a finger to his lips. 'Wait and see.'

'Clarke get a shovel and clear the path.' Erik turned to his father, 'I don't know what you have up your sleeve, but it better be good' he smiled sadly.

Clarke rushed and grabbed a shovel from beside the door where his father had left it the night before. 'Just in case we need it,' Erik had said when his mother had laughed at him. Clarke opened the door and groaned. The snow fall from the night before laid as a thick blanket. He stepped out and sank into it, the snow came up to the top of his boot. He dug his shovel in, it was soft.

'Well, that's one good thing.' He worked in a frenzy, Mooremarsh's threat at the back of his mind.

'I'll have to get you to do that more often. It took me ages to clear that path yesterday,' his father called from behind him.

Clarke stood up and admired his work. He felt a moment's pleasure at his father's words.

I am here, why is the Djinn not. Clarke's moment of euphoria was short lived at the sound of Mooremarsh's voice.

He heard his father and Forrest shuffling to the door, they were ready to leave. Clarke walked carefully back to the house and leaned the spade up beside the door.

'Well, how are we going to get there?' Clarke was not convinced.

'Have faith, smell that crisp air.' Forrest breathed in deeply, then started coughing as the cold air slipped into his lungs. He leaned heavily on Erik.

Clarke looked away embarrassed.

'We all get old Clarke. Time is like a thief, it creeps up behind us, stealing our youth, our prime, before we know it, we are no longer young but staring into the chasm of old age.'

Clarke rolled his eyes and turned away. Forrest seemed to know once again what he was thinking.

'I do believe our transport has arrived.' Forrest pointed at the road.

Hurricane stood there; he gave Forrest a baleful look.

'I know, it's cold and you hate the cold. It is good to see you again my old friend.' Forrest chuckled.

'You have to be joking, you expect us all to ride on that horse to Cirencester, in the snow!' Clarke choked; a wave of desperation started to rise in his guts. He looked at the horse in sheer panic.

'Now Clarke, wait for Forrest to explain.' His father chided him.

'I think it's better if we all get on Hurricane's back and he can show you.' Forrest shrugged with an air of self-satisfaction. 'Son, I will need your help.' He placed his hand under Erik's arm.

Hurricane got down onto his knees and whined at Forrest to get onto his back.

'Thank you, dear friend.' Forrest caressed his mane.

With the help of Erik, he managed to get on the saddle. Hurricane stood up and nodded his head up and down.

'Grab the saddle and get on Erik.' Forrest looked down at his son, 'There's no better feeling in the world than riding Hurricane.'

The horse neighed it's reply.

Erik looked at the height of the horse uneasily. He put his foot in the stirrup, took hold of the side of the saddle an threw himself up onto the horse.

'Come on Clarke, your dad will help you up.' Forrest laughed.

Clarke approached Hurricane; the horse shied away from him, snorting wildly, rolling his eyes at Clarke.

Clarke felt angry, he hid it. 'Stupid horse,' He mumbled to himself.

'Behave Hurricane, you can lift more than this. Be still.' Forrest rebuked him.

Clarke approached once more; Hurricane rolled his eyes at him, his body trembled but remained still. His father held out his hand to him and Clarke took it in his. His father's firm grasp was reassuring. Clarke took a few steps and jumped onto Hurricane's back. The horse moved, adjusting his body under their weight.

'Now, you will see the splendor of Hurricane.' Forrest's chest puffed out proudly as he presented the horse.

He thinks more about his horse than his son. The thought flitted through Clarke's mind. Before he could think about it, the horse started to canter away.

'Good boy Hurricane, back to the circus.' Shouted Forrest in glee.

'For goodness' sake, we will be-' Clarke didn't finish his sentence.

Hurricane spread out huge black wings, tinged with gold, and beat them. The horse took to flight and climbed higher and higher in the air. Clarke heard a screaming; his father was screaming!

'Amazing, amazing!' His father kept shouting.

The freezing air etched Clarke's face and his eyes watered. He held onto his father tightly. He felt the security of the warmth of his body against his. His heart melted. Maybe he should tell him about Mooremarsh, and what was waiting for them.

And see your whole family die?

Clarke closed his eyes. His father would never forgive him, but there was nothing he could do. He had made his choice.

'There it is. Home.' Forrest called out weakly.

Clarke was thrown forward, he opened his eyes to the big-top, lights flashing. As they came closer, he saw a figure standing alone in the snow. Nori stood huddled banging her arms against her body, as they got closer, she waved to them. Hurricane settled onto the ground in front of her. He folded his wings against his body, they became invisible.

'Welcome home Forrest. I never thought I would see you again.' She unfolded her wings and flew up to help him down.

'Neither did I. Clarke wanted to see the circus, and I couldn't resist.'

'I see.' Nori drawled in a way that clearly meant she did not see; she threw Clarke a reproachful look.

Erik slid off the saddle, his feet hit the ground hard.

'Thank you,' Erik patted Hurricane's neck.

Clarke looked around for Mooremarsh, she was nowhere to be seen. He dismounted Hurricane and walked over to Forrest.

Forrest looked down at him. 'I want you to know, even though I have only known you a short time, I love you and your father dearly. I wish we could have spent more time together.'

Clarke looked away uncomfortably.

'So where do you want to go to first?' Forrest asked, taking Erik's arm.

'The ring I think.' Clarke stammered.

'The ring it is.' Forrest hobbled in the direction of the ring; Nori fluttered by his side, chatting at they went.

The ring was dim, lit by a few paraffin lamps. Nori flew to several more and lit them, illuminating the space. For the first time they all could see a large cage in the middle of the ring.

'What is that doing here?' she looked at Forrest.

Clarke had a feeling of dread, the dye was cast, there was no way back.

Nori flew over to the cage and examined it.

'I have no idea why it's been moved here?' She touched the door of the cage perplexed.

'I PUT IT THERE.' Mooremarsh screamed and entered the ring, her eyes flashed triumphantly.

'Who are you?' Nori asked her.

'None of your business. I am here for the Djinn.' Mooremarsh pointed at Forrest not able to contain her excitement.

Erik stood in front of Forrest.

'Oh, don't be stupid. A mere mortal against my magic.' Mooremarsh lifted her hand to send a spell. Nori flew into her and knocked her off her feet.

'How dare you touch me.' Mooremarsh screamed in rage.

Nori came forward again, Mooremarsh, caught Nori's wing, made a slicing motion with her hand. She held Nori's sliced off wing in her hand and dropped it disdainfully. Nori screamed in pain; blood ran down her back from the ragged open wound. Mooremarsh laughed hysterically kicking the delicate wing to one side.

'I can slice the other one off if you would like.' She drawled callously at Nori, raising an eyebrow. 'Now go, and don't bring any of your disfigured misfits with you.' Mooremarsh cackled, she was enjoying herself more than she thought she would.

Clarke stood transfixed at the sight of Nori's torn wing. He watched her stand defiantly in front of Mooremarsh, blood pumping out of the crimson wound.

'Nori, go.' Rasped Forrest, he pushed Erik to one side.

Clarke stood there, his hands hung at his sides, he felt sick at what he had become party to.

'Go now, Nori,' Erik took a step forward.

'You are of no use to me.' She looked at Erik, 'Your son is an imbecilic moron.' She turned to Clarke and stabbed a bony finger at him. 'You really thought I would teach you Dark Magic, magic my family has sacrificed to serve our entire lives. You're the grandson of a Djinn, a half breed, your bloodline is contaminated.' She spat.

Erik looked at Clarke in disbelief, staring at his son as if he were a stranger.

'What have you done!' he asked through stiff lips, the corners of his mouth were white.

'Delivered your father up to me!' Mooremarsh raised her hand up to throw a death spell at Erik, Forrest stepped in the way, the spell graced the side of Erik, he clutched his throat, gurgled a terrible sound, and crumpled to the ground.

'Well, I guess instead of dying quickly, he will now die a slow agonizing death.' She gloated; Erik's pain felt exquisite, she had never experienced the feeling before.

'No, you said you wouldn't hurt my family if I did what you wanted, if I obeyed you. I took a blood oath with you!' screamed Clarke in despair seeing his father's body. He ran over and threw his arms around his still form. 'Dad, I'm sorry, I'm sorry.' He groaned into his father's shoulder, shaking him softly, willing him to respond.

'Well, it's too late for that. You should have stuck to the plan and only brought the Djinn.' Mooremarsh looked at the Djinn as she spoke. He looked old and frail, she only hoped he had enough magic to grant her a wish. Her lips drew into a fine line as she thought about his weakness.

'Get in the cage Djinn. I enslave you for my wish.' Mooremarsh clapped feverishly. Her wish was within her grasp, she trembled with anticipation.

'Don't do it. Don't give her what she wants. She is foul' Clarke screamed thickly, he rocked his dad, trying to bring him back to consciousness.

'There is always your mother left to kill, is that what you want?' Mooremarsh goaded him, enjoying the conflicting expressions on his face.

'It's alright Clarke. Save your mother. Do as she bids.' Forrest implored him, never taking his eyes off Mooremarsh.

Erik groaned; a rattling noise caught in his throat; it was a terrible sound. Clarke stood up and walked towards the cage, the short distance seemed to take forever. He bowed his head, not wanting to look at Forrest.

'Get in the cage Forrest and be enslaved.' Clarke whispered.

He heard the heavy rasping breath and slow amble as Forrest walked towards him. Finally, he stood beside him. Clarke raised his eyes to his, Forrest's were compassionate. Clarke felt his throat tighten; he licked his dry lips.

'Get in the cage and become a slave.' He whispered hoarsely.

Forrest placed his hand on his forehead and rolled a salute at Clarke.

'I do as you ask. Grandson.' Forrest looked gently at Clarke.

Clarke felt sick at the word 'Grandson.' He had been anything but that to Forrest.

Forrest grunted in pain as he bent down onto his hand and knees and crawled into the cage. He sat in its center and slowly crossed his legs. Clarke shut the cage door; the latch clicked as it locked into place. Forrest placed his hands in the air and smacked them together. Two heavy gold bangles appeared on his wrists. The seal of Djinn slavery.

'It is done. I am your slave. You command and I obey.' Forrest's voice was loud.

Mooremarsh clapped her hands, jumping up and down. She danced over to the cage.

'My wish is eternal life.' She commanded the Djinn, she held out her hand as if to receive a gift.

Forrest sat still, saying nothing. Mooremarsh looked at him confused.

'I want my wish now!' she hissed at him. 'My wish is eternal life.'

Forrest still did not move.

'What are you doing? You cannot deny me my wish!' Mooremarsh stamped her foot and kicked the cage.

Forrest ignored her. Clarke could see Mooremarsh was about to explode with anger.

'You must grant her the wish.' Clarke moaned in a panic.

Forrest looked up at Clarke. 'I cannot.'

'Why,' Screamed Mooremarsh.

'Because you are not my master,' he spread his hands wide, his lips in a thin line, 'Clarke is my master. He enslaved me, not you.' He looked at her stonily and turned to Clarke and bowed his head solemnly, 'What is your command, Master.'

CHAPTER 38

MATHEW GIVES THE ALARM

'Forrest is at the circus, that woman, what did you say her name was, Petula Greensborough is there. Nori said he is in danger,' Mathew spread his hands out.

Rutger stood up. 'They are in grave danger. I have a feeling that I know what has happened. Delvera Mooremarsh and Petula Greensborough are the same person. Petula is an alias Mooremarsh has used to pass off as her younger self.' He banged his cane on the floor. 'Bill, will Peter Anderson plough the road so we can get to Cirencester?'

Bill stood up, 'Yes, we can follow his ploughed trail and ask him to get us to the circus.'

'No, that will take too long. Forrest and anyone with him will be dead by then. Thinking of Forrest, I have an idea.' Jasper had sprung to life having said very little during the discussion with Harrow. We have six stones between us. We could use them to enhance air magic. We could get in Bills car and use our staffs to create enough air beneath to travel over the snow, like a plane.'

'Sometimes Jasper, you come up with brilliant ideas!' Rutger patted him on the back.

'We must use extreme caution when we get there, no running off and doing your own thing!' Rutger looked at Joshua and Milly. 'Grab your stones.' He held up a hand at Priddy and Harrow, 'Sorry, but you will need to stay here.' He saw Harrow about to complain, 'No arguments, this is Earth Magic business. Please.'

'Yes, understood.' Priddy looked at Harrow.

Harrow bit the side of his cheek and nodded, 'I don't like it, but under the circumstances, I agree.'

Everyone sat squashed together in the car. Elders in the back, children in the estate car's boot. They sat waiting for Jasper's instructions.

'Hold your stone and close your eyes and think about the air pushing the car up off the ground.' He instructed them.

They all did as Jasper asked. Bill looked at the ground. The car inched off the ground, snow fell off the roof and bonnet. The car rose higher off the snow.

'It's working! We are a good six inches off the snow!' Bill exclaimed.

'Right Bill, you look in the direction you want the car to go, Alana, hold his arm so that a connection can be made with our Earth Magic and Bill's will to direct the car.' Jasper explained.

Bill found the journey nerve wracking, but his every thought was followed, and the car responded brilliantly. He directed the car in the fastest route he could think of.

'There it is!' shouted Mathew, the car jerked and touched the snow.

'Don't break concentration,' admonished Jasper.

Mathew quickly screwed his eyes closed and focused on moving the air under the car. Bill set the car down near the big-top.

'We are here.' Thankful they hadn't had an accident along the way.

Everyone opened their eyes. Alana gave Bill's arm an assuring squeeze.

'Bill, you have to stay here.' Rutger insisted, 'Understand, we have to use magic, and keep an eye on the danger, and the children.'

Alana looked at Bill, he was shocked at her flint like face.

'Yes, understood. But be warned. If Alana or the children are harmed, I am not bound by your laws.' Bill locked eyes with Rutger.

'Understood, I would feel the same way.' Rutger's eyes flicked over Sophia. He grabbed the door handle, opened the door, and got out quietly. He raised a finger to his lips, the others followed and stood by him waiting his instructions. Rutger pointed his cane at the entrance of the big-top, the only sound was the crunching of the snow under their feet. Rutger peeked inside. Mooremarsh was standing in front of a cage. Forrest was inside, and Clarke was standing to one side. He could hear the strands of their voices.

'What do you mean I am not your master?' Mooremarsh's shrill voice smashed the air.

'It was Clarke who trapped me, not you. Clarke is my master.' Forrest's voice rasped.

'It is easy. I will kill Clarke, which releases you, and you are trapped by me.' She laughed, there was a hint of uncertainty in her voice.

'That won't work.' Forrest sounded confident.

'Then I will kill him and his mother any way for deceiving me!' she snarled at him. 'If I can't have your magic, I will kill you!'

Mathew looked at the Elders, they stood there doing nothing, just waiting. He shook his head. The stone felt hot in his hand.

Save them! It called to him.

Mathew ran through the doorway and into the ring. Mooremarsh stepped back.

'You cannot kill Forrest. He is under my protection.' Mathew called out. He saw the hag step out beside Mooremarsh and trembled.

Mooremarsh put her hands on her hips in disbelief and let out a malicious laugh.

'You boy cannot do anything. You are a stupid, stupid child.' She heckled him.

'I am not a child, and I am certainly not stupid.' Mathew held out his hand with the stone and willed it to help him hide Forrest.

Mathew smiled at Mooremarsh. Forrest was gone, he had hidden him with his magic.

'Now, you were saying, I was stupid. Where is Forrest?' Mathew retorted softly, he splayed out his hands.

Mooremarsh whipped around and saw the empty cage.

'Where has he gone!' she screamed at Clarke, saliva drooled down her chin. 'Don't play your stupid games with me!'

'I, I don't know,' Clarke stammered, pulling his hair in despair, his eyes flicked over to Mathew.

'You, what have you done!' Mooremarsh bellowed at Mathew, she came closer to him.

'He is hidden from you all.' Mathew folded his arms and stared at her.

'If I can't have the Djinn, I will kill you.' She smiled a toothy grin at him. 'I know what you are, you are a Doorkeeper.' She snorted, 'If I kill you, he will be vanquished to an eternity of oblivion.' She cackled, 'Now that would be quite delicious if it wasn't that I wanted my wish.'

'I will not release him to you.' Mathew stood his ground.

'Then I have no use for you. Death it is.' Mooremarsh stared at him.

Mathew felt the stone in the palm of his hand getting hot. Forrest materialised in the cage again.

'Thank you for trying, Mathew. Your magic cannot hold a Djinn against their will. I thank you for trying.' Forrest rasped, the effort of releasing himself had taken its toll.

'Clarke, tell the Djinn to give me eternal life.' She commanded him.

Clarke stood silent. He looked at Forrest.

'Clarke cannot command me to give you eternal life for two reasons.' Forrest smiled a cool smile.

'And why is that?' Mooremarsh stepped up to the cage, running her fingers dangerously over its bars.

'Firstly, I can only give him the wish, it belongs to him, no one else.' Forrest looked at Clarke, 'Secondly, you are no longer truly human. The hag standing beside you, that is now your true form.'

Mooremarsh stood still, her heart pounding. She was a hag?

'You tell lies with that sweet tongue of yours.'

'I ask you once more Clarke, Wish the Djinn to give me eternal life.' Mooremarsh's voice was cold and menacing.

'Forrest has just told you it won't work.' Clarke replied.

'Then, I have no use for you.' She lifted her hand to throw a spell at him.

'Stop!' Forrest's voice thundered. 'You cannot harm him; he is under the protection of a Djinn. Go from here you small, minded hag.'

'If I can't kill him, then, I will kill the other one.' She twisted on her heels to Mathew.

Joshua and Milly broke away from their mother and the elders. They ran into the ring. Joshua held up his staff, Milly her stone.

'You cannot hurt us; we have the protection of three.' Joshua warned her.

He held the staff with the stone of Ealdread higher, it glowed a bright blue light.

'Go from here, now.' Joshua commanded coldly.

Mooremarsh walked towards Milly casually.

'Do you really want to be with them.' She nodded towards Mathew and Joshua. 'You are more than they will ever be. They don't even come close to the power you possess. You nearly used that power once on the edge of Dark Magic, use it now, against Clarke who has betrayed his father and Forrest.' Mooremarsh looked at Clarke, her lip curled. 'They are all insignificant, you have the power, Milly. Let me show you how to use it.'

Milly turned her face away from Mooremarsh, her breath was putrid. For a second, Milly's concentration waned. The protection of three was broken. Mooremarsh brought her hand up to strike Milly.

Miskunn flew in between them, she wrapped her wings protectively about Milly.

You will never go to Dark Magic! Miskunn screamed at Milly.

'You touch her, I will kill you.' A man's voice caught Mooremarsh off guard.

'Well, well, Bill Appleby. Did you enjoy the spell from last year?' She heckled him; her forefinger slipped down her cheek.

Bill remembered the Sleep of the Dead she had cast on him. 'Fortunately for me, my wife is more than your match.' He goaded her.

'This time, I will not put you under the sleep of death, I will merely kill you.' Mooremarsh hissed at him.

'I don't think so.' Mooremarsh spun around the sound of Alana Appleby's voice.

Alana stood with her staff held high. Beside her stood Rutger and Jasper.

'I would think again.' Came another voice.

Mooremarsh turned slowly back to Mathew. Sophia stood in front of him.

'You have lost, again Delvera Mooremarsh.' Sophia said calmly.

'So, you finally know who I am. Wondered how long it would take you.' Mooremarsh sniggered. 'Come and play dear Sophia, let us see who is the more powerful.'

'I have no interest in your games.' Sophia watched her walking slowly towards her.

Be careful. She has powerful magic. She is different. Feles hissed beside her.

Sophia ignored him, giving her total focus to Mooremarsh.

'You will be brought before the high council, you are an Energy Vampire, no one is safe with you wandering about. You will be judged by them and the council of Dark Magic.' Sophia vowed.

She saw Mooremarsh flinch.

'An Energy Vampire is forbidden even amongst those who practice Dark Magic. You cannot hide from them.' Sophia pushed the idea knowing it would unsettle the woman standing before her.

Mooremarsh opened her mouth and yawned. 'You can try, Sophia,' she spat her name out, 'But you must have tasted the delight of Dark Magic when you were growing up?' She saw Sophia flinch and smiled; the barb had reached home.

'That was a mistake Delvera, I despise you, even feel sad for you. Contempt may come close.' Sophia kept her eye on Mooremarsh.

'Then it is time for us to find out isn't it.' Delvera screamed at her.

You will not harm Sophia. The deep voice of Sylvester Bluesky boomed from the entrance of the big-top.

Gertie and Prudence stood by his side.

Go from this place, now, you have been warned.

'Well, well, the famous wolf. You're getting a bit long in the tooth for all this aren't you.' Mooremarsh looked across at him. 'Sadly, I will not comply,' a sarcastic smile spread over her lips. She held Sophia's gaze. 'Well Sophia?'

Mooremarsh charged like a bull at Sophia. Her hands raised up, two sharp talons'. She threw a static charge at her quarry. Sophia parried off the static with her staff.

'Now let's see what your friends do about this.' Mooremarsh drew a circle in the air, a red transparent wall went up and over the pair of them. 'They can't get in to help you. Let's see who has the most skill.'

Sophia heard Fele's crying terrified for her safety, she blotted out the sound of his cries.

Mooremarsh slashed the air with her finger, Sophia reached out to stop the blow.

'Hm, been practicing have we.' Mooremarsh laughed.

'Sophia, watch out for the hag beside her.' Mathew shouted out.

Sophia looked towards Mooremarsh's side; she saw nothing. Mooremarsh took advantage of Sophia's laps in concentration and slashed the air again. A slash of blood appeared on Sophia's cheek.

'Gotcha!' Mooremarsh giggled, she lifted her finger in the air and drew the number one. 'One nil I think, darling Sophia.'

'Sophia, step back, the hag is in front of you!' Mathew screamed.

It was too late. Sophia felt a powerful blow, it winded her and she fell to the floor. Mooremarsh kicked her in the head and Sophia fell into darkness.

'Yes!' Mooremarsh raised her fingers to deal a final death blow.

No, we need her. You will not kill any of them! The voice of the hag commanded her.

Mooremarsh lowered her hands, not understanding why she couldn't finally kill her quarry.

'You and I will end this another time, but not today.' Mooremarsh flicked her finger at her magnanimously.

CHAPTER 39

THE LAST FIGHT

Everyone watched in horror as Mooremarsh lowered the red wall between them.

'You were saying Sylvester Bluesky old boy?' Mooremarsh laughed at the wolf.

Rutger looked at Jasper and Alana, he gave a faint nod. They held up their stones and closed in on Mooremarsh.

'Really?' Mooremarsh gibed, 'Have you learnt nothing. I not only have Dark Magic, but something else. Put down your stupid staffs, and canes. Go home.' She flicked her finger at them.

'Bill, stand with the children, in the centre of their stones.' Alana called to her husband.

'Yes, Bill. Be a good boy and do as you're told. Alana, go and pat his head like the faithful little puppy he is!' Mooremarsh curled her lip at him.

'Dad, come over here,' Joshua called.

Bill moved to the children and ducked under their linked hands and into centre. He felt a warm tingle, it must be the protection of their stones, he thought to himself.

'So, what's next?' she jeered at them, 'could we hurry this up, I have a Djinn to deal with.' She gave a bored yawn.

A terrible wail came from Clarke's father, Clarke took a few steps towards him.

'Stay where you are, you little backstabbing creep.' Mooremarsh pointed a finger at Clarke. 'I told you what would happen if you betrayed me.'

Rutger nodded at Jasper. Jasper held his staff higher and threw a binding spell at Mooremarsh.

It didn't work.

'Oh, My, is that all you have?' She bent over double laughing. 'Come on, do you really think a binding spell is going to work?'

Alana stepped forward, Mooremarsh slashed the air. Alana parried the spell easily. She walked forward towards Mooremarsh.

Alana, no. Stay back. Sylvester Bluesky called to her. He covered the space between them. Then he saw her. The hag. He bared his teeth at her, willing her to keep away. The hag ran at him with surprising speed, jumped on his back, and dug her fingers into his shoulders.

You will sleep, the hag whispered, *Sleep!*

Sylvester Bluesky had never felt magic like it.

Dark Magic cannot enchant or kill Magical Animals he mumbled confused.

A warm blanket of sleep washed over him. He felt his limbs become heavy and crumble beneath him; he fell heavily to the floor in a deep sleep.

Alana screamed as Sylvester Bluesky hit the floor with a heavy thud.

'That's the wolf out the way!' Mooremarsh laughed.

Alana raised her staff, 'You will pay for that!' She went towards Mooremarsh, blunting each slash Mooremarsh threw at her.

'Watch out the hag is to your right!' Mathew called out to her. Alana brought down her staff to the right of her.

'You hit the hag; she is on the ground in front of you.' Mathew directed her.

Alana swung her staff towards the ground, a jolt of energy hit her from the ground, and she crumpled in a heap in front of Mooremarsh.

'No!' screamed Bill, he broke out of the ring of protection and charged at Mooremarsh.

Mooremarsh slapped the air, Bill went flying into the seating stands, a sickening snap of bone punched the air. Bill screamed a terrible primeval scream from the pain.

'This is not going very well for all of you, is it' she pointed at them, 'and here is only teensy weensy me!' she pointed her thumb at her chest.

'Let's see, who is next?' She sighed heavily, 'I have to say this is getting a little boring with no real competition.' Her eyes rested on Milly. 'Now, Milly, how about you?'

No, do not rise to her challenge. Miskunn wrapped her wings tighter about Milly.

'No, I do not wish to duel with you.' Milly whispered.

Mooremarsh cackled, held up her hands and shrugged her shoulders.

'She won't but I will.' Joshua stepped forward. His eyes flicked to the still form of his mother.

'You. I always hated you.' Mooremarsh sneered, she brushed away imaginary dust from her shoulder. 'But I will oblige you. Come on then. Your mother was inadequate in her use of magic, your father was like a bull in a china shop.' She cupped her hand to her ear, 'can you hear that, your father's wails,' she said goading Joshua. 'Rather a family of failures,' she eyed him up and down, 'you should be no problem.'

Joshua cleared his mind of her taunts, he took each step slowly, closing the gap between them. Mooremarsh's eyes narrowed as she watched him, her eyes darkened.

'Come closer, I would love to bite you.' Her lips parted; her teeth gleamed in the lamp light. 'Come and do your best.' She turned her chin away, and pointed at her cheek, 'Just there should do it.' Her eyes slid slowly in their sockets jeering him forward.

Joshua stopped, held his staff tightly in his hands. There was a slight shimmer to his right. He thrust the staff at the shimmer just as Mathew called 'To your right.'

A wretched scream cried out, piercing their minds. *That staff has the stone of Ealdread!*

Mooremarsh rushed at Joshua, her fingers hooked like claws. She started to say a spell, before she could finish it, he raised his staff and brought it down on her face with all his might. There was a crack, the staff flashed brilliant blue as it contacted her skin.

'No!' she screamed.

An electrostatic jolt careered through her body causing every nerve fiber to twitch in pain. Mooremarsh pushed her hand protectively on to her face where Joshua had struck her, instinctively lifted the other hand to her other cheek.

Joshua lifted the staff away ready to take another blow. Mooremarsh swayed backwards and forwards.

I told you, you cannot protect yourself against stone of Ealdread!

Mooremarsh ignored the voice, a searing anger ignited within her. She took one hand away from her face, locked eyes with Joshua, defying him to strike her again. The skin on one side of her face crumbled to a fine grey powder, coating her clothes and the floor. The stench of the powder was unbearable. Joshua stepped back in revulsion; bile coated the back of his mouth. Rough scale like skin revealed itself underneath the gap left on her cheek. Mooremarsh gingerly touched it.

'You have taken my beautiful skin. I will kill you and take yours!' Mooremarsh raged, lifted both hands, to cast a spell.

Thud! Thud! Two blows hit her hip, it knocked her off balance.

You will not hurt Joshua! Prudence stood in front of Joshua panting; her long ears stood back from her head like two daggers.

Joshua, go back and make the circle of three! Protect yourself and the others. The hare admonished him.

Joshua ran back to Milly, grabbed her hand, and thrust out his staff for Mathew to take it. Jasper stepped forward, pointed his staff at Mooremarsh, Rutger followed suit.

'We bind you; we bind your Dark Magic.' They chanted repeatedly taking advantage of Mooremarsh's weakened state. Sophia's eyes fluttered open, she pushed herself up, she sat. Through a groggy mist she saw Jasper and Rutger chanting and understood what they were trying to do. She searched for her staff, it was a few feet away, she crawled over to it and grasped it in her hand. She pointed the amethyst stone at Mooremarsh and joined in the chant of binding with the others.

Mooremarsh straightened herself up.

'I will not be bound!' she hissed at them with a serpent like voice.

Sophia's amethyst stone sent out a ray of purple light that touched Mooremarsh. She screamed at its burning touch. Rutgers's cane vibrated in his hand, a sharp white light shot through the air and wrapped around Mooremarsh's body. Jasper's rose quartz stone emitted a pink light. The orbs of light spun around her, increasing in speed.

Joshua caught Milly's pinched face, 'Join in the chant with the Elders.'

Milly's head nodded a fraction, and she began to utter the words. Mathew's voice cut the air; his stone shone. Joshua joined and the stone in his staff shot an orb of light at Mooremarsh and wrapped itself around her.

Mooremarsh twisted under the pain of the contact and screamed in pain.

'You will be the last to die, Joshua Appleby. I will make you watch as I destroy all your family and friends.' She screamed again, saliva bubbled in her mouth, she let out a strangling sound.

Joshua felt sick at the sound of her reptilian voice but held on tight to the staff and continued the chant.

'I will not be bound,' Mooremarsh hissed faintly.

No, you will not be bound! The voice she had heard so often soothed her. *I will look after you.*

The hag materialized. Ugly and hideous. Black empty hollow eye sockets regarded them. A smile split leathered skin and mouthed words they could not hear.

'The Hag is protecting her!' Mathew bellowed.

A high-pitched glass shattering laugh split the air; it stung their ears. Rutger looked over at Sophia, her ears were bleeding.

'We have to stop.' Jasper screamed following Rutger's gaze.

'No, we carry on,' Sophia poured her magic out, desperately trying to bind Mooremarsh's magic.

The hag looked at her, a blistered tongue licked her dry lips, she lifted her gnarled hand and smacked the orbs of light away.

Come with me. She held her hand out to Mooremarsh.

'What are you?' Mooremarsh whispered to the hag.

We are two, who have become one. It is the price of being an Energy Vampire. It was so the day you opened a door between our realms in the library. Now, come with me, into my realm, I will explain everything there. The hag whispered mysteriously.

Mooremarsh looked over at Sophia and whispered, 'We will meet again, you and I. Next time I will finish this.'

She reached out and took the hag's hand. 'I am ready now.'

Mathew saw a shimmer of a doorway. He could see to the realm on the other side, hot and red.

The hag held Mooremarsh's hand tightly.

All will be revealed. The hag pulled Mooremarsh towards her and threw the doorway.

CHAPTER 40
THE LAST GOODBYE

Everyone looked at the space where Mooremarsh had stood. The silence hurt their ears.

Joshua ran to his mother and gently shook her.

'Mum, wake up.' His mother lay still, he touched her face, fearful of her condition, 'Mooremarsh is gone,' he shivered.

His mother whispered something. He put his ear closer to her mouth. 'Milly and Bill, are they ok?'

Joshua looked over at Milly and Sophia. They were already with his father, trying to sooth his pain.

'Yes, Mum, they are ok.'

She patted his arm and nodded.

Sophia called to him. 'Joshua, come here, use your staff on your father's leg. It will heal his broken bone.'

Joshua moved quickly and stood beside Sophia; he hated the look in his father's eyes. Terrible pain.

'Ok, how do I do it?' Joshua asked, not wanting to hurt his father even more. He felt insecure in his ability using the staff to heal him.

'Hold the stone against his leg, think of the bone mending. The stone will do the rest. Believe me, it will work.' Sophia encouraged him.

'Do it son, just do it.' Bill croaked to him.

Joshua held the staff against his father's leg. He closed his eyes and thought of his father's broken bone. *Fix his broken bone.* He willed the staff. *Fix it.*

Bill moaned in pain, he bit down on his lip to contain his moans, for Joshua's sake.

Fix his broken leg. The staff shone.

Ahhh! Bill screamed a crescendo of screams.

Fix the bone. Joshua tried to ignore the terrible sound and pushed the thought harder.

Bill stopped crying in pain. Joshua took away the staff. The silence was deafening.

Alana swooped down beside Bill, she removed a handkerchief from her pocket and mopped the sweat away from his brow.

'My love, I am sorry you endured that,' she placed her forehead against his, 'how do you feel,' she stifled a cry.

Bill moved his leg. 'It feels stiff, but it's mended well. Thank you, son.'

Rutger came over. 'Do you need some help getting up?'

'Yes, that would be great.' Bill accepted his offer.

Rutger put out his hand and Bill grabbed it. He winced as he got up, but he was thankful the bone had mended.

A terrible scream cut the air.

'Dad, dad!' Clarke was crying over his dying father.

'Clarke, let me out.' Forrest calmly called to him from the cage.

Clarke ran to the cage and threw open the latch. Forrest crawled out of the cage.

'Help me up.' He commanded Clarke.

Clarke bent down and hooked his arm under Forrest's, he was heavy, and Clarke nearly fell under the burden of his weight. Forrest winced a shock of pain stung his knees. With Clarke's help, Forrest got up. He looked over at Erik and shook his head sadly.

'Take me to your father.'

After a lot of shuffling, Forrest stood over Erik.

'Help me get down.' Forrest held out his hand.

Clarke took hold of Forrest's hand and helped him down.

Forrest cradled his son. He looked up at Clarke.

'What is your wish?' Forrest asked him.

'Heal my father.' He willed him, 'that is my wish.'

Forrest shook his head, 'I cannot use my magic to heal him.' Clarke went to speak, 'there is something else I can do, but not as your slave.'

'I set you free. That is my wish.' Clarke blurted, 'I do not want any wishes.'

Forrest held out his wrists, the golden bangles dropped off his wrists and onto the floor.

'You made the right choice Clarke, there is hope for you yet.' Forrest wheezed and looked down at his son.

'Erik, it is time. Look at me.' Forrest whispered gently to his son. 'My magic cannot undo Dark Magic. But there is something else I can do.'

'Father?' Erik asked, his face contorted, and he screamed in pain.

'Erik, we don't have much time. I will use the last of my lifeforce to heal you.' Forrest placed his hands over Erik's head. 'I heal you, my son.' Forrest felt the warmth of his life force leaving his body and healing Erik's.

'Dad. What have you done?' Erik choked with a hoarse whisper. He reached up and touched his father's face.

'What I have always done for our family, love and protect.' Forrest whispered. 'I have done it for you son. For you.'

Erik got up off the floor and helped his father up.

'I must go now; I cannot die in this realm.' Forrest whispered sadly.

'I know, I just thought we would have more time together.' Erik pressed his father's hand.

'I must go outside; I need to see the sky to cross over. Help me.'

Erik put his father's arm around his shoulder.

Jasper came forward. 'May I help?'

'Yes, that is kind of you.' Forrest replied wearily, his body felt heavy, and tired.

Jasper walked around, Forrest placed his arm around Jasper's neck, and took Forrest's weight on his shoulder. They ambled to the entrance; Clarke followed behind feeling wretched at what he had done. Outside the bright light of the sun reflected off the snow, blinding them as they stepped out into the open. Forrest stopped walking holding his frail hand up to shield his eyes from the glare.

'Take me further out into the grounds.' Forrest asked.

Nori stood with her family and all the circus folk. Forrest nodded at them.

'Do not grieve for me, love our memories, that will keep me alive.' He looked up at the sky and smiled.

'A beautiful blue sky, it is a good day to go back to my people and die.' Forrest pointed ahead of him. 'Can you see it? The doorway to my realm.'

Erik and Clarke looked. They couldn't see what Forrest could. Mathew walked out of the entrance and saw a brilliant pink and gold swirling doorway.

'That is beautiful.' Mathew murmured.

Forrest looked at Mathew, 'Of course a Doorkeeper would be able to see it.'

'I think I can help them see it too.' Mathew walked over to Erik and Clarke. 'Take hold of my hand.' He held out his hands to them.

Erik placed his hand in Mathews. He saw the glorious colours of the doorway to Forrest's realm.

'Father, its beautiful.' Erik looked at his son, 'Take Mathew's hand, quickly, we don't have much time.'

Forrest looked dreamily at the doorway back to his realm.

'I must go whilst I can.' He held Erik in an embrace. Clarke stood back from them all.

Forrest kissed Erik's cheek and let him go.

'It would be nice to know your mother was there to meet me. I know it is not her realm, but the idea is a sweet one. I will always love you son.' Forrest stumbled towards the doorway to his realm, without looking back he entered the doorway, and was gone.

'Goodbye father.' Erik whispered, choked with emotion. He had lost his father twice.

Mathew let go of Erik's hand, walked back to Joshua and Milly who had been watching quietly in the doorway of the big-top.

Everyone stood in silence, each reflecting in their own way about the time they had spent with Forrest. An earie whining broke the air. Hurricane stood pawing at the snow, tossing his head up and down, crying at his loss of Forrest. Nori ran over to him and put her arms around his neck. She whispered to him, soothing words to try and calm his spirit. Hurricane nuzzled into her neck and stood still listening to her comforting words.

'Forrest left Hurricane to me. I hope you don't mind. He thought I would understand him,' Nori looked over at Erik. 'I have lived most of my life with Hurricane.'

Hurricane whinnied his agreement.

'That's fine, Hurricane I am sure would be happiest with you.' Erik replied. He walked over and stroked the horses back.

Hurricane nudge Erik and neighed gently to him.

'Thank you for the ride over here. Goodbye Hurricane.'

The horse touched Nori and looked into her eyes.

'Hurricane wants to give you one more ride, he wants to take you home.' Nori looked at Erik, 'He will come back by himself.'

'Thank you.' Erik stroked Hurricane again. 'I want to say goodbye to the others.'

Erik walked back to the others.

'We are sorry about your dad Erik.' Sophia consoled him softly, 'he gave so much to the magical community. He loved his family fiercely, which is something special for a Djinn. You should be proud of your father.'

Erik put his hands over his face and cried softly. Sophia stepped forward and put her arms around him, he laid his head on her shoulder. Clarke stood back from them all. Ashamed of what he had done, angry Mooremarsh had deceived him, livid Forrest had come into their lives. He caught Joshua's staring at him. He hated Joshua for pulling him into his world of magic. If he had not met him, would things have turned out differently?

'Dad, we need to go home.' Clarke called dully to his father.

Erik held Sophia at arm's length. 'Thank you, Clarke is right. We need to get home. I need to tell my wife what has happened.'

'You will need to be on your guard. You have made an enemy in Delvera Mooremarsh.' Sophia warned him.

'I know, we don't have magic, what can we do?' Erik spread his hands out.

'Alana will make some protection charms. You must put them around the house. Sadly, dealing with a hag is not something I am experienced with.' Sophia pursed her lips.

'Goodbye Sophia,' Erik looked away at Clarke, he had caused too much pain. 'Keep safe.'

Erik walked over to Clarke, and said hoarsely, 'Hurricane is taking us home.' He looked through his son. 'You will never understand the pain you have caused. You chose to hurt the people who loved you, for what?' Erik shook with despair and rage. 'Get to the horse, I can't bear to look at you.'

Clarke watched his father shuffle away, his step looked laboured as he made his way over to Hurricane. Clarke trembled under an avalanche of consuming rage. He walked stiffly over to the horse, he felt everyone's eyes on him.

Rutger took Sophia's elbow. 'You know if anything had happened to you.'

Sophia put up a hand, stopping him for saying any more.

'Rutger, we decided not to cross that bridge a long time ago. We dedicated ourselves to Earth Magic.' She looked into his eyes, softening the blow, 'I would feel the same way too.' She took his hand and squeezed it in hers. 'I think it's time to go home. I have to consult my history books, so it's back to Salisbury for me.' Sophia placed a finger wearily to her temple and turned to Rutger.

Rutger looked at her. 'Tomorrow, tomorrow will be fine. We rest tonight at Alana's.' He suggested to her.

'For once, I will take your counsel!' she laughed at him.

CHAPTER 41
HOME COMING

Nori stood outside Chestnut Cottage, her back hurt where Mooremarsh had severed her wing and the journey over had been painful. She stroked Hurricane's muzzle, he neighed softly.

'Good boy if we are lucky, they will have some hay for you,' he nuzzled her.

The door of the cottage whipped open; Milly stood on the threshold.

'Come in and get warm, Mum has just made some tea.' Milly beckoned Nori inside.

Nori walked up the path and smiled at Hurricanes whinny reminder he wanted some food.

'It's okay, we have a few bales in the shed. Rutger has some donkeys and stores their food here. You go inside and I will feed Hurricane.' Milly stood to one side to allow Nori to pass.

Milly put her hand to her mouth, shocked by a large opening on the back of Nori's coat. It exposed a livid gash and her torn wing.

Milly took in a deep breath, 'I'll be back in a moment, Mum is in the kitchen, she got your message and is expecting you.'

Nori smiled appreciatively at Milly and made her way to the kitchen.

'Good, you made it. Joshua, get out of that chair and let Nori have it.' Alana nodded her head upwards, 'you sit by the fire Nori, I will get something to clean that wound and some salve for it.'

'Evening Nori,' Grandad Rose looked up from a book he was reading.

'You've never met a fairy have you Marcus.' Grandad Rose grinned at him.

'Er no, no I haven't. You mean they are real.' Harrow wasn't sure if Grandad Rose was jibbing him or not.

'They are real.' Bill interjected laughing, carrying some wood he had just chopped. He started to pile the wood in a neat pile beside the fire.

Nori's nose crinkled, she spread one wing out.

'I thought you might need proof,' she said mischievously.

'Oh.' Harrow was not sure what to say to a fairy.

Bill laughed at Harrow's surprise.

'Marcus, there are a few things you will discover now that you know about Earth Magic!'

Priddy sat snoring gently in an armchair in the living room recovering from the large breakfast he had had that morning. Joshua shut the door to drown out some of the noise.

Nori sat down on the chair he had vacated.

'Thanks'. She gave Joshua a small smile. He walked around her behind her.

'That must really hurt.' He grimaced.

'You don't say! It smarts like mad.' Nori turned her head as Alana returned with warm water and disinfectant.

'You should have come to me yesterday when this happened.'

Nori kept a straight face as Alana cleaned the gaping wound.

'I have to say, this is the first time I have administered to a fairy!'

'The wing will grow back in a few weeks; you would never know it had been cut off.' She noticed Joshua, he looked concerned, 'the colour might be slightly different, but I'm not vain that way.'

She caught his eye and they laughed.

'I could try and heal it with my staff,' Joshua offered.

'Nah, and not be able to flash my war wound around the circus.' She laughed again. 'Any way, I have a feeling your staff would only work on humans.'

They heard Milly coming back in. 'Fed him,' she called from the hall.

'He is magnificent.' Milly sat down at the table.

'Yes, it's a shame you didn't get to fly on him. Now that is exhilarating!' Nori said.

'He flies? No way!' Joshua walked up to the window and looked out at him. 'Where's his wings then?' Joshua examined the horse from afar.

Alana gave Nori a cup of tea and a huge slice of ginger cake. She bit into the cake. 'Now that is amazing! My parents would love this!'

'Good, I will put the rest in a tin, and you can take it home with you.' Alana went out into the kitchen and proceeded to wrap the remaining cake up.

'Well, it's been a heck of a couple of days. Going to really miss Forrest, he was the best.' Nori put down the cake and glugged back some tea. 'You know he left me Hurricane,' Milly and Joshua nodded in unison. 'Well, he also left our family the circus.'

'That's great.' Alana said and placed the cake tin in front of Nori.

'Will you change its name?' Joshua asked.

'No, it's Forrest's circus, so we'll keep the name. It means other magical folk will still know where to find refuge.' Nori wriggled, 'that salve you put on is working a treat.'

'Mum makes the best medicine.' Milly smiled at her mother.

Alana bowed her head at the compliment.

'We will be on the lookout for Mooremarsh or her hag. If we see her, or hear anything about her, we will send Hurricane to you. Get that wolf of yours to come over and talk to him.' Nori saw Alana's eyebrows knit together, 'Oh, you don't know. Hurricane and the wolf know each other from way back. Come on, if he has wings and flies, you don't think he talks too.' She slapped her thigh laughing.

'Ouch,' turning her body had moved the wound on her back.

'How were Erik and Clarke when you took them home yesterday?' Ask Sophia quietly as she came through the door.

Nori's face turned to stone remembering Clarke's treachery.

'They didn't talk to each other all the way home. Not sure how you get over your son betraying you like that.' Nori shrugged, wishing she hadn't and winced at the pain.

Nori stood up and walked over to Milly and gave her a hug.

'I'm going to miss you.' Her eyes slid across to Joshua, 'Don't take any nonsense from those morons at school. Remember, you have a power they don't.' She came a little closer and whispered in Milly's ear. 'Don't let Mooremarsh take away your life, I know you are thinking about her, but leave it. Forrest has just died; he would have said the same. Enjoy your life, Milly.'

Nori held Milly at arm's length, Milly gave a watery smile.

'See you, Joshua.' She gave him a brief wave.' Grabbed the tin off the table, 'I'm going to stop by Mathew's and say goodbye now. Thank you, my parents are going to love these.'

'If you are going to the Anderson's, could you tell Mathew to make sure he gives thanks to Earth Magic.'

Nori gave a little salute, and like a whirl wind she was gone.

Alana looked at the dressing on Sophia's face, she needed to change it.

'Let me take care of that,' she pointed at the dressing, 'Sit down, while I get some herbs to purify the cut again, after I will have to salve it.'

'Thank you, Alana.' Sophia sat down and looked at the children. 'I am glad you are all here. You did brilliantly yesterday. I was proud of you all. You must be on your guard from now on. Mooremarsh has been damaged, it makes her more dangerous.'

Alana returned with the prepared water; the strong smell of sage and lavender radiated from the water. Alana removed the dressing and cleaned the wound, and gently dabbed a salve onto the wound and put a new dressing on. She handed Sophia a small jar.

'Dab it on twice a day, use purified water to bath the wound, and maybe drink chamomile tea, it's good for the nervous system.' Alana inspected her work. 'I think the wound won't scare too badly.'

'I've had worse don't worry.' She placed her hand over hers.

'Where did that hag come from? I thought they had been banished after the five-hundred-day war hundreds of years ago.' Alana sat opposite Sophia.

'When I get home, I will do research on the 500 day Hag War,' she twirled her hair in thought, 'Rutger, you need to contact the council of Elders, they need to be informed that a hag has entered our realm. It is not a good sign.' Sophia stressed.

'And we are staying with you.' Rutger walked in followed by Jasper.

'Yes, we thought, after staying here, it would be nice to enjoy some of your cooking!' Jasper laughed.

'I'm going to be busy with this research, so it looks like you gentlemen will have to take turns cooking for me!' Sophia said playfully, she walked over to the kitchen window and looked out.

'It is snowing heavily again. I think we will be snowed in here with you all Alana for a few more days,'

'You can stay as long as you want!' Alana said, casting an eye towards the window, the corners of her eyes crinkled, 'mind you, Bill could always drive you over air like he did on our way to Tetbury!'

'Trust you!' Bill smiled back at her.

Rutger looked at Milly who was sitting quietly, stroking Miskunn's head.

'I didn't want to discuss it yesterday, but you did well.' He walked over to the fire and rubbed his hands, 'Ignoring Mooremarsh's barbs is the way to defeat her. She feeds on insecurities to get a reaction.'

Milly said nothing, she was exhausted, and terrified Mooremarsh wanted her magic so badly. She continued to stroke the eagle's head.

He is right you know. Mooremarsh wants you. She wants your magic. Always keep vigilant. I will always be by your side; I am here for you. Miskunn rubbed her head on Milly's knee.

'Before you leave, we need to give thanks to Earth Magic.' Alana opened a cupboard and took out three brown paper bags. She handed one to Sophia, Milly and kept one for herself. I have some plant pots that we can plant up with these in. Joshua, get some buckets of compost from the shed.'

Plant pots filled with compost, all planted with their bulbs they gave thanks to Earth Magic.

'We replenish the energy of the earth with these offerings.' Sophia sang, 'We are thankful to have survived.' Sophia held Rutger and Jaspers hands. 'Light of Winter.'

Alana, Bill, Joshua, and Milly held hands and sang,

'Light of Winter. We replenish the energy of the Earth.'

'We will be able to beat Mooremarsh, won't we Mum.' Joshua asked.

'You have all grown up so much this past year. You each have a stone which will amplify your magic. Anything is possible, anything.' She said encouragingly.

Practice using Earth Magic and the stones, knowledge will be your power in defending against Mooremarsh. Prudence leaned against him.

Joshua stroked her ears; the touch of her fur was comforting.

'Well, who's for lunch?' Jasper put up his hand playfully.

Joshua and Milly made snowballs and threw them at him.

Rutger held Sophia's hand a little longer. She squeezed it in hers. 'You know, I think we will be all right.'

EPILOGUE

Clarke hid in the early morning shadows. He held his bicycle against him and stood looking up at the house shrouded in darkness. A milk float hummed past; he hid to make sure he wasn't seen by the milkman on his delivery. He stepped out into the rays of the rising sun, it felt good on his face. A March wind picked up and tore at his body, he pulled his coat tighter about him, to protect against the bitter cold. Heavy snowstorms had prevented his journey until now. It had been perilous to cycle on the ice crusted roads from Tetbury to Malmesbury, it was only now that it had been safe to make the journey. Clarke shuffled forwards from his hiding place and looked around; the street was thankfully empty. He adjusted his hands on the handlebars, walked across the road pushing his bike beside him. Tapping the gate with his foot, it opened, he winced as it whined under his boot. He pushed his bike onto the path of the house, his breath come out as white whisps, ragged in his anticipation at finding what he needed. Leaning his bicycle against the fence and walked up to the door. Standing in front of it he thought briefly of the woman who had lived here and caused so much harm. 'That will end,' he whispered.

Clarke took off his gloves, the wind nipped at their exposed warmth. Touching the door, the cold bit his skin. He slipped a hand into his coat pocket and fiddled around until he felt cold metal, he grasped the metal and took out a small bunch of skeleton keys. He had been practicing opening locks for months, just for this moment. Examining each key, he decided which one would be best to pick open the lock. Sliding the key into the lock he felt it slide into position, he held the key firm and turned it, eyes opened in surprise; the lock snap open with more ease than he expected. Looking around once more he scoured the area; he was still alone in the street. Blowing out his cheeks he pushed the door gently open, it creaked on its hinges, the sound boomed the screeching sound down the hallway. Entering the house, he shut the door quickly behind him and listened for movement. There was none. His heart beat wildly in his chest, his breath was ragged.

Why are you here? The echo of her voice taunted him.

'I will destroy you.' Clarke spat out to the silence.

Fortunately for me, I am elsewhere, but we will meet, I have a score to settle with you. The voice taunted at him.

'And I with you,' he hissed back at the voice.

Clarke walked into the tidy sitting room. It reflected Mooremarsh's personality, ridged and stern. He walked over to a walnut chest of drawers. Large shiny brass knobs embellished each drawer. His fingers touched the smooth wood, it felt warm under his fingers. Pulling out the drawer, he rifled through their tidy contents, his quarry wasn't hidden there. A tall welsh dresser stood against the opposite wall. He took down framed photographs of Mooremarsh's family from its shelves. He shuddered, they all had the same eyes, dark and dead. What he was looking for wasn't in this room. Moving into the kitchen, he put his hand over his nose. A sickening smell issued from somewhere. He proceeded to open the cupboards, not mindful of what was spilling out of them.

'Hell!' he jumped back as a jar fell out the cupboard he had just opened. A slimy liquid spread over the counter. He ignored it and looked at the rest of the contents.

'Guess I will have to get used to all this stuff.' He shivered not from the cold of the house but revulsion. He poked the odd jar around.

'I will have to come back for all of you.' He shut the door.

One more glance around the room and he decided he had seen everything he needed to see. Proceeding to the hallway, he looked up the stairs at the dingy landing above him. A creak vibrated as he stepped onto the frayed stair carpet. He winced at the sound, stopping for a moment.

'There's nobody here, what is there to be scared about?' he mumbled to himself.

Clarke carried on to the top, his eyes glanced at the three doors in front of him. He walked to the first door and opened it. It was a Spartan room, wallpaper peeled off the walls, black mold creeped down from the corners. Forlornly, a bare bed and chest of drawers graced the room. He quickly examined the drawers, but they were empty, so he made his way to the second room. Clarke pushed open the door. There were a few more items in this room. A tortoise shell handled brush, silver handheld mirror and a flat screwdriver adorned a chest of drawers, above it hung a mirror. A neatly made bed and a wardrobe. He entered this room and was hit with a feeling of revulsion, this was Mooremarsh's bedroom. He went to the drawers and began to look through them, he closed each drawer aggressively, he didn't want to touch them any longer than he had to. Opening the heavy door of the wardrobe, a few clothes hung neatly from a rod. He saw nothing special there, he slammed the door shut. He looked around once more and shook his head.

'Where are you?' He called out desperately not expecting a reply.

He walked over a small floor mat and heard a creak, something wobbled under the mat.

'That doesn't sound right,' he said feverishly to himself, 'maybe this is the spot.'

His fingers clawed at the corner of the rug and whipped it away. He banged the floorboards with his fist. One floorboard bounced and he sat back on his haunches looking at the floorboard.

'Now, I need something to lift you up with.' He felt the thrill of finding what he was hunting for.

He took out a small pen knife from his pocket he used to whittle wood, but pushed it back, deciding he didn't want to blunt its edge. Standing up he scanned the room for an implement he could use. He spied the screwdriver and grabbed it quickly.

'This should do it.' He grasped the wooden handle tight and dropped to his knees in front of the floorboard.

Clarke stabbed the screwdriver into the crack and banged the screwdriver to prize the floorboard up. He felt elated as it moved, he thrust his fingers under it and ripped it open.

'Yes!' his fist thumped the floor in excitement.

Mooremarsh's Dark Magic books lay there proudly. He grabbed the first one and stroked the red leather.

'I have been looking for you.' He whispered.

He took each book out, quickly flicking through the pages. From inside his coat, he removed a string bag. He stuffed all nine books into it. Standing up, he kicked the floorboard unceremoniously back into place and pushed the mat back. He checked the third room, it was bare. Just in case there were any more treasures he stamped on the floorboards to make sure none were loose.

'Time to get you lot home.' He looked at the books in the bag. Taking the stairs two at a time, he ran to the door and whipped it open. He gave the street a cursory glance to make sure it was clear. Stuffing the books into the bicycle pannier he pulled the bicycle away from the fence, lifted his leg over the bicycle cross bar, and straddled the seat. Clarkes face hardened as he sat there in the cold.

'You may not have wanted to teach me Dark Magic Mooremarsh, but I will teach myself.' He whispered into the silence, 'I will protect my family from you. My life is dedicated to Dark Magic. I am the sword of your destruction. I will crush your heart, send you to oblivion, to live alone in the darkness where you can do no more harm.'

Clarke kicked the peddle into position, slid his foot under the peddle strap and rode off along the icy road lost in thought.

A shadowy shape slipped out from behind a bush on the opposite side of the road. The sun unmasked him as he stepped into its light. Sylvester Bluesky avoided snowy patches and watched Clarke riding off into the distance. He sat down lost in thought, thinking over what Clarke had said. Clarke would embrace Dark Magic to protect his family from Mooremarsh.

There must be something we can do. A familiar voice sliced through his thoughts.

The wolf sighed and shook his head. His fur rippled from side to side.

We do not deal with those who do not have Earth Magic. Sylvester Bluesky finally answered.

Clarke was their friend. He has been damaged by Dark Magic. We share some of the responsibility, don't we? Prudence pressed on.

We cannot break an ancient covenant. It is not our place to help Clarke. The wolf replied sternly.

Prudence raised onto her hind feet. *That boy needs our help. He is alone and he may have lost his family by his actions. We cannot leave him to the mercy of Delvera Mooremarsh.* Her ears stood up defiantly and her eyes blazed into his.

Earth Magic and Dark Magic do not mix. Oil and water, they are immiscible. We share our magic with our magical human no one else. Sylvester Bluesky raised his regal nose.

A shimmer of purple spread over them and Gertie landed gently in front of Prudence.

We must have some obligation to the boy. From what Mathew's says he was drawn into a fight that wasn't his to have. Joshua should not have exposed our world to him. She preened her feathers. *But he did, didn't he. Joshua must take responsibility for Clarke.*

Prudence glared at Gertie, as she hopped closer to Sylvester Bluesky.

It wasn't Joshua who caused Clarke's life to be threatened this time. Clarke wanted to learn Dark Magic from Mooremarsh. Prudence expanded her chest.

But why did he want to be taught Dark Magic? Who was by his side when he was in the hospital after the fight in the barn? Gertie looked at them both accusingly. *Delvera Mooremarsh.* She let the name hang in the air. *Did it never occur to you that he might have needed some protection?* Her beak snapped at Prudence. *Joshua made a mistake, we let it happen, the Elders did not stay to help Clarke whilst he was in hospital. The mistake is ours. We need to help Clarke not to walk the path he is taking.* Gertie flew over to a gate post.

Are we responsible? Did I not instruct Joshua in the ways of Earth Magic? Is this my fault? Prudence looked soulfully up at Sylvester Bluesky; her ears lay flat against her back.

I suppose it is really. Gertie's head waved from side to side.

Sylvester Bluesky growled at the crow.

No Prudence. It is not your fault. You instructed Joshua and he chose to ignore you. We can guide and protect them, not enforce them.' He cocked his head to one side.

Prudence nodded, looking a little less upset.

Our duty is to warn the others of Clarkes intentions. I will tell the Elders the direction Clarke is taking with Dark Magic. I hope it is enough. He looked at Gertie, *our obligation is to our Earth Magic Human. They are our priority.*

I understand. Prudence nodded.

Gertie flew down and settled in front of Sylvester Bluesky.

Mathew will always be protected and guided by me. I swore an oath once and I swear it again. Her head nodded several times.

We understand each other. Now go and keep watch on the others. He dismissed them.

He sat alone in the street for some time thinking about the past. The cold seeped into his paws and he stood up. He was fearful of the future, fearful for the Appleby's but also Mathew and his family. A cold knot tightened against his chest. His breathing became short, he lay down feeling dizzy.

Am I to die now?

The smell of rose petals drifted into his nostrils. A golden light shone around him.

No, it is not your time yet Sylvester. We still have work to do.

Sylvester Bluesky looked around; he recognised the voice speaking to him.

I have missed you. Sylvester Bluesky hoarsely whispered.

We will have enough time to talk. Now, we need to plan. The Earth Magic humans will need us, as well as the young ones, Prudence and Gertie. Miskunn came closer to him and wrapped her wings around his body.

There she stood. Miskunn. Beautiful and wise

We face the future together. Come, it is time for me to tell you where I have been. She unwrapped herself from him, nudged his chest and flew away into the sky. *I give you a gift, you will be able to see me. It is not a gift I can share with many, but your magic is strong, and I believe our bond will keep this gift alive.*

Sylvester Bluesky watched her flying away not sure if he believed she had been there. Her eagle song reached him, sweet and beautiful.

I will follow you, Miskunn. He stood up, shook his fur, *we will make a battle plan to keep them safe.*

He looked up into the sky once more, listening to the echo of her song, and made his way in the direction Miskunn was flying.

Books In the Joshua Appleby Series

Joshua Appleby and the Flaming Sword

Joshua Appleby and the Ruby Dragon

Joshua Appleby and Sigrid's Lantern
(Available Autumn 2022)

KIM LANGLEY

If you would like to follow Kim Langley and enjoy finding about her new books as she creates them.

www.kimlangley.com
Facebook/kimlangleyauthor
Instagram/kimlangleyauthor

About the Author

Stories have been in Kim Langley's mind forever! From an early age, she would take herself off on a London Routemaster Red Bus, along with her younger brother, Steven, to central London. Here they would spend their time in the Natural History, Science and Victoria and Albert museums exploring the magnificent halls, fascinated by amazing curiosities on display in grand wooden cabinets. They would make up stories about exhibits when they had no idea what they were. Those musty corridors allowed them to dream of long-gone days and a future yet to arrive. Art was also a huge part of her life and during these adventures, she would visit The Tate and National galleries, each picture was a magical story, and what wonderful stories could be made up! Sundays the greyness of London was swapped for a day in the countryside or watching the ocean in nearby seaside towns. Those long walks made a lasting impression on her, and she joined Green Peace as soon as she was old enough. Kim developed a love of cars as her father had one rickety car after another. Watching the repairs of cars alongside motorbikes, and the sound and smell of roaring engines is a memory that will stay with her forever. In 2009 she moved to the dreamy Cotswolds and lives with her husband and their two dogs, River and Darcie. It is during her long walks and doing art she dreams of magical fantasy adventures and plots for her books.

KIM LANGLEY

www.ingramcontent.com/pod-product-compliance
Lightning Source LLC
LaVergne TN
LVHW091529060526
838200LV00036B/536